PENGUIN BOOKS

# The Boy That Never Was

Karen Perry lives in Ireland. *The Boy That Never Was* is her debut novel.

# The Boy That Never Was

### KAREN PERRY

PENGUIN BOOKS

PENGUIN BOOKS

Published by the Penguin Group

Penguin Books Ltd, 80 Strand, London WC2R ORL, England

Penguin Group (USA) Inc., 375 Hudson Street, New York, New York 10014, USA

Penguin Group (Canada), 90 Eglinton Avenue East, Suite 700, Toronto, Ontario, Canada M4P 2Y3
(a division of Pearson Penguin Canada Inc.)

Penguin Ireland, 25 St Stephen's Green, Dublin 2, Ireland (a division of Penguin Books Ltd)

Penguin Group (Australia), 707 Collins Street, Melbourne, Victoria 3008, Australia
(a division of Pearson Australia Group Pty Ltd)

Penguin Books India Pvt Ltd, 11 Community Centre, Panchsheel Park, New Delhi – 110 017, India

Penguin Group (NZ), 67 Apollo Drive, Rosedale, Auckland 0632, New Zealand
(a division of Pearson New Zealand Ltd)

Penguin Books (South Africa) (Pty) Ltd, Block D, Rosebank Office Park,
181 Jan Smuts Avenue, Parktown North, Gauteng 2193, South Africa

Penguin Books Ltd, Registered Offices: 80 Strand, London WC2R ORL, England

www.penguin.com

First published in the United States of America by Henry Holt and Company, LLC, 2014
First published in Great Britain by Michael Joseph 2014
Published in Penguin Books 2014

001

Copyright © Karen Gillece and Paul Perry, 2014

The moral right of the authors has been asserted

The line from the Patrick Kavanagh poem 'On Raglan Road' is reprinted from
*Collected Poems*, edited by Antoinette Quinn (Allen Lane, 2004), by the kind permission
of the Trustees of the Estate of the late Katherine B. Kavanagh, through the
Jonathan Williams Literary Agency

Set in 12.5/14.75 pt Garamond MT Std
Typeset by Jouve (UK), Milton Keynes
Printed in Great Britain by Clays Ltd, St Ives plc

A CIP catalogue record for this book is available from the British Library

ISBN: 978-1-405-91404-8

www.greenpenguin.co.uk

MIX
Paper from
responsible sources
FSC™ C018179

Penguin Books is committed to a sustainable
future for our business, our readers and our planet.
This book is made from Forest Stewardship
Council™ certified paper.

# The Boy That Never Was

# Prologue: Tangier 2005

A storm is rising. He can feel it in the strange stillness of the air. There is no movement, no flutter of clothing, not a whisper of a breeze along the narrow streets of Tangier.

Beyond the lines of washing strung between the buildings, above the tiled roofs, he sees a patch of sky. There is a strange luminous quality to it, a bluish hue and lights that look almost like auroras.

He stirs a cup of warm milk, blinks, and looks out again on to the changing and otherworldly colours of the sky.

Setting the spoon down on to the counter, he turns from the open window and crosses to where the boy is sitting, his face tightened in concentration at the jigsaw puzzle before him.

'Here,' his father says, holding out the cup.

The boy does not look up.

'Come on, Dillon. Drink up.'

The boy looks at him and frowns.

'No, Daddy, I don't want to.'

His father hands him the cup again. The boy hesitates before reaching out, and in that moment, Harry feels the faintest beat of indecision. He ignores it and nods his head at the boy in encouragement. The boy takes long, slow gulps. A small dribble of milk escapes from the corner of his mouth, and his father wipes it away. Dillon gulps again and hands the cup back. 'Here, Daddy,' he says. 'Finished.'

Harry takes the cup and walks to the sink to rinse it. At its bottom there is a fine residue of powder. He fills the cup with water and watches the residue flow up and out of it and down into the drain.

Leaving the tap running, he fills a pan and sets it on the stove. The gas is not easy to light, and he pushes the knob and presses the ignition switch several times before it takes.

The couscous is out. Next, he takes a handful of raisins and places them in a bowl. A half-full bottle of brandy stands on the counter by the olive oil. Harry takes the brandy and covers the raisins. Before placing the cap back on to the bottle, he holds its opening to his nose and inhales. Then swiftly, almost surreptitiously, he drinks from the bottle before screwing the top back on to it and returning it to its place beside the olive oil.

He looks out again at the changing colours of the sky. He wants to say something to his son about it, but he does not. Dillon is completing his puzzle, becoming drowsy.

Harry returns to his cooking. He pours a small amount of olive oil into his right hand and smears the chopping knife with it. He chops dates, gathers them into a bowl, and slides his finger across the knife blade before placing the apricots on the chopping board.

Beyond the window, the streets are quiet. Usually, at this time of the day, in neighbouring apartments, there are the busy sounds of people preparing meals, but this evening there are no raised voices, there is no clanging of dishes, no hissing of cooking fat, no crying of hungry babies. A hush has descended upon this part of the world. It is as if all the inhabitants of Tangier are holding their breath.

He turns to Dillon. 'Time for bed.'

There are no protestations from his son, just a vague nod of consent. Harry picks him up and carries him to his room. There he undresses the boy. He leaves him in an undershirt and underpants and eases him under the covers. He strokes his cheek and leans over to kiss his forehead. 'Night night, sweet prince,' he whispers, but the boy does not answer. He is already asleep.

Back in the kitchen, Harry fixes himself a gin and tonic. The day has been long and difficult. The heat, his son's demands, and his own inability to concentrate cling to him, making his skin feel tight.

The air remains heavy, although the heat has dissipated. Now that the boy is asleep, he can finish cooking dinner. It is Robin's birthday, and he has planned a special meal to celebrate.

He turns the oven on, removes the cover from the lamb on the counter, and seasons it with roughly ground salt, then massages the meat with rosemary and oregano and slides it into the oven. As he does so, he glances at the sky and wonders when the clouds will break and the downfall begin.

Rain in Tangier can be biblical. The torrential downpours can last for days. It is one of the things that surprised them most when they moved here, five years ago. He longs for one of those rainstorms now to clear the air and lift this dull, oppressive atmosphere.

The pain around his head has not abated, despite the gin. He glances at the old clock above the stove and refills his glass.

The phone's ring startles him.

'Everything all right?' asks Robin.

'Yes. Dillon's asleep, and I'm getting dinner ready.'

'He's asleep?'

The surprise in her voice unnerves him.

'He was exhausted.'

'Listen,' she says then, and he can tell from her tone that she has some favour to ask. 'Simo has gone home sick, so I told Raul I'd stay on a while longer to cover.'

'But it's your birthday.'

'It'll just be a couple of hours, that's all.'

He is silent.

'It'll still be my birthday when I get home,' she says.

He drains his glass and agrees that yes, it will still be her birthday when she gets home.

He says goodbye, hangs up and makes himself another drink. It will have to be his final drink before she arrives. He doesn't want to get drunk and spoil things for her.

Tonight, with his headache, with the uneasy feeling in the air, he is as jumpy as a cat and craves the reassurance of her presence. For some reason, he does not want to be alone. So he distracts himself by putting away toys and gathering up books and returning the cushions to the sofa.

He clears clutter from the coffee table and sweeps the tiled floor. The place is coming back to itself, back to the tidy space that has become their home – the shabby

4

yet comfortable sofa, the bead curtain that separates this room from the cubbyhole kitchen, the corner by the window where stacks of canvases are propped up against the wall. Even the wooden table they dine at is cleared. Harry is annoyed at Robin; perhaps he would not have made Dillon go to sleep so early if he had known she was going to be late.

Still, he tries not to be downbeat and goes about setting the table. Knives, forks, napkins, but where are the candles?

Earlier that day, he'd bought four white unscented candles at the souk, a roll of saffron-coloured linen to throw over the sofa, and a large, ornate serving tray cast in silver, decorated in a fine filigree of scrolls and curlicues. The tray is a gift for Robin, one he spent twenty minutes haggling for, but it is only now that he realizes he has left it and the other items at Cozimo's.

He had not planned to go to Cozimo's. It was a spur-of-the-moment thing. Almost immediately, Harry had regretted bringing Dillon. Cozimo was not used to having children around, especially in his own home. Dillon had grown bored and irritable while Harry sat chatting with Cozimo, and as the time passed, the boy began pulling at his arm, complaining loudly, so that their visit had ended abruptly, Harry sweeping the boy up into his arms and carrying him away, leaving his friend in a grateful peace.

'Fuck,' he sighs, trying to think what to do.

The obvious thing is to call Cozimo. But Harry knows what this would mean: Cozimo would insist on delivering the forgotten items, request a drink for his efforts, and before either of them knew it, they'd be deep in conversation – the dinner spoiling, Cozimo settling in, the evening on its way to being ruined.

Harry goes to check on the boy. He is in a deep sleep, and Harry knows better than to disturb him. Besides, Cozimo's house is not far – a short walk down the hill. He can be there and back in ten minutes. Best to go now, quickly, before the rain comes.

Taking one last look at the sleeping child, he hurries down the stairs and into the empty bookshop, which is cast in shadow now that the evening light is fading and the sky beyond has grown dark and brooding. He steps outside, locking the door behind him, and strides purposefully through the narrow street.

The lingering quiet in the streets unnerves him. He looks up and catches sight of a veiled woman peering down at him. Quickly, she draws back from the window, disappearing from view.

Somewhere nearby in the warren of alleyways a dog is barking, and he cannot shake the sense of unease. The gin, instead of taking the edge off things, has somehow sharpened his anxiety.

But what has he to be anxious about?

He has left the boy alone. Pangs of guilt make him increase his pace, and he half-walks, half-runs to the corner.

The neon sign above the bar gives off a loud, sibilant hum as he passes. He is aware of the strange figure he cuts – a white man hurrying through these streets. He doesn't stop until he reaches the ornate gate, where he leans heavily on the doorbell.

6

A moment passes before he hears the *shush shush* of soft leather slippers on the stone paving beyond the gate. A small figure clothed in a djellaba appears, and, as Cozimo approaches, his wizened features clear of confusion and he raises a hand in greeting.

'My friend,' he says, and opens the lock.

It is as the bolt is drawn back, sliding through the return with a rasping clink, that Harry hears it: an answering sound, louder, more violent and more frightening than the first.

This is no crack of lightning, no roll of thunder. The break, when it comes, is not above his head, as he imagined it would be. Instead, he feels it in the soles of his feet.

A low rumble rises from the bowels of the earth. The ground begins to shake. He reaches for the wall, but the wall shifts, and the gate jangles on its iron hinges.

The ground beneath his feet moves like liquid. There is a sickening swaying of the earth. The world is filled with a guttural roar and the sounds of breaking glass and falling roof tiles and the shrieks of rending wood.

Beneath Harry, the ground is pulsing, the earth slipping away from his feet, his heart catapulting in his chest.

Somewhere on the street, he can hear gas hissing out of broken pipes, and as he turns himself against the wall, he can see the building opposite veer and sway. It rocks back and forth on its foundations, smoke rises in the distance, the air fills with the smell of gas, and just as he thinks the building will topple, it stops.

The ground grows still. The roaring is silenced. The rage beneath the earth recedes.

He stays where he is, flattened against the wall, his

7

hands splayed on either side of him. The building he has been watching settles.

His whole body is paralysed by fear, and it takes a few moments for him to calm himself. His muscles unclench; movement returns to his joints.

'That was a bad one,' Cozimo says, his face ashen, his eyes still wide with fear.

Harry is about to say something, but does not.

*What*? Cozimo wants to ask, but his throat is parched and Harry is already gone.

He runs past the bar, where the neon sign has fallen on to the road. It fizzes and spurts with bursts of electricity before going dead. All along the street, the lights cut out. There is silence now, a veil of uneasy calm, but it does not last.

The fragile peace is broken as people begin to stream past him. Down the hill they go, fleeing their homes, propelled by fear: fear of the aftershocks that will come, fear of the imminent collapse of these flimsy buildings.

He alone seems to be charging uphill, his breath caught in his chest, his heart beating like a madman's.

As he runs, Harry hears the shrieking and the crying begin. Doors open, and people emerge from their homes, some dazed and confused, others driven by panic. A man rushes past him, carrying three children in his arms. A woman stumbles on to her doorstep, crying and bloodied, a crimson gash above one eye.

On the corner, a man calls out over and over again, 'Allah sent it, Allah.'

Harry stops to catch his breath. A woman throws her arms about his neck. He pushes her away and flees.

All around him, buildings are rocking and flames shooting up. People on all sides are crying, praying and calling for help. Animals too, fowls and beasts, are crying out.

He runs on frantically. And then at the Hotel Mediterranean, there are three men on the roof. Rather than see the crazed men fall in with the roof and be roasted alive in the blazing building, a military officer on the scene directs his men to shoot them, which they do, quickly and accurately, before a dumbfounded crowd of spectators.

It feels like the end of the world.

Everywhere there is dust.

He inhales it, coughing and spluttering, his eyes streaming, his mouth dry. Smoke invades his nostrils. He sees buildings alight, flames licking at windows and doors.

In the distance, there is the whine of sirens. Other sounds too: sudden crashes as buildings collapse in on themselves, the thump of bricks toppling on to the street, the snapping of wood as eaves buckle and crack.

Still he runs. A building slumps against its neighbour, as if tiredness and old age had weakened it, and it could simply bear up no longer.

From cracks in the pavement, water bubbles up – water and sand. A foul sludge fills the alleyway and sucks at his feet.

At the corner to his street, the bakery's façade has fallen away, revealing rooms with their furniture still standing.

He sees a bed and a sofa, curtains fluttering in the open air.

As he reaches the street he lives on, the dust in the air thickens. A great cloud of it rises to meet him.

He stands still.

About his feet, there is a shuffle and flutter. He looks down and sees hundreds of books strewn about the road.

In the clearing, the sky is flat and dark. The buildings that have remained standing look yellow and barren.

He scans the wreckage. An image from earlier in the evening returns: he is standing in the narrow passageway, holding his sleeping son in his arms – he can almost feel again the softness of his flesh, the warmth of his body.

And yet another astonishing reality confronts him. The building where once he worked, slept, loved, fathered, painted, put his son to sleep, where he lived and called his home, is simply and irrevocably no more; it is sunken into the earth, swallowed, gone.

Dublin 2010

# 1. Harry

Robin was still asleep when I left the house. I wanted to wake her, to tell her about the fresh arrival of snow. But when I turned from the window and saw her lying there, her hair spread over the pillow, the gentle rise and fall of her breathing, eyes closed and her face at peace, I decided against it. She had been tired lately; at least, that is how it had seemed to me. She had complained of headaches and of not sleeping well. And so I let her be, closing the bedroom door softly behind me. I walked downstairs, took the empty wine bottles from the kitchen table, placed them outside and went out without breakfast or coffee. There was no need to leave a note. She would know where I was.

The cold air was refreshing. I had the same regret having drunk so much the night before that I've had on many other occasions, but in the crisp, cold air, I experienced a renewed sense of well-being. I was full of good intentions. I was going to turn over a new leaf, get healthy, live my life more fully and honestly. It wasn't just the morning air. Hadn't I said as much to Robin the night before?

'You're a man with good intentions.'

'The best of.'

Robin smiled when I said this. Hers was a generous smile, a smile that recognized the weakness within me and forgave it all the same. After Dillon, her gentleness had not dissipated, when it easily could have. I would not have blamed her. She had not become hardened. She had mostly remained herself, despite everything we had been through.

Though there were times when something she said or did came as such a surprise that it gave me pause and made me consider my wife anew.

'That's what you call being married,' my friend Spencer once told me. As a single man, or *bachelor*, as he liked to insist, he often had insights into married life. To the complaint one day that my wedding ring was too tight, his pithy reply was: 'It's supposed to be.'

Robin and I still talked the way we used to, still opened up to each other, but like with any couple which has been together for a long time, there comes a point, sometimes, in a night's conversation when you anticipate what the other person is going to say and you stop listening and you go to bed. And that night – last night – well, that was exactly what happened. I was mid-flow when Robin stood up abruptly, leaned over and silenced me with a kiss before saying, simply and blankly, 'Good night.' I shouldn't have let it bother me. I had been gabbling, talking nonsense most probably, and her sudden departure from the kitchen turned me to another bottle of wine and another late night.

Today, however, was different. Today was to be a day of new beginnings. The snow was there to announce it, to wake and remind me of our fresh start. I was closing up shop and locking the doors to my central Dublin studio. 'The end of an era,' Spencer had joked. From now on, I was going to work from the garage at home. It would save us the much needed cash to renovate the house we had recently moved into. It had once been Robin's grandparents' house, and now it was ours. For Robin, the house held memories. And though the suburbs of Monkstown were a far cry from our time in Tangier or even the times we had spent in Dublin together, I was not ungrateful. It's a big old house. And Robin had plans. She wanted to get her hands dirty. Her excitement was infectious. What could I say but yes, yes, let's get our hands dirty.

The crunching sound as I walked through the snow put a smile on my face. There must have been two or three inches of it, and, by the looks of it, I was the first to venture out on our street. When I got to the van, the old Volkswagen's door wouldn't open. I tugged at it, finally wrenched it open, started the engine and went back for a kettle of water to pour over the windscreen. I loved the old orange van. Robin had pleaded with me not to buy it. Had it broken down once? Had it stalled, stuttered or wavered in its time? No. It had been fail-safe and hardy. We had even slept in it. I won't pretend that it was comfortable, but it could have been. I put the key in the ignition and turned the engine over a couple of times before backing out of the driveway slowly, cautiously, feeling the snow compacting under the tyres.

I got into town that cold, beautiful morning with little bother. The roads were deserted, and I made good time, parked outside the studio on Fenian Street and walked down to the basement for what would be, I imagined, the last time.

The studio had at one time been a basement flat, but Spencer had gutted it. The walls were bare, the floor concrete. The toilet cistern gurgled all day and all night too, whenever I slept over. I had an old mattress, a couch, a kettle, and a camping stove. I liked the place to be this bare, and I stretched my canvases and stuck them on the floor to work on them. I didn't use an easel. I didn't use a palette. Sometimes I didn't use brushes. I used sticks and knives or broken glass to create the paintings. The sparseness of the place let my imagination do its work, and I'd sketched, drafted and completed canvas after canvas here. And now it was all over.

I didn't have a system as such, but I spent the morning packing the van with canvases, frames, paints in pots and tubes, brushes, sticks, catalogues and finished and unfinished paintings. I don't consider myself sentimental, but I did feel a twinge. The studio had served me well since we had moved back from Tangier. I'd produced all my new work there. It had added up to two solo shows and a bunch of group efforts. Spencer, who had made some shrewd business decisions in the past, owned the building and lived on the top floor. He'd rented the studio to me for a song. He also liked to remind me that he was my landlord and that I was his tenant. By eleven a.m., I had been there for over two hours. That was when he rang.

'This is your landlord speaking. Eviction orders are in motion.'

'You're a funny man,' I said.

'I don't need you to tell me that.'

He arrived ten minutes later to help, wearing a black

silk dressing gown and a pair of old leather slippers, a cigarette dangling from his lips. I say he arrived to help: he
brought a snare drum and a crate of beer. 'I'm the boy
who bangs the drum,' he said.

'Start lifting.'

'I could have been a wealthy man if I had charged you
what I should have for this place.'

'You *were* a wealthy man.'

'I worked it out last night. I could have had quite the
stash put away.'

'I'm afraid renting one small basement to a friend was
not your downfall.'

'Here we go – now you're going to tell me . . . you, the
lowly tenant.'

My phone rang.

It was Diane, the manager of the gallery I show at.
'You won't reconsider?'

'I'm packed.'

'You know I think it's a mistake.'

'So you told me.'

'And not only because I won't be able to stop by . . . but
business-wise.'

'It's done.'

Diane wanted all manner of things then. I told her I
had to go.

'Who was that?' Spencer asked.

I wasn't inclined to hear the tirade he would inevitably
deliver about Diane if I told him it was her, so I lied. 'Just
Robin,' I said.

'The lovely.'

When Spencer had lifted his last box and chosen a painting he liked the look of – 'Either I'll sell it for you or take it as a Christmas present' – I stopped what I was doing and made us a pot of coffee.

'The strongest coffee this side of the Liffey,' Spencer said. He took a silver flask from his pocket and poured.

'Whatever that means.'

'This is what it means.' He held the flask out to me, but I covered my cup.

'Driving,' I said.

'Why anyone would want to drive on a day like today is beyond me.'

'Have you forgotten? I'm moving out.'

'Now, listen to me. I have a question for you.'

'Go on,' I said, wrapping a number of brushes in a rag.

'You'll please tell her ladyship, queen of the damned, that you have vacated the crucible of creativity and for-sworn my great generosity.'

'Has anybody ever told you that you are a verbose fucker?'

'Don't insult me.'

'I don't mean to. Are you talking about Diane?'

'If that's what you want to call her. I like –'

'She knows well I'm moving out,' I said, reaching for Spencer's flask and splashing a dash into my cup. I felt, in that moment, in need of something to steady the sudden and unexpected quiver of nerves.

'But you know what I'm afraid of? Late at night, she'll come round here looking for you. She'll find me instead, and then what? She'll try to sink her teeth into me as well. She will try to suck the blood out of me.'

'The way I see it, someone's already beaten her to it. Have you looked in the mirror?'

'You cruel fucker.'

'I tell the truth.'

Spencer shook his head. I watched as he lit another cigarette, then stood up and sauntered around the empty space. A hollow feeling had come over the room; and I felt lonely. The whiskey burned a hole in the coldness of my stomach, and I watched as Spencer stopped and peered into one of the few boxes still waiting to be loaded into the van. Plucking the cigarette from his lips, he reached down and began rifling through the sheaf of drawings held there, and I felt my insides contract with grief and rage. They were my drawings of Dillon. He picked one out and held it up in front of him, examining it through narrowed eyes. Before he had a chance to comment, before he could say anything at all, I was on my feet and crossing the room, snatching the drawing from his hands.

'Those aren't for you,' I said sharply, turning away so that he couldn't see the burning in my cheeks or the tremble of my hands. I placed the drawing back with the others, my fingers lingering briefly.

I felt his silence and reckoned that he was considering whether to say anything. He knew me well enough to understand when to back off. Then I heard the slow shuffle of his slippers, the scraping of a cup against the table as he reached for his coffee and downed what was left of it.

'Does this have a name?' he asked, and I looked and saw him holding aloft the canvas he had chosen.

It was one of my Tangier paintings: indistinct figures, a market square, the sun's light beating weakly in the background. In the distance, the sea.

'No.'

'I'll give it one,' Spencer said. He pointed to his snare drum. 'And I'll pick that up later.'

'Mind yourself,' I said, and he was gone.

The door slammed shut, and I waited a moment or two before returning to Dillon's box. It was a large wooden container, aluminium hammered around the corners. I dipped my hands in and took out a handful of loose sheaves and looked at them. For a brief moment, I considered throwing them away, destroying them. I had a vision of a burning barrel. All those images turning to dust. *Put it behind you. Get on.* These are the things people have said to me. Reasonable people. People who cared about me and my well-being. People who cared about Robin, cared about us.

All that time I had kept my grief hidden, but still those sketches continued; something I didn't fully understand had drawn them out of me, guiding my hand across the page, time and again. Somehow, I couldn't seem to stop myself. And I don't know how long it was, that day, I sat there looking at them. I didn't weep. Instead there was a wholly other feeling. I'm not sure I can describe it. A feeling of recognition. The sketches were the truest thing I had drawn in years. I don't believe in the soul, but if I did, I would say there was a soul within those pencilled lines.

My sketches of Dillon were all dated. And I sat there sifting through the years, sifting through the hundreds of pencil drawings and charcoal impressions I had of the boy as he might have aged. *The boy*. Do you hear me? Call him what he was: my son.

These sketches were not something I had painted. They were not something I had shown anyone, not even Robin. Especially not Robin. The drawings were a secret. That is why I could not bear to hear Spencer's voice saying anything about them. I don't know why, but on some level they had kept me going.

So I didn't bundle them up and burn them. I laid them out carefully in their dated order, spread them out across the concrete floor. I had tried to capture my son as he might have been, getting older with each month, with each year. And as I stood there, looking from one to the next, there he was again, growing before my eyes.

Enough, I told myself, and, hunkering down, I picked them up and slowly returned them to their calendar of despair. The lid closed over the box, and I carried it out and locked the studio behind me.

I decided to leave the van where it was. The thought of driving home and having to empty the damn thing just made me feel tired. Instead, I walked along while following the hum of a low-flying helicopter as it circled above O'Connell Street. My plan was to get something to eat, to fill the gaping hole in my stomach, but I was entranced by the whirr of blades overhead and found myself instead walking down O'Connell Street and

21

meeting the demonstration against the government head-on. Caught up in my own private drama, I had forgotten that the protest was taking place at all. On another day, I might have made a point of being there, adding my voice to the collective exasperation at the government. Fury, even. I was as angry as the next man. All over the country, people were united in their feelings of frustrated anger at the bailout. The terms were stringent, so in a way I was glad to be walking down O'Connell Street, an accidental protester of sorts.

There were no cars, no traffic, but thousands of people marching and chanting and bellowing in protest. News crews from around the world placed their cameras along the protesters' route. Tourists stopped to take photographs and video footage. Wherever they were from, what they saw can't have been that surprising. Ireland's financial woes were international news, after all.

The Guards were out in force, too. They wore luminous yellow jackets over their uniforms and huddled in twos and threes at intervals along the route, chatting and stamping the ground to keep warm. They didn't have much to do. The demonstration was good-natured and benign. For all the rage, there was a dignified restraint to it. As a protest, it was more mannerly than riotous. One protester held a home-made placard that read, REPUBLICAN IRA: EUROPE OUT, BRITS OUT. The letters had been scrawled in a black marker. On a piece of paper slipped under your front door, it might have looked threatening. But on the end of a stick in the middle of a peaceful demo, it just seemed pathetic and out of place.

I walked along with the protesters and thought about joining in with the chanting and the singing. The crowd moved and flowed along the thoroughfare, pooling by the General Post Office, where a stage had been set up, and from behind the outstretched arms of Jim Larkin's statue, a large screen flickered with the black-and-white footage of demonstrations from the past. Ghostly images. The past resurrected, played out once again in a strange and unearthly light, sending shivers up my spine.

Then up on stage, where everyone's attention was now directed, a man took the microphone, rallied the crowd to cheers and boos and introduced a woman, who sang a long and ranting song of remonstrance. The guitar shook in her hands. A helicopter flew over the crowd, and for a few moments the noise of its turning blades drowned out the singing.

I was caught in a throng of people, swaying this way and that. I suppose I allowed myself to be carried away with it all. Joining in with the applause and chanting. Adding my voice to the chorus of others. The woman finished her long lament to cheering and whistles. 'We've been sold down the river!' the man with the microphone boomed. 'It's time we stood up for ourselves!' He introduced another woman; she told her story, about hospital cuts and waiting lists. And then a man took the microphone and told his story, about small communities and closing post offices. And another man told his story, and so on, a line of people on the stage, each with their own tale, and every tale greeted with roars from the crowd, applause and cheering, heads nodding and arms raised in solidarity.

Time passed; how much time, I don't know. But after a while, I began to grow weary and hoarse. Somebody somewhere was beating a drum, and I felt the reverberations of it in my head and started to think about leaving. The strangeness of that morning – the surprise of snow, the clearing of my studio, whiskey poured into an empty stomach, Spencer's hands on those drawings, and now the push and roar of the crowd. *Bang, bang, bang* went the drum. It was too much. I was hungry and tired. I needed to get home, or to the warmth of Slattery's. I needed to see Robin.

As I turned to go, I noticed a flash of colour. A scarf wound around a woman's neck, the ends of it loose and billowing in the breeze. A diaphanous material, silk perhaps, the colour blue like smoke on the air. The woman, tall and attractive, was holding a boy by the hand, the two of them walking purposefully up O'Connell Street. The boy turned and looked at me, and everything slowed right down. The drumbeat stopped. The roaring hushed. The crowd fell away. In that moment, there was nothing but me and the boy, our eyes holding each other's.

Dillon.

My heart gave a frightened beat. I sucked in my breath, and the blood roared into my ears.

My son. My lost boy.

Someone passed in front of me, and for an instant I lost sight of my son, and into that sudden vacuum, it all came rushing back: the clamour and screech of the crowd, the thundering pulse of the drum, the push of bodies and the oppressive hovering of the helicopter above us.

I strained to see him again, sweating profusely as I began to push through the crowd. The blue scarf rose like a puff of smoke, and I felt a kind of panic. I pushed people out of the way, jostled and shoved to get past, driven by a new and unfamiliar urge. I was heckled: 'Hey, watch it, pal.' 'Calm the fuck down.' 'What's your hurry, chief?' But I didn't care. I heaved and shimmied, dodged and darted my way through the slew of people. It was hard going. But it didn't stop me. Nothing, I felt, could stop me.

After all these years when I had hoped and wondered, searched and questioned, after all these years when I had followed the smallest of clues, walked through the solemn streets of Tangier, kept sleepless vigils in unholy places and been disappointed time after time by a trail gone cold, he'd presented himself to me. He'd walked past me. Now, of all times, when I'd least expected it, he was there, before me, in Dublin, a place he had never been.

The crowd seemed to thicken and clot about me. The atmosphere changed. It grew hostile and forbidding. I was working hard to keep them in my sights – the boy and the woman – to hold on to them as I battled my way through. Their pace had quickened. They walked at a clip; distance began to open up between them and me.

'Dillon!' I screamed. 'Dillon!'

I can't be sure whether he heard me or not, but there was a moment when it felt like he turned in response to my shout, and our eyes met. There, among the heaving crowds, his blue eyes somehow found mine, at least for a split second. Was there a hesitation, a moment of resistance on his part, an instance of recognition? I can't say, though I have asked myself since a million times or more. And as quickly as he turned to look at me, he was gone. Swept away from me all over again, my son, my disappeared boy, leaving me trapped in the crowd, caught like a piece of meat in a snake's body, stunned and struggling to get out.

# 2. Robin

I woke to find Harry sitting on the edge of the bed, pushing his feet into his shoes and reaching for his jacket. Pretending to sleep, I secretly watched from my nest of blankets, taking pleasure in the sight of him slipping his cigarettes into his shirt pocket, his wallet into the back pocket of his jeans – his morning ritual – before pushing himself up and rising to meet his reflection in the mirror. His height meant he had to bend down to examine his appearance, passing a hand roughly through his hair. His hands were large and powerful, paint and pigments permanently caught around the nails, and his body appeared lean and angular in the cold light of the morning. I watched as he ran his fingers over his unshaven jaw, dark with three days of stubble, held by the same fascination that had bound me to him when first we met, sixteen years ago.

Opening the curtains, he sucked in his breath with amazement. Beyond him, I could see the tree outside our window weighed down with snow. On the windowpane there was a bloom of frost, and he ran his hand over it and looked out.

It was the last Saturday of November, and the first snow had fallen. I watched him at the window, and the glare of sunlight reflected off the white surface of the garden below seemed to illuminate his face, briefly clearing it of all traces of the burden he had been carrying for some time. He was thirty-six years old, though he looked older, but that morning his delight at the sudden snow — the surprise of it, lying thick and unspoiled, making everything clean and new — was so open and unabashed and boyish that it brought a smile to my lips. I was about to drop my pretence and say his name, maybe join him at the window, wrap my arms about him, whisper against his ear, 'Don't go, my love,' then drag him back into the warm funk of our bed, when I remembered how Dillon used to sleep between us.

Something cold slipped down into my stomach, and instantly I knew I would not go to him. Much as I wanted to, I couldn't. Instead I had to lie very still with my eyes closed, concentrating hard on shutting out the image that had entered my head. The softness and warmth of our son's little body lying between us. The sound of his breathing. The smell of him.

My mind came down on the image like a steel trap.

I stayed where I was. I kept my eyes closed.

The moment passed, and I lay listening to Harry padding quietly down the stairs and felt the twinge of regret at not keeping him here. Still, I had held it together. That was the important thing. I would make it up to Harry later. Besides, there was something I had to do first. From downstairs came the clink of bottles and the sound of the door closing after him. Eventually the van coughed and spluttered to life, and then he was gone.

\*

With Dillon, I knew it right away. It was as if I woke up one morning and all the molecules in my body had shifted slightly during the night – a small, almost imperceptible restructuring – so that I felt different, but in a way I couldn't quite put my finger on. I felt changed. Within days the nausea started – waves of it at any time of the day or night. And along with it came a sweeping tiredness so that I, who had always had difficulty finding sleep, suddenly found myself nodding off at bus stops, in bars, over dinner with friends. I felt it – I felt him – even before I realized I was late. With Dillon, I felt like my body had been pounced on by pregnancy. This time seemed different. I was over a week late, and there were no symptoms – no nausea, no sudden assaults of fatigue. It was different from the first time, and I was grateful for that. Because I didn't want this pregnancy, this baby, to remind me of Dillon. I had put all that behind me.

Ten minutes after I listened to Harry's old Volkswagen groaning and screeching out of the driveway, I sat shivering in the bathroom, staring at the thin pink line that confirmed my suspicion.

'Steady,' I told myself, feeling my heart rocking in my chest. 'Take it easy, Robin.'

I put the wand down, washed my hands at the sink and looked at myself in the small, cracked shaving mirror. I'm normally quite pale, but that morning the face that looked back at me was flushed, blood rushing up from my neck and suffusing my cheeks with colour. I put my fingers to my face and smiled. A murmur of happiness started inside me. I began to laugh. In that cold, damp bathroom, with

29

my breath clouding out on the air, I hugged my arms about myself. A brand-new life. A fresh start. I felt it like the blanket of clean, white snow outside making everything new.

There is one room in this house that is devoid of any evidence of DIY. It is a sanctuary, a place to avoid the snaking cables of power tools that lie like nests of vipers across the bare floors, or the scarred walls where half-hearted attempts at stripping wallpaper have been started and then abandoned, or where tiles have been hammered away, leaving globs of old tile adhesive and flaking plaster. We use this one room as an office, and it was to this room that I went, still wrapped in my bathrobe, long socks pulled up over my knees. I sat there, shivering in front of my MacBook, scanning the Internet for an ovulation calendar, a menstrual cycle graph, some means of indicating when this child might have been conceived. Then I checked the calendar on my phone and flicked back through the weeks. I did all this as if someone were watching me – making a great show of my careful calculations – when really I knew. I put down my phone and closed my MacBook. At the window, I watched the skeletal tree filling up with snow. I had known all along.

It was the anniversary. Our annual celebration had reached its sixth year. It was something we'd decided one night not long after he was gone. The two of us sitting together in a café, nothing stronger than coffee between us, and Harry hammering the table with his fist, tears in his eyes, hissing angrily that he did not want us to be defined by the tragedy we had suffered. He refused to live his life governed by grief, to become one of those people paralysed by the past, caught in the amber of loss. He said it, and I watched him shaking with grief, barely able to control it, and I put out my hand to steady him. I held on to his arm, whispering to him, as he sobbed, that we didn't need any anniversary Masses or weekly visits to a grave to get us through this. No reliving of all the fond memories; it would not bring Dillon back. Instead, I suggested that we would have one day every year – Dillon's birthday – and it would be a day of celebration, just the two of us. He looked up at me then, caught by the idea, and listened as I went on: Each year, on that day, for the rest of our lives, no matter what happened between us in the future, on that one day we would go somewhere together for a meal, for a night, for a drink and a long walk; we would talk about him, about how much we had loved him, about how happy he had made us; we would get drunk, we would make love, we would cry, we would do whatever was needed to get through that day. It was a chance to distil and contain all the love and longing left after him.

Dillon was three years old when he died. And every year since we have observed this anniversary. Strange, as we no longer celebrated or even acknowledged our own birthdays. After what happened in Tangier, I couldn't.

A month ago. Driving to Kilkenny, where we were booked to spend the night in a stately home – log fires and tartan rugs and stags' heads mounted over the billiards table, that kind of thing – we were talking about how some people would think us morbid, the way we still celebrated our son's birthday five years after he had died.

'Take your brother, for instance,' Harry said.

'Mark? You've spoken to Mark about this?'

'No, but he did ask me once in that awkward way of his whether he should, "you know, send birthday cards for Dillon and stuff".'

Harry had drifted into a mock imitation of Mark, with his halting speech and the nervous way he chewed his lip whenever dealing with something serious. I feigned shocked indignation, then broke into laughter, telling him to stop taking the piss out of my brother.

'No, seriously, Robin! And as for your mother – Christ! When I told her we were going to Kilronan House for the night, she began waxing lyrical about how she had seen an article about it in *Image Interiors* and how some friend from her bridge club raved about it, and when I said that we were going there to celebrate Dillon's birthday, her face kind of froze in horror. Seriously! I'm not making this shit up. It was like a death mask. That waxwork of Robespierre's head after the guillotine. That's what she reminded me of.'

'Stop. You love her really. Admit it.'

He smiled, and I turned my attention back to the countryside viewed through the windscreen.

Something was nipping at the edges of my happiness. All the way from Dublin, I had harboured the feeling that I had forgotten something, and we were halfway to Kilkenny when I realized what it was: my birth control. I didn't say anything to Harry, just sat there biting my lip and jigging my crossed legs, watching fields and hedgerows strip past and trying to calculate how great a risk would it be if I took my pill tomorrow at lunchtime, when we got back home, rather than at nine o'clock that night, when I would normally take it. Was fifteen hours a big risk? Surely not. Not after nine careful years?

I told myself that as soon as we got home the next day, the minute I walked into the house, I would go upstairs and pop my pill.

Only I didn't.

We got home after a night of too much wine, of making drunken, messy, soppy love. We both felt tired, and a little sad as we always did after that day, yet renewed as well, somehow fortified by it. I went upstairs and I stood in the bathroom, looking at the foil pack of pills, seven empty blisters, fourteen bulging. I stared at the tiny letters – SAT – printed on the foil, and I thought to myself: no.

I suppose you might say that it was then that I made my decision. At that moment, it felt like the right thing to do. I didn't discuss it with Harry; I knew already what his answer would be. In the past, whenever I had broached the issue, it had always been met with a refusal.

*'I wouldn't trust myself.'*

That was what he always said. But the look in his eyes when they met mine said something else: that really what he was afraid of was the thought that I couldn't trust him with another child. Not after Dillon.

But I did trust him. I understood somehow that it was guilt that held him back from wanting another baby, as if he needed to punish himself for leaving Dillon alone that night. And after five long years of watching him trapped and struggling with the burden of his self-loathing, I felt that something had to be done to release him from it.

I flushed the pills down the toilet. What the hell, I told myself as I watched the water swirling in the bowl, each little blue tablet washed away. Let's just see what happens. That was a month ago, and in all that time I hadn't said one word about it to Harry. I kept searching for the right moment to bring it up, but it never came. Now the fuse was lit, and it was too late for a discussion. And when I considered that in the coolness of our little office on that snowy morning, I felt the first quiver of doubt passing through me.

'Hello?'

'Hello, love. I'm glad I caught you.'

'Mum. How are you?'

'Frozen. Your father keeps turning off the heat. All this talk of austerity has gone to his head.'

I sat on the bottom step of the stairs and cradled the phone to my ear. In the background I could hear the clink of cutlery against crockery and pictured my mother at the kitchen table with her blonde hair neat as a wig, her face fully made up, and a cashmere shawl draped over her shoulders as she wrapped herself around a steaming mug of coffee.

'The only room in the house with any warmth is the kitchen. Jim has this notion that if we turn off the range we won't be able to turn it back on again.'

'And I suppose you're happy to perpetuate that myth?'

'Of course. Not a word to him, now, do you hear me?'

'Your secret is safe.'

'How about you, love? How are you coping with this cold weather?'

'Well, I'm sitting here in the hall, and there's a crack above the front door and the back door won't close properly, so it's a bit like sitting in a wind tunnel.'

'I can imagine. That creepy old house. I feel cold just thinking about it. Why you didn't find yourselves a nice modern place with insulation and central heating is beyond me. I said it at the time, but you insisted on buying Mark's share of that house and living in it. There was no reasoning with you. And I know, I know,' she said, cutting me off before I could offer my defence. 'It was Granny's house, and you didn't want a stranger living in it.'

'We love this house, Mum.'

'Love is all very well. I just hope you are warmly dressed.'

'I'm wearing tights under my jeans, and a thermal vest underneath a flannel shirt and a fleece.'

'You sound like a dustbin man. What are you two doing with yourselves today, anyway?'

I stared at the scraper in my hand.

'I'm stripping wallpaper, and Harry's gone into town.'

'Oh.' There was the slightest pause, and then she said, 'He hasn't gone on that march, has he?'

The march. The Irish populace rising up in protest at the government and the banks and the IMF and the EU and all the other bogeymen who claimed to be rescuing us. I could see my mother clearly, fingering her pearls like worry beads, a look of distaste spreading across her face at the shameful prospect of her son-in-law caught on TV looking militant behind an Irish Congress of Trade Unions banner or tossing a petrol bomb or attacking a Guard with a bottle.

'No, Mum. He's gone into the studio. He's clearing out the rest of his stuff today, remember?'

'Ah. Yes, I'd forgotten.' Then, after a pause, she added, 'He'll miss that place.'

'I know. It's hard for him.'

'Still,' she continued, more briskly now, 'no point wasting money on rent for a big cold cellar in town when you have all that unused space at home.'

'Yes, Mum,' I replied, but even as she said the words and I knew they made sense, I felt that small niggle of doubt, and thought of how quiet Harry became lately any time we talked of moving his work space to the garage adjoining the house. He loved his studio. He loved the solitude and privacy of it. I knew that. But it didn't make financial sense. And then I remembered that last night, as we were standing alongside each other at the sink, doing the dishes, I had offered to help with the move. 'No, Robin,' he had said, his voice deadened and flat, his eyes fixed on the dish in his hand, and I had felt the defeat coming off him in waves. With a sudden twinge of remorse, I'd sensed that perhaps it was a mistake. He could be so vulnerable.

'Mind you,' my mother was saying, 'if anyone should be marching, it's you.'

'Me?'

'Yes! Haven't architects been hit badly by this crisis?'

'Well, yes, but —'

'How many days a week are you working now? Four? Three?'

'Three and a half.'

'Three and a half. And a mortgage to pay on a house that's falling down about your ears.'

I felt my heart hardening, and knew the conversation was reaching that tipping point beyond which it would descend into irritated sniping on her part and sullen bullishness on mine.

'Look, Mum, I really should get back to my —'

'Of course! Sorry, love. But look, before you go, can I just check with you about Christmas?'

'Christmas?' I said, my heart giving a little lurch at what I knew was coming next.

'I thought I would make sure that you and Harry are still coming here for Christmas.'

'Well —'

'Because Mark rang last night and broke the news to us that he is going to be spending Christmas in Vancouver with this new squeeze of his, Suzie.'

'Her name is Suki, Mum.'

'God, yes it is. Although I can't say it with a straight face. It's like something you'd call the cat.'

I laughed despite myself and then I decided it was best just to tell her, rather than avoiding the issue for weeks and forcing myself to blurt out on Christmas Eve that Harry and I had decided to spend this Christmas at home, in our house.

There followed one shocked moment of silence.

Then she said, 'But you always come to us.'

'I know, Mum, but this year, we thought it would be nice to spend it in the house, especially after all the work we've been doing . . .'

My voice trailed off. It sounded pathetic and threadbare, even to me.

Into the silence, my mother breathed her discontent. She said, 'I suppose this is Harry's idea?'

A flare of annoyance sparked inside me. Not this again, I thought.

'Actually, it was mine,' I said archly. 'I was the one who wanted to spend it here.'

'I see.'

She let a minute pass, then spoke with weary resignation: 'Well, you always were headstrong. Never one to seek advice, or take it when it was offered. Insistent on doing your own thing, regardless of the consequences.'

The words hung in the air between us. We both knew she was thinking about Tangier. I felt a tightening around my heart. For five years there had been an unspoken 'I told you so' hovering around her – words that, if spoken, would poison the love between us.

I almost hung up the phone. But instead I did something even more foolish.

'Why don't you and Dad come to us?'

'Come to you?' she asked. 'But you have no heating!'

'I promise, Mum,' I told her, 'if you come to us for Christmas, we will have heating. There will be roast goose and wine and champagne and a Christmas tree and presents and heating.'

'Well, I don't know, love,' she said, her voice thin and doubtful. 'I'll have to see what your father says.'

'Okay. Just think about it, Mum.'

'I will. Thank you. Take care now, love. And stay warm!'

She hung up, and I sat on the step, looking at the phone and thinking: *Fuck*.

Now I had two things to worry about telling Harry.

I spent the morning hacking away at wallpaper, and in the afternoon I took a long, hot bath. It is one of my favourite things – a hot bath while listening to the radio and drinking a glass of red wine. I avoided the wine, and after ten minutes of radio commentary that covered the freezing weather conditions along the east coast and the advance of the march towards Government Buildings, I switched it off and wallowed in silence. In the stillness of the water, I peered down at my body, looking for symptoms of pregnancy. My tummy was flat and smooth – no stretch marks, no telltale signs of a previous birth. I tested my breasts for a new fullness or sensitivity, but there was nothing different.

The water was cooling, but I didn't want to get out yet, not ready to bare my naked flesh to the cold air of the room. And as I looked about – at the mould spots on the ceiling, the walls weeping with damp, the ancient avocado bathroom suite, the lino on the floor curling at the edges – I was overcome with a sense of panic. Every room in this house was still a work in progress. But now there was a clock ticking. How on earth were we going to get it ready in time?

Calm down, Robin, I told myself. The baby will be born in the summer. At least we won't have to worry about the heating until the autumn. But the worry had started, and now I was like someone picking at a scab. I couldn't leave it alone.

I thought about the house falling down around us. Mum was right: we should have sold it when we had the chance. We would have got a decent price for it – enough to buy a small but comfortable house in a nice area, with no mortgage to worry about. Instead, we were stuck with a crumbling old pile whose value had plummeted in the four years we had owned it. And while at the time of purchase we had thought it the bargain of a lifetime, now that my working week had been cut back and there was talk of further reductions, or even redundancies, it all seemed like a terrible risk. I had not factored in a pregnancy – how would work respond to that? Plus, the art market was suffering with the recession, so Harry's future seemed uncertain. He was excited about the new stuff he was doing, yet it felt like a long time since he had sold anything major.

Everyone is in the same boat, I told myself. The trick is not to panic.

But it was hard to stay calm in a climate of fear. You couldn't turn on the TV or the radio without hearing about spending cuts, the budget from hell, tightening our belts, sharing the pain. People were screaming blue murder about our loss of sovereignty, about how our forefathers who had given their lives for our independence would be spinning in their graves. The French and the Germans were hounding us over our low corporate tax rate, and if they succeeded in ridding us of it, then the country would become an economic wasteland. And into this panicked, embittered, frightened world, I wanted to bring a child? What on earth had I been thinking?

'Hello?'

'Robin, it's me.'

'Where are you?'

'I'm in town. At the protest.'

'Harry, I can hardly hear you. Can you call me back from someplace quiet?'

'I just saw –'

'What's that?'

'I saw –'

A crackle on the line, a roaring crowd in the background.

'What did you say?'

'Come and meet me.'

'In town?'

'No. I need to get out. I've got to see you. Meet me in Slattery's.'

'Are you all right – Harry?'

He'd hung up, and I stood there with the phone in my hand, looking out at the tree caught in the early-evening sunlight, casting a cold shadow on the snow.

# 3. Harry

I broke free of the crowd and ran blindly down an alley-way. At the corner I stopped, my chest heaving, looking left, then right, wildly searching. Nothing. Instinct told me to go right. I ran up that street, panicking now with each passing minute. Where was he? Where had they gone? I recognized the acrid taste of fear in my mouth, like smoke, and suddenly I was back in Tangier again, running up the hill, my heart on fire, a kind of prayer ripping through me, a plea, as I raced back to him.

A couple was strolling hand in hand, coming towards me, and I shouted out to them, 'Have you seen a boy in a red jacket? He was with a woman.'

The blank expressions on their faces were answer enough. I didn't stop to hear their reply, running on up the street, rounding another corner now and finding myself in the wide-open expanse of a square. There was a church on one side, a shopping centre on the other, and groups of people idling in the snow-covered space. I scanned the faces of those gathered there, desperately hoping to catch a glimpse of him again, but I could feel him slipping away from me.

'Fuck!' I shouted. There was no time to panic. No time to think. No time for anything except action. Every second, he was getting further away from me, slipping from my grasp.

I was running again, back towards O'Connell Street. By the time I reached Henry Street, there was a searing pain in my side. Sweat had soaked through my clothes, and my coat and boots felt too heavy. Still, I kept on. I needed help. There was a police station at the top of O'Connell Street, and when I got there, my limbs were shaking, my mouth and throat scratched dry.

The station was busy. Not one of those quiet nests of indolence. Not this central in the city. A man who had had too much to drink was being asked to sit down. His legs looked like they were about to buckle beneath him. A child in a buggy was roaring while her parents exchanged insults. There was a queue, but I was too agitated, too desperate to wait my turn. Instead I marched straight up to the counter and told the Guard behind the desk, 'You've got to help me.'

'Do you mind?' the woman I had elbowed past demanded in an aggrieved tone, and behind her there were shouts of indignation: 'What the fuck?', 'Listen, pal, there's a queue.' I didn't care. I didn't give a flying fuck.

'My son,' I said urgently. 'My missing son. I've just seen him.'

And it hit me then, the magnitude of it, like a fist in the guts. The Guard behind the counter gave me a weary look.

'Your son,' he said slowly.

'Yes, my missing son – I've just seen him,' I said

stupidly. And then I gestured with my thumb to the street outside, where the roar of the crowd could still be heard, and said, 'Out there. At the march. I saw him. He was with a woman. I don't know who she was. Please, you've got to help me —'

The Guard held up his hand to halt my flow, and I became aware of how fast I was speaking, how panicked and breathless I sounded.

'Just back up there one moment. Your son – how long has he been missing?'

'Five and a half years. He'd be nine now.'

'And what were the circumstances surrounding his disappearance?'

'It was in Tangier. Look, I don't have time for this now – we need to do something before it's too late to find him.'

'Please lower your voice, Mr –?'

'Lower my . . . ? Lonergan. Harry Lonergan.'

'Lonergan,' he repeated slowly, writing it down carefully. I watched him with a rising impatience. His calmness was maddening. 'Address?'

Patiently, I stated my address, trying to keep my cool, aware all the while that my son was getting further and further away from me.

'Have you filed a missing persons report, Mr Lonergan?'

'Can't you get on the radio, issue a description of him? The city is crawling with your lot today – one of them is bound to spot him.'

'One moment.' He gave me a cool glance before turning from me and disappearing through a doorway into an

44

office. The door shut slowly behind him, and I was left there, brimming with anxiety and crazed with a spiralling panic.

Beneath my fingertips, I felt the rough, grainy surface of the plastic countertop. In the queue behind me, I heard the irritated scuffling of feet and heavy sighs of indignation. Not that I cared. It was all I could do to remain still and to wait for what seemed like the longest time before that door opened again and the Guard emerged with a folder in his hand.

'Now then,' he said slowly, fixing me with a look I couldn't quite get a handle on. 'You say your son went missing in Tangier.'

'Yes.'

'And I see you have been in to see us before. It says in your file that your son's disappearance coincided with an earthquake.'

He looked up at me with a cool, implacable stare.

'Look, I know what you're thinking. I know that there is an assumption that he was killed that night, but a body was never found, and just now, not half an hour ago, I saw him. With my own two eyes. He was there, alive, breathing. He looked at me and I knew –'

My voice broke off. Judgement had crept into his eyes and pity, too. That Guard was regarding me like I was some poor demented fool, and I knew exactly what he had read in that file. What they had written there about me. I had been in so many times over the years. I could tell he thought I was a crank.

'Mr Lonergan, you would have been told on those

other occasions that this matter was handed over to Interpol. I suggest you contact the National Central Bureau in the Phoenix Park.'

'Listen to me,' I said slowly, keeping my voice low, trying to sound reasonable, knowing that this was my only real chance of finding Dillon. 'If you could just get on the radio, please. Please, I'm asking you. Just issue a description. Have your guys check it out.'

I held my breath.

'Mr Lonergan, you must have seen the demonstration outside. Every Guard in the city is on duty today. All leave has been cancelled. There are no available resources, and even if there were, this would not come under our remit, because as I stated, Interpol . . .'

I was clenching my fists as he spoke.

'If you wish, you may fill out this form, and I will add it to your file. When Sergeant Sayer gets in on Monday –'

'Monday'll be too fucking late.'

'Watch your language there, Mr Lonergan.'

I pushed myself angrily away from the counter and, ignoring the gawping bodies in the queue, flung wide the doors.

Outside, cold air rushed back into my lungs. I felt a sudden crushing despair. I should have known better. The pain of the dismissal was nothing compared to the thought that it was too late. I had blown it. After all this time, the one chance I had – the only opportunity to present itself in five and a half long years – had been wasted. In that moment, I didn't know what to do. I didn't know whether to ring Robin or get in the van and start driving through the city to look for my son. I did know that I needed to steady my nerves, so I went into a pub and ordered a drink.

Some football fans were screaming at a huge TV screen. There was a demonstration outside, where the buzzwords were 'loss of economic sovereignty', but inside nobody gave a crap about economic sovereignty. They cared about whether Arsenal were going to score the next goal and who was going to buy the next round of drinks. That was all. The atmosphere was oppressive. I drained my lager, felt it swirling around inside me, but with no effect. A trickle of doubt had started to work at me. Before the day was out, it would build to a full-flowing river.

I went back outside. It was still bright, and the light reflecting off the snow made me squint. I walked around Parnell Square, then for some reason went into the Rotunda Hospital. I walked up and down the wards, stuck my head into room after room. Nobody asked me anything. I left feeling dejected and tripped back down O'Connell Street, looking out all the way. At one point, I called Robin. The need to see her was building inside me – the need to share this burden with her. A hurried arrangement to meet in Slattery's, and then I hung up, still casting my eyes around me. But there was nothing, no sign of Dillon – his dark hair, the red jacket he was wearing – or the woman he was with. I could have searched up and down that street until nightfall, for all the difference it made. They had simply vanished.

*

When I got back to Fenian Street, I was shaking. Had Spencer left any booze? My hands were cold, and I rubbed them together vigorously. They looked red and old. The hands of another person, not mine. They were always shaking these days. Too much drink, too much stress, too much worry and fear. It had become an aesthetic of sorts. The hazy brushstrokes of my paintings, thick with egg yolk, vinegar and sand, were not an act of the mind. They came not out of an intellectual context, a framework of notional and conceptual investigation. No. The paintings, the work, the vision, if anyone really wanted to know, came out of the delirium tremens of my life, the hangover, the morning after, the shake in my hands causing the brush to waver and tremble over the canvas, giving everything a shadowy, uncertain and unreal aura. All tremor and nerve.

I lit a cigarette as I walked up to the building. I had an idea. Spencer, as a businessman, as a man of means, well, he had connections. He knew people. Detectives. Someone who might have access to the CCTV cameras on O'Connell Street, someone who might, without causing too many waves, without letting too many people know, inspect them closely, follow it up, help me track Dillon and that woman down or give me an idea of where they were going, which direction, which bus, who they might have met. A terror rushed through my body, but it was a terror mixed with a thread of hope. I felt manic as I pushed open the door to the studio. When I saw a figure standing at the other end of the room, the mania changed to dread.

Diane was trailing her finger over the worktop in the kitchenette.

'I wouldn't say you've done a great job cleaning this place up.'

'Diane, what the fuck?'

'I have a key. You know that, Harry. All your stuff may be gone, but there's still something of you about the place.'

Even on a Saturday she wore a suit, a stiff black jacket and skirt. She brushed her hair out of her eyes and smiled. I picked up some folders I had left and turned to go.

'I wanted to say goodbye,' she said.

'What?' I asked, turning back to her.

'To your place, the place where you worked. To the memories.' She was walking towards me, holding up a bottle. 'I brought this, as a kind of bon voyage.'

I said nothing.

'Har . . . Harry,' she said coyly.

'Look, I have to go,' I said, but she was already coaxing me back into the room, pouring two short glasses of whiskey. I don't know if it was the lure of another drink, or the shock I'd had, or the immediacy of my need right then for any human company, but it made me think, I don't know, that I could linger at least for a moment, that I needed to, in order to calm down.

'You made some of your best work here,' she said, passing a glass to me. 'Do you remember your first solo show? *The Tangier Manifesto*. I made it happen, Harry.'

I drank the whiskey and felt suddenly exhausted. Her hand had come to rest on my thigh.

'It was a great show, Harry.'

She was right. I had sold a lot and, yes, I owed Diane a great deal. But that was all in the past.

'Diane, I thought we decided.'

'I know, I know we did. But I thought –'

She was an aggressive lover. Coy at one moment and ferocious the next, and always candid in her sexual communication. She could be modest without being shy, seductive without being sluttish, and when she moved her hand along my leg, I felt the tug and urge to be with her again, though I knew it was wrong.

'Have I ever let you down? Have I ever disappointed you, have I ever let your wife know? And I won't, I still won't, but, Harry, I want you to do this one last thing for me. I want you to give me this one final farewell.'

It had never been an affair. At least, I had never considered it as such. A fling. A series of bad decisions, misjudged ends of nights, lustful moments, stupid sex. She had been there when we got back from Tangier. I suppose she supported me when I was in a bad way, when I was in a dark place. She became a confidante, bolstered my spirits, gave me some hope, put on my first show. She was available. I can still remember her coming to the studio that first day. 'It's more of a bedsit than a studio, but it will serve you well,' she'd said authoritatively. 'I've brought you a little something.' It wasn't a bottle of wine, a contract, a business proposal, or any painting materials; it was a fax machine, wrapped in Christmas paper. It wasn't Christmas. 'It's all I had,' she said, meaning the wrapping paper, making herself comfortable and smiling at my bewilderment.

'All the artists have them now.'

'In their studios?'

'In their studios. You can receive communiqués.'

'Communiqués?'

'Contracts and the like. It'll be less intrusive than a computer.'

And that's how it started with her. Week after week she would visit; we would talk. One thing would lead to another. 'Tell me about Tangier,' she would say, and we would fall on to the mattress at the back of the studio, and it had continued like that, haphazardly and foolishly, until now.

'I can't.'

'Harry . . .' I thought she was going to say I owed her. Her hand moved further up my thigh, slow and insistent. I felt the steady pressure of it tugging at me, drawing me to her, not taking no for an answer.

'I saw Dillon.'

Her hand stopped.

'I saw him. He was there, at the march. Some woman had him by the hand.'

She held my gaze for a moment; then her eyes flickered over my face. She sighed and looked away. 'Not this again, Harry.'

'*Not this again*? What are you talking about?'

Her hand, withdrawn from my thigh, was now raised in a calming gesture.

'You know what I'm talking about, Harry.'

'This is ridiculous. What am I even doing, sitting here with you? I have to get going. I have to find him.'

'Harry, sit down and relax.'

'Relax? Don't tell me to relax, Diane.'

'Harry, come on. We've been through all this before. Dillon is dead. He was killed by an earthquake in Tangier.' She enunciated each word slowly and carefully, as if talking to a child.

'They never found a body.'

'Well, there were lots of people in that earthquake whose remains were never found. That doesn't mean they all survived and were spirited away to different countries, given new identities and began living different lives.'

I heard the mocking tone in her voice as I crossed the floor.

'I saw him.'

'Have you asked yourself, if by some miracle your son did manage to survive an earthquake, how on earth he could have made his way to Dublin, of all places?' Her question lingered in the air. 'It's just not possible, Harry, is it? You're stressed, under pressure . . . It's not the first time. When you were in the hospital, in St James's, didn't I visit you?'

I turned and gave her one last look, and in a voice that I struggled to keep calm and firm, I said, 'Diane, I saw him.'

She didn't even look up. She just shook her head and drained her glass. But I had had enough. I needed to get out of there. I was late and wanted desperately to see

Robin. I stood, walked away and, without a backward glance, I let the door slam behind me.

I drove to Slattery's too fast. The van slid on one corner, but I held it together and drove more slowly until I found a parking space outside the pub. I knew Robin would be there. I was full of nerves. I wasn't sure what I would tell her, but as soon as I saw her I could see that Robin had something to tell me.

She looked up at me expectantly as I approached the corner booth. She said nothing about me being late, just raised her face to accept my kiss. As I drew away, she smiled and handed me a menu and began to talk. I took the seat opposite her, eased my coat from my shoulders and felt the hammering of my heart as I considered what I was about to say.

'I've ordered champagne,' she said. 'You don't mind, do you? I know it's extravagant, but still.'

'What's the occasion?' I asked.

She shrugged. 'A girl doesn't always need an excuse to order champagne.'

'True.'

She must have heard the doubt in my voice. She leaned across and took my hand and said, 'I'm just happy. Isn't that worth celebrating?'

I looked at her then, and I don't know if it was the strangeness of the day or the renewed guilt I felt over Diane, but it was as if I were seeing my wife with fresh eyes. In the shadowy dimness of the pub, she seemed to radiate a warmth. I felt the turmoil inside me grow calm.

I loved how she had eased into her thirties, growing into herself, becoming the woman I loved and not just the girl I had fancied. Dillon's loss had aged us both; there was no doubt about that. When I looked at photographs of the two of us in Tangier, we seemed to be kids. We were students when first we met. Bright-eyed and all that. Now, well, yes, there were lines of age on her face, lines of sadness. In the dark blue-grey of her eyes, I saw an extra depth of melancholy, but not despair; instead, there was a depthless sympathy, a forgiving and timeless patience. The difference between us was, whereas I looked ragged and rough around the edges, Robin had aged gracefully.

'I'll drink to that,' I said.

We raised our glasses to each other, and I drank and felt the bubbles fizz on the back of my tongue. For a brief instant, the room seemed to swirl. I closed my eyes. When I opened them, I noticed that Robin's drink was untouched.

'So, what's your news? You sounded frantic.'

I didn't know what to say. The expectant look in her eyes, the champagne – it unnerved me momentarily.

She was staring at me. 'Are you all right?'

'I'm fine. Tired, that's all.'

'Are you sure? You look flushed.'

'Do I? It's probably just the heat in here after the cold outside.'

The look of concern lingered on her face.

'I'm fine, really. It's the champagne.' And I reached across for her hand, felt the answering squeeze, and she smiled.

But I wasn't fine. I was overrun by a strange mixture of

emotions. One moment I felt elated: I had seen Dillon, after all. The next I sank into the depths of something I couldn't quite climb out of. I knew that I had to tell her, but I couldn't find the right words. I wanted to reveal the news carefully, so that she would trust the news I gave her and believe me. But part of me dreaded her reaction. A big part of me. While she was talking, I waited for the right moment to tell her, the pause in conversation when I could reveal what was on my mind. That our son was alive. That he was close by. That he was, after all these years, finally within our reach. But after one drink and then another, it was she who told me what she had wanted to tell me all day.

'Harry,' she said. Whenever she uses my name directly, I know it is something important. Usually, it's something serious. She wants to, as gently as she can, suggest that I drink less, or spend more time at home, or consider going away with her for the weekend, or have dinner with her parents. Oh fuck, I thought, not Christmas; she wants us to have Christmas with her folks. She's going to pay the bill and plead. *Please, Harry*, she'll say. *Do this for me.*

But she did not ask me. Instead, she said, quite matter-of-factly, 'Harry, I'm pregnant.'

I stared at her. Not in surprise, really. Shock, more like.

She gave me a nervous smile, then bit down on her lip. 'Did you hear what I said?' she asked softly.

I had heard. It was crystal clear. But somehow I couldn't respond. My mind filled and surged; it opened like a dam, a dam spilling out doubt and quandary. Finally I managed, 'I don't know what to say.'

I felt a strange mixture of emotions. Something rose in me, a wild excitement. I was to be a father again. Seeing Robin look so happy, radiating new possibilities for the future, made me doubt myself. It dispelled the thoughts that suggested that I did not want her to be pregnant. She reached out her hand, and the gesture brushed away my doubts, dismissed the afternoon, my visions, because that is what they must have been. The trickle of doubt I had felt over my sighting of the boy now strengthened. It became a rushing river. All my certainty was washed away, and with it my fury at the Guard's inaction, my guilt over Diane, my own frustrated urge to comb the streets of Dublin to find my missing boy. The image dwindled and faded.

'You're going to have to say something, you know,' Robin said.

I knew in that moment that I would not tell her about Dillon. About what I thought I had seen that day, *who* I had seen. I would have to keep that from her, because what she had told me made it so much more unlikely.

I said, 'I can't believe it.'

'Believe it,' Robin said. 'It's true. It's going to happen. Harry, I'm so –'

I thought she was going to say 'happy', but she didn't. She said something that surprised and puzzled me. She said, '– relieved. I'm so relieved.'

She was close to tears. Her hands were shaking. I got out of my seat and rounded the table. I slipped in beside her and took her in my arms, felt the warmth of her there, the brush of her hair against my face. I whispered to her that it was wonderful news, that I couldn't believe it. I tried to say all the right things, to use all the right words. I felt her hands on my back, the pressure of her fingertips against my spine, and all my hopes seemed to anchor themselves to her.

For the rest of the night, we talked about the baby. We talked about dates, night feedings and nappies, yet all the time, the ghosting image of Dillon wavered in and out of my consciousness. I could see, at different points in the night, his gaze, unsure but still and fixed.

Later, I stood in the bedroom, and the world spiralled about me as I tried to make sense of everything in and outside my head.

Robin got into bed. In her hands was a book, a book on pregnancy. I had never seen it before. Or had I? Was it an old one? Was it the one she had found in Cozimo's second-hand bookstore in Tangier?

'Are you coming to bed?' she asked, putting down the book. She smiled. Her hands beckoned me to her, and I found myself reaching for her and pulling my clothes off within her embrace. Our bodies knew each other's pulse, and we moved this way and that and found the groove and spell our love had known for so long. Her hands held me firm against her, her fingertips sinking into my back. Spent, we lay side by side, breathing heavily and sweating. Robin turned over and gradually fell into a deep sleep. After some time, I got out of bed and went to the bathroom.

On the way back to bed, I found a bottle of water on

the floor, knelt and drank every last drop. I lifted myself on to the bed. Robin stirred. Her arm reached for me. I could see the book about pregnancy on her side of the bed. The spine of the book wavered in my tired mind until it became any number of book spines, and before I knew it, I was falling surely and fitfully asleep, with the image of Cozimo and his dusty bookstore spinning and swirling in my already dizzy head.

# 4. Robin

When I woke on that snowy Sunday morning, I was immediately aware of what had gone between us the night before – my revelation and all that followed. In the quiet of the early-morning bedroom, I lay there and thought about it, about what it would mean for us, about how things would be different now. It was as if the house itself felt changed. It seemed enveloped in a new calm. This house, with its ancient walls, its creaky floors, its shifts and moans, had always seemed to be a living, breathing thing. Sentient, almost. The life force of the previous inhabitants had seeped into the raw materials of the house, the sheen of their spirits adding another layer to the multiple layers of paint and varnish and the stains of generations. But on that Sunday early morning, as I silently pulled back the covers and put my feet to the floor, I listened to the silence around me, and it was as if the breathing of the house had slowed, had grown easy. There were no creaks or moans as I got out of bed and padded across the floor, closing the door softly behind myself, leaving the room and Harry sleeping peacefully together.

Downstairs, I put the kettle on and looked about. I was taken with a new energy, a sense of urgency about my need to tackle the house. This restlessness rumbled about inside me as I walked from room to room, assessing the varying degrees of dilapidation and making a mental list of what needed to be done. I looked through the doorway that led into the garage, and in the half-light I could see the cold, quiet space that would soon become Harry's studio. It seemed to be waiting for him to begin, and I thought of how this room would soon be transformed into a place of creativity, of art, and I pictured Harry working away in here, deep in concentration, a quiet contentment possessing him and seeping out to every corner of our home. I thought of this, and felt a tingle of excitement pass through me: things were about to change.

The kettle whistled; I turned away, back towards the kitchen. I put a mug on the counter, and it was as I was pouring water over the teabag that it came for me – that old memory, swooping down out of nowhere – and all at once I was standing once again in that tiny bathroom in Tangier.

It had been hot. Even in that room, the one cool spot in the apartment, the air had felt heavy and dull with heat. Outside, in the hallway, I could hear Harry pacing up and down. Every couple of minutes, his footsteps stopped, and I knew that he was right there, right on the other side of the door, and that he was listening for me, for some clue as to what was going on. I had locked him out, had told him to wait, but his impatience and his barely contained excitement seemed to push up against the closed door. I could feel the insistence of it. Inside, I held myself very still, sweat gathering on my forehead and upper lip as I stared down at the white stick in my hand.

'Well?' he asked through the door. 'Have you done it yet?'

His voice hit a nerve. Something inside me seemed to plummet.

'Just a minute,' I said, my voice thin and stretched.

I needed to compose myself.

I put the stick down and leaned against the sink. It felt cold to the touch. I would have liked, then, to lie down on the tiled floor and press my face and body to the cool ceramic. I was so tired I could have fallen asleep right there, right then, and maybe, when I woke, I would have found that everything was all right, everything was as it should have been. I could have been myself again.

'The instructions said you'd know within two minutes.'

That insistence again, the weight of it pressed against the door.

'Come on,' he said, tapping softly but impatiently. 'You're killing me here.'

There was a mirror above the sink. The face that stared back at me was pale and drawn. The eyes had a haunted look to them.

Robin, I said to myself. What on earth have you done?

I left the teabag on the draining board, my hand shaking. Get a grip, I told myself sternly. The tea made, I took it with me to the armchair drawn up to the window and I sat down and stared out at the frozen garden, feeling the mug warm between my hands. The memory had rattled me. Why had it come to me now? And in its wake, I felt unsettled, deflated, my energy draining away, leaving me in a lethargy of discontent. One memory followed another. They tumbled up from the past, demanding recognition. I sipped my tea and allowed my mind to wander.

I thought of that first pregnancy, the craziness of it. Stumbling and lurching from month to month, my mind struggling to catch up with the changes sweeping through my body. Harry had accepted it far more quickly and easily than I had. He had jumped at the possibility of a baby – pounced on it. From the very start of my pregnancy with Dillon, Harry was there, ambushing me with his eager anticipation, his hunger for it. And yet, last night, when I'd told him my news, he had not been like that at all. Instead he had grown still and silent. He had stared at the table in front of him for the longest time, and I had felt the reluctance coming off him in waves. What was it he had said?

*'I can't believe it.'*

Now, sitting in my armchair by the window, the mug of tea cooling in my hands, those words came back to me, and I felt the chill echo of them in that silent room. I considered again what that reluctance might mean. I told myself that it was the suddenness of the news, coming on a day that had been difficult for him, what with moving out of his studio and all the complex emotions that entailed. I told myself that after Dillon, even good news brought on a strange mix of feelings. I told myself that, given time and space, he would come around to the idea.

And I knew from experience that it was best not to push it. Better to let these things lie. He was a man with a particular vulnerability. I knew the signs. Funny, the things you learn about yourself when a tragedy takes over your life. Who would have thought that I would turn out to be the strong one, while Harry fell to pieces.

A creak of floorboards overhead alerted me to his rising. I sat there listening to his movements in the bedroom, a pause before the groan of the door, and then the sound of him coming down the stairs.

'Jesus, you look terrible,' I said as he emerged from the hallway, a greenish tinge to his skin, his eyes bleary and bloodshot. He was holding himself carefully, as if every movement threatened the delicate balance of his hangover and it was a great effort to keep himself from veering over the precipice.

'Tea,' he croaked, his voice hoarse from a dozen cigarettes. 'I feel like something's died in my mouth.'

'Kettle's just boiled.'

I watched him there, pouring hot water into a mug, and I had the thought that the years might have fallen away and we could be students again. From where I was sitting, he seemed the same tall, somewhat gangly youth, with that unruly dark hair, the square set of his shoulders, a skittish energy running the length of his long, taut body. But I wasn't eighteen any more, and he wasn't twenty. He tossed the teabag and spoon into the sink and grimaced as his mouth met with the lip of the cup. Then he came and sat down opposite me, giving out a great sigh as he did so, running a hand over his face, rubbing his eyes, and I remembered how agitated he had been the night before, his eyes darting around the room, unable to settle. He has cold blue eyes, like shallow water touched by sunlight. One iris is flecked with an amber flame. Last night they had seemed very bright, but now, in the cold light of morning, they looked dull and ringed with fatigue.

He leaned forwards, putting his mug on the floor by his feet, then straightened up, taking his cigarettes from his pocket.

'Harry,' I said, watching him put one to his mouth, a wry smile starting on my lips. 'Haven't you forgotten something?'

He looked up, puzzled. And then he saw my amusement, and the confusion cleared from his face.

'Christ. The baby! I'd forgotten.'

He shook his head and laughed, returning the cigarette to its pack, and then sat there, a little stunned, as if processing anew the information, and all the while I looked on, willing him to be pleased, willing him to show some indication that he could be happy about this.

And then he ran a hand through his hair and said, 'A baby. I still don't believe it,' and the smile broke out on his face – a grin that sliced through the hangover and the tiredness and the tension – and this time the words seemed to have a different meaning. It seemed, in fact, that what he meant was that he couldn't believe his luck. That after all we had gone through, to be given a second chance, the gift of this new little life – it seemed too much to grasp.

I felt an answering jump of excitement inside.

'You're not angry, are you, Harry?'

'Angry? No! Of course not. Why would I be? I'm a little surprised, that's all, but not angry. Not in the least.'

'You're sure?'

'Robin, it's great news. I'm thrilled. I swear.'

He said it and smiled and reached for my hand, and we

sat like that for a moment, and I believed he was pleased.
I really did.

'So how are you feeling? Any nausea? Any sickness?'

'No, nothing at all. I feel absolutely fine – great, in fact.'

'Lucky you,' he said, referring to his hangover.

For a while we talked about the pregnancy, picking up
our conversation from last night. We discussed what hospital should we go to, what kind of care we wanted, when
should I tell them at work, what would we do once the
baby was born.

'We'll have to do something about this place,' he said,
casting his eyes about the room, as if noticing for the first
time the snaking cables, the holes in the walls, the whole
shambolic array of projects started and stalled.

'Jesus, where to begin,' he added.

'If we can just work out the more pressing things that
need to happen, and focus on them.'

'Right. Well, you'd better make a list.'

'Me?'

'You are the architect, sweetheart,' he remarked, not
unkindly, and yet I felt a slight sting in his words.

My decision to study architecture after returning from
Tangier had not rested easily with Harry. I had tried to
explain to him my need for something stable, something
dependable in my life, in my career, and while on one level
he seemed to understand, I'd always felt that a part of him
resented me for my change of heart. It was as if he perceived some kind of accusation in my decision to abandon
my art for the safety of a profession, while he continued

with his. The truth was, I had needed, more than anything, to put Tangier behind me. To create a life utterly different from what we'd had there. I needed to forget. And while I had set about constructing my new existence, Harry had clung to what he had of the past. In his cold studio in Spencer's basement, he'd persisted with his paintings of Tangier as if the world around him did not exist. It seemed, sometimes, as if he had never really left Morocco at all.

But that was not worth bringing up, particularly that morning, when he seemed focused on our future. So we talked about insulation and heating, about bathrooms and plumbing, about getting our bedroom in order so that we might make room for a cot.

'A cot,' he said as he finished his tea, giving his head a baffled shake. 'That's something I didn't think I'd ever have to consider again. Can't we just put the kid in a drawer?'

I took his empty mug from him and said, 'Why don't I get you some aspirin. Your hangover looks like it's going to linger.'

'Thanks, babe. I'll just nip out for a smoke.'

I went to the sink and left his mug there. Then I fished in the cupboard for a pint glass and, as I was filling it with water, I looked up and caught sight of him outside in the garden. He was drawing deeply on his cigarette; then he breathed out a plume of smoke into the cold morning air. And what he did next was this: he took the cigarette from his mouth and dropped it on the snow. He stood perfectly still with his head bent, as if staring at the butt on the ground. Then he closed his eyes and brought both hands up to cover his face. His bent neck, the slump of his shoulders, his face hiding in those cupped hands. Something about it made me go cold. It was a gesture of despair.

'Freezing out there.'

He closed the back door behind him and stood there shivering.

I found the packets in the cupboard. The tablets plinked as they hit the water, and I handed him the glass, and he swallowed down the contents with a groan, as though the effort had drained him of any last scrap of energy.

I put my hand against his brow and felt the heat there despite the enveloping cold. Then I leaned in and wrapped my arms around him, pressing my body against his, needing to feel close to him to dispel the despair that still clung to him.

'I know something that's good for a hangover,' I said slowly, and when I drew back, he met my smile with a broad grin of his own.

'Oh yeah?'

'Yeah.' I reached up and kissed him then, slowly, savouring the taste of him, sour with alcohol and cigarettes, but I didn't care. My desire for him licked like a flame inside me.

And so it was not until later, when we lay against each other in our bed, naked and exhausted, a quiet contentment falling over us like a happy sigh, that I remembered our phone call of the previous day.

'Harry?' I said, watching the strand of my hair that he was idly spiralling around his finger.

'Hmm?'

'You never did tell me.'

'Tell you what?'

'Yesterday, on the phone, you said something had happened.'

'What's that?'

'Remember? When you rang to ask me to come and meet you? You said something had happened. But you never said what it was.'

'Didn't I?'

'No.'

'I thought I did.'

'So?'

He stopped playing with my hair and rubbed a finger in his eye, frown lines puckering his brow.

'I bumped into someone.'

'Who?'

'Eh, Tanya – that girl from the Sitric Gallery. The one with all the freckles. Do you remember her?'

'Vaguely. And?'

'And we got talking and I told her about the stuff I've been working on . . .'

'And . . . ?'

'And she sounded interested.'

I pushed myself up on to my elbows to look at him.

'Do you think they might give you a show?'

He saw my eager expression and let out a burst of laughter.

'Look at you, counting your unhatched chickens.'

'Seriously, Harry. Do you think they might?'

His laughter died away, and he gave me a slow, hazy smile.

'They might. They just might.'

Then he pulled me back down to him, and we lay in silence for a minute, both of us considering the possibilities.

'Harry?'

'Go to sleep, baby.'

I felt the weight of his arm slung over my hip and the tickle of his rough chin nestling into my neck.

'We're so lucky, Harry.'

His body lay cupped around mine, so I couldn't read his expression.

'Yes,' he said slowly, before drifting away to sleep. 'Yes, we are.'

# 5. Harry

The first time we met Cozimo, he had been knocked over by a passing bicycle on one of the narrow alleys of the medina. His straw hat lay beside his outstretched body. He didn't cry out or seem inconvenienced in any way. Staring blankly upwards as if considering his predicament, he was humming something to himself. When I bent down to see if he was all right, he looked up at me and said, 'It's not like I've been drinking.'

I reached my arm down, and he grabbed it and I lifted him up. Robin handed him his hat.

'Your health,' he said, reaching into his waistcoat. He took a swift slug from a small silver flask before blurting out that he was 'much obliged'. But as he turned to walk away, he fell to the ground like a deck of cards. 'Perhaps,' he said, never losing his decorum, 'you could call me a taxi or an ambulance, even.' He was very polite, always polite.

We went with him to the hospital, much to his surprise. It was Robin's idea. The hospital was small and unclean. Robin spoke good French and told a nurse how we had found the man. By this stage, Cozimo was somewhat delirious and speaking – or, rather, slurring – in a number of different languages and at one stage humming and what can only be described as chirruping in a language resembling Arabic.

That night we left him sedated and cheerful. When we returned to see him the next day, he was garrulous and appreciative. Robin asked if there was anything we could do for him.

'There is one thing,' he said.

'Anything,' she said, taking a shine to him or feeling sorry for him or some mixture of the two.

'Can you check on the shop?'

The shop was his bookshop. Robin, of course, said yes. She is always talking to strangers and saying yes. She doesn't know how to say no. Generous to a fault.

He handed us the keys and a scrap of paper with the address. 'It's in a state, but it'll be good to know it is still standing.'

We took off in a taxi and found ourselves travelling through a network of narrow streets until the car stopped and the driver pointed. 'You walk now,' he said, and we did and found the old building tilting at the end of a small laneway. We let ourselves in – into the ramshackle old bookshop, into Cozimo's life, and into, without knowing it at the time, what would become our home for the next four years. You see, one upshot of Robin's generous spirit was that Cozimo offered us, by the time he was leaving hospital, a place to stay. 'It's my pleasure. You'd be doing me a favour.'

'We can't,' Robin said.

'You visited me every day.'

And that was the start of our time in Tangier, something that began as a dream and ended a nightmare. I can't tell you everything that happened there. I can give you an

71

idea, a sense of what the place was like – that's all. I'd go mad if I had to delve into all the details again. It's strange, because I remember it now as if it were someone else's life. To put it simply: we had wanted to come to Tangier because of the light.

Back then, both of us were artists. After art college, we had travelled a bit through Europe – Spain mostly – ending up in Tarifa on the Costa de la Luz. We liked its hippy feel, it was cheap, and it gave us a chance to paint with the luminous coastal light of Andalusia. The century was drawing to a close, and after a weekend in Tangier, where we celebrated the start of the new millennium, we knew it was for us. The cultural mix was more interesting, and more importantly, there was something magical about the light there. It wasn't until we returned to Ireland that Robin gave up on her art. After Dillon, she somehow lost the heart for painting. Maybe she associated the painting with him. She kind of co-opted his contributions to her paintings, you know, included them as part of the process. Ours was a free household. We weren't fussy about the paintings. If Dillon wanted to dip his hands in and spread them about the canvas, well, so be it. At least, that's how it became. Sure, when I started, I liked to have a closed-off space, but as I realized that Dillon was less of a distraction and more of an asset, I loosened up and let him throw whatever dollop of paint my way whenever he wanted.

I think Cozimo liked the idea that there were two artists living in his apartment. 'Talk about landing on your feet,' I said to Robin, but she thought it a poor choice of words after Cozimo's accident.

'Some broken ribs, maybe an internal thing or two, they don't know. How could they? Tangier is a wonderful place to live, but not if you are a medical patient. Or a medical specimen, as they would have it.'

Cozimo talked with an affected English accent. The sinking couch in the apartment was where a prince of Morocco had been conceived, he whispered confidentially to us, lounging and downing his pills with a heady mixture of cocktails. He liked martinis most of the time, and he could often be heard calling out for vermouth.

'Where is the vermouth? Olives, where are the olives?'

We were intrigued by this eccentric yet austere-looking man. His hair was receding at the front, but he wore it long at the back. He wore slippers and silk trousers. We visited him in the hospital every day for a week before he came to convalesce with us. 'Look here,' he said, 'stay – we'll come to some sort of arrangement.'

'Arrangement?' I said a little dubiously.

'A rent agreeable to both parties.'

I remember Robin asking him, in those early days, how long he had been in Tangier. He answered her while mixing another martini. 'Since God was a child, my dear,' he said. 'Since God was a child.'

That's the way he spoke. He was theatrical. He owned the bookshop, but it seemed to do very little trade. Was it a front, a hobby, something to keep the lord himself occupied? 'One can't be sure,' he said, answering my indirect question obliquely on one of those smouldering afternoons. 'The truth is, I can hardly remember when or why I opened the place myself.'

The apartment was large, with three rooms. In the back room, where we painted, there was a stack of old typewriters. 'I used them once, I think,' Cozimo told us. 'Now I collect them. I must have used them once. Maybe I wrote a book on one of them.' He balanced his gold cigarette holder between his fingers like Garbo and blithely flicked the ash on to the ground.

Tangier. It was another world away. Another lifetime. We had freedom. We had Dillon. We had everything we wanted. Yes, we arrived without Dillon. And we plunged into life in Tangier without him, but in a way, I remember that time as if he had been there all along. Laughing, mischievous, unfettered.

We worked hard there, but we enjoyed ourselves, too. And even though one painting followed another, it seemed as if the days were longer, languorous, hazy and golden, that we had time for everything we wanted to do.

We wrote *The Tangier Manifesto* there. It was a co-authored missive of free living. A poster stuck to one wall of the kitchen. We scratched mottoes, dictums, words of encouragement, reminders, jokes and phrases we heard:

Paint or die.
Wake early.
Meditate.
God give me the strength to lead a double life.
Milk, please, we need milk!

Sometimes the phrases were crossed out, and over time 'paint at first light' was replaced by 'bottle at 3 and 6 a.m.!,

74

Harry's turn!' Or: 'nappies, we are out of nappies and the water has been cut off.'

But more often than not, they were madcap phrases of the moment: 'What is Buddha?'

The next day the answer might be scribbled by the same person or someone else: 'Three pounds of flax!'

Thinking back now, it seemed as if Robin never fully believed in Tangier. Maybe she thought it was too good to be true. Maybe it was. Maybe she thought, life can't be like this. Of course, her mother didn't help. Ringing her all the time. Asking her to come home. Guilt-tripping her. 'Your father's sick.' 'I miss you.' Or 'How can you deal with the heat of that country while you're pregnant? That's no place to bring up a child!' And so on, ad nauseam.

Her one and only visit was a complete train wreck from start to finish. Jesus, what can I tell you now? The essentials are: her flight was delayed. I was to meet her. Robin had picked up a few hours working in Caid's Bar, so she'd sent me. I waited for the plane dutifully. It was delayed further. I went for coffee. I went for a drink. The plane landed. We missed each other. Robin's mother did not speak to me when I saw her later that night. Neither did she like our digs, so she wasted money on a four-star hotel an expensive taxi ride away. She spent the weekend weeping, beseeching Robin to come home. 'Beseeching' I say, because she is the kind of woman to use the word 'beseeching'. I thought she might develop a rapport with Cozimo, but she found him small and vile. Her words. The weekend passed dismally, and Robin accompanied her mother back to the airport, and I never said goodbye.

Robin hardly ever mentioned the visit, and we settled back into our life. But I knew, or I sensed at least, that the wobbles were there in Robin. Her mother had only exacerbated her anxiety. It was not the middle-class life our parents might have expected of us, but we were doing what we had dreamed about in college. Tangier was not an expensive place to live, and we had, from what I had made from my first show out of college, enough to get by on, I reckoned, for at least three years. That had been the plan, but within eighteen months of our arrival there, Robin told me she was pregnant.

Not that that changed things for me. I was elated. But when she suggested moving back to Ireland, I resisted, to put it mildly. 'Why would we go back?' I said. 'What have we got to go back to?'

'Family.'

'Your family?'

It wasn't hard to figure out why I did not get on with Robin's parents. They resented me for taking their daughter away from them, away from Ireland, away from everything cosy and comfortable. An artist has to go away, I told Robin. She didn't disagree, and I remember talking at length on the subject. She wasn't objecting, but it didn't stop me from making my point, even after we had absconded.

But I'd always suspected that Robin had her eye on our return. Whereas I wasn't sure I would ever go back. What for?

To say it was not an ideal place to bring up a child just suggested you were from somewhere else. Dillon's first years passed in a blur of night feedings, sleeplessness and walking, always walking, in a buggy, in my arms, on my shoulder, whatever it took to get him to sleep.

Cozimo was bewildered but charmed by the presence of a child. He lived within walking distance of the book-shop in a detached and gated house he was curiously private about, and though we saw him nearly every day since our first meeting, he rarely asked us to his home. That was something Robin and I talked about, but never with Cozimo. He was generous enough as it was and brought gifts for Dillon on a regular basis, but he looked at the boy strangely, as if he had never encountered a child before. 'Amusing little things, aren't they,' he said to me once after I found him blowing smoke into Dillon's face. 'Doesn't like that,' he said wryly.

'No, I wouldn't imagine he does,' I said, assuming Coz-imo's arch tone. There were plenty of oddities about Coz. Where was he from? Where had his money come from? What was his own house like? Why did he spend so much time with us at the apartment? We had our own theories about him, but Cozimo for the most part remained elu-sive, and though I can say that he was probably my best friend from that time, I also feel like I hardly knew him. Take, for example, his bizarre interest in the occult.

I'm not sure how he persuaded me, but one night he wanted to have a séance. 'I have some questions for the dead,' he said. The truth was that he was off his head most of the time, and I suppose I was overindulging myself. Tangier was a transit point for all sorts of drugs; the place was drenched in them. There were parties where you could hardly avoid cocaine, pills, hash – anything you wanted or had ever heard of was there.

'I don't think Robin will be into it,' I said to Coz.

'Okay, so we'll do it when she is out.'

After work, Robin often liked to walk at night. I'm not saying it was safe or that I approved, but she took in the sights, cleared her head and very often went to an Internet café or somewhere she could make or receive a phone call. She liked to stay in regular contact with her parents, and when I say 'regular', I mean every second day. I did not have that problem. Even if my parents had been alive, I don't think I would have been in touch that often. But it was Robin's business. In any case, that and her work at the bar allowed me to join in with the séances. I remembered something about Yeats getting involved in séances, way back when, and I thought Cozimo's flighty idea might generate some ideas for my own work, my painting, and that it might be some fun. Yes, I was curious. And I was high.

The thing was, before that first séance, Dillon had fallen asleep on the dinner table at the apartment. I know it sounds strange, but things were free and easy and out of kilter. The large oak table we ate at also had a dip at the end of it, where Dillon sometimes climbed. I often put a cushion up there, and late at night he would climb up and fall asleep. I think he was about two when we had this first séance. Two Spanish sisters I had never met before and a local couple Cozimo had befriended the previous week were there, too. 'What about Dillon?' Cozimo asked. 'Can you put him to bed?'

'I'd hate to wake him,' I said.

Dillon was a bad sleeper. Straight and simple. In the past it had had nothing to do with teething or growth spurts or the noise from outside, the hawkers or touts, the music from across the street, the heaving mass of the city, none of it; he was like his father, pure and simple, a bad sleeper. No, wait a minute; he was worse. Probably, if we had gone to check it out, we would have been told it was some kind of condition. But we didn't. We struggled on. It was like this: he could stay awake for hours. I'm talking all night. Now, Robin and I had been night owls, back in our college days, but in Tangier we were super-conscious of the light, the daylight. We had to have as much of it as possible. That's what we had come for. That's what made the paintings possible. The strange and beautiful light of Tangier, its radiant and dusty history.

But we became exhausted. Missing the morning light because of lack of sleep made me sick. I started taking pills either to keep me going when I woke or to get me to sleep at night so I could be up to catch that fiery dawn light I wanted in my paintings. Cozimo had a cabinet full of pills. In one pencil case, he kept the pills he needed for a week; a generous soul, he offered me pretty much what I wanted or what he thought I needed. Of course, I didn't tell Robin about taking these pills. But to paint, to be ready for the canvas, I needed to be there; I couldn't afford to be exhausted from lack of sleep.

The first pill I tried was a sleeping pill. I took it at half eleven at night and slept till seven a.m. Robin wasn't suspicious. She was happy I had got some rest. 'If only I

79

could sleep like that,' she said. 'Dillon was awake half the night.'

When the lack of sleep started to take something of a toll and Robin lost weight and dark rings formed about her eyes, I thought that, rather than offering her a pill, I would get the little man to sleep with a quarter of a pill. Then maybe she could rest. I crushed the pill up in the kitchen and poured it into a glass of warm milk. It dissolved, and Dillon never noticed. I know I should never have done that. But it felt almost as if someone else was doing it. Somewhere in the back of my mind a voice was saying, *Bad idea, very bad idea, stop*, but the other Harry, the one who moved and spoke and did things, he carried on regardless, and after that first night, when our Dillon slept properly, heavily even, and woke up with a satisfying yelp and smile, I thought, well, lucky, good, no harm done.

Then our séances became a monthly thing. Cozimo managed to contact his great-uncle and a childhood friend named Albert who he had not saved when he could have. It sounds perplexing now, but at the time it all made sense – either that or I didn't think so much about it and went along with it. I mean, why weren't we doing these dodgy séances in his more private, more spacious and comfortable house? But then, that first night there was an element of spontaneity about it. Anyway, one of the beings Cozimo wanted most to contact – and I am not joking when I say this – was his childhood pet beagle. That's how our monthly meetings became known as the Order of the Golden Beagle. It sounds ludicrous now, and even then the ridiculous title and name – well, it was all a bit of fun, another excuse for a late-night party. Robin never participated, and I did not discuss the details of those supernatural evenings with her, even if she suspected something.

I didn't administer the crushed pills to Dillon every night; I wasn't that far gone. But I did start to give them to him more than I might have, more than I should have – I know that now. I take the responsibility, even if it is not something I found the nerve or courage to tell Robin about. I suppose I gave them to him once a month. Cozimo became convinced that the sleeping child on the table – Dillon, in other words – was instrumental to the success of the séances. So as we got bedtime together and after I had read him his storybooks – he liked the tales from Narnia; Aslan was his favourite – I gave him his milk, with the crushed quarter pill, and deposited him on the oak table before the Order of the Golden Beagle met. Cozimo even made him an honorary member of the order and procured a special pillow, embroidered with the order's name, and that is where Dillon's head rested on those particular nights.

And so we got started. It was all more or less nonsense: the joining of hands, the murmuring. One of the Spanish women – Blanca, I think her name was – acted as medium. Is this something she volunteered for or Cozimo suggested? I can't be sure, but either way she assumed the role. I remember she mumbled and hummed and told us all to close our eyes while Cozimo was relighting the candles, which had been blown out by a dry, swirling wind that had come through town. The noise from outside seemed deafening at times: footsteps, people walking, people talking, car horns blaring, and engines revving. Then something very strange happened. During the séance, the other Spanish woman started wailing. Her name, I can't remember, but Cozimo joined in. 'Don't break the circle,' Blanca said. 'Don't.' But it was too late, and everyone was standing about, shifting from foot to foot, looking for another drink.

'I felt something,' Cozimo said. 'Something powerful.'

Blanca told him that he should not have broken the circle. But the séance was over, and we started drinking more. Cozimo had a great record collection. He had a wonderful old record player made in the shape of an old gramophone, and that is where you could usually find him after the séances had ended, bent over his old records, both classical and jazz. But he was too moved by this experience, he told us, while pouring more wine into everyone's glass. Instead, I knelt by the player and changed the record.

Cozimo looked over. While it was now our place, mine and Robin's, he still felt possessive about his vinyl. He eyed me suspiciously and made some comment about being careful as to what I chose. Then there was more music, more dancing, more talking. The song I remember from that séance was 'Turn Out the Stars'. I remember swaying to its languid rhythms, my eyes closing slowly to its lulling beat. I remember the song for another reason too: it was playing in the apartment the last time I saw Dillon.

He had been asleep, his head sinking into the embroidered pillow, which he had taken into his bedroom. How still he looked, lying there, eyes closed, long lashes dark against his skin. And vulnerable too, with his hands thrown up above his head, fingers curled. I looked at him and felt the slow burn of love.

And then there was my foolish dash to Cozimo's and the devastating earthquake. All the time, the music ghosted through my head; the slow syncopation of jazz played counterpoint to my panic, to the fires, to the hissing gas, to the falling dust and shuddering buildings, to my frantic race back to the apartment.

The night it happened, Robin was working late. It's ironic, but that week, that month, Robin had come round; her doubts and worry had somehow dissipated in the weeks leading up to that fateful night. She was more resolute about staying in Tangier – not for ever, that was not the plan, but for a time, the time it took to finish another show, one I was calling *The Tangier Manifesto*. It was her birthday. On her break, we had spoken briefly on the phone – a casual conversation, no hint of the great drama that was just around the corner for us, a drama that would come to be the central point of our lives. Afterwards, she would have returned to the bar and continued serving the scattering of customers there that night; perhaps some of them might have commented upon the strange stillness in the air, the charged atmosphere that lingered in the streets that night. And then she would have felt the tremors, been caught up in the commotion, seen the growing and distressed crowds, the shifting buildings, the smoke, the rising flames. She would have left the bar, run through the streets of our neighbourhood, passed the pharmacy, the leather shop, the launderette, raced down the dip to the bakery, and then she would have seen me.

I say 'would', because to be honest, I can't truly or completely remember that night. So much of it is a blank. Shock, rage, panic, fear, grief, disbelief – they all swelled together to numb my mind and blacken out the last parts of the night as if the stars themselves were extinguished.

What I do remember is her calm and even voice asking me, 'Where is Dillon? Harry, where is he? Where is Dillon? Where is our son?'

That's it. How the night ended? I can't tell you, because I don't know.

But let me tell you this, let me tell you something I do know: I have the same dream again and again. I am asking Dillon to close his eyes. He is not sleeping. I am trying to get him to sleep. His warm body is next to mine. We are lying together in his little bed. It is Tangier. His arm is cradled about my neck. A feather has escaped his pillow and is resting in his hair. I turn the bedside lamp on. Close your eyes, I say to him, and in the dim blur of the light, I see that his eyes are closed and that he is sleeping after all.

And then I wake.

# 6. Robin

Two days later, I stood in the kitchen of my oldest friend, Liz, and listened as she pulled apart two screaming six-year-olds who were trying to maul each other to death in the next room. On the floor by my feet, four-month-old Charlotte cooed to herself and sucked her fingers, a wide necklace of drool soaking into her bib. She gazed up at me with a curious stare as I made tea and listened to her mother shrieking at her brother.

'For Christ's sake, Isaac! If I have to come in here one more time to sort you boys out, I will take those light sabres and bin them! Do you understand?'

Sounds of muted disgruntlement followed in her wake as Liz returned to the kitchen, a look of weary exasperation on her face.

'Give me strength,' she said dramatically, approaching the table and throwing herself into the chair opposite mine. 'I don't know what possessed me when I bought those light sabres.'

'Sleep deprivation does strange things to a person.'

The lull in the next room exploded as the two pint-sized Jedis resumed their brawl, but this time, Liz made no effort to move.

'Let them kill each other,' she said with an air of surrender.

'Boys,' I said sympathetically, pouring tea into her cup.
'They always play at killing each other. At least my boys do.'

Liz and I went way back. We had been at school together, our friendship enduring the teenage years, when she was a Goth and I was a boho bookish sort, and then through college, when I studied art and she read history. The years I spent in Tangier, she spent getting married to Andrew, buying a large house in Mount Merrion and filling it with a succession of boys before finally having Charlotte, a chubby, wide-eyed baby who smiled and gurgled, oblivious to the clamour and chaos that whirled around her brothers.

'Biscuit?' I said, offering Liz the open packet of Rich Tea I had found.

'Sod that. There's a Toblerone on top of the fridge.'

I reached for the giant-sized bar and whistled.

'The size of this thing. You could club a small child to death with this.'

'Don't put ideas in my head!' Liz laughed, before adding, 'Andrew gave it to me as a peace offering.'

'A peace offering?'

'Oh, we had this massive argument on Tuesday evening. He accused me of being more interested in drinking a glass of wine while watching *Grey's Anatomy* than in having sex with him.'

'Is he right?'

'Of course he's bloody right, but I'm hardly going to admit to it. And besides, that's not the point.'

'The point being . . . ?'

'I have four children under the age of eight! Two of them I seriously suspect have ADHD or Asperger's or some bloody thing. And one of them is waking up twice in the night for a feed. What does he expect? That I sit around daydreaming about jumping his bones? Please. All I want to do is sleep.'

'Or eat chocolate,' I said, snapping off another triangle.

'It's depressing,' she said. 'One time he would have come home with Chanel. Now I get a bloody Toblerone.'

'At least you get something.'

'That's true. And how *is* Harry?'

I felt the barb in her comment and chose to let it go.

'He's fine.'

Liz sat and watched with an impassive expression as I explained how he had moved out of his studio and set up in the garage. There was no love lost between my husband and my best friend. Liz had always been protective of me, suspicious of any man I showed an interest in. 'Where men are concerned, you have terrible taste and rotten judgement,' she told me once by way of explanation. Harry provoked a kind of wary curiosity in her. That is, until Tangier, which she thought was madness. I still recall that heated phone call between us when she called him a selfish sod and told me that I was a fool to allow myself to be dragged to some seedy shithole for the sake of our art and I accused her of selling out, with her big house in the suburbs and her middle-class snobbery. It took some months before I was able to speak to her again. And yet, after Dillon she was one of the few people I could really talk to. Over the years, I had sat in her kitchen more nights than I can remember, drinking wine and reminiscing about him, crying about him, opening up to her about my deepest wound. And yes, I had told her things about Harry that perhaps I shouldn't have. But there was no one else I might have turned to. And when I thought about all the things I had said in this kitchen – about Harry, about his behaviour, about my suspicions, about how sometimes he frightened me – a wave of regret came over me, so strong that I felt physically weakened by it.

'Steady on,' Liz said, taking the Toblerone from my hands. 'The way you're working through that, anyone would think you were pregnant.'

I blinked with surprise and stared at her, and she stared back, her eyes widening.

'You are? You bloody *are* pregnant! I don't believe it.'

'Oh God. Is it that obvious?'

'Only to a trained eye. How far gone are you?'

'About five minutes. Shit, Liz, you can't tell anyone. I haven't even told my mother yet.'

'Don't worry. Your secret's safe.'

Her eyes, ringed with tiredness, were suddenly lively, and her voice dropped to a whisper as she leaned over the table and drew me into a conspiratorial hush.

'So, tell me all. Come on, I want details.'

'There's really nothing to tell.'

'Oh bollocks to that! Planned or accident?'

'Accident.'

'Yikes! I bet Harry was pissed off.'

'Not really. Actually, he seems happy about it. Elated, in fact.'

'Really?' She raised an eyebrow, and I felt the scrutiny of her gaze and shrank from it.

'Okay, I admit it – he was surprised.'

'In a good way?'

'Yes, in a good way.'

'What did he say when you told him?'

I remembered again his blank expression, his voice as he said, *I can't believe it.*

'He'd had a crappy day, and my news came out of left field, so he was taken aback. For a minute he couldn't speak.'

'And when he found his voice?' Liz prompted, her tone acidic.

'He was thrilled. And ever since he's been so excited about the baby, about the pregnancy. He can't stop talking about it. Can't do enough for me.'

'Well, good. So he should.'

'Please, Liz,' I said then, suddenly tired of this. 'Don't be like that, okay? He's changed. Whatever you may think, I know this baby is going to make all the difference. I don't know why, but I feel like we've been waiting for something like this to happen for a very long time.'

'I just want him to realize what he's got,' Liz replied, her tone lightening. 'I don't want him retreating into that artistic solipsism of his – "Oh, woe is me" and all that. Not now. Not after all that's happened.'

'He won't,' I said firmly. 'I know he won't.'

Her eyes flared briefly with concern, then softened.

'Good.' She reached out and put her hand over mine. 'I'm happy for you, Rob. Really I am.'

'Thanks, Liz. I am, too.'

I felt her eyes on me, her lingering concern, and experienced a little stab of guilt over what I'd said about Harry, his enthusiasm for the baby, his elation.

'Now tell me you're not about to run off into the desert to have this baby, are you?'

'No!' I laughed, and she grinned back. 'No, not this time.'

When I got home, I could hear Harry at work in the garage. I had decided, on the drive home from Liz's, that I would not tell him that I had shared our news. Somehow, I knew that it would bother him, get under his skin. Besides, I had the sense that he needed a little more time himself to digest this development, and I was more than willing to grant him that.

I closed the door behind me, hung my bag on the newel post and went down the steps and opened the door to the garage. I didn't knock, didn't call out his name, and when I went in, he looked up at me, startled, and I had the impression that I was interrupting something.

'Hey there,' I said, walking over to him and kissing him lightly. 'What're you doing?'

'Getting set up,' he replied, and I saw on the floor behind him the boxes and crates filled with his paints and pigments, his brushes, knives, canvases, sketch pads. In another corner he had stacked against the wall all the unsold paintings. He had laid a rug on the ground underneath them – a small touch of tenderness in this cold, hard space.

'The light in here is terrible,' he said, reaching up to flick a finger at the bare bulb hanging from a wire. A puff of dust came away as he left the bulb swinging.

'That's what you said about Spencer's basement, remember? But you sorted it out, didn't you?'

'It's bloody freezing in here.'

'You can take the plug-in heater from the office to warm things up.'

He gave a sound that might have been agreement or a grunt of disapproval. He seemed prickly and moody, distracted, but I wouldn't allow my optimism to be dented.

'So-o-o,' I said, drawing out the syllable as I leaned against the table and faced him, my smile surfacing again, 'I've been doing some thinking, and I've decided to have the baby in Holles Street and split my care between Dr O'Rourke and a consultant at the maternity hospital.'

'Great. Sounds like you have it all worked out.' He fixed his gaze on the wall opposite. 'I think I'll put shelves there. To tidy up the clutter a bit. And this stuff has got to go.'

He turned and indicated with a sweep of his arm the pile of junk that had accumulated over the years, gathering and filling the space, growing like a living organism.

'We can get a skip,' I said. 'Do a big clear-out. It's about time we tackled it.'

He began shifting things around, hauling sacks towards the door. A toolbox fell on the ground, its contents clattering across the concrete floor.

'I have to register at the hospital this week. Do you want to come?'

'Do you need me to come?'

'No, but –'

'It's just filling out forms, isn't it?'

'I guess so. It's too early for anything else.'

'Well, you don't need me to do that.'

I looked carefully at him.

'I'll come for the scans and the check-ups and that.'

That was all perfectly reasonable. Perhaps I was just imagining the hint of aggression in his voice.

I let it go.

He began piling chairs up in a corner, clearing a space in the middle of the floor.

'Want me to help?'

'What? Have my pregnant wife haul some furniture about?' he asked, flashing a grin at me. 'What kind of a dick would that make me?'

'Fine,' I said. 'I'll make some coffee.'

It was giving up the studio that had brought it about – this minor estrangement of ours. He had always been sensitive to his environment, his work space in particular. I had expected him to react badly to the move. It needled me a little that he could not accept it with good grace, but the argument was not worth having.

I filled the coffee pot with water and spooned the coffee into the basket and wondered how long this little rift would continue. His moods could sometimes last for days. It was as I set the coffee to boil on the hob that he stepped into the kitchen. He stood by the doorway, his hands in his pockets, looking sheepish. His tousled hair, the way his eyes swept over the floorboards – he was a little boy again, ready to confess, needing to be forgiven, and I felt a tug on the thread that held us together, pulling me back to him.

'I am happy about the baby, Robin,' he began quietly. 'You do know that, don't you?'

'Of course I do.'

'I've been thinking,' he went on, 'now that I'm working here in the house, and now that you've a shorter working week and will be at home more, I think we should have some ground rules.'

'Ground rules?' I said, confused.

'Yes.'

And I realized that what I had thought was sheepishness was something other than that. He looked shifty. He looked sly.

'I need my space, Robin. I need privacy in order to work. You can't just walk in for a chat whenever you're feeling bored or lonely.'

Anger began to rise inside me like mercury in a thermometer.

'So what should I do?' I asked, keeping my voice cool and level. 'Should I knock first? Make an appointment for coffee? Tiptoe around my own house?'

'Come on, Robin, don't be like that.'

'I'm not being like anything. You're the one who's acting weird.'

'Look, all I'm asking is that you treat my work space here the way you treated the studio in town.'

'Like a sanctum, you mean?'

'Not a bloody sanctum,' he snapped. 'You never popped

in for coffee there, did you? Never just dropped by for a quick chat.'

'You never let me.'

He stared at me. 'Why do you do that? Say things like that. *I never let you.* Making me out to be some kind of control freak.'

The coffee pot was spitting and hissing, and I turned and removed it from the heat, placing the cups on the counter with a clatter.

'You don't have to make this into a big thing, Robin,' he said.

I felt those words, the accusation they held, release into the air like a tiny puff of poison. Something snapped within me, and I knew I was going to ask him one of the questions I had never asked but always wondered about.

'Why didn't I have a key to your studio?'

'What?' He looked wary, confused.

'A key. You never gave me one.'

'Why would you need –'

'Diane had one.'

Her name hung between us like a threat. Her name in my mouth felt sharp. Everything about Diane is sharp, from the pointed tips of her Cupid's bow mouth down to the spike of her heels.

'That's different,' he said softly, stepping past me and pouring coffee into his cup.

'How is it different?'

Raising his voice and speaking slowly, as though talking to a child, he said, 'She needed to have access to my paintings when I wasn't there, that's why.'

'Does this mean she'll have a key to this house?'

'Of course not. What the fuck is wrong with you today, Robin?'

My eyes flared and I felt my heart thrum with fury.

'What's wrong with *me*?'

'Every time Diane is mentioned, you do this. Every fucking time.'

'Do what?'

'Bring on the big freeze. Give me the thin-lipped, disapproving look. It pisses me off.'

'I've got good reason to disapprove.'

'Why? She's never done anything to you. So far as I can see, she's only ever been nice and polite to you.'

'Ha!' I gave out a shout of mocking laughter. 'Oh yes, very nice. God, Harry, you're so blind. Nice to me? Every word she says to me is tainted with her condescension. I am the little wife of the great man, and doesn't she love to remind me of it.'

'It's all in your head, Robin.'

'All in my head, oh sure. Tell yourself that. Don't you remember the one time she was in this house, and some of my old canvases were stacked against the wall, and she deigned to look through them and give me her professional opinion? Don't you recall what she said?'

He gave me a weary, guarded look and drank deep from his coffee cup.

'She cast her imperious gaze over them and told me that they were sweet. *Sweet, cosy, and parochial* – that's what she said. *Parochial!* She actually used that word!' As I thought of those words, I remembered again how small

95

she had made me feel. I had seen my work through the sneer of her gaze and felt the awful deflation of failure.

'So she didn't like your stuff. So what?'

I held his gaze for a moment, and then, in a low voice, I said, 'I don't like the way she looks at you.'

Instantly he straightened up and slammed his cup on the counter. Giving me a dark look, he turned to leave.

'I don't have time for this crap.'

I stood there shaking my head, my hands squeezed into fists as the blood pumped hotly through my body.

'That's right, Harry. Walk away. God forbid you should stay and actually talk about it.'

'We've been through this before! There's nothing to talk about, apart from your paranoia.'

'My *paranoia*? How dare you!' My anger was brimming over, taking possession of every pocket of space within my body. I felt swollen with fury. 'I am not paranoid! I know the two of you were fucking! I know it, Harry! I might not know the details, when it began or how long it went on for. I don't even know if you're fucking her still! But I know you two have been together, even if I can't prove it. And it's not paranoia, and fuck you for saying that it is! The very least you could do is show me just a little bit of respect and admit to it instead of lying to my face and dismissing me as some paranoid, neurotic little wife!'

'That would make you happy, would it? That would get you off my back? All right then – I fucked her. There now. Happy?'

He spat the words at me and held his hands up in a gesture of mock surrender.

'Make a joke of it then,' I said, shaking my head and looking at him anew. 'But you weren't always like this. I never would have suspected you of sleeping with someone else – never. Not until Dillon –'

'Don't you mention him,' he growled, raising a finger in warning. 'Don't you bring him into this.'

'Is that why you do it?' I went on regardless. 'Does fucking around take your mind off the guilt? Does it numb the pain? Does it help to blot out the details of that night even for just a brief instant?'

He stared at me from the doorway. He looked tired, bleary and wild with pent-up rage. I wondered if there was a bottle somewhere in the garage, in among his things, that he would go to now and draw strength from.

'Don't be so bloody stupid,' he said in a thick voice, then closed the door softly behind him.

It took me a long time to calm down after that. I felt my anger stalking around inside me like a big cat, clawed and dangerous. It snarled and paced, and I felt restless and distracted.

We don't often argue, Harry and I. Neither one of us likes confrontation. But that day, in the kitchen, I was taken by a sudden rage, and, if I am honest, it had nothing to do with Diane. God knows, we have had that argument often enough. Nor did it have anything to do with the studio or what I saw as Harry's adolescent sulk at having to give it up. Him and his bloody ground rules. The real root of my anger that day concerned my pregnancy and Harry's apparent ambivalence towards it. No – more than that: his studied refusal to engage with it, whatever he said otherwise.

With Dillon he had wanted to know everything. Back then, he had pored over the pregnancy book I had found at Cozimo's. He was relentless in his questioning, eager for details of the changes I was feeling. He had encouraged me to keep a diary, documenting my pregnancy so that we would always have some way of remembering it, long after the details had faded from memory. At that early stage, he was already planning for posterity. He had wanted so badly to connect with the life growing inside me that it almost broke my heart. It almost suffocated me.

Now he seemed unable to connect with me or the pregnancy. He was caught up within his own thoughts, distracted by something he wouldn't share with me. And what bothered me most, the thing that niggled away at me constantly, was worrying just what – or who – was causing his distraction.

Later that week, when there was a lull in activity at the office, I slipped out and walked briskly down Parliament Street, out on to Dame Street. I had spent the morning digitizing up drawings for one of the senior architects, and my eyes were watering from staring too long at the screen. Lately, I seemed to be doing little more than data-entry work, and it was getting to the point where even working on door schedules sounded exciting. But as the most junior member of the staff in a small practice, I had little choice in what work I did, and I knew, deep down, that I was lucky to have a job at all.

A heavy snow had fallen during the night, and the city felt blanketed – muffled. There was an air of desertion about it. What traffic there was moved slowly, and people picked their way carefully through the snow and the slush. It took me half an hour to reach Trinity College, and fifteen minutes more to make my way across the slippery cobblestones and the cricket pitches, out to the Lincoln Gate. I hadn't thought of it until then, but my journey led me on to Fenian Street and past Harry's recently vacated studio. It was just around the corner from Holles Street and the hospital. I looked up as I passed, up at the closed, opaque windows. I half-expected to see Spencer's leathered features staring out. But the windows were blank, reflecting the dull glare of the sky. As I passed, I thought of Harry. Our argument had been patched up and yet something remained, like a lingering smell.

I reached the hospital and was directed to a prefabricated building behind an archway – the clinic I would be attending for my check-ups. At first glance it seemed a flimsy, temporary structure, not weighty enough for the serious business of having a baby. Inside, a hassled woman whose hair had been scraped back in a ponytail took my details and then set about putting together a folder for me. I watched in amazement as she amassed a sheaf of variously coloured pages, hastily leafing through and stabbing different sheets with labels in the harried yet bored manner of someone who has done this a thousand times. Then she handed it to me, along with an appointment card, and asked me to wait. Several minutes later, I was taken to a cramped office, where a brisk but cheerful woman proceeded to register me in more detail.

'First baby?' she asked brightly.

'Second.'

'Ah, so you know what you're about, then.'

'Yes, I suppose so.'

'Boy or girl?'

For a second, I was confused, and she looked up at me and said, 'Your first child. Is it a boy or a girl?'

'Boy.'

'Ah. How old?'

I swallowed hard. After all this time, I am still not good with questions like that. My mouth went dry, my tongue sticking to my palate. I thought of Dillon, an involuntary memory of him in those last days before we lost him. His soft hair, how it curled about his neck; his chubby limbs, dimples on the knuckles of his fleshy little hands. That was how I thought of him – how I remembered him: a little boy, forever trapped in childhood.

'Three,' I said.

She smiled warmly, then directed her gaze from me to her computer monitor.

'I'm sure he'll be very excited to find out he's going to have a brother or sister.'

'Yes,' I said weakly.

'Now then. You've opted for combined care, so you'll need to fill out this form and send it off to the Health Service Executive.'

The rest of the appointment was a blur, for I spent the whole time worrying about how I had lied about Dillon.

Not an outright lie, but a lie of omission. Why had I done that? Because I could not bear to watch her face losing its brightness and taking on a mournful, sympathetic look, that's why. I have been treated to that look more times than I care to think about. But then, throughout the course of the interview, I began to worry that the lie might have consequences, later on, throughout my visits here. I began to imagine coming in here and bumping into this kindly woman and having her ask about my pregnancy and did my son know about it yet, asking me in a corridor crowded with expectant women and their partners, all half-listening, watching idly, and then I would have to explain that Dillon had died, and the very thought of mentioning a dead child in front of a group of pregnant women seemed outrageous.

'– and that will all happen at your first appointment. Now, let me write the date down on your appointment card, so you won't forget.'

I handed it to her, watching her neat writing fill up a white square, still thinking I should say something to clarify things, something about Dillon.

'So, when you come back for your appointment, go straight up the stairs there, and the nurse will see to you. Okay?'

'Right. Thanks.'

I left her to her cheerful administration, still chewing my lip with indecision and regret, and that is when I heard my name being called.

'Robin? Is it you?'

A woman in a blue dress with a neat, round bump like

a Christmas pudding was approaching me with a hesitant, timorous smile. Her auburn hair was swept over one shoulder. Her face was crazy with freckles. It was a face I knew but couldn't locate in memory.

'It's Tanya,' she said. 'From the Sitric Gallery? We met at your husband's exhibition some years ago?'

'Tanya. Yes. Yes, of course. I'm so sorry.'

'That's all right!' she laughed, adding, 'Pregnancy has a tendency to scramble your brain, doesn't it?'

'I suppose it does. When are you due?'

'March. And you?'

'Not till the summer. I'm actually just here to register.'

'Ah,' she said.

For a moment, neither of us said anything, both tacitly acknowledging the awkwardness of the situation. It is something you hope won't happen – bumping into someone you know when going to register your pregnancy. Not yet ready to share your news, and yet there is no denying it once caught on the premises of an ante-natal clinic. I had the strange, almost shamefaced feeling of being caught with my hand in someone else's purse.

'How is Harry, anyway?'

'He's good, thanks. Busy,' I added, remembering now what Harry had told me. 'He mentioned that you might be interested in looking at some of his new work.'

A look of mild consternation crossed her face.

'When he met you last weekend,' I went on. 'He was quite excited, in fact, although he'd kill me for saying as much. But you know he'd love the chance to exhibit again at the Sitric.'

The look on her face stopped me. Consternation had changed to genuine confusion, and she was shaking her head slowly.

'You must be mistaken, Robin. I haven't seen Harry in ages. In fact, it's a good two years, at least, since we last met.'

'Oh,' I said, momentarily thrown. 'Well, perhaps it was someone else from the Sitric Gallery that he was referring to. There's another girl who works there – Sally or Sarah? I forget!'

I laughed, yet still she looked at me strangely.

'The Sitric Gallery has closed,' she said softly.

'What?'

'Another victim of the recession,' she continued with a little mirthless laugh. 'No one has money to spend on art any more.'

My mind raced. The Sitric had closed? My thoughts whirred back over what Harry had said – Tanya from the Sitric. The day of the march. I was sure that was who he had mentioned.

'Well,' she said, shrugging. 'It was nice to see you. And please give Harry my best. Perhaps, when things pick up, our paths might cross again.'

'Yes,' I said with a smile. 'Good luck.'

As I walked away, picking my way carefully through the snow, I thought about Harry, about what he had said, and wondered why he had lied. And if he hadn't seen Tanya the day of the march, then who had he seen, and why did he not want to tell me?

Perhaps I was mistaken. I told myself that it was

possible he had meant someone else from a different gallery and I had just misheard or misinterpreted his remarks. But even as I turned the thought over in my mind, I knew it wasn't true. He had lied to me. And I remembered how he'd been that day – agitated, distracted – and the memory stayed with me on the long, slow walk back to the office, creasing itself into a little furrow of worry: one more to add to the rest.

# 7. Harry

I woke up to 'Fairytale of New York' playing on the radio. That was it. As soon as you heard 'Fairytale', you knew Christmas was on its way. I felt rough. I felt like the scumbag in the song. The strung-out tones were fitting. Nothing like Shane MacGowan singing how he could have been someone on a bleak Monday morning in December to make you think of taking to the drink again. Hair of the dog was on my mind.

Beside me, the bed was stone cold. Robin must have been up for a while. I stumbled into the bathroom and got the water going. Standing under the shower with the jets of water spraying painfully across my face, I thought of what my life had come to, the point in the path that I was at. I thought of my work, the opportunities that were opening up to me now with this trip I was about to take. I was off to London for a meeting with a gallery about a show I might do, a follow-on from *The Tangier Manifesto*. A part two, if you like. I was nervous but excited, too, conscious of all the possibilities swirling about me. I thought of Robin and the baby growing inside her. I thought of this old house and the future that lay within it. All of these things flitted across the corridors of my mind. But a shadow was cast over them. The shadow of the boy I had seen. His face rose up amid the steam of the hot water, and I turned away from it, flicking off the water and stepping out of the tub. I did not shave, just dressed quickly, grabbed a few things and threw them into an overnight bag.

Robin called up the stairs to me:

'Harry? Are you ready?'

'Yep,' I said, taking the stairs two at a time, pressed by a sudden need to get going.

'I'll drop you at the airport.'

'What? In this snow?'

'It's not too bad. We can go for breakfast in the airport before your flight.'

'Okay. If you're sure?'

She gave me a warm smile of reassurance, then skipped past me to the van. As I locked up, I could hear her turning the engine over, bringing it to life.

'Tickets? Passport? Wallet?' she said as I got in beside her.

'Check, check and check.'

She seemed so breezy that morning. An air of optimism hovered around her, giving off warmth on that cold, cold day. I felt so grateful for it in that moment that it was enough to dispel all my thoughts about the boy, about what I had seen or what I thought I had seen. Delusions, that's what they were, brought on by guilt or fatigue or a combination of both.

Robin had turned her head to back out of the driveway when I saw the expression on her face change, the frown forming on her forehead. I turned, too, and saw the long snout of the old Jag pulling up, blocking our exit. I heard the creak of a hand brake and watched as the door opened and Spencer stepped out, fag clamped in his mouth, loose strands of uncombed hair lifting in the breeze.

'Great,' Robin declared in a flat tone as he raised a hand in salute.

'I'll get rid of him,' I said.

She looked at me with a weary expression. 'If only it were that simple.'

He was at the driver's window now, tapping on the glass. Dutifully, she wound it down. I could smell his breath cutting across her, bitter and sharp.

'Where are you off to?'

'Airport.'

'Come on. I'll give you a lift.'

He turned and stalked back to the Jag, not waiting for an answer.

Robin stared at her knuckles, her hands still gripping the steering wheel.

'Sorry, love,' I said, and I kissed her goodbye. She sighed. 'I'll make it up to you. Forget breakfast at the airport – I'll take you out somewhere nice when I'm back.'

Robin didn't respond. I climbed out of the car, feeling like I had let her down again, and stepped into Spencer's. He had on a camelhair coat. Peeking beneath the lapels was a flash of black silk: he was still wearing his dressing gown. His eyes were bloodshot. He looked like he had not slept in a month.

'Are you sure you're okay to drive?'

'What? Course I am,' he said, holding up a breathalyser. 'I have the system sussed.'

He drove so I had to clutch the door handle. My foot pressed to brake more than once. But we made it with time to spare.

'I have talked with McDonagh, my mate in the Guards, and he has managed to source the CCTV for the hours in question. It's all digitized these days.'

'Oh. Right. Excellent.'

'The man owed me a favour, so here, my friend, are half a dozen DVDs.'

I looked at the stack of them, bound with an elastic band, and a tide of mixed embarrassment and regret washed over me. Why had I asked him for these? What purpose could they possibly serve? At that moment, my suspicions seemed so patently absurd, let alone my desire for some amateur sleuthing.

'These were not easy to come by, favour or no. Seems like they are hot property. Austerity measures, protests. Forget *The Tangier Manifesto*, that's what you should call your next show.'

'*Austerity Measures*?'

'Bingo.'

'Maybe I will.'

'Listen, you'll have to analyse those discs yourself. McDonagh may have owed me one big favour, but he was not about to look through three hundred hours of people walking up and down O'Connell Street.'

'Three hundred hours?'

'Give or take. There's, like, three or four cameras, so . . . I don't know, you do the maths.'

'Right you are. Thanks again. You're a mate.'

'I've been called worse.' He parked. 'Look, are you going to buy me a drink or what?'

'What about the car?'

'I'll leave it. And . . .'

'And what?'

'Say it was stolen or something, I don't know.'

I checked in, and we went to the nearest bar.

'So?' Spencer said, an expectant look on his face.

'What?'

'Are you going to tell me what the fuck this is all about?' He pointed at the discs, then reached for his pint.

I knew I couldn't tell him. Mostly, because I was embarrassed – afraid, perhaps, of the conclusions he might draw from my behaviour, the references he might make to all the trouble in my past. Besides, he had not known Dillon. Not really. He had visited Tangier once, shortly after the birth, and we had spent a memorable weekend wetting the baby's head. He had been the only friend to make it over and he'd seemed genuinely happy for us. After that, he'd doted on Dillon but from afar, sending gifts and cards. He hadn't been anything as official as a godfather, but he'd held a special status for Dillon. He'd been 'Uncle Spencer'.

Before I had a chance to dodge the question, Spencer butted in: 'You know there's more than fifty fucking CCTV cameras in the city centre? Not to mention the rest of the country. Big Brother is watching you.'

'You said it.'

'What about our civil rights?'

'Spencer, you don't give a fuck about civil rights.'

'How do you know? How do you know I don't care about my civil rights?'

'You are just looking to pick a fight.'

He glared at me as if I had insulted his mother.

'You're contrary today,' I added.

'No, I'm not.'

My phone rang. It was Diane. She knew about the Golden Clock gallery in London, but I did not really want her involved. I did not want her on the scent, representing me as if she owned me. The more distance I had from her, the better. I let the phone keep ringing. Spencer picked it up and saw Diane's name. He pressed the reject button. 'The less said, the better.'

I agreed.

More beers arrived.

'You're in a generous spirit,' I said.

'It's my Christmas cheer.' He picked my phone up again and logged on to the web comic Wheel Spinning Hamster Dead. 'That's us, my friend. That's Ireland.'

'Yeah, that's hilarious, Spence. Really charming stuff,' I said.

'There's no app for loneliness,' he quipped.

'You're jealous you don't have an iPhone,' I said, but the truth was, I couldn't afford it myself. Money was tight. My overdraft had an overdraft. We had been given a house, but it was a poisoned chalice of sorts. The place's upkeep threatened to wring us dry. It had leaks and draughts. This was broken, that was malfunctioning. I'd never say this to Robin, but we had inherited a wreck. 'It'll make a good home,' she'd said. 'It'll serve us well. Why can't you be more excited?' I know I sound like a miserable sod, but it was the sense of not having earned it, or made it ourselves, that sat uneasily with me. We'd even taken out a mortgage to buy Mark's half, to do the place up; taken out a mortgage on a house that had been given to us. Utter madness. And yet, mortgages, phones, none of it mattered – not right then. The glimmer of possibility still flickered and shone. Hope, I suppose you might call it.

'You realize all the music you own is from the 1980s?'

'Yeah?'

'You sad fucker. Your music-listening life ended in 1989.'

'Well, they are the vintage years.'

'Howard Jones, Nik Kershaw. Please.'

'The Cure, The Smiths.'

'Lloyd Cole.'

'Fucking love Lloyd Cole.'

'Lost weekend in a hotel in Amsterdam.'

'Story of my life.'

Out of the corner of my eye, I saw two figures – a woman and a child – and I spun in my chair to look at them. But the boy was younger than he should be, only about three or four, and the woman was different too, the wrong hair colour, the wrong height.

I turned back and saw Spencer staring at me.

'What is with you today, bud?' he asked, looking me square in the face.

'Nothing.'

'You're twitchy as hell.'

'I'm not.'

'Yes, you are. Every time someone walks past, you're swinging around in your seat. Are you expecting someone?'

'No!' I said, indignant and flustered. 'Here, finish this for me. I've got to head out.'

The flight boarded after a delay. The hold-up had something to do with de-icing the runway and the wingtips. If you thought too much about it all, you'd never go anywhere. I got on to the plane and sat down beside a woman whose first greeting to me was 'Cold enough for you?'

Her perfume was so strong I could taste it. Even the gin and tonic I ordered did not help. Across the aisle, a man was coping with a crying child. He dipped the child's dummy into his drink and popped it into the child's mouth. The child stopped crying. The man saw me watching, smiled and gave me a wink. I turned away. It seemed that everywhere I looked, there were children. I couldn't escape from them.

By the time I made it to London, it was too late for the meeting. I rang Daphne, and we rescheduled for the next afternoon. I had the half-formed notion to take in some of the sights, a museum maybe, or a walk down by Waterloo Station. But drinking so early in the day had left a fug of inertia within me, so instead, after checking into my hotel, I lay on my big boat of a bed, flicked on the telly and spent a mindless twenty minutes watching Nigella Lawson spoon one creamy concoction after another into her mouth. Spencer's DVDs sat on the bedside table. I tried to ignore them, but I felt their presence nonetheless, drawing me to them like a scab demanding to be picked. It was a bad idea and I knew it, but after a while I turned the TV off, switched on my computer and fed the first DVD into the slot.

At first, I watched with half-hearted amusement. The images were grainy and of poor quality. I paged through a magazine, aware of the flickering movements across the screen, my attention snagging occasionally before it drifted away again. I'll turn it off in a minute, I said to myself, but the minutes became hours, and soon I found myself ejecting a disc only to replace it with another. Trapped by boredom or torpor, my magazine discarded, I let myself get sucked into that screen and the images it conveyed.

One shot showed the Liffey. Three men rocked back and forth in a boat, waving banners. I had missed that one on the day. But there it was. I made instant coffee with the small kettle in the corner of the room. I kicked off my boots and propped the computer on a pillow. Hours passed, and the footage became a blur, people milling this way and that. Talking, moving on. It grew tedious.

The computer was like a hot rock on the bed. Wary of burning the hard drive out, I turned it off and took a break. I had watched hours of footage, and I was tired, but that didn't stop me from going out. A beer at the hotel bar and then out to wander. I didn't really know where I was going, but it was a chance to get out and clear my head. The city was under a veil of snow. Solitary walkers passed in lonely silhouette as they crossed the deserted parks. Black cabs moved slowly over a tide of slush. I wandered from bar to bar, images of the demonstration streaming through my head, before I looped back to the hotel with pains in my calves and knees from walking so carefully and sank dog-tired into bed.

I woke to the sound of my laptop humming. It blazed on the bed beside me as my head pounded. In the bathroom I gargled with mouthwash, then swallowed painkillers. No stomach for breakfast. I took my bag and walked towards Soho.

I was miles too early for the meeting, but I couldn't spend another second in that hotel room. I needed to get away from my laptop and those DVDs. They contained nothing there but images to feed my already overextended delusion. It was unhealthy. I had to clear my head, to focus on the future. The past held only heartache.

With a view to killing some time, I wandered into the British Museum and found myself straying into the Egyptian exhibition. The painkillers had worked to a degree, but my head felt fuzzy, clotted with too many thoughts. I tried to concentrate on what I was viewing, but there was too much coming at me, elbowing for room in my crowded brain. I walked around in a daze, untouched, unmoved, until I came across the mummy of a child, from Hawara, Egypt, and stopped suddenly, riveted.

The mummy had been discovered in an excavation of a Roman cemetery near the pyramid at Hawara towards the end of the nineteenth century. It was elaborately wrapped, and there was a portrait of the child sketched into the outer layers of the wrappings. Over the torso of the mummy, a shroud had been painted with various scenes of the Egyptian religious tradition. The sky goddess Nut was at the top. I read the placard and learned that the child was the offspring of a woman whose mummy was housed in the Cairo Museum. Something about that caused an unexpected stab of pain. The child in London, the parent in Cairo. Separated, even in death.

I gazed at the mummy for a long time. For a while I could not understand why it commanded my attention, why it caused my heart to quicken. The placard said the portrait had been done in tempera on linen. The large eyes and dark hair were spellbinding. And then it dawned on me: it was the portrait of the boy's face that took my breath away. It was astonishing. The boy's face was so similar to Dillon's that I felt as if someone was playing a cruel joke on me. The universe, the cosmos, what was it saying to me? I don't know. But maybe not; maybe it was a reassuring message. I wanted to reach through the glass and touch the child's fragile bindings.

I looked about myself, as if to say, *Do you see this, do you see the boy prince from Hawara?*

*He is my son.*

I felt elated. My mind raced. My hands shook. I caught sight of my reflection in the glass case and saw tears coursing down my cheeks.

I read the placard again, hungrily this time, scouring it for information, for some kind of pointer or clue. I don't think it was any coincidence that the man who'd discovered this child mummy, a man called Petrie, had described Egypt as 'a house on fire, so rapid was the destruction'. A house on fire. If that wasn't a sign, then what was it? It was all coming together. Petrie also wrote: 'I believe the true line of research lies in the noting and comparison of the smallest details.'

The smallest details. I thought of the DVDs, which, without realizing, I had slipped into my bag, and felt them drawing me back to them like a magnet.

I was ready to give up on the gallery when Daphne texted a confirmation through to my phone.

I took a photo of the child mummy with my phone and tore myself away from that bright face. On my way out, I bought a postcard of the child and placed it in my jacket. I walked to the gallery with a strange sense of elation and desertion. It felt like I was floating.

Daphne was charming, all lovey-lovey and full of yes, darling, of course, darling, let me give you a tour of the gallery, darling. There wasn't that much to see, but I suppose I was seeing history, or at least that's what they kept telling me. History, they seemed to be clinging to history, her and her assistant, Ian. This building . . . blah blah blah. I heard none of it. Dillon and the child mummy of Hawara were melding in my mind.

I sat in the boardroom with Daphne, Ian and a man named Clive to talk about the future, my future. It was flattering how seriously they were taking me. My head was pounding. I tried hard to pull myself together. They dithered about, getting coffee and notes and slides and other nonsense while I plugged my computer in and went through another section of CCTV. I became engrossed. I was back there on the day. The light, cold and heavenly. The strange and ghostly movement of the people up and down O'Connell Street. It looked almost funereal, a great procession for the dead or of the dead.

'New project?' Clive asked, leaning over me, watching the footage on my computer screen.

'I love it,' Daphne said. Clive and Ian were quick to join in.

'You're moving into video.'

'Good choice.'

'A collage?'

'CCTV.'

'Big Brother.'

'Genius.'

What the fuck?! I looked at them and closed over my PC. 'Let's get down to business,' I said.

They all sat back down at the oval table and began their agenda. The shows, the rights, the sales, the cut, the five-year plan. Ian went to get more coffee. Daphne suggested wine, and I nodded my consent. I drank, and they kept talking.

'Harry?'

'Yes?'

Jesus, had I fallen asleep? Were they waking me up? What had they been talking about?

'You were considering?'

'Yes, yes, I was.'

My phone rang. It was Robin. 'Everything okay?'

'Good, yes, very good.'

'And you're –?'

'At the gallery. Long meeting.'

'Late night?'

'Well –'

'Harry?'

'I'll call you back.'

'Are you okay?'

The concern in her voice touched something deep inside me, and I hung up quickly, afraid that if I held on, she might tap into some well of pain within me.

Daphne, Ian and Clive brought me to a posh restaurant after the meeting. I struggled to be sociable and say the right things. The bottle of wine at the gallery had levelled me off, but I needed something else to give me a second wind.

Not long into the appetizer I excused myself and went to the bar, where I ordered a brandy and then an espresso. I was under the impression that this might keep me awake. I was wrong. Daphne prodded my resting head with her finger as the main course arrived. 'Come on, sleepy, wake up and eat.'

I roused myself and went to the gents and splashed water on my face. When I returned, everyone looked surprised to see me. Pretty quickly, Ian and Clive excused themselves. 'Have to be up early,' they said. Daphne dangled her gallery credit card and suggested a cocktail bar. 'Sure,' I said, 'because we both really need another drink.'

I felt wretched. A text from Robin said she was missing me. I tried to text back; I typed that I had had a good night and was on my way back to my hotel room, but for some reason, the text would not send. Then I said I was in bed.

Didn't send. Then I rang. Bad idea, but no answer. So I left it. Face the music tomorrow.

Lloyd Cole was blasting through the speakers of the cocktail bar we walked into. He was asking us all if we were ready to be heartbroken.

'Your show is going to be great,' Daphne slurred into my ear. She ordered a bottle of champagne. The lights were kaleidoscopic. The music was so loud it pounded in my chest. And then I thought of the child mummy, alone now in the dark, echoey space of the deserted museum, its mother in another sarcophagus in a glass case with thousands of miles separating them. My heart brimmed with a new and sudden grief. Then Daphne looked into my eyes and said, 'Are you ready to be heartbroken?'

When I woke up, two texts were waiting. One from Daphne. It said sorry. The other was from Robin: 'You probably know this already, but your flight has been delayed. You'll be lucky to get home today or tomorrow.'

I swallowed some painkillers and crawled back into bed. Images from the night before flashed in and out of my mind. Daphne might as well have been Diane. I tried to lose myself inside these meaningless trysts, as if such a loss of control could help me forget about Dillon. But it didn't help. It just made everything worse.

When I woke again, it was dark.

I showered and went out to get more booze. There was no point in trying to work through the hangover; I needed the hair of the dog. I needed the dog's bollocks.

Back at the hotel, *The X Factor* was on TV. The world was falling apart. Ireland was bankrupt. I had seen my dead son. But all the whole of fucking Ireland and the UK were talking about was *The X Factor*. So I sat there, sipping from a bottle of no-name whiskey, guilt scratching around inside me, ill to my core, watching a flurry of lights and hysterical voices.

It was all too much – too loud and too bright. I flicked off the TV and went back to the CCTV footage. I had to. It was what I was there to do, in a way. I took the postcard of the child mummy and stuck it to the wall by the desk. I ordered room service and watched another two hours of footage, barely touching the food. All I was good for now was alcohol.

I drank whiskey and watched. At some stage, I checked my e-mail. In my inbox, I recognized the usual slew of gallery invitations and junk mail. There was an e-mail from Diane, too. I didn't open any of these. But one e-mail stood out. Under Sender it read, 'COZ'. In the subject heading were the following words: 'Tangier Manifesto'. The message was to the point: 'Daphne tells me you're in London. It would be lovely to see you. – C.'

I hailed a taxi and handed over the slip of paper.

The car drove carefully from one traffic light to the next, its headlights ghosting through the snow. The streets were almost deserted. I wasn't sure where we were going. The roads seemed to narrow and twist. I closed my eyes and almost fell asleep.

When the taxi stopped, I thought there must be some

mistake. It was not what I had expected: a housing estate in the East End.

'Are you sure this is right?' I asked.

The taxi-driver nodded his head and pointed to the meter.

When I paid him, he handed the piece of paper back to me, and I stepped out into the cold again.

I checked the number on the door and shook my head. This couldn't be right, could it? A small, terraced house. Cozimo here? I was perplexed.

I rang the doorbell.

'Harry, you are most welcome.' It was Cozimo; his face was in shadow, and he seemed to be shorter than I had remembered, but there he was, beckoning me to follow him, repeating to me, 'Most welcome.'

The voice was as grandiloquent as it had been in Tangier, but it was also more shrill somehow. I followed him down the narrow passageway, listening to the *shush shush* of his leather slippers, the weary drag of his feet over the tiled floor. We entered a cluttered living room where a fire was lit, but I felt little heat from it.

'It's good to see you,' I said.

'And you, my friend.' I was expecting an embrace, but instead Cozimo held out his hand with the old grandeur I remembered, the way a king or pontiff might. And sure enough, there was a dazzling ring on his hand. I was going to make a joke about kneeling and kissing the stone when I saw the speckled and frail hand tremble. I took his hand gently then and held it for a moment.

'It's been too long, Coz.'

'It has,' he said, somewhat out of breath. He wore an old paisley dressing gown and seemed somewhat lost within it. 'Please sit.' He went to shift a stack of yellow newspapers from the couch on to the thinly carpeted floor. I noticed that his face was marked with deep grooves; it looked like a map of wrong turns, detours and cul-de-sacs. I felt as if you could almost trace its contours of sadness, joy and disappointed ambition. There was only a faint glimmer in his eyes, no sparkle. The mischievous joy had gone. As if to accentuate the loss, the low hum of a cello came from a stereo buried in one corner of the room.

'Here, let me,' I said.

He took a step back and let himself fall into an old, dark-red leather armchair.

'You must tell me all your news, but first let me get you something to drink.' He tried to hoist himself up.

'Don't,' I said. 'Just point me in the right direction.'

He did so and placed a fresh cigarette into a gold cigarette holder.

There was a bottle of gin on the table, but there was not enough for two glasses. 'The fridge,' he said. 'There's another bottle and some tonic in the kitchen. Do you mind?'

Gone were the martinis; it was gin and tonic now.

I walked into the dark and cold kitchen. The fridge was almost bare. A carton of milk, some soft cheese and a tub of yogurt. Jesus, I wondered, was this the same man at all?

The soles of my shoes stuck to and unstuck from the linoleum. On the yellow wall by the fridge, there was a dust-covered mirror and, next to it, a collage of framed photos. Many were of Cozimo looking dapper and smiling, cheering or lending his salutations to the company at hand. One Polaroid showed a group of us: me and Robin, Cozimo, Simo, Garrick, and Raul. It looked ancient and faded, as if the sun had shone too long on its flimsy surface. What struck me most was how happy Robin looked. I didn't know why, but something about the photograph bothered me.

Without wanting to dawdle, I found the bottles and brought them back to the living room. Cozimo's eyes were closed. His skin had lost the tinge of the sun and gained the hue of jaundice. His head swayed back and forth in a gentle motion – to the music, I supposed, though his syncopated nodding was not keeping time. He opened his eyes as I started to pour the gin.

'No ice, I'm afraid.'

'Not to worry,' I said and sat down. Much of the clutter in the room looked like it had come from Tangier: trinkets, souvenirs, paintings – one of the casbah and the complex of castles on the hill overlooking the city. Another painting displayed three figures at dusk; they stood, facing the viewer, as if the painting were in fact a photograph. Was it one of Robin's? It must have been – the deep ochre hues were all hers, and she'd gone through a period when she'd etched her paintings with words. Somewhere in this painting, in its skyscape, were the words 'love' and 'dusk'. I had a vague memory of Robin giving the painting to Cozimo after he had first let us stay at the apartment. It took me unawares. It had been so long since I had seen it. Out of the corner of my eye, I spied a tarot deck on the table, too.

'You have a show?'

'Upcoming.'

'*The Tangier Manifesto*?'

'A sequel.'

'I will be a guest of honour.'

I smiled, and he reached out to hand me his glass. 'This time make it a double, Harry, for God's sake.'

I laughed.

I wasn't sure what to say or how to ask – but I desperately wanted to know how he had found his way back to London. I was about to pose the question when he must have read my mind, because he said, 'There's something about returning to where one first started, I suppose.'

I nodded.

'You know, I remember less and less of Tangier, but I can't get its smell of sulphur out of the nostrils. Strange, isn't it?'

I was going to say something about Tangier, something about the earthquake, when he asked about Robin.

'She's . . . good, very good,' I said, looking toward the painting. Cozimo seemed to smile, but I couldn't be certain. 'We have a nice place in Dublin, not far from the sea.'

I wasn't quite sure what to say. Do I tell him she is pregnant? I wondered. At the same time, I felt like he was going to tell me something, something important. He hesitated, dithered and gulped down his drink with awkward, uneven breaths, wheezing heavily. He was like an unwell, lame dog, lapping at his gin and tonic.

I, too, felt on the brink of divulging something. The something of my year. I felt that, unlike Spencer, he would not make fun of me or doubt me. I felt that, unlike Robin, I could trust him fully to understand what I had seen. I knew he would understand.

More than anything, I wanted to tell him how I had seen Dillon.

Through the walls, I could hear a dog barking. Cozimo looked up at me. He smiled weakly. Had he lost his teeth? His face was shrunken.

'I'm afraid of dogs,' he said, quite blankly and unfamiliarly.

I felt a little weepy. I wanted the old Cozimo back. I wanted his strong, blithe spirit back.

'I meant to keep in touch,' I said.

There was a long, strange silence. The haunting tones of the cello echoed through the small living room. I felt claustrophobic and short of breath.

'I saw something yesterday, in the British Museum. A child mummy. It looked like Dillon.'

'Ah,' he intoned, nodding thoughtfully, a sad smile coming over his face.

My heart was beating high up in my chest, and I felt his little eyes alight on my face, curious now, snagged by my hesitation.

'And I saw him. I saw Dillon, too. In Dublin. At least, I think it was him.'

Cozimo sat forward now, his eyes narrowed with concern or suspicion. I was unnerved by the look but ploughed on regardless. I told him where it had happened.

I told him about the woman, about calling out, about how the boy had turned around and looked at me, and the fleeting instance of recognition in his eyes. I told him all of it and then I paused, hearing his breath rasping across the distance of space between us.

He didn't speak, and I let out a nervous laugh and said, 'I feel like I'm going out of my mind, Coz. My dead son resurrected. I know it sounds unlikely.'

'Very unlikely,' he said, not unkindly, but something sank within me nonetheless. I gazed into my empty glass and felt my grief plumbing a new depth, before he added, 'But not impossible.'

I looked up then and caught his gaze, which was unreadable, and waited for him to say something more.

He exhaled slowly and uneasily. 'There were things I knew which perhaps I should have told you.'

'Like what?'

'I'm not sure it matters now.'

His lungs wheezed and rattled, and he shrugged his narrow shoulders, his face set in an expression of weary acceptance.

'Maybe it does matter?'

'I'm tired,' he said sadly.

I'd leaned in to press him on the point, to prod him to reveal what was bothering him, when I heard a key unlock the front door. Then somebody walked down the hallway and into the living room.

'This is Maya,' Cozimo said by way of introduction. 'Do you remember each other?'

I looked up and saw a short Spanish woman in her early

126

forties. I did not remember her, nor did Maya say anything about knowing me. She took off her coat, threw a log on to the fire and took the glass from Cozimo.

'It's nice to meet you . . .'

'Harry.'

'Harry . . . but Cozimo is not to drink.' She put his glass down on the table and, without reproach, said, 'He needs to rest now.'

Cozimo smiled indulgently. 'But Harry has only just got here.'

Maya placed a footstool beneath Cozimo's feet and fixed a blanket over his legs.

'He and Robin and their son, Dillon, lived above my bookstore.'

Maya said nothing. Cozimo looked to me with something like pity in his eyes.

'Before the earthquake. Everything changed after that. It still haunts me, Harry.'

'Yes.'

'But we had some good times, didn't we, Harry?'

The desire to press him about what he had said, what he had intimated, drained from me. Maybe because he had mentioned Dillon to Maya, because he had said the word 'earthquake'. Maybe I didn't think in his state of health he would be able to handle it. I lost my nerve and let it go.

'The nights we had chez Cozimo.' He seemed to sink into a reverie, further into the chair, further into himself.

Maya stood, waiting for me.

'Well,' I said. 'Perhaps I will call tomorrow.'

'Thank you for coming, Harry,' he said after a moment, now looking into the fire. The cello suite had ended, and the needle of the record player lapped over the lip of the final groove of the record with the sound of a lulling tide coming in.

I gathered up my coat, and Maya walked me to the door.

'I do hope we see each other again,' Cozimo said, his voice barely audible, before I walked back into the snow.

I picked my stuff up from the hotel and reached the airport only to discover that my flight had been cancelled.

'The morning looks better,' an attendant told me.

I went in search of somewhere to sit or lie down. Bodies were strewn about the airport as if after some kind of natural disaster.

I found a corner and threw my coat over myself, but it was too cold to sleep. I dug my computer out and pressed play. Time passed in a deadening blur. Sometime in the hour after dawn, my head fuzzy with fatigue, the sky beyond the airport terminal turning from black to violet, sounds of an industrial vacuum humming over the cold, hard floor, something on the screen made me sit upright. Two spectral figures, a boy and a woman, hand in hand, walking up O'Connell Street among the protesters.

The woman stops to look into a window. The boy is pulling at her. They walk on. They reach the top of O'Connell Street.

And then the DVD ends.

My heart was racing, and my mouth was dry. Jesus, I

thought. That's them. That's him. That's Dillon. I did see him. I am not going mad. I rewound. The software on the computer allowed me to zoom in on them. Yes, it was him. Tears welled in my eyes. I felt a curious mixture of joy and fear, panic and relief.

I scrambled furiously to find the next disc, slotted it into the computer, and feasted once again on the sight of my son. I could see them as they ambled up O'Connell Street; a car was waiting for them. It was an old red Ford. I strained to see the licence plate. I paused the video and scrambled among the mess in my bag for a pen and paper. I could not quite make out the numbers. The battery on my computer was about to die. Still, I rewound, pressed play again. I had the year, 01. I had the county letters, and the next four digits were there. The last digit was blurred, though, vague and indistinct. I rewound the disc, played it once more. Finally I had it.

# 8. Robin

When I got home that Wednesday evening, the street was in darkness. House alarms were screaming a few doors up, and a dog was going nuts in somebody's rear garden. There was a dull ache in the small of my back as I unlocked the front door and stepped inside, flicking the light switch redundantly up and down.

'Great,' I said aloud to the dim, empty hall. 'Just great.'

I knew there was a flashlight somewhere in the kitchen, and I fumbled through the hall, inching my way along, the dark all around me growing black and dense. In the kitchen, things were a little brighter. The moon was casting a cold glow on the garden, which remained covered in snow. The light reflected off it gave a blue sheen to the hard surfaces of the countertops and cupboards. I fished in the drawers until I found a small black flashlight and some candles and matches, and for the next ten minutes I set about filling the rooms of the house with flickering light. The place was freezing, so once I had completed that task, I lit the radiant heater in the kitchen and set a fire in the fireplace of the sitting room, and another one in the narrow fireplace of our bedroom, my need for light and warmth overpowering my worry over the risk of setting the place ablaze. I rooted through the mess of clothes strewn around the bottom of our wardrobe until I found one of Harry's woollen sweaters big enough to suit my purpose and, having wrapped myself in it, I burrowed my nose into the rough knit of the sleeve and inhaled the musky scent of cigarettes and the chemical odour of oil paint, which seemed the very essence of Harry himself, and felt warmed and comforted.

There was something nostalgic about being plunged into darkness like this. It reminded me of power cuts when I was a kid, back in the eighties, when Ireland was in a deep recession. I had a memory of being huddled around the kitchen table, playing Scrabble by candlelight with my mother and father and brother.

But there was no one to play Scrabble with that night. Harry was stuck in London, stranded by the snow. In general, I don't mind being alone. There are times, in fact, when I crave it. In Tangier, when we were living in that space, eating together, sleeping together, working together, it felt claustrophobic, stifling. I had to get out of there regularly, away from those rooms, away from Harry even. Just to be by myself for a while. He has a powerful presence. He fills a room. Sometimes I felt the force of his personality so strongly, the relentless punching of it, I thought that if I didn't get away from it, my sense of myself would become so porous that I would lose myself in him. But that night, sitting there in the red glow of the heater, I became aware of how large this house was. The high ceilings, the cavernous rooms above and behind me. Space and more space. I felt the first pang of loneliness.

*

I rang Harry, but it went through to his voicemail.

'Hey there, you. Hope all's going well in London. I'm sitting here in the cold and dark in the middle of a blackout. It really is the eighties all over again. Hope it's luminous where you are. Anyway. I miss you. Ring me if you get a chance.'

I hung up and thought about my message, hoping I sounded upbeat and not needy or lonely. Harry would hate that.

The power cut meant I couldn't cook, so I grazed on stuff from the fridge – a yogurt, the ends of different cheeses, a slice of melon that was almost dried out, a couple of squares of chocolate. There was nothing much else to eat in the house, and it left me feeling light and insubstantial. But the snow made me reluctant to venture out again, and I couldn't be bothered getting a pizza delivered. I sat at the kitchen table, feeling restless.

What happened next was not planned. It was the restlessness that started it. I browsed the Internet until the battery of my laptop ran out. Then I tried reading, but the candle kept wavering, and I had to squint to make out the text, so pretty soon I gave up, sat back and looked about. I looked at the old cupboards, at the paint peeling off them. I looked at the long tube of the fluorescent light fixture on the ceiling, which was coated in the grime of generations but was dark now, the kitchen strangely silent without its constant buzzing or the sibilant hum of the fridge. I looked around at everything I wanted to get rid of, to peel off and strip away, to throw out and paint over, and then my eyes came to rest on the door to the garage.

As I sat there staring at it, I began to think of the distance that had sprung up between me and Harry lately. He'd seemed harsh in recent days – surly and morose. And I was skittish with nerves. There was a coolness between us, a sensitivity that seemed to cling to our conversations, so that I felt the need to tread carefully, that each word spoken between us was laden with meaning, that the most innocent facial expression or casual gesture could be misread out of all proportion. I don't know why, but the thought came to me then that all of it could be made right if I were to go into the garage now, into the space that was becoming his studio. I had a half-formed notion that if I were to spend some time there alone, among his work, among the things he created his art with, I would gain some new understanding of him, some feeling of empathy that would soften things between us. Perhaps it was snooping. And certainly there was an air of distrust between us that might have driven me in there. Or maybe it was just curiosity. Either way, it got me out of my chair, holding on to my candle in a jar as I pushed the door open, flicking the light switch out of habit, and stepped down into that cold concrete room.

I don't know what it was I went looking for. I really don't. And standing there with my candle held aloft, looking about at the heaped-up pile of junk in one corner and the spread of contents from Harry's studio sprawled all over the ground like a spillage, I said to myself, Robin, this is ridiculous. You are being ridiculous.

But instead of backing out of the room, I stepped in further and found a place to rest my candle. It was freezing in there. I took Harry's jacket from its hook on the back of the door and slipped my arms into the sleeves. Then, hands on hips, I looked around, trying to work out where to start. There were some plastic crates stacked against one wall, and it was to these I went first. One contained the fax machine. Another held coils and coils of wires and cables, and batteries that skittered and rolled as I lifted the crate and put it to one side. The crate underneath contained paperwork, and I sat down cross-legged on an old roll of carpet and set about going through it, anxiously scanning each receipt, each fax and letter and bill, anything that might give me some clue as to why my husband was behaving in such a strange manner. I must have spent a half-hour going through it, growing colder and more exasperated with each minute. And guilty. The shade of guilt grew darker the more I looked. At this stage, I was snooping. I could admit that much to myself. And at the end of it all, I'd barely turned up anything. A receipt for a night out at La Cave that amounted to almost three hundred euros was the only incriminating thing. Well, that and a cryptic fax from Diane: 'What a night! A triumph! You were really something . . . as always. Dx.'

I sat there looking at it. 'Bitch,' I said aloud to the empty room. 'Poisonous bitch.' And taken with a cold rage, I held the corner of the fax to the flame of my candle and watched it blacken and crinkle, the flame eating up the page. There was a bucket in the corner by the stack of canvases, and I took the smoking page over and dropped it there, watching the last of it shrivel and burn against the cold enamel. There was some satisfaction in that, but still the restlessness lingered, and as I looked about I saw a wooden box, the corners sealed with hammered metal. It was half-hidden by a roll of canvas, stashed away beneath some storage shelves. Drawn to it, I set my candle down on the ground beside it, moved the canvas to one side and slid the crate out from beneath the shelf. As I pulled it towards me, I felt the roll of the bottle within, heard the clink of the glass against something metal. I reached inside and, from among the rolled-up sketches, pulled out an almost empty bottle of Lagavulin. I stared at the honey-coloured liquid gleaming in the light of the candle. It was so obvious and expected, it made me suddenly depressed. Why had I gone looking through all this stuff? What had I hoped to find? I should have known that nothing good would have come of it, that all I could possibly find was something else to cause me pain. With a heavy heart, I put the bottle back, and it was as I leaned forwards to push the crate back into its hiding place that I caught sight of them. It made me stop cold. I held my breath.

The first one I drew from the box was dated April 2005. Barely a month after Dillon had died. It was a pencil sketch, and the likeness was so clear and immediate it caused a tightening around my heart. Those eyes so black and luminous in the round saucers of sockets. Harry had used a pencil with a soft lead, and this softness made Dillon's eyes seem dreamy and plaintive, as though they were looking out from beneath a film of water. His mouth was open a little, a smudge on the lips giving them the appearance of wetness, as if he had just licked them. A faint flick of the pencil had given his chin a cleft – the chin dimple I had worried so much about. His hair was tousled, as if he'd just been woken from sleep. I stared hard at the sketch. It was a mask of innocence.

The next one was dated November 2005. We would have been back in Ireland by then, trying desperately to piece together a life for ourselves from the shards and fragments left in his absence. Harry had drawn this one as if Dillon had been caught by surprise. His body was facing one way; only his head turned to stare back at the artist. And in this sketch the pencil used had been harder, darker. Sharp lines carved out the hollow stare, picking out the questioning shine of his eyes, the straight line of his closed mouth. His hair was a little longer; it curled under at the nape of his neck.

May 2006 then. Again, the same hard pencil, the same sharp lines. This time Dillon was facing the artist full-on. And there was something angry about his face. His eyes seemed flatter, colder. A feeling of distance had come into this drawing, and I couldn't tell exactly how. The hair was even longer, more dishevelled. It had a grubbiness that suggested a tougher existence, mirrored in the look in Dillon's eyes. A defensive look.

The sketches continued. They went on and on. Year after year. And each one showed him a little older. Each one showed him a little more distant, a little harder. Something about his face seemed to be closing itself off, shutting itself down, so that by the time I reached the last one – dated July 2010 – it was as if the very spirit of my son had been extinguished. A hard, sharp face stared out at me. All the softness had been erased; the innocence had disappeared. I saw a tough, angry boy. A boy who looked like Dillon. But not the Dillon I knew, not the Dillon I remembered, not the Dillon I loved.

The light came on, and I gave a little cry of shock. With the electricity restored, I was plunged into the stark brightness and, looking around, I saw that I was kneeling in a corner of the garage surrounded by all the sketches of Dillon. Under the harsh light of the bare bulb, with all those portraits scattered in a semicircle around me, as though they were closing in, I experienced a tightening under my ribs like panic.

'Why?' I said aloud. 'Why has he done this?'

All these sketches, all these years. The labour and the longing that must have gone into them. I looked at the wooden box he had shoved in under the shelves – that he had hidden – and thought of all the pain he kept squirrelled away, hidden from my view, and it filled me with sadness and that age-old remorse. Slowly, I gathered the pictures together and put them in their box, pushing it back in place and returning the roll of canvas so that the box was once more obscured. It was as if I had never touched them.

I couldn't sleep. For hours, I tossed and turned, trying to find a cool spot on the pillow. My limbs kept creeping across the mattress, trying to find Harry's sleeping form. I have always found it difficult to sleep when alone. I stared up at the dark ceiling and tried to drag my mind out of the corridors it kept travelling down. Ancient, dusty passages filled with shadows. Tangier. Old memories, old faces – Cozimo, Raul, Garrick . . .

One memory I kept returning to was a night in Tangier during the time when Harry and I were separated. It was not a long separation – three or four weeks. Long enough to feel lonely. Long enough for my anger to bloom and then wither. Dillon was three years old at the time – I mention this, because he was the cause of our estrangement. Or, rather, it was what Harry did to him that prompted my furious response, that caused me to snap and throw him out of our house.

Those pills.

I can still remember it. The horrible plunging feeling when I held them in my hand and realized what Harry had been doing.

Cozimo had taken him in, of course. Cozimo, his friend and ally. An accomplice of sorts. And it was Cozimo who came to me after three or four weeks to plead Harry's case and ask me to take him back.

I remember the night. The alleys dark and quiet. The soft sounds of Dillon playing quietly with toys in his bed. Cozimo sprawled on the couch, languorously sipping the martini I had grudgingly made for him. All the while I sat opposite him, my arms folded across my chest, unsmiling and staring implacably at him, quietly enraged by his presence – the gall of the man.

'You know you won't be able to keep this up for ever,' he remarked.

'Won't I?'

'No, of course not, my dear. You are angry, and that is fine. You have every right to be.'

'Yes, I am aware of that, Cozimo.'

He ignored the pointed remark and continued: 'But such anger is exhausting. It will wear you down. And the single unalterable fact remains that you love Harry and Harry loves you, and that, as they say, is that.'

He raised his eyebrows as if to say, *end of argument*, and sipped his drink, sinking a little deeper into the sofa.

'I would question the "unalterable" part of your statement.'

He smiled and gave a little wheeze of a laugh.

'Your love for each other has been tested, granted.'

'Tested?'

'But such trifles are not the stuff that breaks a marriage.'

'*Trifles?*' I unfolded my arms and pushed myself forwards so that I was perched on the edge of my chair.

'Yes. Trifles,' he replied, unfazed.

'He gave our son sleeping pills, Cozimo. *Your* sleeping pills, I might add, and you think that is a trifle?' My voice rose with anger, driven by the infuriating little smile on his lined face, his shrugging manner. 'The two of you drugging a little boy. I ought to report you.'

'Ah, now there I must correct you, my dear. I never drugged anyone. I merely supplied the pills, and it was up to Harry what he chose to do with them.'

I narrowed my eyes at him.

'You slippery old sod,' I said. 'The way you oil your way through life, allowing responsibility to slide off you –'

'It is my life, Robin, and one of the things I like most about it is the precise lack of responsibility. I have never understood why any man would want to shackle himself to another person – I certainly have never felt the urge.

139

And it is no concern of yours how I choose to live my life.'

'It is when you start interfering in mine.'

His eyes squeezed shut for a few seconds, and when he opened them again, he seemed more composed, colder perhaps.

'We are straying from the point, my dear.'

'How so?'

'The fact remains that you are still here, in Tangier, and that more than anything else tells me that you still love Harry and there remains the distinct possibility that you will take him back and thus relieve me of my houseguest. Much as I love him, one must have one's own space, after all.'

'Bothering you, is he? Cramping your style?' I was beginning to enjoy myself.

'Oh, Robin, what kind of debauched life do you imagine I lead in my little palace?' He gave me a wistful smile. 'In truth, I lead a simple life. No, Harry is not cramping my style. In all seriousness, it pains me to see him so sad, so morose. He is bereft without you, and distraught over what he has done. If you would only see him, talk to him, listen to what he has to say –'

'What is the point, Cozimo? It's all just talk. Words and more words. Promises and apologies, but underneath it all, something has been broken that cannot be fixed.'

'And what is that?'

'Trust.'

He stared at me across the distance of the room, and the word seemed to hang in the silence between us.

Slowly, he got to his feet, putting the glass down on the

table. A thoughtful look came over him as he moved towards the window and gazed down at the alley below.

'Trust,' he repeated softly, his gaze caught by something outside that I couldn't see.

Turning back towards me, hands behind his back, still with that pensive look on his face, he said, 'I have always thought that trust is a funny thing – a curious thing. The weight people put on it. The immense proportions it takes on in a relationship. And what strikes me is that we all have a great desire to trust others. We want to trust the ones we love even when we know we shouldn't, even when past experience has taught us not to. We say, "I can never trust him again," but then time passes, and we let them back into our hearts. We forgive, and we get on with things.'

He moved towards the door, and I watched him, feeling that he was working up to something.

'And then there are those who we trust because we have no reason not to. But who knows? Perhaps there is a reason we shouldn't trust them, but we are unaware of it? After all, none of us are saints, are we? Even the most saintly among us can slip.'

He fixed me then with a piercing gaze, and I saw something in those hard little eyes – something dangerous.

'I don't know what you mean.'

He straightened up and smiled.

'Haven't you ever committed a misdemeanour, my dear? Hmm? Are you quite sure Harry can trust you?'

He held me in his gaze, and I felt the cold plunge of fear in my heart.

'Giving a pill to a fractious child to help him sleep

might not be the worst crime in the world, don't you think? You and I both know that there are far greater breaches of trust.'

His eyes, in that moment, seemed as grey as gunmetal, and I felt the cold glare of the threat coming off him.

Then he smiled, and I knew he had accomplished what he'd come here to do.

'I'll let myself out,' he said, and I listened to the *shush* of his leather slippers all the way down the stairs.

Now, across the distance of years, I could still hear the drag of his slippered feet, even as I lay alone in my bed in the dark, snow outside the window, Dillon, Cozimo and Tangier all long gone. Don't go there, I told myself. Leave those thoughts where they belong – in the past.

I turned over once more, resolved to fall asleep, and it was then that I felt it. A bubble bursting inside me. A pocket of liquid suddenly voiding itself. It gushed from me, warm and wet against my thighs. Panic came quickly as I reached to touch the dampness of my pyjamas and then hurriedly groped for the light.

The first thing I saw was the bloody handprint I had left on the sheet.

'No!' I cried out, ripping back the covers.

The sudden violence of it was shocking. So much blood, so quickly – it did not seem possible. Flinging myself from the bed, I raced to the bathroom, crying, and there I was confronted by my reflection in the mirror: tears streaming down my face, pale as a sheet, the blood below my waist a violent contrast.

'No,' I said again, a plaintive cry to an empty house.

142

I felt like I had been punched. Everything drained away inside me. I sat on the edge of the bath, the dampness of my pyjamas clinging to me like a bad conscience.

'It isn't fair!' I cried. 'It's not fucking fair.'

And I knew then, in that moment of loss, how badly I had wanted it. The baby. I understood then that I had come to think of it as more than just a second chance. I had come to think of it as a redemption.

I waited until after dawn to go to the hospital. It hardly seemed worth a mad dash into Holles Street in the middle of the night just to have confirmed what I already knew. I spent the night on the couch, wrapped in the duvet, trying to comfort myself.

At first light, I dressed and got the van to start. I drove slowly, mechanically, my face set in a dull, numbed expression. Driving, parking, talking to the woman at reception – all of it felt slightly surreal, as if I were outside my body, watching myself going through this set of actions. I felt I couldn't possibly cry any more. And yet, when I spoke to the midwife on duty and told her I'd mis-carried during the night and she turned to me with an expression of such pity, I found fresh tears brimming over once more, all my emotions rushing to the surface.

'Oh, you poor pet,' she said. 'Have you other children at home?'

I shook my head, no, and she rubbed my back comfortingly.

'Let's get you sorted out,' she said, handing me a plastic container and directing me to the bathroom.

When I came back with my sample, she told me to sit in the waiting room, which was already filling up with women there for their ante-natal check-ups.

'No,' I said, surprising her. 'I'm sorry. But I just can't sit out there in that room full of pregnant women.'

And then the tears came all over again. Perhaps it was because of that, or maybe she just felt sorry for me because I was there alone; in any case, she ushered me through to an examination cubicle straightaway.

'Sit tight there, love. The doctor will be along to you in a minute.'

She left me alone, and I sat on the examination table and looked at the grey walls around me, and I had the thought that this would be it for me. A cursory examination. An appointment made to flush away the remaining traces of my pregnancy. My last chance gone. There would be no more babies. No more children. I wondered how things would be with Harry now. His behaviour since I'd become pregnant had led me to understand that he did not want the child. Well, now that had been neatly taken care of for him. A spiteful thought, but I was hurt and angry. All night I had tried phoning him, getting his voice-mail every time. What was he doing? Why, at the moment when I needed him most, could he not be there for me? I dreaded seeing him again. I couldn't bear to hear whatever worthless words of comfort he would try to offer. It would all sound fraudulent. I didn't want to be comforted, anyway – not by him. And it struck me that this time I would have to grieve alone. After Dillon, we were at least able to share our pain, confide in each other, get angry with each other, hammer against the walls, scream into the night, weep in each other's arms. Whereas now, I knew that I would keep my grief separate from him. I had a vision of the days and nights to come – Harry circling me with his concern, trying to keep his relief hidden from me, while I remained aloof, holding my sadness away from him, maintaining the distance between us. A distance that, I knew, would grow and grow.

I staggered out of the hospital. Staggered – that is the only way to describe it. Stunned, confused, blinking in the light of the new day. My mind was awash with all that had just occurred. The doctor, a tall, solemn black man with a firm, confident voice, slightly accented, peering through to that most private space, saying: 'Your cervix is closed.'

'Is that a good thing?'

'Possibly.'

Still I could not fathom it. All that blood. The terrible rush of it.

An ultrasound. A hazy image like a TV with poor reception. The dark cavern of my womb appearing – a pocket of blackness. Then I saw it. A tiny shape curled into one corner. A caterpillar. A bean. A fern waiting to unfurl.

'There!' the doctor said, a note of triumph in his voice. 'You see? There is your baby.'

'But . . . is it . . . ?' I couldn't say it. I couldn't ask if it was alive.

'You see this here?' His dark finger pressed against the screen. 'You see?'

And then I saw it. A flickering. A rapid pulse.

'Your baby's heart beating.'

And I felt my own heart quicken.

'I don't understand. The bleeding. There was so much of it. How can –'

Busy taking images from the ultrasound, he shrugged his reply.

'Who knows why these things happen. Who can say?'

He handed me a small black-and-white print. The little bean resting, waiting, in that dark space inside me. I held it in my hand and swallowed hard.

'So what now?' I asked.

'You have had what we call a threatened miscarriage. But your baby is still alive. And your cervix has closed. Hopefully, the bleeding will have stopped.'

'So what should I do?'

Again he shrugged.

'It is up to you. Some say that bed rest helps. But there is no real scientific evidence to back this up. Try to stay calm. Try to stay positive. It is in the hands of God.'

The hands of God. Strange words coming from the mouth of a doctor. I had long ago stopped believing in a God. And yet, when he said it, I felt a strange tug inside me. A kindling of the hope I'd thought was dead. I had something to cling to once more, something to put my faith in.

# 9. Harry

Spencer was there when I got back. Not standing at the gate like every other welcoming friend or relative but hunched over in the bar, struggling with the crossword. The same robe, the same tangle of hair. It was as if he hadn't moved since I had left. When he saw me, he winced, shaking his head in disapproval at another of our country's woes.

'Did you see this?'

Not how was the trip, not how was the gallery, heard you were delayed, how did you fare, what about the CCTV footage – no, none of that. Instead, his hoarse voice could only manage the vituperative 'Did you see this?'

In his hand was the smudged and ragged front page of one of the national newspapers. He pointed to a headline about a well-known broadcaster's autopsy. The word 'COCAINE' was writ large. The rumours had been confirmed.

'What did you expect?' I said.

'They've come down a bit hard.'

'You reckon?'

'People died to feed his habit.'

'What?'

'That's what the papers say.'

I shrugged, and Spencer stood up a little unsteadily. He took my bag, and we walked out of the airport.

'Here, give me the keys,' I said. 'You look like you've been here all week.' He handed the keys over without a fuss and shot me the kind of look that suggested he might indeed have been there the whole time I was away. I actually couldn't be sure.

Dublin seemed tired as we drove towards it. It may have been my passenger, but there was a mangy look to the city. Even the WELCOME TO DUBLIN sign looked jaded.

'Take the tunnel,' Spencer said. 'I'll pay.'

After being roombound for several days, I found it strange to be driving. In fact, after all of my discoveries, the whole sensation of travel was dreamlike.

'The Port Tunnel, another colossal waste of money. Did you hear they're moving the fucking port to Balbriggan?'

'You're turning into a grumpy old man.'

'I am a grumpy old man. You'll also have noticed, it's been three days, the snow has gone nowhere!'

He said it as if the snow had slighted him personally. As we coasted through the tunnel, Spencer looked at his phone and sighed. 'Here, let's ditch the car and go for a pint. I've an awful headache.'

'Somewhere by the Point Depot?'

He rubbed his hands together. 'Yeah, brill. Maybe someone will nick the car. I'm sick of it.'

We found a small pub, one of the old early houses

where the dockers went, and slipped into a private corner. Spencer ordered two pints.

'Get that into you,' he said, gulping greedily at his.

It felt odd, sitting there in the semi-darkness, the two of us huddled over our pints while outside the morning was just getting going: trains pulling into stations, commuters spilling out, people hurrying towards offices while the wind whipped across the Liffey. I hadn't slept in over twenty-four hours, and my body cried out with fatigue, yet a kind of crazed energy fizzed through me, a manic desire to keep going, to get moving, to pursue this one lead before it went stone cold. My son was alive. I had seen him. He was out there. He was close – I could sense it.

'So. Are you going to tell me why it is that you needed to see me so urgently? It's not often I get a call at dawn demanding a lift from the airport.'

'Yeah, I know. And listen, thanks. I appreciate it.'

'No problemo. So, what? Things a bit tight, are they? Couldn't make the fare for the Aircoach? Had a barney with the missus and she refused to pick you up?'

The mention of Robin brought a tinge of remorse. I hadn't called her, hadn't even texted. I had ignored her calls, her messages, some part of me needing to shut down against her and avoid contact. Part of it was cowardice – this I was fully aware of. After Daphne, well ... I could hardly look at myself in the mirror, let alone speak to my wife. I was afraid of what my voice might give away. But part of it had to do with this new resolve I had, this burning need to find Dillon. To track him down. What I had seen the day of the protest – it wasn't a delusion. I was not going mad. The CCTV footage confirmed what my gut had registered long before. He was alive. That was the important thing. And now I needed to find him, to bring him back, to reunite him with his mother so that maybe, just maybe, she might finally be able to forgive me. I had the thought that if I could bring Dillon back to her, it might be possible for me to erase the look of horror that had contorted her features when she'd discovered how I had left him alone.

'You haven't used up all your favours with the Guards, have you, Spence?'

'For fuck's sake, Harry.'

'The DVDs you got for me. I went through them. I found what I was looking for.'

'That's wonderful, Harry,' he said sarcastically. 'But I still don't know what the fuck you're up to.'

'It's a licence plate. I need to find out who owns the car and where they live.'

'Right you are.'

'Really?'

'No, not really, Harry. What the fuck? Who do you think I am, Columbo? I don't have any favours left – I'm all out of favours.' He was exasperated. Something was annoying him, something apart from me. I had a hunch. Money was always on Spencer's mind. It was probably that. I ordered another round and pressed on.

'It's important.'

'It always is with you.'

I wasn't entirely sure where Spencer's contacts came from or why any Guard would do anything for him. He'd always been vague on that. He had a variety of interests, as he called them. He was part of a syndicate. They owned a horse together. Went to Cheltenham to watch it race. That kind of lark. McDonagh owed him money because he'd borrowed some to bet on one or two horses too many. I got that story piecemeal. He also owned or had an interest in a property that may or may not have been a brothel. The client list included names he could use. It's not like he would, because he knew there'd be consequences for him if he did. But he could, if he had to, if you know what I mean. Something like that. It was a tangled mess really, and if he did a favour for someone, they'd usually do their best to help him out with something. But whatever tangle Spencer was in, I needed him. I have to tell him, I thought. It's the only way.

'Spence?'

'What?'

My mouth dried up, and my voice didn't sound like my own. It was as if I were watching myself act and talk in this strange manner. 'I saw Dillon,' I said.

'Who now?'

'I saw Dillon. At the demonstration. The day I moved out of the studio. My son. I saw him.'

Spencer didn't seem to be taking in the weight of what I was saying.

'He was with a woman, holding her hand. They were walking up O'Connell Street.'

'If you have a fiddle, I have a cello.'

'Spencer, do you hear what I'm saying? I saw my son. He's alive.'

'Jesus, Mary and Joseph. Not this again.'

'I saw him. I saw Dillon.'

The barman looked over to our table. I had raised my voice. Spencer signalled to me to keep it down. 'Now, hold on a minute, chief. Have you been taking your fucking meds?'

That was a cheap shot, and Spencer knew it. The six weeks I had spent in St James's had been a nightmare. I had been diagnosed with depression and a thought disorder. It's not something I liked people to joke about. But I let it go; I pressed on. 'Spencer, I saw him. I saw Dillon, and I need that fucking licence plate traced, and you're my man.'

For a time, Spencer said nothing. He looked about himself as if he were consulting invisible presences, waiting for their approval. They gave it, apparently. Because the next moment, he was smiling and asking me, 'I'm your man?' I didn't think he was mocking me.

'You are.'

'Harry, we need to talk. Are you sure you're all right?'

'I've found my son, Spencer, that's all.'

Spencer peered at me seriously. The lopsided sneer erased itself from his face. A look of concern came over it, and then a sudden exhaustion.

'Listen,' he said, his voice low, his eyes liquid and staring. 'You've been going through some kind of a rough patch – I can see that. You've been under strain. The house, Robin's work being cut back. Shit, I didn't realize how tough things were till you told me you were closing up the studio. Don't you think there's a chance that this, this . . . sighting,' he said, alighting on the word, 'might have something to do with that? You wouldn't be the first man who thinks he sees things that aren't there. Christ, think of all the fuckers who spot ghosts or UFOs or moving statues of the Virgin Mary. Paranoid delusions. The thing is to recognize them for what they are – a sign. A wake-up call that you need to destress, sort your head out, slow down.'

'A wake-up call to destress? Can you even hear yourself? You sound like a self-help book. Do me a favour and spare me the amateur psychobabble, will you?'

He nodded his head slowly, looked down at the glass in his hand and seemed to consider what I'd said. We had been good friends over the years. He was loyal. One of the few visitors when I was in hospital. One of the few who was not scared off by my monologues or dismissals, my lack of insight, my psychosis. It felt as if we had known each other all our lives. But then sometimes, I felt like my life had started only when I began art college and met Robin and Spencer, and took the apartment Spencer offered me to rent.

I waited a long moment for him to speak. Then he looked up at me, one eyebrow raised, a grin starting out of the corner of his mouth. 'I don't suppose you've told your wife any of this?' he said.

'Nope.'

'Nope?'

'Just you.'

'I'm fucking privileged.'

'So, are you going to help me, or what?'

He sighed heavily, considering the question, then put his glass down. Reaching into his jacket, he took a cigarette packet from the pocket and ripped the back off it.

'Write the number down on the back of that. I'll get on to Fealty.'

I cast a look of gratitude across the table, then scribbled down the digits I had memorized.

He picked up the card and squinted at it. 'This'll cost you, by the way.'

'Sure.'

'I'll want payback. It's not something for nothing.'

'Whatever you say.'

He could have asked me for anything right then and I would gladly have given it. Anything to get Dillon back. Nothing was too high a price.

We sat in silence then. In the corner of the room, a TV was on, tuned to a news report. A man was driving a cherry picker into the gates of the Irish parliament as a protest against the government. The high-reaching crane had all sorts of slogans on it. I couldn't make them all out. But one of them read 'ANGLO TOXIC BANK', and another had something to say about Bertie Ahern's pension plan. One more I caught out of the corner of my eye: 'ALL POLITICIANS SHOULD BE SACKED'.

'Apparently,' Spencer said to me, nodding his head at the cherry picker, 'he was a property developer.'

We parted company then. I stood on the slushy pavement, watching Spencer's hulking form as he ambled down Pearse Street, his overcoat pulled tight against the cutting wind coming in off the quays. I had done what I had intended to. Tapped Spencer for his contacts in the Guards. Set in motion my plan to track the licence plate of that car. I should have been filled with a sense of accomplishment, but instead I just felt deflated. Some remnants of nervous energy still whisked around inside me. I knew I should go home, try to patch things up with Robin. I wasn't exactly sure how I would explain it – my wilful refusal to take her calls or reply to her messages. How could I justify that? This strange urge to focus all of my being on this one slippery goal, finding my son – this urge demanded that I turn my back on my other responsibilities, so afraid was I that I would become distracted and lose my nerve. So I didn't call her. I didn't return home. Instead, I went to Mary Street to see Javier.

Javier is a fortune-teller. He runs his operation out of a basement beneath a hair salon. He's well known. He reads tarot cards and palms and does charts and all that kind of thing. He's nothing like a crystal-ball reader in a tent. He is one of the few people to have given me hope over the years. I rang, and his assistant said he could fit me in for a half-hour reading.

The steps down to his place always give me goosebumps. A woman sat in his waiting room, ahead of me. She had travelled from County Clare, she told me. 'He's the best.' She looked distraught, and I wondered what she was hoping to learn in this basement, what supernatural knowledge was about to be imparted to her and whether it would change her life.

I had promised Robin I wouldn't waste money on Javier again, after our last wedding anniversary. She was sensible like that. But that was before I had seen Dillon.

Javier welcomed me into the back room. It was dimly lit, with a table and two chairs, the table draped with a red velvet cloth. I could smell the odour of a rich, dark tobacco. Javier had a calming presence. His hair was greying, and he spoke with a heavy Spanish accent. He asked me what sort of reading I would like. Years ago, I had become fearful of the tarot cards. As well as a sizable occult section, in the bookshop, Cozimo had kept a deck of tarot cards in our apartment above it; he sometimes dabbled. But whenever I went near them, they scared me. I'm not sure why. I remember him playing with them on our kitchen table one morning. 'Don't worry,' he said, 'I am not going to tell you your future. I don't need the cards to do that.'

When was it he said that to me? Our first year? Robin was pregnant, and our futures lay ahead of us. 'These beautiful cards were given to me by a wise old man in the old quarter,' Cozimo said. 'We were playing poker, and he ran out of money, so he gave me these. Said they're hundreds of years old. From up where the Taro river runs in northern Italy. "Pathways" is what he said the word "tarot" meant in Arabic. Pathways.'

But Cozimo did try some form of divination with them in the months to come, and he taught me to use them, too, though I always resisted. That morning, he held my hands in his and said, 'They are not a toy; it is not a game.'

I looked at him, a little surprised. His earnestness

seemed sincere. 'I would gift you this pack, but I'd be afraid what you would see.'

I asked him to explain.

'They are a special and peculiarly honest and insightful deck.'

I laughed and reached for the cards.

'They will tell you things you do not want to know. They have told me things I did not want to know.'

My hand retreated. 'Like what?' I whispered.

'Can you ever imagine me back in London?'

We both laughed then, but in Cozimo's laughter there was a knowingness. I could see it in his eyes, too. He kept on smiling and picked up the cards and slipped them quickly into his breast pocket, as if to say, *'Safer here.'*

Somehow, in Javier's hands the tarot looked more trustworthy, less severe, and so I succumbed to something inside me, some need, some indefinable pull, and asked for a card reading, and without any small talk Javier took the cards into his hands and shuffled them languorously. Now, there are several readings you can get with a tarot pack: a twelve-card spread, a horseshoe spread, a full spread, and so on. But this time, Javier said, 'It will be a one-card reading.'

He held the deck out to me. I hesitated, then chose. I had picked the Sun card, one of the Major Arcana. On it was an image of an infant riding a white horse under the sun, with sunflowers in the background. In the child's hand was a red flag. The sun looked down with a human face.

I caught my breath and nearly told Javier everything – about Dillon, about the child mummy, about Tangier. It seemed as if images of children were all around me, as if they were trying to tell me something, to help me. But I held my tongue, and Javier started his forecast.

'The Sun card,' he said, 'is considered by many to be the best card in the tarot. It is associated with attained knowledge. The conscious mind prevails over the fears and illusions of the unconscious. Innocence is renewed through discovery, bringing hope for the future.'

Javier didn't so much tell you your future; he interpreted the cards for you. He had insight, a sense of things. Ultimately, he left it up to you to make out of the reading what you would. But he gave you clues and indicators to suggest ways of interpreting decisions that had to be made. Some things were more specific. He told me there was a strong pull from a foreign land. He said I was still working something out. That it remained unresolved. That it would come to a head soon. But that I must have an open heart. He said the sun was a positive symbol. I don't recall what else he said. He didn't say, 'You're going to find your son.' But he did say, 'There is a child, and it is no longer yours.' That hurt. I think he saw that. I was sweating, trying to stop my hands from shaking. Jesus, I don't know what was happening to me right then.

Before I left, Javier gave me a green amulet. 'For luck,' he said. I nearly hugged him, I was so far gone. He saw me blinking at a copy of a book on his table. It was *The Book of the Dead*. 'Take it,' he said, and I did, thanking him. I walked through Dublin in a daze, my fingers worrying the stone. All these people out? How did they get here? How did they make it through the snow? I stopped to listen to a man sing 'On Raglan Road'. When the fellow sang, 'I loved too much and by such, by such is happiness thrown away,' I felt a lump in my throat. Fuck, I felt as if I was falling to pieces. Had anybody touched me right then, I would have disintegrated.

I don't know why, but I didn't think I could go home right away. Even though I knew Robin wanted me to. In a quiet basement bar off Grafton Street I ordered a drink, took the postcard of the child mummy out of my pocket and looked for information about it online on my phone. What I came across was something about how green magic protected a child mummy: the discovery of a rare mummified child with a bright green amulet stone, once thought to hold magical powers, had led archaeologists to believe that the ancient Egyptians thought that the colour green would protect children from unwanted influence and ensure their health in the afterlife.

Was that, I wondered, why Javier gave me the amulet? Maybe it was a gesture; it was to protect me, to protect Dillon because he was still alive. That was how I saw it. That was how it made sense to me. You know, I'd never believed Dillon had died in the earthquake, though Robin had tried for months, for years, to persuade me that he had. Eventually I had to pretend that I accepted that he had in fact died, but not before I had filed missing persons reports both in Tangier and in Ireland. I made calls, wrote letters and e-mails, contacted my local politicians, joined survivors' and victims' support groups online and listened to and read whatever news I could in the months that followed the earthquake, seeking survivors' stories and information about bodies found, alive or dead.

I contacted Interpol, the Moroccan police force, the Guards. The best I got, the only thing I got, was 'Your son died tragically in an earthquake. The building was destroyed. It was swallowed by the earth. It was an act of God.'

Robin left Tangier three weeks after the earthquake. I don't think I ever forgave her for that. I stayed for another few weeks. 'He could have survived,' I said.

Robin shook her head. 'Harry, don't.'

'I'm not leaving him,' I said.

But Robin was having none of it. She said, 'It's the grief, Harry. The grief is unbalancing you.' The grief had ravaged me, I'll admit that. But her protestations were not enough to assuage my doubts. How could she know he had not, by some strange circumstance, survived the earthquake?

'Hundreds died,' she said, as if statistics were somehow the answer.

Then she told me she wanted to have a service for Dillon when I got back to Ireland.

'What kind of service?' I asked.

'A service,' she said.

'A funeral?'

She said nothing.

'Because we can't have a funeral if he is not dead.'

'Harry.'

'Or if we do not know . . .'

I was ordering another drink when my phone lit up. It

was a message from Diane. She must have rung right through to my voicemail. 'I know you were in London. Word travels. Harry, call me. I miss you.' I ignored the message and turned my phone off. I watched the snow start to fall again. The Met Office's forecasting skills were weak. It fell heavier that day than they had predicted. It fell and fell, heavy, luxurious and effacing snow. Their equipment was unsound or their interpretations too narrow. I knew Javier's readings of what was to come had a vagueness about them. I'm not a fool. But they suggested rather than dictated; they imagined rather than declaimed. And that postman from Donegal had as much accuracy, if not more, in his predictions of the snow. I remember him saying that when the sun shines on to the Blue Stack Mountains and down to the lowlands and it turns a reddish-brown colour, that's a sign of snow. He'd said something about the sheep and the cattle going mad too, shaking themselves, coming down from the mountains. That, too, was a sign.

The signs were there. What mattered was how you interpreted them. Suddenly, involuntarily, a memory came back to me as I sat there watching the snow: We are in Tangier. I am lying in bed with Dillon. We have the television on. It is a news bulletin. 'Is she speaking to us?' says Dillon about the newsreader. I tell him she is talking about a political party. 'They can come to my party,' he says. He will be three next week. 'That's very good of you,' I say. He strokes my face. From one cheek to the other. Intimately, lovingly. He says, 'Daddy, I love your beard.' He says, 'Daddy, I love you.'

I finished my drink and walked up the stairs from an alcoholic underworld and wondered about where the licence plate would lead. What pathway would it take me on? Was the sun to shine? And the boy on the horse, was that Dillon?

# 10. Robin

In the end, Harry was gone for four days. When he finally got home, he appeared in the doorway dark-eyed and bleary, several days' worth of stubble shadowing his face. He looked like someone troubled, someone who was letting himself go, a shadow of the man he'd once been. And I thought back to how he had been in Tangier – so vibrant and alive, full of bright colour, awake and instinctive, inquisitive and hungry. Not this tired, worn-out, beaten-down person with a hollow stare. Part of me strained towards him with a terrible pity for all he had become.

After I told him what had happened – the bleeding, the hospital, the threatened miscarriage – he sat down heavily on the couch beside me and stared blankly ahead. He didn't say a word. And then he lowered his head into his hands and started to cry. Silent tears. I didn't see his face, only his body shuddering and his hands shaking.

'Harry.'

'I'm sorry, Robin.'

'Baby, don't say that. Come here. Show me your face.'

I felt the pull of his resistance, but slowly he yielded to me, letting me take his hands in mine, looking down shyly, unable to meet my gaze.

'I can't believe you went through all that on your own.'

He looked at me then, and I felt I had a chance in that one moment to make things right between us.

'I have been so angry with you, Harry,' I began tentatively. 'All that time you were away, I kept trying to call you. Last night I left messages, sent texts, and yet there was no response from you. I couldn't believe you would be so callous — so cold. And after the way we left things, well . . . you can imagine what I was thinking. Things have not been good between us lately, not really. Ever since you moved your studio. Ever since I told you about the baby.'

He shook his head and stared at the floor. I saw the movement of muscle along his jaw as he clenched his teeth, but still I went on.

'I had the impression that you viewed your London trip as a welcome escape from me.'

'That's not true, Robin.'

'Isn't it? In these last days, I've felt that I've been losing you.'

He didn't say anything, or try to deny it.

'You've felt it, too?' I asked, and he nodded slowly. I found my lip starting to tremble, the tears coming unbidden, but I swallowed them away.

'We can't lose each other, Harry. Not now. Not after everything we've been through.'

'I don't want to lose you, Robin. It's just that . . .'

He stopped, and I had the notion that he was on the verge of telling me something, confessing something to me, and I thought again of the drawings of Dillon and all the secret pain he kept hidden from me. I took his face in my hands and looked into his eyes.

'This is a new start for us, Harry. A new beginning. This baby is real. It is happening. When I saw that ultrasound, that little heartbeat, it made me realize – all the other shit doesn't matter. This is what matters. So I'm not going to ask you about London. I'm not going to demand an explanation as to why you didn't return my calls or why you've been so distant lately. We need to put all of that behind us. Because this is our future.' I reached for his hand and placed it on my belly, still flat, and yet I thought of the child embedded deep within me, the little bean nestling into the soft layers of my body, silently growing in the darkness. 'I know you weren't happy about the pregnancy – no, please, let me finish. I know you weren't. But if you had been there, Harry. If you had seen what I saw, I know you would feel differently. This child isn't Dillon. No one will ever take his place. But we can still have this baby and love him or her as much as we loved Dillon.'

'I know. I know.'

'Listen to me now, Harry. No more lies. No more deceits. I don't want us to keep things hidden from each other. We used to be so open with each other. We used to be able to tell each other anything. Do you remember?'

'I remember. I just can't seem to remember when that stopped.'

He looked up at me then, his eyes so plaintive and forlorn, and I experienced a rush of guilt so strong, it almost made me tell him.

The moment passed. We sat together. I felt his hand moving over my tummy. I heard the logs in the open fire cracking and spitting.

'A new start, Harry.'

'Yes,' he said. And then he fell silent.

It snowed again – heavier and softer than the earlier fall of snow. For the first time in many years, we would have a white Christmas. I watched it come down, heavy and thick, filling up the garden, easing a soft blanket over every surface, every shrub and bush, clinging to the crooks of branches and the tiles of the roof, frosting the window-panes. We had the fires lit all the time. We tried to keep the house warm and our spirits light, and yet still the cold air crept in through crumbling window frames, whistling through the cavities in the brickwork. The tide of Christmas parties swept us along, and I felt an attendant tiredness, irritability I put down to pregnancy hormones and the pressures of work. The office had grown more stressful. A project we had successfully bid for had fallen through, and there was talk of coming pay cuts.

On a cold Thursday evening, Harry and I put on our hiking boots and trudged down through the snow to Blackrock College, where they were selling Christmas trees for the Society of St Vincent de Paul. We picked one out – a large, bushy thing – and half-carried, half-dragged it home. There was a silence between us that day that I couldn't account for. I was tired and anxious. Our office Christmas party had taken place the previous night. Usually a lavish affair, this year it had consisted of a few drinks and some sandwiches in our local pub. I had felt like the only sober person there. At one point in the night, one of my colleagues, the worse for drink, had passed on a rumour he had heard that there would be lay-offs in the New Year. When I'd pressed him on the issue, he had given a hollow laugh and said, 'CAD monkeys like me and you, I suppose.' And then he saw the anxiety on my face and instantly changed the subject. I thought of mentioning it to Harry, and yet I didn't want to worry him. He seemed caught up in his own thoughts that day, and I couldn't quite muster the effort required to dispel the weight that was between us.

Back home, I sliced oranges and studded the slices with cloves, then baked them in the oven. The dried-out wheels I strung with twine and hung from the tree. The whole house seemed to smell of Christmas – the pine needles, the spices, the sweet orange tang – and my spirits lifted a little. Harry went up to the attic and brought down the lights for the tree and the box of decorations, and then he sat on the floor and drank coffee laced with whiskey and watched me untangling the strings of lights.

'That tree is fucking huge,' he said, casting his eye over it. 'I think we got carried away.'

'It's a big room.'

'It's not that big. You'd need a ballroom to fit that tree.'

'I love it. I think it's perfect.'

'The angel will have vertigo. Maybe we should cut a bit off the branches?'

'No! Leave it! Wait until I've the lights and the decorations on – then it won't look so monstrous.'

'Do you think that's why they call it "trimming the tree"? Because you always end up hacking bits off it just to get it to fit in the room?'

'No hacking bits off it, Harry. Just leave it be.'

I had the lights untangled and was standing on a chair, trying to loop them around the top of the tree.

'Are you sure you should be doing that?' Harry asked, watching me with a doubtful expression. 'A woman in your condition?'

'Oh, please. Don't start that now.'

'Start what?'

'The overprotective routine.'

'Why? Did I do that before?'

I turned and looked at him.

'Harry? Are you serious? With Dillon, you hardly allowed me to move. I couldn't leave the house without an escort. You'd have a fit any time I carried a few plates from the table to the sink!'

'Did I?'

'Yes!' I laughed. 'You were a nightmare.'

This was something new. Dillon had started creeping back into our conversations. For such a long time, I had closed my mind to that whole chapter of my life. I had buried it deep down in the dark recesses of memory. But now, with this new life started inside me, I found I was able to open the door just a chink and let a little light in. Gradually, bit by bit, we were reclaiming ourselves as parents. We were reclaiming our son – our memories of him. The pain was still there – it never really went away – but it had softened. The sharp edges of it had grown blunt. I was finding that I could say his name and hear it said back to me without feeling that instant rush of sadness, that well of melancholy springing up.

'So do you think you have enough decorations?' Harry asked, peering into the large box stuffed full with angels and Santas, reindeer and bells and stars.

'It is a big tree, need I remind you?'

He had picked out a wooden angel with movable arms, and with one finger he was causing the arms to rise and fall, rise and fall.

'Seriously, how long have you been collecting this stuff?'

'I don't know. Years. What can I say? I love Christmas.'

'Other people love Christmas. With you, it's an obsession.'

He paused and looked down for a moment, his eyes growing dreamy with some old memory.

Then he said, 'Do you remember that Christmas tree we had in Tangier?'

I stopped draping lights over the branches.

'We must have been the only people in the whole of Morocco who had a real Christmas tree. Jesus!'

'Yes,' I said.

I stared at the string of lights in my hand.

Harry said something else, but I had stopped listening. I turned the lights over in my hands, and ever so slightly my hands began to tremble.

'Robin? Are you all right?'

I looked down at him and saw the concern in his eyes. My hands were steady now, but something had come over me.

'I'm tired,' I said. Getting down from the chair, I dropped the lights on to the couch. 'I'm going to lie down.'

I didn't look at him as I left the room.

*

On the last Saturday before Christmas, I was in the home-ware department of Brown Thomas with Liz, both of us attempting to cram all of our shopping into a couple of hours. Guilt plagued me as I eyed the price tags and thought about my mortgage repayments and my reduced working hours and wondered how on earth I was going to stretch my budget to buy presents for my family. I was flustered and hassled and overheating.

'What do you think about this for Andrew's mum?' Liz asked, holding aloft a blue bread bin with a walnut lid. 'It's ridiculously expensive, but does it look it? I don't want her to think I picked up some cheap tat for her, especially as she's cooking Christmas lunch for my whole brood.'

'It looks fine.'

'Hmm.' Liz frowned and returned the item to the shelf.

'Can't Andrew shop for his own mother?'

'Ha!' she laughed. 'If I left it to Andrew, he'd just get her a gift card. Or, worse, he'd present her with a cheque.'

'What's he getting you?'

'A gift card,' she intoned humourlessly. 'Don't say it, Rob. I know – the romance is dead.'

I smiled and picked up a jug, turning it over to check the price.

'How about you?' she asked. 'Are you still dead set on having your folks over for Christmas?'

'Yep. It's all arranged. The goose has been ordered, the wine and champagne have been bought –'

'Fair play to you. Just don't kill yourself.'

'What do you mean?'

'Oh, Robin, you know what I mean. Cooking,

entertaining, preparing the house. You're like Nigella Lawson on speed when it comes to these events. I just don't want you overdoing it, that's all. Not in your condition. Not after the scare you've had.' She eyeballed my belly dramatically, and I laughed in response.

'Relax. It's nothing lavish. Just Christmas. And besides, Harry is digging in to help.'

'Is he now?' she remarked sceptically. 'I bet he's overjoyed at the prospect of Christmas with the in-laws.'

'Actually, he's been fine about it. I expected some resistance, but he's been great. Brilliant, in fact. He's taking care of the shopping and cleaning up the house. All I have to do is cook. So between us, we have it all covered.'

'Good. Glad to hear it.'

She picked up a Le Creuset pot with an air of mild distraction and asked, over her shoulder, 'How has the move worked out? Has he sorted out his studio yet?'

'Yes, I think so.' My mind went instantly to that box of sketches I had discovered, the drawings of Dillon, and I wondered whether they still sat there, hidden away in the dark. Since that night, I had not set foot in the studio. Resolve had gathered inside me to ignore all that. To put my back to it and face the future. That was what mattered now.

'His London trip went well,' I carried on in a voice full of optimism. 'I think some work will come out of it.'

'Oh yeah?' She glanced across at me. 'Well, that would be great. So long as he's not spreading himself around too much. His work is wonderful, of course, but hardly prolific in recent years.'

'Listen to you! Worrying about Harry's workload.'

'Yes, I do worry,' she replied sharply, suddenly serious. 'I don't like the thought of him committing to things he can't deliver on. Not with his history.'

'Liz . . .'

'Tell me to piss off and mind my own business if you like, but you're my oldest friend, Robin, and I wouldn't be that friend if I didn't tell you that I worry about Harry when he's put under pressure. I know how sensitive he is. And I can't bear the thought of his old trouble returning. I hate to think of you having to go through all that again.'

'It won't,' I said solemnly, and in that moment I believed it. 'He's fine. We're fine. More than fine, in fact. All of that is behind us now.'

Instinctively, my hand went to my belly. She caught the movement and nodded slowly, her expression softening.

'It's funny, I didn't think you guys would have another baby.'

'Really?'

'I wasn't sure if either of you had the heart for another go on the merry-go-round.'

She smiled then, the brightness coming back to her face. Glancing down at the Le Creuset casserole dish in her hands, she remarked, 'Right then. I'm getting this. She can always return it, can't she?'

'Yep.'

'Here, hold it for me a sec,' she said, dumping the heavy dish into my arms and rooting in her bag for her wallet, and it was as I stood there, clasping the dish to my chest, that I saw him. My heart beat wildly, and the casserole dish almost slipped from my grasp.

He was leaning forwards, peering with great concentration at a display of coffee machines, and as I moved towards him, he looked up and I caught the sudden flash of consternation crossing his face.

'Hello,' I said, trying to sound calm, trying to keep cool, but all the while I stared at him, not really believing it to be true. Everything about it was wrong: the wrong time, the wrong place. After all these years, here he was standing before me, in a department store in Dublin – it seemed incongruous, perverse almost.

The look on his face changed then, something about it closing down. A defensive look.

'Don't you know me?' I asked with a nervous smile. He was still just standing there, spooked into silence, and I felt my face burning.

'Of course I know you, Robin.'

My mouth was dry as paper, my body steaming under my clothes.

He looked older, his hair running now to grey at the temples, lines fanning out from his eyes, and two deep creases travelling from either side of his nose down to the corners of his mouth, like brackets. His clothes looked expensive and warm. I found myself more distracted by this than by the rest of his appearance. I guess it was because I had never known him to wear anything other than cotton or linen, fabrics flimsy and cool enough to cope with the muggy Moroccan heat. It was disorienting, seeing him muffled up in cashmere and wool.

'What are you doing here?' I blurted out, the words sounding rude and abrupt. I was flustered, acutely aware of Liz looking up from her bag, her eyes passing over this tall stranger with the American accent who had brought flaming colour into my cheeks.

'Shopping,' he remarked with a shrug that seemed to express discomfort more than nonchalance. 'Same as you, I guess.'

'No, I mean in Ireland.'

'I know. I was just kidding.' His eyes flickered over me, and I felt my cheeks glowing crimson and regretted my lack of make-up, my choice of shoe, the shabbiness of the coat I was wearing, my dishevelled hair.

'Eva's mom is sick. We came over to be with her.'

'Oh. I'm sorry to hear that.'

He shrugged then. 'She's old.'

'Is she in the hospital?'

'Yeah. That's why I'm in here,' he added, his gaze wandering briefly around at the brightly lit store. 'Killing time while Eva visits.'

'And your son?'

'He's with her,' he said quickly, his eyes looking past me to a point over my shoulder.

Something froze inside me. The shock of seeing him again robbed me of even a solitary thing to say. Beside me, Liz cleared her throat, and I turned to her, distracted, and saw her offering him an inquisitive smile and watched as they introduced themselves, shaking hands across me, but it was all a blur, too bizarre to be real, and there followed a long, awkward pause before he nodded with an air of finality and said he'd better get going. He told Liz it was nice to have met her, and then he fixed his eyes on me and I felt his penetrating stare.

'It was good to see you, Robin.'

'Yes. You, too.'

He turned and walked quickly away, and it was only as I watched his retreating form that all the things we should have said to each other came rushing back to me: he hadn't inquired after Harry, we had barely talked at all about Eva or Felix; I hadn't asked how long he might stay.

'So?' Liz demanded, looking for gossip. 'Are you going to tell me who that long, cool drink of water is or not?'

He was at the top of the escalator, not turning to look back. A few seconds later, he was gone.

'He's no one,' I said flatly, but my heart was racing. 'Just someone I used to know in Tangier.'

I remember it. I remember it like it happened yesterday.

A café near the Place de France. The air stale with smoke. Shadows gathering in the corners where the walls met the ceiling. A lizard skittering over the floor. Cozimo was reclining languidly on a couch; Harry was leaning forwards, leafing through some old book of Cozimo's with a growing excitement. They were all there – Sue, Elena, Peter, our little coterie of expats – and others whose names and faces I have since forgotten. I was sitting on the floor, cross-legged, sipping my beer in a silent rage.

'You're very quiet tonight,' Cozimo said, and I looked up to find his bright little eyes fixed on me with an inquisitive stare.

'She's sulking,' Harry said, not looking up from his book. 'Cozimo, these pictures are amazing. Where did you get this book?'

'I won it in a card game,' he answered quickly, his eyes still on me.

I wondered if this was true. I wondered whether half the words that came out of that dry little mouth contained the slightest grain of truth.

'Why are you sulking? Surely you have not been arguing? You are both too young and too beautiful to waste time on such nonsense.'

'Christmas,' Harry said, casting a glance in my direction before returning to his book.

I rolled my eyes and let out a small sigh of exasperation. I hated the way Harry did that – shared our arguments with everyone else. He couldn't respect the privacy of our conflicts, didn't even seem to understand why I should want them to remain just between us.

'Christmas?' Cozimo repeated, confusion clouding his sharp features.

'She's pissed off because I won't go home for Christmas.'

Cozimo looked from one of us to the other, his palms held up to signify his lack of understanding. Why should something so trivial cause us to argue?

'Harry, please don't,' I said in a low voice, but he didn't seem to hear me.

'Robin is your typical Irish atheist. There is no God except at Christmas. And then it's all about the baby Jesus and midnight Mass and the turkey or goose dinner with the family and all that bullshit.'

'It's not bullshit.'

'It's "Ave Maria" and "O Holy Night" and "Hark! the Herald Angels Sing" until you want to kill yourself.'

'Stop it, Harry.'

'And of course you can't have Christmas in a warm climate,' he went on. 'Even though Jesus was from the Middle East. No, no. Christmas must be cold. It must be celebrated with trees native to Scandinavia. You don't tart up your mantelpiece with olive branches or palm leaves. It's holly and ivy all the way.'

'What's wrong with that?'

I looked up. I didn't know the voice – low tones and the slow drawl of an American accent. The face was new to me, too. Cold blue eyes, high cheekbones, a cleft chin beneath a wide, unsmiling mouth, blond hair worn long and slick, swept back off his face to reveal a widow's peak. A face that was knifelike and sharp, yet there was no denying he was handsome in a boyish kind of way. His age was difficult to guess at – he could be twenty-one or forty-four. He lounged on a sofa, holding himself perfectly still, his shoulders giving a slight shrug as he repeated his question.

Harry looked up at him and let out a soft chuckle.

'Don't tell me. It's got you all misty-eyed too, huh? Feeling a longing for the snowy hills of Vermont, are we?' he asked, not unkindly.

Again the shrug. 'Sure. Why not? Christmas means home to me. Home and family. Although I'm from Oregon, not Vermont.'

'Vermont. Oregon. What does it matter? Surely you'd prefer to be here in Tangier, where life is real, where life is happening, than wrapped up in some Coca-Cola-inspired festivities with a bunch of relatives you can hardly bear to be in the same room with?'

'Yeah, I understand why you might think that. And I respect that that's the way you feel. But I have to admit that those Coca-Cola ads really get me going. They always have. It's the same with Budweiser Christmas ads. If that makes me some kind of consumer sucker or sad fuck, then whatever; so be it.' His hands rose in a brief gesture of *mea culpa*. He added, 'And I happen to like my relatives, too. I guess that makes me really uncool, huh?'

Harry was staring at him, mystified. I could see that he didn't know what to make of this guy with the casual manner, his direct approach, his 'I am who I am and I don't give a fuck what you think' attitude. I could tell Harry felt a longing to mock him, and yet this man, this stranger, could not be easily dismissed as another sap, another dim American. His quiet conviction and solid confidence gave me to understand that he was the type of man to stand his ground, the kind who would not back down from confrontation. He had a direct stare that might be seen as a challenge.

I don't remember much else about that night. I know that I didn't speak to him – Garrick – nor he to me.

The days and nights passed, and Harry and I reached a kind of unspoken truce on the subject of Christmas. I agreed to stay in Tangier with him, and sometime in the New Year we would have my parents over – a compromise then.

I saw him sometimes – Garrick – in the bars and cafés

we used to go to, mixing with the same crowd. Another hanger-on, another one of Cozimo's eclectic gang, although even in a crowd, he always seemed alone to me, aloof and isolated. We never spoke, and I felt he hardly noticed me. I noticed him, though – the tall, faintly bored American with the piercing gaze. I learned about him through titbits of gossip I gleaned from other people's conversations. The picture that emerged was incomplete and conflicted. He was a rich kid, a trust-fund baby, with nothing to do except wander around Europe and North Africa, spending his money. He was a poet, a philosopher, an art dealer. He worked for an NGO. He had dropped out of Cambridge or Yale or the Sorbonne. He had been a successful financier before burning out and growing disgusted with capitalism. He had lost his wife in a tragic accident and was looking to lose himself in Tangier. Like so many others drifting through this continent, he was running away from himself.

To me, he was a distraction. Nothing more.

Life went on. I worked hard at my painting, although I knew I was floundering. Tangier had not turned out to be the artistic awakening for me that it was for Harry. I was often lonely. I went to Internet cafés frequently, needing to touch base with home, with my friends. A strange envy took hold of me whenever they e-mailed back the news of their continuing lives, their new jobs, their fledgling careers, the money they were earning, the mortgages they were taking on, the men they were meeting and falling in love with and getting engaged to, the babies they were making. I felt outside of it all. I felt as if life was happening elsewhere. I kept all of this to myself. With Harry, it was different. I had never seen him so happy – so alive. The work he was producing was vibrant and passionate and evocative, light and colour dancing through his paintings. You looked at them and felt yourself getting pulled in.

One evening in late December, I came back to our flat feeling that strange sense of emptiness that often took me after hearing from home. I climbed the stairs and entered the living room and came upon a scene I had not expected to find. Cozimo was sprawled on the couch, peeling an orange; Garrick was sitting opposite him, hands held in his lap, passing one thumb over the other in a slow meditation. And in the middle of the room, Harry was struggling with a Christmas tree. He was stuffing sweaters around the trunk in an effort to get it to sit up straight in a bucket.

'Where did you get that?' I asked.

'There you are!' he exclaimed, crawling out from underneath the branches. He looked from the tree to me. 'Well, what do you think? Is it straight?'

'What do I think?' I looked at the little tree, the straggly branches, the bald spots where the needles had been completely shed. It was a small miracle, this little spruce in the middle of dusty Tangier. 'Baby, it's wonderful! It's amazing! How on earth did you get it?'

I rushed to him and wrapped my arms around his neck and reached up to kiss him about his head, moved to this public display of affection by the thoughtfulness of his gesture. And he laughed at me in an almost bashful way and caught me about the waist.

'Calm down there,' he said, swooping down to kiss me on the mouth. 'But don't thank me. I had nothing to do with it. Your fellow Christmas obsessor is responsible for this.'

I looked across. He was staring at the tree. His thumbs had stopped moving. And then he raised those gleaming blue eyes, and it seemed as if that was the first time we had ever looked at each other. He lifted a hand in greeting, and the corners of his mouth moved to give the briefest of smiles. He held me there for a moment before I had to turn away.

I went to the bedroom to drop my bags and take off my shoes. I sat on the bed and held my face in my hands and felt my cheeks hot with the blood rushing to the surface.

Back in the living room, Cozimo was draping orange peel over the branches by way of decoration.

'That won't do,' I told him. 'This tree deserves to be properly dressed.'

I set about rooting through my art supplies and Harry's for any bits and bobs I could fashion into baubles and ornaments to string from the branches. Harry got some beers from the fridge, and the men began to talk of a forthcoming trip to Casablanca in the New Year, and soon I felt forgotten in my solitary work.

Later, as he was leaving, he came and stood alongside me as I hung my improvised decorations on the branches.

'Do you like it?' he asked quietly.

'It's wonderful.'

'I wasn't sure. You seemed reserved. I couldn't tell if you approved.'

'I do like it,' I said, before adding softly, 'I love it.'

And then I brought my eyes up to meet his, and he was gazing at me so intently, in a way I had never experienced before, like his eyes were reaching right into me, trying to touch some hidden point inside me. I had to make myself keep looking. I had to force myself not to turn away.

'Good,' he said, nodding. And I found him so solemn in that moment. Solemn with a trace of sadness. I felt his remoteness. He seemed unknowable.

He left, and I carried on as before, dressing the tree, accepting another beer, sharing a joint with the others on the couch. But something had changed in me. The person who went to bed that night was not the same person who had awoken that morning. The person who went to bed that night was someone sleepless and fretful, with a dark longing growing within her.

# 11. Harry

The days passed. No word from Spencer. No phone call. No address. Nothing. I sat at home. I brooded. But still I didn't let Robin know. I hid my thoughts. I hid my feelings. I didn't say anything about having seen Dillon. Even when she said his name, I remained silent, revealing nothing about him, nothing about the CCTV or the licence plate or an address I was waiting impatiently for. I drank coffee. I drank tea. I smoked cigarette after cigarette. I sat in my studio and did the crossword. But there was always the unsettling, restless urge to do something, to get going, to find out where Dillon actually was.

I drew and sketched. The child mummy mostly, images that had lingered in my mind since London. It was one way of dealing with the recurring visions. A catharsis, if you like. Drawing the images out of myself, literally. But even that was superseded by the run-up to Christmas. Then one day, not long before Christmas Day itself, like a heavy cloud, the load burst.

Robin's peaceful demeanour of the previous week had vanished. Christmas was starting to stress her out. Her parents were coming for Christmas dinner, and she was taking it seriously. She had lists. And more lists. Shopping lists. To-do lists. Recipes. Presents to buy. Things not to forget. She was starting to look drawn and tired.

'This house is a disaster,' she said, glancing about in despair.

I was about to say something when my phone rang. It was Spencer.

His gravelly, surreptitious tones smoked their way through the receiver: 'We're in luck.'

'What?'

'I have an address.'

My heart gave a sudden kick. An address. It was all I had been thinking of. I had almost lost hope, and now I was grateful and dumbfounded.

'You can thank me later. I'll pick you up this afternoon.'

Robin looked up. 'Who was that?' she asked suspiciously.

'No one,' I said.

'No one? It must have been someone. What's with all the secrecy?'

'It was just Spencer. Nothing important.'

She squinted at me, nodding slowly.

I was nervous as a cat, listening for the hum of Spencer's Jag drawing into the driveway. I could sense that Robin was looking forward to a night in, but she was also agitated. She sat down in the living room. I lit a fire, then fixed myself a coffee with a dash of whiskey.

'There's so much to do, Harry,' she said.

She sounded a little sad. I wanted to reassure her, but before I could, the doorbell rang. I shot up from my chair and out into the hallway.

When I opened the door, two carol singers stood before me. A pair of young girls with hungry faces singing

'Jingle Bells' at breakneck speed. They finished and one of them said, 'Hey, mister, happy Christmas,' and shook a plastic jar at me. It jingled with coins. At the end of the driveway, I could see a bullish man leaning on a stick, waiting for them. I fumbled in my pocket and gave them the few coins I had. They rushed out of the drive towards their minder and the next house.

'Who was that?' Robin said looking out the window.

'Carollers,' I answered.

The evening drew in around us, and we settled into a kind of amicable silence, broken only by occasional chitchat. It was weird, though; it was what most people think is normal chitchat, but for me it was just outward chatter from someone who was called Harry, spoke like Harry and moved the way Harry moved. Otherwise, I was somewhere else, someone else. A man on the edge. A man waiting. In the last few weeks, I hadn't been sleeping well. I kept dreaming that I was back there on that empty street in Tangier, dust choking my lungs, the flutter and shuffle of hundreds of books strewn about my feet. When I woke I could still taste the dust, a chalky deposit coating the roof of my mouth, and the gaping maw of emptiness was still there inside me, and I knew that for more than five years I had been trapped in that place, standing still while the awful reality consumed me. Now I had a chance to change all that. I wanted to be there for Robin, but with everything else going on, it just wasn't possible. Every minute we spent in each other's company, I was on the brink of telling her what I was up to, but I thought that it would only upset her, so I kept putting it off for a better moment, for the right moment. Which is nonsense, I know; it's not as if I waited for the right moment to ask her to marry me; it's not as if I waited for the right moment to first approach her or kiss her or any of those things. I acted spontaneously and impulsively, and when the doorbell rang I acted in the same way. I got up without saying anything to Robin and grabbed my coat.

'Harry?'

'I'll be back soon.'

'What is it?'

'There's something I have to do.'

'What?'

'I'll tell you later.'

'Can it wait?'

'Not this time.'

She followed me into the hall.

'Harry, what's going on?'

'Nothing. I'll be back soon.'

I should have made up a reason. I should have given her an excuse. But I mumbled my way through leaving. Disappointment crept into her voice: 'If you're going for a drink with Spencer, why not tell me?'

I shut my eyes, my heart pounding. I told myself that this would all soon be over, and then she would know. Then I could tell her. But right at that moment, I just wanted to get away.

I pulled the door open and saw Spencer sitting in his car, hunched over the steering wheel, a grin lighting up his tired features. Behind me, I heard Robin huff out her irritation. Spencer's presence, his brash braking, his old Jag, his blithe demeanour – none of it helped my departure. I turned to kiss her goodbye, but a look of reproach had come over her face.

'Go then,' she said, then tied her dressing gown tighter about her waist and watched me leave with a disappointed air. I had let her down again. But it would be worth it, I told myself. It would be worth it this time.

'Trouble with the missus?' Spencer asked when I got into the car.

'Shut up and tell me where we're off to.'

'Well, I have the address. It was a pain in the arse to get. Need I say, you owe me. Anyway, when we get there . . .' He let the statement hang, and we drove on in silence. All the light had gone out of the day, and the city looked washed out and colourless as we passed through the empty streets. I leaned my head against the window, relishing the coldness of it against my temple. All my excitement had dissipated, leaving me hollow inside. Spencer accused me of sulking, but I ignored him, my eyes passing over the blurry smudges of streetlamps and the grey buildings streaked with rain.

A memory was pulling at me: the day of the memorial service we had for Dillon. A group of us gathered in a room in Robin's parents' house – friends, family, people who cared about us, who were moved by our pain. Words were spoken, poems like prayers, silent weeping. Robin beside me, dry-eyed and staring, her body rigid with the discipline of controlling her grief. I reached for the hand resting upon her thigh. I held it for just an instant, but long enough to feel her flinch. Long enough to feel her

anger, her pent-up unexpressed rage, in the sudden with-
drawal of her hand from mine as she snatched it away. I
remember the shock of it – the strange violence contained
within that one small gesture – and I knew then that she
blamed me and that she would always blame me. That no
matter what words were spoken to smooth over the pain,
to soften my distress, she would hold that reproach within
her, carrying it alongside her pain. I sat there, stunned,
blinking away tears of shock. And then, as if overcome
with regret, she relented, reaching for my hand and holding it within hers. I let her take it, sitting dumbly through
the rest of that service, feeling my hand hot and limp
within hers, knowing all the while that there, within the
core of our mutual love, the rot had set in.

'Here we are,' Spencer said, pulling into a housing estate
behind a bleak-looking hotel and parking beside a patch
of wasteland. 'The house right over there.' He pointed
across the street.

Nerves roused me from my daydream. I felt unpre-
pared and uncertain, in that moment, about what to do. I
looked at Spencer. 'So? What now?'

'Wait and see. Wait and see. Nothing rash.' He hadn't a
clue, either. 'It's confirmation we're looking for, nothing
more. Once we can confirm, then we take it to the next
level.'

'The car isn't here,' I said, suddenly panicked.

'That means nothing.'

We sat there for a few moments, Spencer drumming
the dashboard with his fingers while I smoked another
cigarette and tried to work up a plan.

'Fuck this,' he said, reaching for the door handle.

'What are you doing?' I said, grabbing his arm.

He shook off my grip. 'Wait here. I'll be back in a sec.'

I watched him slam the door and cross the road. He rang the doorbell and then stood there, picking at the cuffs of his coat sleeves while he waited. An old woman answered, staring up at him with an expression of confused suspicion. There was no sign of the woman I'd seen on O'Connell Street, nor was there any sign of Dillon, just this old woman. I watched Spencer turn on the charm, and after a moment, she beckoned him in, and the door closed behind them. I shifted in my seat. Something about this situation made me jumpy. For all that I knew of Spencer, he was deeply unreliable, dangerous even. I thought about getting out and following him into the house. But I didn't.

I took out another cigarette, but my lighter spluttered and died. The car lighter was missing. I reached for the glove compartment, hoping for a book of matches. What I found took my breath away.

It was a gun. A black handgun with a brown grip nestled in among receipts and sweet wrappers and empty cigarette packs. I bit my lip and passed a hand over my face. What on earth did Spencer have a gun for? He had to be into even dodgier dealings than I had imagined. Curiosity got the better of me. I picked it up and weighed it in my hands. Heavier than I'd thought it would be; the cartridge must have been full. 'Fuck,' I said aloud, gingerly putting it back.

At the sound of Spencer jerking back the door handle I closed the glove compartment quickly.

'She sold the car,' he said, climbing back in. 'But without the registration certificate. She did have a number, you know, for the person she sold it to. But not his address.'

'A wild goose chase,' I said.

'Don't worry.' Spencer started the engine. 'Leave it to me. I'll suss this out. But not tonight.'

I asked for the number, but he wouldn't give it to me. I was too tired to argue. 'I'll have that address in no time. And we won't need Fealty,' he said.

Spencer dropped me off; he said something about a love song tattooed on to his palm. He held up his hand. On it was written a phone number.

I stood in the driveway, the house looming in front of me. It seemed deathly quiet. When I jammed my key into the lock, it snapped. I left it there and walked around to the back, my footsteps crunching in the snow. I didn't want to ring the doorbell and wake Robin. Great, I thought, I am going to have to break into my own house. And that's exactly what I did. I swung my elbow at the back door window and . . . nothing: a simple thud. I picked up a stone, broke the window, reached my hand in, and turned the key.

Robin didn't wake. My hand was smarting with pain, and I looked down and saw tributaries of blood running between my knuckles. In the kitchen, I ran the tap, waiting for the water to get hot. My body ached with tiredness, but my head was swimming with thoughts, clamouring with all the chaos of the evening, and I knew I wouldn't sleep. I thought about a sleeping pill. But no, I could never go near them again. Not after Tangier. I sat in the kitchen with the lights off, a towel wrapped around my bleeding hand. Illuminated by my iPhone, I flicked through the book Javier had given me: *The Book of the Dead*. The section I opened to was a chapter that was to be recited over a boat seven cubits long, made of the green stone of the Tchatchau. It entranced me with its poetry: 'Make a heaven of stars, and purify it and cleanse it with natron and incense. Make then a figure of Rā upon a tablet of new stone in paint, and set it in the bows of the boat. Then make a figure of the deceased whom thou wilt make perfect, and place it in the boat. Make it to sail in the Boat of Rā, and Rā himself shall look upon it.'

I fixed myself a whiskey and read further: 'The heart is not taken out of the body because it is the centre of intelligence and feeling and the man will need it in the after-life.' I took a piece of paper from the bookshelf and drafted an image of Dillon. I drew his heart and shaded it.

'Make a figure of the deceased,' the book said. 'To make it perfect. In a boat.' I fixed myself another drink and dozed and read and sketched. Lost in something of a trance, reciting a prayer from the book, I fell into a fitful sleep.

I dreamed of the earthquake in Tangier. This time I did not go to Cozimo but stayed with my son and walked through the burning building, into the bookshop. The flames did not burn me. I was immune to their heat. I walked through them. On my chest hung the green amulet. I was protected. I found my son hiding behind a bookcase. He did not see me. I tried to say something to him, but he did not hear me. My mouth was dumb, my words silent. I tried to lift him, but my arms went through him. And then I watched as a man stole into the shop and walked brazenly to the counter, bending without a second thought to lift Dillon away.

I awoke with a jolt, confused to find myself sitting in the dark at the kitchen table, all the hard surfaces around me cast in a patina of cold, blue light. I was not alone. Robin stood by the window, her back to me, staring out at the garden. I hadn't pulled the curtains, and it was a clear night. The moon was close to full, and with the snow falling again, the light was silver and shining. She held herself as if she were cold. She was wearing one of my T-shirts, her legs slender and bare, and her small feet looked cold on the hard tiled floor. She stood still as if lost in thought, as if watching the snow fall, as if steadying herself against something. The intensity of her stillness made me think she was watching someone move out there. I craned my neck to see if there was anyone outside, but there wasn't. It was all darkness, snow and moonlight.

And then she turned, and I saw the tracks of tears on her face, and it made me flinch. In that moment, she looked cold, and beautiful, and sorrowful.

'What is it?' I asked, my voice hushed and hoarse. 'Sweetheart, what's the matter?'

She dropped her head, shook it, and when she spoke it was with such melancholy and such regret that it pained me. There was a tinge of sadness to her voice that seemed to say, *I thought we had moved on; I thought we were over this.*

'I was dreaming about him,' she whispered. 'After all

this time, I still dream about him. It was so real. He was here. Dillon was here. Out there, playing in the garden.'

'Robin . . .'

But she shook her head and turned away, casting her gaze back out the window, and there was something incredulous in her manner, the way her eyes scoured the frozen ground as if she might find evidence there – footprints in the snow, something to confirm the impossible.

I went to her and put my arms around her. Not long, I thought to myself. Just hold on.

'It's Christmas Eve,' she said flatly. And then she slipped from my grasp and walked away.

# 12. Robin

My parents arrived just after twelve on Christmas Day. I was leaning into the oven, draining fat off the roasting goose, when Harry opened the door to them.

'Isn't this lovely?' I heard my mother declare to the hall.

'Avril,' he said in reply, and there was a brief pause where I could tell he was leaning down and offering his cheek to her and she was planting a warm kiss near his ear. 'It's good to see you.'

'Harry.'

'Jim. Here, let me help you with those.'

'Good man. Heaven knows what's in all these bags. Avril came prepared for a nuclear winter.'

'It's just a few bits and bobs. No need to make a big fuss, Jim.'

The front door closed, and I wiped my hands on my apron and came out to meet them.

'Darling!'

My mother looked smart in a red wool dress with matching lipstick, diamonds twinkling from her earlobes, her hair perfectly set. She handed her coat to Harry and came forward to offer me a hug.

'Happy Christmas, Mum,' I said, feeling her warm embrace and catching a whiff of sherry off her breath. 'Drinking already? Whatever will the neighbours say?'

'Oh, now! It was just the teeniest glass of sherry. And it was the neighbours that forced it on me.'

'Forced, indeed. They were fighting you off. Where's my girl?'

My father is a smallish man whose hair disappeared sometime in my childhood. He has a rather stern carriage – an almost military bearing – and a hard voice that belies his soft nature. He hugged me tight, held me at arm's length while he cast his shrewd little eyes over me. Then he nodded firmly, which could be taken as approval or a dismissal – sometimes, I just couldn't tell.

Behind him, my mother was complimenting Harry on his appearance, and it was true that he did look well. His hair had been recently cut, and he had shaved that morning and was wearing a black cashmere polo shirt. I felt a sense of relief, now, when I looked at him. He glanced up and caught me gazing at him and smiled, and all the worries I'd had about this day dissipated.

It had been some time since my father had been in this house – his childhood home – and he wanted to see what changes we had made. And so the four of us set about going through the rooms, pointing out the work we had done and what we were planning on doing next. Throughout the tour, my father nodded sternly, and again it was difficult to tell whether he approved or was simply reserving judgement. My mother, on the other hand, kept up a series of cheerful rejoinders and enthusiastic compliments. She had clearly set her mind to being positive and optimistic. I knew that this forced cheerfulness would wear a little thin after a while – it drove Harry crazy – but I was grateful to her for her efforts, for her determination to make the best of this day.

Our tour ended up in Harry's studio, and we stood in that cold concrete space as he pointed out the new shelves he had put up, the work space he had cleared, the new lighting he'd installed. As he spoke, my eyes cast about, searching for the crate of his secret drawings. It was nowhere to be seen.

My mother gave a dramatic shiver.

'Lord, it is cold in here, isn't it? Shall we go back inside?'

'You girls go on in,' my father said. 'I want to take a look at some of these.'

He was hunkering down in front of the canvases lined up against one wall. My father had always shown an interest in Harry's work, and Harry, in return, seemed to welcome Jim's attention. It gave me a feeling of warmth, that clear bond between the two men I loved most in the world.

Back in the kitchen, I checked the oven.

'Smells delicious,' my mother said.

I was roasting potatoes with parsnips, butternut squash, shallots, and garlic. The mingled smells filled the kitchen.

'You're a great cook,' my mother said, 'when you put your mind to it.'

'Thanks, Mum.'

'Mind you, that's true of most things with you. So intelligent, so talented.'

I glanced up and saw her looking at me wistfully.

'Oh, Mum, now don't.'

'Don't what?' she asked and smiled. 'It's Christmas Day. Let's have a drink. Where's your corkscrew?'

I went to fetch the glasses from the dining room while she uncorked the wine. She poured out two glasses, and when I asked about wine for Dad and Harry, she swatted away my concern. 'They're well able to take care of themselves. Leave them to it, and let's enjoy this moment, just the two of us. Cheers, my love.'

'Cheers.'

We clinked glasses, and I watched her drink. And when we returned our glasses to the kitchen counter, I told her.

'Mum, I'm pregnant.'

She held me in her gaze for a second. Her hand went to her chest and she emitted a sound somewhere between a sigh and a suppressed sob. Then, without saying a word, she came to me and wrapped her arms around me, and I felt the force of her hug, the ferocity of her embrace. When we drew away, the tears had started in her eyes, and she shook her head and said, 'That's wonderful. Oh, darling, that's wonderful.'

And then the sob escaped from her, and I watched in amazement as she shook her head violently, her hands flapping about her face as mascara streaked her cheeks.

'Here,' I said, ripping a paper towel from the roll and offering it to her. 'Are you okay?' I asked, stroking her back as she dabbed beneath her eyes and tried to compose herself.

'He was a beautiful child – Dillon,' she said, still shaking her head. 'I adored him, you know. I just adored him.'

'I know you did, Mum.'

'And I never know with you whether I should say any-thing about him. The last thing I want is to upset you. But it's just that . . . I have missed him so much.'

There was such force in her words that the tears came again. I felt my own emotions rising to meet hers and bit down hard to keep them under.

'It's been hard for you, Mum. I know.'

'Darling,' she said, turning to me and taking my face in her hands, and she smiled at me through her tears. 'Another baby. You have no idea how much this means to me. No idea.'

The door opened, and Harry came in, my father behind him, still in conversation. But when they saw the two of us there together, and the tears running down my mother's face, they both stopped.

'Oh, Jim,' my mother exclaimed as he moved towards her, his face concerned and confused. 'The most wonder-ful news.'

She told him, and my father came and wrapped his arms around me, and I believe that in the moment of our embrace, I could feel his body shaking with some deep-buried emotion. Again he gripped my arms and looked at me, nodding.

Behind him, my mother was hugging Harry, laughing and wiping the tears from her eyes. She reached for her wineglass and then stopped herself, saying, 'Wine? We should be drinking champagne! This is a celebration!'

This roused my father from his momentary paralysis, and the two of them set about finding champagne flutes and unwrapping the foil from the Veuve Clicquot, both of them taken with a new excitement, an almost childish giddiness.

Harry and I looked at each other. I smiled at him as if to say: *Isn't this wonderful? See the happiness this baby is bringing already? The healing?*

His face was set and unreadable. And then my father put a glass of champagne in his hand and he turned away.

The dinner was a lavish affair. It was – I admit it – slightly over the top. Candles and linen napkins, bouquets of flowers and white china, silver cutlery and a starched white tablecloth, Bill Evans's piano playing softly from the stereo. There was smoked salmon to start, followed by a terrine, then a lemon sorbet to cleanse our palates. The conversation around the table was lively and brisk. At first, we spoke a little of my pregnancy, Harry and I filling them in on all the details, before the talk turned to more serious matters: the state of the economy, how long before the government would fall, who we would vote for in the next election. There was only the four of us, though we made enough noise for eight, the tone bright and cheery, despite the subject matter.

In the kitchen, Harry carved the goose, and I spooned the vegetables into warm serving bowls.

'It's going well,' I said to him.

'Hmm,' he replied, intent upon his work.

'Are you all right?'

'Me?'

'Yes. You seemed a little quiet earlier, when I told them.'

'Oh. Yeah. I just didn't know we were telling people yet, that's all.'

'They're my parents, Harry. They're not just people.'

'I know. I just thought we should have discussed it in advance.'

'You're not angry, are you?'

He put down the carving knife and he kissed me.

'Of course I'm not angry.'

'Good. Did you see their reaction? Did you see how happy it made them?'

He smiled at me then.

'Yes.'

And then he turned and picked up his knife and renewed his efforts with the goose, and I brought the vegetables through into the dining room.

It was just after we had served the chocolate amaretto trifle for dessert that Harry's phone beeped. It was on the mantelpiece behind him, and after reaching for it and checking it, he stood up and excused himself, the expression on his face changing.

'Harry,' I said quietly. 'It's Christmas Day. Can't it wait?'

'I'll just be a sec,' he said, squeezing my shoulder as he moved past me. 'Promise.'

We continued talking in his absence; my mother had moved on to the subject of my brother, Mark, and his new girlfriend, Suki, and we were speculating as to how long this relationship would last. All the time I was aware of the conversation taking place in the next room. The tones were muted; I couldn't make out what was being said. But when Harry returned to the room, there was a new light in his eyes, a quickness and agitation in his movements. He sat with his chin resting on the back of his hand, elbow on the arm of his chair, the fingers of his other hand drumming the table, over and over. His eyes had a faraway look, and I could tell he was finding it hard to sit still, that his mind was elsewhere. It made me uneasy. Something about him made me uncomfortable. I thought of how he had been for these last few weeks – nervy and unpredictable – and I remembered what Liz had said: his old trouble. I watched him carefully, so much so that neither one of us paid much heed to the conversation.

When my father asked Harry a question, and he seemed completely oblivious to the fact that he had even been addressed, I felt a spark of anger. Why was he behaving like this? Why, when this day was going so perfectly, was he now threatening to make a scene?

When Harry went into the kitchen to make coffee, I followed him. I found him standing in the middle of the room, staring at his feet and scratching his head.

'Who was that?' I asked.

'What?'

He glanced up at me, and I caught a certain wildness in his eyes. His hair, which had been neatly combed, was now dishevelled. In the glare of the kitchen light, his face looked pale and creased with worry, shadows lurking beneath his eyes.

'On the phone? You've been completely distracted ever since. Who was it?'

He took a breath.

'It was Spencer.'

I made a face and he saw it and a shadow of annoyance crossed his features.

'It's not like that, Robin.'

'Oh, come on. With Spencer, it only ever means one thing – trouble.'

He looked at me for a moment, chewing on his lip, and it seemed that he was weighing whether or not to tell me something.

'What?' I asked, growing impatient.

He came towards me slowly, his eyes passing over my face, and I realized that whatever it was he was about to tell me, it was serious. And my heart tightened.

'It's Dillon,' he said quietly. 'I've found him.'

For a moment, there was complete silence. Neither one of us spoke.

When I finally found my voice, it emerged as a whisper, low and hoarse.

'Dillon is dead,' I said.

He shook his head slowly.

'No, Robin. No, he's not. He's alive. He's alive, and I've found him.'

He spoke softly, but his words held a quiet conviction. His eyes seemed lit from within. It chilled me to the bone.

'It's true, Robin. Listen to me – I know it's hard to believe – but you have to get your head around this.'

'Stop it, Harry.'

'No, really. I know it sounds mad, I know you think I'm crazy, but just hear me out. You remember the day of the march? Back at the end of November? That's when I saw him. In a crowd with some woman. He's older now, obviously, but I still recognized him. I knew him straightaway – the same eyes, the same face. He looked right at me, and I immediately knew it was him. He was with some woman I didn't recognize. She pulled him away before I could get to them. But then I got on to Spencer and he got on to his contacts in the Guards, and they got hold of this CCTV footage and . . .'

On and on he went. His voice rose on a tide of mounting excitement, the words coming out quickly, a frantic babbling rush. His eyes grew wide, and his hand gestures became more rapid, more expansive. I watched his mouth moving, felt the words brushing past me like dandelion seeds caught in the wind.

I felt suddenly exhausted. All the labour I had invested in the preparations for this day, and even before that – I felt like for the past five years I had been climbing a hill, dragging something heavy behind me – and now that I was so close to the summit, I had met a barrier that I was just too tired to overcome. I thought of those weeks after Harry came home from Tangier, how dangerously unhinged he was then, those weeks that were a living hell for me – I had been so sure we had put it all behind us. I had convinced myself that the healing was almost done. But now I saw the wildness in his eyes, and I knew that the wound had not been healed. He'd ripped the plaster off, exposing an ugly weeping sore. I felt all the energy drain from me.

He stopped speaking and waited for my response.

'No,' I told him, shaking my head slowly.

And then I turned and walked away.

He followed me into the dining room, where my parents were sitting awkwardly, passing little worried glances between them. How much of our conversation they had overheard was unclear.

'Don't walk away from me, Robin. You've got to listen. You've got to understand.'

I whirled around to face him, finding a pocket of strength from the anger churning inside me.

'All I understand is that you've had too much to drink.'

'What? No! No, listen. I'm not drunk —'

'Well, then you're insane. Either way, I don't want to hear it!'

My father stood up. He nodded to my mother, who was looking from one of us to the other with a tight face of anxiety. 'Come on, Avril. Let's make a start on those dishes.'

They brushed past Harry, but he hardly seemed to notice them, he was staring at me so intently.

'Why are you doing this?' I asked him, feeling tired and sorry for myself and in no way prepared for this situation. 'Why are you trying to sabotage this day?'

'I'm not trying to —'

'You didn't want my parents to come, I know. You hate Christmas. But this? To do this? To say these things to me? About Dillon?' I shook my head vehemently, feeling emotion rising up my throat. 'Harry. It's too much.'

He stood there for a moment, weighing things.

'Wait here,' he said, and left the room.

I dropped into my chair, made a nest of my arms on the table and rested my head there. I felt I could sleep for a week and still it wouldn't be enough.

He came back with his laptop, and I raised my head wearily as he fired it up and fiddled with a DVD, scanning through until he found what he was looking for.

'There!' he said triumphantly, and turned it so I could see.

A grainy image taken from a CCTV camera showed a woman with a boy, walking hand in hand. Harry pressed play, and I watched as their images flickered across the screen, briefly showing them walking towards a car.

'Do you see?' he asked.

'It's just a boy,' I said. 'It could be anyone.'

'I was there, Robin. I saw him. It was Dillon. I swear on my life it was.'

The brightness in my husband's eyes was frightening. I felt myself shrinking from it.

'And this! Look.' He flicked through images on his iPhone, pausing when he reached the one he wanted. Another blurry picture of a seven- or eight-year-old, taken from a distance, the boy facing the camera this time, a faint expression of curiosity on his face. 'Can't you see the similarity? Look at his chin. Look at his eyes.'

I began to cry then. I couldn't help it. The thought of Harry going out into the world, day after day, convinced that his son was still alive, taking photos of random boys in the mistaken belief that they were – all of them – his dead child, was just too sad for me to bear.

'Dillon died,' I said. 'There was an earthquake, and he died. It was awful. And I miss him every day, just as much as you do. But, Harry, he's gone.' I put my hand on his arm and added quietly, 'You have to let him go.'

'I've been thinking about it,' he went on, as if I had never spoken. 'What if he didn't die? There was never a body. They pulled other bodies out of the rubble but not his. Doesn't that tell you something? Doesn't that make you even slightly suspicious?'

I watched him with growing horror as he laid out his case.

'What if Dillon didn't die but was kidnapped instead? Think about it. Whoever abducted him would have the perfect cover. Who would ever suspect? What if all these years he's been growing up and living somewhere else, with other people acting as his parents? What if all this time we thought he was dead, our boy was really alive?'

His face strained with the effort of telling me this, a vein pulsing at his temple. I thought of all the pictures he had drawn over the years, pictures of Dillon, a reimagining of how our son would have grown and developed. It seemed dreadfully sad – this pathetic attempt at keeping a dead boy alive.

'Can't you hear yourself, Harry? Don't you know how crazy you sound?'

He drew his arm away from me then, ferocity in the gesture.

'I'm not crazy. I know what I saw.'

'You want to believe he's alive because you can't accept that he's dead.'

'Because I don't believe he is dead.'

'Jesus Christ, Harry. Enough! I understand why you're doing this. I know you've been under strain these past few weeks, what with moving your studio, worrying about money, and now the baby, but –'

'It's got nothing to do with the baby!'

'Doesn't it? Isn't it possible that this pregnancy has triggered something inside you, some fear of getting hurt again? Bringing a new child into the world and falling in love with it and the risks involved in that, after the pain we suffered with Dillon?'

'For fuck's sake!' he hissed, getting up so swiftly I had to reach to stop his chair from toppling over.

He paced to the window, talking all the time, saying that this had nothing to do with the pregnancy or anything else.

'Please spare me your diagnosis, Robin, and do me the favour of actually considering that what I'm saying might actually be true!'

'No,' I said. 'I am not going down that road with you again, Harry.'

'What?'

'The last time. Those weeks you spent in St James's. All those counselling sessions we went through together – dredging up the past, picking over the memories. God! You promised me – do you remember? You promised me that there would be no more of it. No more wild notions or crazy ideas. You told me that you accepted that Dillon was dead. You told me, Harry. You made me a promise. And now I find out that you have been lying to me all these years?'

'I haven't been lying to you –'

'I found the pictures.'

He froze.

'The pictures you drew of Dillon.'

Still he didn't respond.

'Aren't you going to say anything?'

'They're just pictures,' he said with a shrug. 'That's got nothing to do with this.'

'Yes, it does! Don't you think I understand? You have been keeping him alive in your head all this time –'

'No, I haven't –'

'All this time, perpetuating this fantasy that he didn't die that night, that he didn't get crushed to death in his sleep, all because your conscience won't allow you to!'

I stopped, both of us staring at each other, stunned.

'My conscience?' he asked slowly.

'Yes,' I said firmly, driven inevitably towards what I would say next. 'This is about your guilt, Harry. Your guilt and nothing else.'

He looked at me, speechless.

'I want to ask you something,' I said quietly. 'Something I've never asked you before. And I really want you to answer me truthfully. Would you do that for me?'

I swallowed hard, but he just kept looking at me, not saying anything.

'That night – before the earthquake hit – did you give him something to make him sleep?'

He let out a sigh and hung his head, and when he lifted it again, it held an expression of weariness, of exasperation.

'Not this, Robin.'

'You had said you'd stopped. When I took you back. You told me you'd never do that again. But –'

'But?'

His voice was defiant, but I could see the creep of fear around his eyes, and so I went on.

'It was my birthday, you were making a meal, and when I rang to say I'd be late and you said he was asleep already, there was something in your voice, something . . . I don't know, but I've never been able to shake it from my head. Your voice. It sounded . . . guilty. I'm right, aren't I, Harry? You drugged him, and it meant that when the earthquake happened, he could not rouse himself to escape. I know it's true. Try and tell me that it isn't.'

I said this quietly but with defiance, and something about his expression changed. He became grave and strangely still.

'Say it,' he said quietly.

'Harry –'

'Just say it.'

And then I felt it bubble up, pushing its way to the surface, demanding to be spoken – the dark thing I had kept inside me since the night of Dillon's death, the thing so black and ugly that I couldn't bear to shed light on it, to give voice to it, for fear that it would destroy what was left between us.

My tears broke, and it came out in a gulping sob: 'Why did you leave him there? Why could you not have taken him with you? Jesus Christ, Harry! You left him! You left him there, my little boy. My baby boy. You left him to his death!'

As soon as I said it, I knew I had gone too far.

He held me there for a moment longer with his cold stare, as I wept in front of him. Then he walked past me. A moment later I heard the front door slam shut behind him, and the choking sound of the van starting, the angry hiss of the wheels turning over in the snow.

Then there was silence.

I sat still for a moment, paralysed by the shock of what I had done, what I had said. All this time I had kept that thought inside myself, and now that it was out I imagined I should feel something – relief, guilt, regret? Instead, I just felt numb.

The slow opening of the kitchen door revealed my mother's face peeking nervously at me.

'Robin? Are you okay?'

I shook my head and started to cry again, and she came and leaned over me, holding my head against her chest and stroking my hair.

'It will be okay,' she whispered, over and over. And I remembered how she had said this to me once before, after Dillon died. I remembered standing in the arrivals hall at Dublin Airport, all those people staring as I cried my eyes out, my mother rocking me back and forth, repeating those words to me: 'It will be okay. You will be okay.'

And I was okay. It had taken time. It had taken a lot of time. And I'd thought that we had finally turned a corner. But now I knew that I had been mistaken. While I'd believed we were moving on, the wound had been festering in the dark all the time.

'Come on, sweetheart. Pull yourself together.'

I drew my head away from her. All I wanted was for them to go home and let me go upstairs and sleep. I looked up at my mother, overcome by a sensation like dozens of needles prickling my face.

She regarded me with a pinched, anxious expression.

'Come into the kitchen.'

I followed her through the door and watched as she went and stood by the kitchen counter, chewing her lip, her brow knotted.

My father was standing with his back to the sink, one hand covering his mouth, his eyes fixed on me with a grave expression. I had expected voices of concern, words of comfort. But the minute I laid eyes on my father's face, I knew this was something different.

'What?' I asked him. 'What is it?'

'You need to come home with us.'

'For God's sake, Dad.'

'I can't leave you here. I *won't* leave you here.'

'This is my home!'

'Robin,' my mother said slowly, 'we all saw how he was behaving.'

'He's just a bit stressed right now . . .'

'It's his old trouble,' my father continued, his expression solemn, something ponderous in his voice. 'This paranoia or neurosis or whatever it is he suffers from. It's back. But it's worse this time.'

'Oh, Dad . . .'

'Robin, I want you to come home with us.'

'But Harry might come back . . .'

My father stepped away from the sink and came towards me then. I felt the firmness of his grip on my upper arms, the intensity of his gaze as his eyes searched my face.

'Yes, he might,' he whispered. 'And that's exactly what frightens me. Now, please, love. Get your things.'

# 13. Harry

I drove without thinking, my eyes swimming with tears, so that I could barely see the road. A fire burned in my head. I heard myself gulping liquid breaths, great heaving sobs emerging from my chest and filling the cold space around me. *You drugged him. You left him to his death.* Over and over, her voice played in my head. Words of accusation that cut to the quick, cut to the very heart. The look on her face – regret mingling with a ferocious anger, eyes ablaze. My foot pressed down on the accelerator, as if I was trying to drive away from the words, trying to escape the heat of accusation, the burden of memory, the echo Robin's words had created in my mind. It was as if all those burning questions were again rekindled. *You left him! You left him there, my little boy. My baby boy.* All the insomniac hours I had spent thinking the same thoughts, asking myself the same questions, came back to me in a dark wave that threatened to drown me.

The roads were practically empty. Hardly a sinner out. A few cars. One or two couples walking before or after dinner. Otherwise, it was a ghost town. I drove down to the coast, the light still strong, though it wouldn't be for long. The snow had been pushed on to the verge into great mounds that were starting to turn black. The wind was up, and the spray from the water was high and blowing skywards.

I parked at the rocky inlet at Sandycove and tried to pull myself together. Switching off the engine, I heard the whine of the wind, the roll and hiss of the waves. My tears had stopped, but something remained. A line had been crossed. Words spoken that could not be erased from memory. My thoughts teetered and brimmed, and fear nipped in about the edges – fear that maybe Robin was right. Maybe all this really was a figment of my imagination? The product of a guilty mind to protect myself from the awful thing I had done.

I needed to clear my head. But my mind was racing. I sat in the van, watching the waves come in and out. I breathed deeply. I tried to calm myself, to still my shaking hands. I reached into the glove compartment for the flask I kept there. I gave it a good shake to see if there was still some left, unscrewed the top and gulped. The whiskey made me shiver and gag. The second gulp eased me.

There were a few people in the water. Splashing about and swimming out to the rocks. My father used to bring me here, to the Forty Foot, before Christmas dinner. Just the two of us. We always had a late dinner on Christmas Day. There are fewer people, he'd say, and I knew by the way he said it that he meant it as a good thing.

Caught by a sudden impulse, I reached into the back and grabbed a towel that had been stuffed into one of the moving boxes. Then, leaving the van behind, I made my way down to the water. With all the food I had eaten and the wine I had drunk, with the nervy distraction and anxiety I was feeling, it was probably the worst thing I could have done: gone for a swim. But that's what I am telling you: I was not thinking straight. I was determined. And the questions had gathered again, gathered to a chorus of accusation: *You, why, you, you.*

I made my way to the rocky changing area, a concrete shelter with stone benches. A man in a pair of orange trunks was beating his chest. 'It's the only thing for you.' He pointed to the woman sitting beside him. She had a scarf wrapped around her head and a mildly amused look. 'As for my wife,' he said, 'there are two chances of her getting into that water: Bob Hope and no hope.'

She nodded to me, and the man chuckled and started to sing, 'I'm dreaming of a white Christmas'. Their cheer bounced off me. I was impervious to anything but my own loneliness.

I stripped. The woman took a sharp intake of breath, and her husband said something about 'old school'. I walked naked towards the rocks, braced myself and jumped in. The water was freezing, and I sank with a gasp. Surfacing, I sucked air into my lungs and gave a yelp. I swam out a distance, then began to feel sluggish. *You drugged him. You left him to his death.* My stomach ached. I counted twelve strokes, thought about turning back, but as I did so, a sharp pain struck in my side. I braced myself, and the pain struck again. *Why did you leave him there? Why could you not have taken him with you?* In that moment, all the fight went out of me. I took a deep breath and relaxed. There was no point in struggling any more. My arms floated outwards and my head went under again. Strangely, the water didn't seem so cold to me then. I pointed my toes and sank deeper into the sea. Down, down, I went, giving myself to the water, feeling it closing in above me, claiming me. My eyes opened, and I could see a dark, grainy sediment. It was like the texture and quality of the CCTV footage. Then my body shot upwards, towards the light, and I bobbed out of the water before going down again. *My baby boy. My baby boy.* This time, the water's grainy texture yielded those very images I had saved and replayed for Robin. I felt like I could have kept on falling towards the seafloor, but I shot up again like some kind of buoy, and this time my head was not plunged back into the water's steely embrace.

I swam back to shore and climbed out. The man in the orange trunks handed me my towel. 'Here, have a wee dram of that,' he said, passing me a flask of hot coffee laced with whiskey. 'You scared my wife off,' he said.

I apologized. He laughed. 'You're all right?'

'I am,' I said, still shivering, and handed back his flask. The few who had been in the water when I'd first jumped in had disappeared. The man told me I was the last of the day. 'You had me worried for a moment, bobbing up and down like that. Best to swim with someone watching.' He wished me a good Christmas and headed off towards his car, where his wife was waiting. I felt their eyes on me as I walked back to the van.

I got dressed and called home. I don't know why. The phone rang, but there was no answer. I pictured it clanging away in the empty house, echoing from room to room; the dusk settling, dessert half-eaten.

There in the car, I closed my eyes. I tried to put myself

back in time. I tried to peer into the rubble with my mind's eye to see the lifeless body of my boy. Dust clogged the image, and I struggled to find some sense of acceptance. My son's body, pulled down into the yielding earth, covered over, decaying, turning to dust. I kept my eyes shut, trying to feel it, trying to believe it. But it would not come. Something within me prevented my accepting it. Instead, I opened my eyes and fumbled in my jacket. Hands shaking, I pulled out my phone.

There within my list of messages was the text from Spencer: 'Is this him?' The image attached showed a blurry and distant shot of the boy. I stared at the picture and felt a glow of conviction gather within me. It was him. I knew it was him.

I rang Spencer. 'The address, I need the address.'

'And a merry Christmas to you too. I'm not giving it to you over the phone, Harry. Why don't you stop over tomorrow.'

I hung up.

The cold of the sea had entered my bones. My body shook. I looked at my hands; they were mottled and blue, and I couldn't help but think of Cozimo's hands, speckled with liver spots, frail, the hands of an old man, and I remembered his words to me: 'Very unlikely. But not impossible.' There was only one place I could go now. I eased the car back on to the road and headed into the city.

Spencer answered the door wearing socks, a Lloyd Cole T-shirt and a Santa hat. He was holding a can of beer. 'Harry. Jesus, are you okay?'

I walked past him, into the warm fug of his flat, needing some heat to penetrate my bones. Spencer's latest girlfriend, Angela, was sitting on the couch. I knew her from a long time ago.

'Hello, stranger,' she said.

She wore Spencer's dressing gown, and the way her hair was tossed, she looked as if she had just climbed out of bed. I stood there, stunned and confused. At my elbow, Spencer looked sheepish, eyeing me with an air of mild apprehension.

'Harry, is everything okay?' he asked again.

Angela got up and reached for my arm. 'You look cold, pet. Your hair is wet.' She shot a glance at Spencer.

'Christmas swim,' I said, laughing, but the laugh came out hollow and forced, and I saw the look of alarm that passed between them. I was hanging by a thread.

'Christ, Harry,' Spencer said. 'Sit down there and I'll get something to warm you up.'

Smoke wafted from the kitchen.

'The turkey is incinerated,' Angela said.

Spencer shrugged. 'Burnt to a sausage.'

'I don't care,' Angela said. 'I'm going to have a shower and get dressed. Then I'm ringing the Shelbourne and booking a table.'

'Last of the big spenders,' Spencer said.

His blithe tone was betrayed by the concerned expression on his face. Was he talking to Angela under his breath? I couldn't be sure. I was so far gone.

'Can I get you a sweater or a towel, something to make you warmer?'

'I'm fine, Angela,' I said.

She shrugged and left the room.

'I've come for the address.'

'Harry, it's Christmas fucking Day.'

'I can't wait any longer. I know you have it – now, cough up.'

'Listen, pal –'

'Don't tell me to listen, Spencer.'

'All right, all right!' He put his hands up in a gesture of surrender and crossed to the other side of the room, where he lifted his jeans off the back of the couch and fished in the pockets until he found a scrap of paper. I kept my eyes fixed on the note as he returned to me, passing it from one hand to the other, his reluctance apparent. It felt like he was taunting me with it.

'I'm not giving it to you without going with you,' he said.

'Let's go, then.'

He sighed and shook his head. 'You know, Harry, I think this might be a red herring.'

'What?'

'The address, the boy.'

'You've seen him. The picture you sent me –'

'I saw *a* boy, Harry –'

'You went there. You saw him with your own two eyes. The picture –'

'It's not him, Harry.'

I stopped. I held my breath, waiting for him to say more, wanting him to speak, even as part of me shrank from what he might say.

'Look. When I got the address, I decided to take a drive down there and check it out myself before passing the information on to you. So I went. I checked it out. The house is a cottage in the middle of nowhere. There's nothing sinister about it. There was a couple there with their kid.'

'With Dillon.'

'There's a vague likeness. But I'm telling you honestly, I don't think it's him.'

I didn't speak, just stood there withstanding his concerned gaze.

'You've got to let it go,' he said gently. 'This obsession you've developed . . . it's not healthy. I'm worried about you, Harry.'

He went to put his hand on my shoulder, but I raised my palm, warning him to back off.

'Listen, I'm sure Robin is worried about you. Why not head home? We can talk about this tomorrow.'

I hung my head; something within me was starting to give way.

'I need a drink,' he said then. 'How about it?'

'Yeah. Sure.'

He went to the fridge and set about fixing gin and tonics, and I stood there listening to him talk about a total lunar eclipse, how the moon turns red, how we were about to have one, and something else about the moon passing through a shadow created by the earth that I did not understand.

At the same time, my eyes were fixed on the kitchen counter and the scrap of paper he had left tucked behind a coffee cup. Rattling ice cubes into each glass, Spencer kept talking, and for once I was grateful for his verbosity, as it meant he didn't notice me leaning forwards to pluck that note from its hiding place. He was slicing limes and cucumbers and rattling on about God knows what while I passed my gaze over the scrawl of his handwriting, absorbing that address into my memory. Not an easy thing to do when you're full of goose and booze and still shivering from plunging into the frigid waters of the Irish Sea, but I managed it.

And then with the address in my head, I slipped out the front door, Spencer's voice trailing behind me as I left.

Downstairs, I found the van where I had left it, parked alongside Spencer's old Jag. Before I got the key into the lock, a sudden impulse overtook me. I walked over to the passenger side of the Jag and tried the door. Locked. I looked about, found a fist-sized rock by the car's front tyre and, with barely a moment's thought, I smashed that rock through the passenger side's glass window with one heavy swipe. Reaching in, I opened the door while the car alarm screamed around me. I lunged towards the glove compartment and found what I was looking for. I didn't stop to check if it was loaded, just jammed the gun into my pocket, jumped into the van and took off without once looking back.

On the road again. Darkness was falling, and the streets were silent and empty. My phone lit up. Someone had rung through to my voicemail and left a message. In fact, there were two messages. I was sure one would be from

Spencer. He had tried to play it cool at his place, ease me into trusting him again. But it wasn't him. The first message was from Cozimo. His voice sounded frail and far away. I could barely make out what he said: 'Harry, I'm sorry. I should have liked to have talked more. I should have liked to have told you . . .' The sentence ended in an excruciating incompleteness, much like our last meeting. The next message was from Robin.

She sounded hoarse, as if she had been crying. 'Harry, I've left with my parents. I'll be staying with them tonight. I don't know what else to say.' That was it. The phone went dead. I pulled over and rang her back. There was no answer. But I kept dialling. Ten, twenty, who knows how many times. Finally, she answered in a whisper, 'Harry?'

'Robin.'

'Harry, I don't want to hear it.'

'What?'

'Whatever you're going to say.'

A long sigh came out of her. I don't know why, but I was smiling. It was time to come clean, and I felt strangely exhilarated. I knew she wasn't going to hang up. Wait till she hears what Javier said, wait till she hears about the green amulet, the tarot card, the Sun card, for Christ's sake, wait till she hears all that, I thought. And the child mummy in London and *The Book of the Dead*, all of it leading me to Dillon. She would be convinced, won over – not swayed but swept away by the guidance I was receiving. Surely with her own intuitive sense she would realize all this. But before I could tell her anything she said, 'I'm worried about you.'

'Don't be.'

'You've been acting so . . . erratically.'

'I have an address, Robin. *The* address.'

A pause.

'This has to stop, Harry. You need help.'

'Don't you see? Everything is so clear now. He's so close, Robin. After all this time, I'm almost there. I've almost reached him.'

'Jesus, can't you hear yourself? This is exactly like last time.'

'Last time?' I said, momentarily thrown. 'What are you talking about? Today is the first day I've told you about this.'

'You're confused, Harry. You're not well. You need to see someone.'

'Robin, you don't understand.'

'I can't handle this by myself any more. I've tried to pretend that you're all right, that this is just a blip – a temporary lapse brought about by stress. But it's more serious than that. I finally realized that tonight. Harry – I'm frightened for you.' The pitch of her voice shifted, and I heard genuine alarm in her tone.

'Frightened *for* me or frightened *of* me?'

She ignored the question.

'I've come back to my parents',' she whispered desperately into the phone.

'But I want you to come home.'

'No, Harry.'

'Are you leaving me?' I asked, jolted suddenly by the possibility. 'Is that what you're doing?'

She paused, as if thinking about what I had asked. I waited to hear what she would say next, waited to hear the bend in her voice as she denied it, as she cleaved to my request to come home. But she did not say what I thought she would.

'Maybe I am. You need help, Harry. But you won't admit it. You can't seem to understand how far gone you are. Maybe leaving you is the only way I can help you.'

I held my breath and then slowly, exhaustively let it out again. The line went dead.

I drove, but it was as if the van were driving itself, as if the steering wheel spun this way and that and my hands just happened to be on it. We turned left, turned right, slowed, speeded up, stopped when necessary. But it was not me, it was the van; it carried me; it was the vehicle, I was the passenger.

When I got there, the lights were out, except for one downstairs, in the living room. I could see a figure pacing. It was Jim. He was gesticulating, glass in hand, talking to no one but himself. I tapped on the window. He turned and saw me. I must have given him a fright; he spilled his drink. I pointed to the front door.

'Harry,' he said, opening it. His tone was weak and resigned. I expected him to be confrontational, but instead he fixed me with a look of sadness and utter disappointment. I would have preferred it if he'd punched me. He turned from me then, leaving the door open so that I could follow him into the house. I stepped inside, cleared my throat, and said, 'Where's Robin?'

He winced slightly at the mention of his daughter and my claim on her; then he gathered himself, setting his shoulders back. 'We've always understood each other, Harry. At least, I've always thought so.'

'Where is she?'

One of his hunting trophies, a springbok's head, hung ominously on the wall on the landing.

'I'm very fond of you, Harry. I like the way you have taken chances in your life. But I want you to stay away from Robin —'

'Stay away from her? She's my *wife*.'

The slump had returned to his shoulders. I could see his mind going through all the possible outcomes.

'I think you should leave now, Harry. She doesn't want to see you tonight.'

'But I need to see her.'

He nodded slowly but he couldn't look me in the eye.

'If I could just see her to explain.'

'Give it a day or two, Harry. Go home. Get some rest. You look like you need it.'

He wasn't going to budge. He met my gaze and held it for a moment, but something else was tugging at me, pulling me away from him. I had the address and felt again a keen sense of urgency.

'Tell Robin . . . tell her that whatever else happens, I want her to know that I'm sorry,' I said.

Then I walked back to the van, and Jim shut the door and turned off the porch light.

*

The night was pitch-dark. There wasn't a soul on the roads. I raced back along the M50 towards Wicklow. It felt like I was the last person left in the world. The map was on the passenger seat. I studied it as I drove, making a mental note of how I needed to take the M50 until it turned into the N11, past Arklow and west towards Aughrim. The landscape was mostly blank and dark. The roads were clear until I exited off the N11; then they turned suddenly treacherous. Too little traffic and no grit made it a difficult drive. Once or twice, the car skidded on ice. I was so tired, I could hardly keep my eyes open. The day seemed to have lasted a lifetime. The wipers flicked a fresh fall of snow from the windscreen. In the distance, I could see the soft lights of houses waver and fade as families settled into Christmas evening.

When I got to the intersection I was looking for, I drove off the main road and down a narrow lane into what seemed like a valley. It was not a housing estate I was looking for but a single standing house, a lone dwelling. I could tell that much from the address. In fact, I could tell a great deal more, if I am honest. The house itself was not far from a house my parents had owned when I was very young. They had stayed there for only three or four years, from what I can remember, but I had strong memories, so in a way it was like I was coming back to my own childhood place. It was like I was coming home. How strange, I thought. I remember a small red bicycle, my right ankle scabby from banging and grating against the chain ring. I remember the thread of white dandelion seeds blowing into the air, and I remember, one summer day, running away. I had a black sack filled with sweaters and sandwiches. My mother, when she found me, was smoking and talking to one of the neighbours. I was hiding in a bush, still hoping she had not seen me. Then, bending to peer down into my hiding place, she said, 'Come on, love. Time to go home.'

On the final stretch of road to the house, the van skidded into a shallow ditch. I pressed on the accelerator, and the engine revved. The tyres spun, but the van didn't budge. I tried a few more times, but it was hopeless. It didn't matter. I was nearly there.

I clutched the steering wheel one last time and looked out on to the dark expanse of the night. The trees and shrubbery about me held their dark outlines, but barely; their forms were slowly dissolving into the night. Beyond them I could make out the Wicklow Hills, the headlamps of cars appearing and disappearing in the distance. I felt like the darkness was entering me. Shivering and exhausted, I climbed out of the van and left it behind. I followed a dirt path for a half-mile. At the end of it, there was a wooden gate and a long driveway. The house was partially hidden by dense trees. Red fairy lights covered a spruce tree in the front garden. A television flickered in one of the front rooms, where no other light was on. A car was parked further in. I couldn't tell what colour it was or whether it had the licence plate I had been looking for, so I crept past the gate to the fence, climbed over it, in case it creaked, and fell to my hands and knees.

The grass was covered in hardening snow. I crawled slowly. My face and hands were wet. In the distance, I could hear a neighbour's voice carry. Someone was saying goodnight. Someone was laughing. The stars were out. A galaxy of stars. I started to shiver again. I got closer to the car, but I still couldn't make out the numbers. Finally, I made my way to the grass verge and on to the gravel. I shifted my body as quietly as I could over the stones, to the back end of the car. I felt exhausted, dazed as though my head had taken a heavy blow. No one saw me. I crouched there in the darkness and tried to focus. It was the right make of car. I felt a surge of relief and held my phone up to the licence plate. I read each letter and number, one at a time. Yes, I thought. This is it. I leaned back and let out a great sigh.

Then the front door opened, and a man walked out.

# 14. Robin

*Are you leaving me?*

I lay there, the phone still in my hand, the echo of Harry's voice still travelling through my head, and felt a weary resignation. I wished he hadn't asked me that question. And I wished I hadn't said what I had said. This terrible gamble after all the years of love and tenderness and affection, after all the hurt and grief and shared pain. That was it. There was nothing more to be done. For all the questions that littered my mind, I hadn't the heart or the energy right then to chase answers.

Still, I couldn't sleep. I lay there tracing patterns across the ceiling. I wanted to get out of bed, go downstairs and sit in the kitchen and try to work this thing through. But there was a bar of light under my bedroom door that told me my parents were still up. I listened to the hum of their voices coming up through the floorboards. Their conversation was low and hushed. It went on long into the night. I imagined their anxious faces, their bewildered questioning: Had there been any inkling, any foresight of this coming? I imagined them asking themselves how had the child they had reared so carefully, so lovingly, the child they had invested so much in and had such hopes for, how had she come to this? I imagined all this and shrank from it. Sometime later, I heard my mother going to bed and downstairs I heard the sounds of my father lingering, pacing, worrying. I didn't want to face him again that night. Somehow, his unspoken disapproval hurt more than the harsh words exchanged between Harry and me, and part of me was just so bone-weary, I felt my legs could hardly bear the weight of my body. I lay on the bed and stared at the ceiling and asked myself how things had come to this.

My mind drifted through memories. I thought back to a night in this room, many years ago, the first night I brought Harry home. I was nineteen, caught up in my first real love affair, made reckless by it. I smuggled him up the stairs, both of us drunk and giggling. He fell on to the bed while I stood with my back to the door, chest heaving with the effort of suppressing my laughter. He lay on his back, legs crossed at the ankles, hands behind his head, a large, sloppy grin on his face. Already he was assuming ownership of the room. There was no lock on the door – my mother didn't agree with them – so I took a chair and shoved it under the doorknob. When I turned back to him, his smile was still there, less sloppy now, a serious glint in his eye.

'Now take off all your clothes,' he said.

I remember his body, the discovery of it that night, long and rangy and taut. Skin smooth over hard, lean muscle. The line of black hair from his navel down. Thighs that were thick and strong. The surprising weight of him as he lay on top of me, the sharpness of his pelvic bones as he moved above me, into me, slowly at first, with rising vigour.

Our lovemaking was nervous on my part; I was overly conscious of every moan and sigh, every shudder and creak of the bed, keenly aware of my parents asleep across the hall. On his part, it was mischievous and irreverent. He was a confident lover, one who saw sex as entertainment, something to be enjoyed and not taken too seriously. He liked to nuzzle and lick and tickle, and my laughter aroused him. That was how it was between us back then. In time, he would grow more serious. The humour drained from him as the years passed. After Dillon died, we stopped making love. For a long time, we remained untouched, held apart by our grief – or by something else? Resentment? Unspoken blame?

But thinking back to that night, I recalled how afterwards, before we drew apart and lay back against the pillows, two separate bodies again, he kissed me along my neck and my shoulder blades – softly, slowly. There was reverence in that act – tenderness – a marked contrast to the mirth and frivolity that came before. It was at that moment that he felt open and vulnerable to me, and I knew how serious things were for him. It was then that I felt the pull towards him, a cord binding us to each other, and I knew it was something lasting, something that would prove painful to break. It was then that I had a glimpse of how much I could hurt him.

Sometime in the night, a car door slammed shut, and I woke. Confused at first, then surprised that I had managed to drift off to sleep at all, I lay there listening to the noises of the house around me, the pipes ticking and the groan of the sycamore outside, bearing its burden of snow. I tried ringing Harry again but just got his voice-mail. I had no idea where he might be. I hardly knew what to say to him. Perhaps I should have said that I missed him, that I didn't mean what I had said. That I wanted him back – not this new, crazed, secretive Harry but the old Harry, the one that was funny and generous and bursting with life and humour, the one everyone loved. The one I had loved. In the end, I didn't leave a message, just hung up. I think I slept.

I woke to a dark sky, an unfamiliar room. I checked my phone, but there were no messages. I lay there for a while, watching the dark shapes around the room announcing themselves as a wardrobe, a chest of drawers, a long mirror. The room had long ago been stripped of the posters and the toys; the accumulation of junk over the years had been culled, so that it now seemed bare and somehow diminished. I looked around at the rosebud-print wall-paper, at the tufted headboard and waffle-patterned linen, all of it unfamiliar. This room contained no trace of my past existence here. This wasn't my home – not now, not any more. And I thought of the house we had left and how I was estranged from it, after what had happened yesterday. I felt, in that moment, alone and completely unmoored.

Getting out of bed, I pulled the curtains and looked out at the empty suburban street, a faint granular light beginning to tinge the night sky, casting the drifts of snow and the skeletal trees in a ghostly shade. The events of the previous day seemed so distant, so completely removed from any reality, that I could hardly believe them. I thought about how Harry had walked out; I thought about my father's face full of anger and confusion and my mother paralysed with fear.

'You need to come home with us,' he had said sternly. The way the kitchen light caught his face made his cheeks seem puffy and his eyes look old.

'For God's sake, Dad.'

'I can't leave you here,' he said sharply.

That's when I saw how worked up he was, how deeply this rift that had come between my husband and me had affected him. I saw his sadness and recalled my mother's words, about how much she missed Dillon but felt unable to ever admit such to me. And I wondered how much they kept hidden from me, my parents, of their own losses and grief, their own sadness and worry.

As I came downstairs, I heard sounds from the kitchen. It was barely six, but I knew my mother was in there, venting her worry by cleaning the oven or defrosting the fridge. I paused on the bottom step, feeling like a child again, under the shadow of disapproval after some disappointment that had tested my parents' love for me, for which I would have to strive to redeem myself.

I pushed the door and found her spooning batter into a muffin tin. She looked up at me and smiled. The brightness of her dressing gown seemed lurid in the early-morning dimness. Her hair had lost its shape, and there were small traces of mascara under her eyes. She looked old and tired and small. Her shoulders seemed slumped, and I saw for the first time that her upper back had grown curved. I had a glimpse of her as an old lady, still glamorous, with her cashmere sweaters and brooches, her lipstick a valiant banner, but shrunken and hunched, hands gnarled at the knuckles, lines fanning out from her eyes.

'Robin, how did you sleep?'

'Okay,' I said.

'Bed all right?'

'Mm-hmm.'

'Lucky I changed the sheets on Christmas Eve.'

'As if you were expecting me,' I said drily.

She looked at me warily, then gave me a tight smile of reassurance.

'Sit down, love, and I'll make us both a cup of coffee.'

'Where's Dad?'

'Still in bed. Enjoying his lie-in.'

I didn't ask when he finally went to bed. I didn't want to know how long he had paced the floor. Instead, I watched as she flicked on the coffee machine, then slid the tray of muffins into the oven. Her easy domesticity had never given me much pause for thought, but now, in the light of everything that had passed, I looked upon it as a sort of triumph. She had come through almost forty years of marriage intact, with her home and her family still around her. For the first time, I saw the value of such an achievement.

'I've made such a mess of things, Mum,' I said then.

Hearing the break in my voice, she came and sat next to me, wrapping her arms about me, and drew my face down to the crook of her neck.

'Robin . . .'

'Yesterday, I had wanted so badly for the day to be perfect. It couldn't have gone any worse.'

'Don't be so hard on yourself, Robin. You cooked a lovely meal. Let's not forget that.'

I drew back from her, momentarily dazzled by her ability to gloss over the negative when she needed to.

'Mum, my husband walked out on me. Tell me how this is not a disaster.'

'Well, when you put it like that . . .'

She stood up and busied herself pouring the coffee, returning with two steaming hot mugs, and we sat there together on that cold winter morning, warming ourselves around them.

'What am I going to do, Mum?'

'I don't know, love. But you're welcome to stay here as long as you like. This will always be your home.'

I shook my head. 'No. I don't think that'll solve anything.'

'Well, you can't go back to that house.'

'Why not?'

'For heaven's sake, Robin. With Harry acting the way he is? Don't be ridiculous. You must think of the new baby.'

'I am thinking of my child. I owe it to him or her to try and sort things out with Harry. Jesus,' I said then, my head sinking into my hands. 'A baby. What a fucking mess.'

Neither of us spoke. And then I looked up and told her about Harry.

'He thinks Dillon is alive.'

Anxiety clouded her face, and she put down her cup.

'He says he saw him.'

'When? Where?'

'Does it matter? The whole thing is a fantasy.' I relented and then told her: 'In Dublin, he says. In the city. He saw a boy he swears was Dillon with some woman he didn't recognize.'

'My God.'

'The frightening thing is how far he has taken it this time. Before he just talked about the possibility of Dillon having survived – talked and talked about it until it became an obsession, until it made him sick. But this is different.'

'How?'

'For a start, he didn't tell me anything about it, not until yesterday. For weeks he has been acting weirdly, but he never mentioned a word about it. And then yesterday I found out that he has spent the last month playing detective and doing things that don't sound legal. He somehow got access to some CCTV footage and is convinced it shows Dillon. But the worst thing was the picture.'

'Picture?'

'On his phone. He showed me this picture on his phone of a young boy. It was blurry and distant. He claimed it was Dillon, but it wasn't. It was just a boy the same age Dillon would have been had he lived. I keep thinking about Harry going out there in the world, looking at young boys, taking pictures of them with his phone, just because they bear a vague resemblance to his dead son. It's so sordid. So sinister. It's not like Harry. I just can't understand what has driven him to this. Is it the baby? Is that what caused him to crack?'

My mother shook her head.

'You think he's having another breakdown?' she asked softly.

'Oh, Mum,' I said, surprised by my sudden tears. 'I hope to God he's not.'

All the signs were there. It was starting all over again – another breakdown. I gazed beyond my mother, through the glass doors closed against the frozen garden. I could see the swing hanging from the sycamore. I looked at it and remembered those weeks Harry had spent in St James's, all those counselling sessions. I remembered how he had held himself, hugging one arm protectively about his ribs, staring hard at the ground, one finger compulsively rubbing at his lower lip, how intensely caught up he was in his own fevered imaginings, how locked in he was by the illusions he had created. I remembered the anxiety of friends and relatives as they asked tentatively about his progress, their naked concern for him. And I remembered how angry it made me – how furious I was. Our son had just died. He had died a horrible and tragic death. My heart was shattered. I would wake in the night and remember all over again, and the shock of the realization was like a hammer blow, so intense I could hardly breathe. And through all of that, I was alone. Harry retreated behind his wall of illusions, his refusals to believe that Dillon was dead, his crazy theories of abduction and mistaken identity. I tended to him patiently, I was present at all the counselling sessions, I held his hand and listened to the doctors, I answered everyone's questions, gave regular updates as to his progress, I waited and waited, but inside I was engulfed by rage. That white-hot anger burned and burned, and I kept it hidden from everyone, while secretly it consumed me. Now I watched the dawn creep coldly over the silent garden and I thought of how his behaviour over the past few weeks had been erratic and strange, how moody and uncommunicative he had become. Clearly, he was unhappy, depressed even. A jolt of panic thundered in my chest. I turned to my mother and said, 'Jesus. You don't think he's planning to kill himself, do you?'

'No,' she said, moving quickly to reassure me.

'Christ, I don't know. He rang me last night, and there was something about his voice . . . something so final in it.' My heart was beating crazily in my chest, and I felt nauseous. My mother didn't answer, and she seemed suddenly pale, as if all the blood had drained from her face.

'Mum? What is it? You look like you've seen a ghost.'

She swallowed. 'He was here last night.'

'Who was?'

'Harry.'

Something sank within me.

'Why didn't you wake me?'

'I didn't see him. I didn't even know he was here until afterwards. He spoke to Jim.'

'What happened?'

She bit her lip and looked down at the place mat she had begun fiddling with.

'Mum?'

Cold plunged through to the pit of my stomach.

'He told your father . . . he said to tell you that he was sorry. That whatever else happens, he wanted you to know that.'

I turned from her then and ran out into the hall. Her car keys were hanging by the door, and I snatched them as I went past.

'Robin, don't do this . . .'

'I'm not going to do anything,' I said, trying to sound calm, trying to sound like a woman who was in control of things, although we were well past that now. 'Please, don't worry.'

That was the last thing I said to her as I headed out the door.


I drove in a daze, feeling light-headed and dizzy. The snow hurt my eyes. There was a hole in my stomach, and my head was blurry from lack of sleep. I drew the car up in front of our house. There was no sign of the van. I stared at the front door from behind the steering wheel. What waited for me inside?

The first thing I noticed was the cold. The fire had gone out, and the heating had been off since the previous evening, and the last of the warmth seeped away as I closed the door behind myself. I kept my coat on as I pushed the kitchen door open and saw saucepans piled up by the sink, upturned glasses on the draining board. The light had been left on all night, and its sibilant hum echoed and bounced off the cold, hard surfaces.

In the dining room, things were exactly as we had left them. There were bowls of half-eaten trifle, glasses of wine waiting to be drunk, cold coffee in espresso cups, cream turning sour in the jug, napkins bunched and left lying on the table. A fork rested on the side of a plate as if whoever had been sitting there had just popped out of the room for a minute.

I took each room in turn, and with every door I opened, I felt myself holding my breath, not knowing what I would find, fearing the worst. When the last room had been checked, I came back to the dining room, feeling myself grow calm again. For a moment, I stood there, taking it all in, trying to feel relief, or at least some resolve – the push of determination to clear up this mess, to get on with things, to sort myself out.

Instead, I sat down on one of the dining-room chairs and listened to the house around me. The tickings and creakings. Dust drifted through the air. This house was old, and full of memories. I listened hard and tried to be still, straining to feel some trace of the past, of the people who had once occupied these rooms, of my grandmother and grandfather, some whispery echo of their voices. The air smelled empty. Harry had not been home. I wondered where he was. He seemed entirely remote from me now, cut off, falling through his own crazy universe.

His laptop was on the table, right where he had left it. Looking at it now, I recalled the vigour and spark of his actions the day before, how excited he had seemed as he'd scanned through those grainy images, how triumphant his response on finding the right one, and how hurt and offended and indignant he had become when I'd refused to see what he saw, when I'd denied what seemed so blatantly obvious to him. Casually, half-heartedly, I reached for the laptop and drew it towards me. I turned it on and waited for it to hum to life. The DVD popped out of the drive and I pushed it back in and waited for it to reload. Absently, more out of a half-formed curiosity than anything else, I began to flick through it, trying to summon from memory where he had paused, what part of this recording held his fascination. I fiddled with it for a few minutes, telling myself that I was crazy, that I was as bad as Harry, and yet I felt myself getting sucked in.

I don't know how long I sat there. Long enough to grow cold. Long enough for the battery to run out. I got up and turned on the heat. I made myself a mug of tea. I looked at the dishes stacked by the sink and told myself to get cracking on them. But instead, I found the cord for the laptop, plugged it in and kept looking.

I don't know why I did that. Some need to understand, I suppose. Some need to connect with Harry, to find a reason to explain his behaviour. Maybe I was grasping at straws in some pathetic bid to prove to myself that he was not crazy, that there could be a simple explanation to all this. But in my heart, I knew I was fooling myself.

The DVD was long and mind-numbingly boring. I skipped through it, fast-forwarding and pausing. I wondered how much of this Harry had sat through – all of it?

A picture formed of him in my head, huddled in the cold concrete space of his studio, his eyes growing red and squinty with fatigue as he scanned through these images, watchful of the door in case I made an appearance, furtively seeking the boy, whoever he was, who had so captured his imagination. The thought depressed me enough to want to stop looking.

But just before I gave up, I found the image. A boy of about eight or nine, walking hand in hand with a woman, presumably his mother, both of them stopping and getting into a car. The image was grainy, and when I paused it to examine the boy closely, I found it impossible to see any real likeness, so poor was the quality. It was a blanked-out face. It could have been anyone.

I sat back and folded my arms. I closed my eyes and pressed my fingers into the sockets. The house was warmer now, and I thought I would go upstairs and sleep.

But when I opened my eyes and again saw that image, something came to me. Something I had not considered before. I sat forward suddenly. I looked at the boy. I looked at the woman. There was a question in my head, the possibility of something so remote. My stomach gave an answering lurch, and immediately I got to my feet.

I half-ran to the kitchen. My heart was pounding now, blood thundering in my ears. The number was in my phone, and once I had pulled it from my handbag, I scrolled hurriedly through the address book until I found it. My hands shook as I dialled and waited for a response.

'Hello?'

'It's me. It's Robin.'

A pause. A hesitation.

'Robin. Are you okay?'

'I'm sorry for calling you like this – out of the blue. But . . .'

'What is it?'

'I'm . . . Listen, I want to ask you something.'

'Okay?'

'When we met, the other day, you said you'd been in Ireland for a while. How long?'

Again the hesitation.

'A few weeks,' he said slowly. 'We came just before Halloween –'

'Do you remember the march? The protest against the austerity measures in the budget? It was back at the end of November.'

'Sure. I remember it.'

'You weren't, by any chance, at that march, were you?'

Sweat had formed on my upper lip, and I tasted the saltiness of it now as I waited for his answer.

'No.'

I closed my eyes. Breathed out a sigh.

'That is, I wasn't at the march,' he said, as if to clarify. 'But I was in town that day. Eva was visiting her mom at the hospital. I went to pick her up.'

Tightness clenched around my heart.

'Oh, no.'

'Why? What is it?'

'Harry,' I said. 'Harry was there. He saw her. He saw her with a boy.'

I heard his breath draw in quickly.

'Fuck.'

'The boy's age, the likeness . . . He's jumped to a conclusion. I need to see you,' I said then. 'Tell me where you are.'

'Robin, just hang on . . .'

'This can't wait. I need to get to you before Harry does. Now please, tell me where you are.'

# 15. Harry

A porch light threw the man's shadow on to the gravel before me. I could hear a lighter unlatch and fire. Then I heard the crackling hush of a cigarette as it burned and was inhaled.

Crouching to one side of the car, I stayed as still as I could, a stinging pain starting in my thigh muscle. With one hand, I reached down and felt the rip in my jeans and the smarting pain of a flesh wound. My hand came away wet with blood. It must have happened when I jumped the fence. Wincing, I tried to keep the wound clear of the ground. The effort of staying still was exhausting; every inch of me strained toward this man, this stranger, exhaling a solitary plume of smoke into the night sky. Someone must have called out to him from within the house, for he turned and answered, 'Just getting the fireworks from the car.'

Fuck, I thought, panicking as I heard the car door creak open. Without thinking, I threw myself on to the snow and rolled underneath the car. I held my breath. Staring up at the shadowy undercarriage, I strained to hear the voice again. It had a familiar ring – a self-assured tone, the accent a curious mixture of places. I knew the voice, or it was recognizable to me at least, but I couldn't place it. I thought of Cozimo and what he had said. *Very unlikely. But not impossible.* In a way, his words had carried me here.

A woman came to the porch. I could make out her out-line only. It resembled that of the woman I had seen on O'Connell Street. 'Find them, Dave?' she asked.

'Got them. It's freezing out here. Go back inside.' The man's voice again; I knew it. But from where?

The creak of springs above me, and then his feet on the gravel beside me. Brown hiking boots. I let out a silent breath and held it again, as if I were underwater. I tried not to move a muscle.

The light from the porch went as far as the car, but beneath it I remained in shadow. I let out another silent breath and inhaled the dank smell of rust and oil.

'Are you ready to go?' he asked.

'Gimme one sec,' she said, disappearing into the house, and panic rose up inside me while the man leaned against the car, his feet crossed at the ankles, waiting.

A wave of nausea came over me. What was I going to do when he started the car? I opened my eyes to see if there was anything on the undercarriage that I could hang on to if the car did move. There wasn't. The exhaust was old and rusty. Maybe I could just lie still and pray the fucker wouldn't drive over me.

I didn't know what I was going to do. Maybe I should just step out and confront them right now? But I hadn't formulated a plan. Before I did anything, I wanted to see Dillon. I didn't know whether I was going to take him or talk to him or what. I needed to think, but there was no time. The man, Dave, who was he? I'd known Daves, and at some time, I knew that voice, but no, I couldn't be sure.

He had sat down into the driver's seat and was turning the key in the ignition. I closed my eyes and braced myself.

But then, as the engine hummed above me, I felt the undercarriage lift again, and saw the man's feet emerge. I watched those feet walk away through the snow, back to the house. I didn't watch for long. No sooner were his feet out of the range of my vision than I shuffled out from beneath the car and hid among the fir trees that lined the driveway.

Crouching beneath the dense boughs, I let out a sigh of relief. Still no sign of Dillon, but at least I had not been seen. I waited for my breathing to slow, trying to collect myself. My mind was all over the place. I reached into my pocket. Thank fuck I had remembered to stash the flask of whiskey. Left pocket: whiskey. Right pocket: gun.

The silence was interrupted by the chirruping of my phone. The damn thing nearly gave me a heart attack. I fumbled to silence it and saw the caller ID. Spencer. Shit! One way or another, he seemed determined to get me killed. I peeked out through the bushes, but there was no sign of either the man or the woman. Then my phone lit up with a text.

'Don't do anything stupid.'

Rich, coming from him. But that thought died as I watched the front door open again. The man stood in the doorway, smoking another cigarette. He had a hood pulled over his head, so I couldn't make out his features. His shoulders seemed square within his jacket, and he held his body tensely, like a boxer. He finished his cigarette, tossed the butt aside, walked to the car, its engine still running, and sat into the driver's seat. The woman locked the front door, hurried down the steps and operated the gate. There was no sign of the boy. I didn't know whether to feel relieved or crushed.

I waited until the red taillights had disappeared down the blackened driveway. I gave it a couple of minutes more, just to be sure they were not returning. At first, when I went to move, nothing happened. I thought I had been paralysed. I tried to move again, and this time I managed to slowly crawl from the undergrowth. I was stiff and aching. I stood up carefully. The cold felt like it had seeped into my bones. I took one step and then another. Gradually, sensation returned to my legs. Then I crossed to the house. All the lights were out. I was enveloped in the thick black cloth of darkness you find only deep in the countryside. There was no sound of a television and no voices.

I walked around the house. It was a small, ivy-clad cottage, with maybe two or three bedrooms. I tried peeking through the windows, but all the curtains were pulled. I saw nothing but the pale moonlit outline of my own frightened face.

My feet crunched on the gravel. The gravel yielded and carried me around the cottage. I thought about getting in, wandering about, tiptoeing through someone else's life. I went to the back door and reached for the handle, and the door creaked open. For a moment I stood stock-still. There was no movement from within the house. I stepped in and felt for a light switch and found one, then flipped it. There was nothing unusual about the kitchen – other than the fact that it looked like a couple had been in the middle of dinner and had left suddenly. Plates with half-finished food lay on the wooden kitchen table. A bottle of wine stood uncorked. Chairs were pulled out.

In a room adjoining the kitchen, a number of canvases leaned against the wall. The first paintings I inspected were bright, garish abstract things. I flicked through the work, which seemed to be a catalogue of fads and fashions in contemporary art. There was nothing real or original in there – that is, until I stumbled upon a large canvas. My breath quickened when I saw it because the thing was, it was one of mine.

I remembered making this painting like I had painted it only yesterday, in fresh and running watercolours, confident, strident strokes full of the vibrant, pulsating light of Tangier. But more important than the context was the subject: it was the first painting I had ever done of Dillon. He must have been only six months old. I had no memory of selling this painting, no recollection of parting with it, and as I contemplated how it had arrived here, at this most unexpected place, something moved within my chest, the shifting of my understanding, and it came to me at once who Dave was.

We had never known him by his first name, if what he went by back then was indeed his name at all. But the low intonation, the self-satisfied inflection – it all spoke of one person. I knew then that it was Garrick, the American in Tangier, the miracle man, the man with a Christmas tree in the desert, the poet, the painter, the dilettante, and that he was living in Ireland, with this woman and Dillon.

I felt suddenly weak. My stomach heaved. I was weary, worn and exhausted. I remembered again the photo in Cozimo's flat: me, Robin, Cozimo, Simo, Garrick and Raul. Cozimo saying, *There were things I knew which perhaps I should have told you.*

I walked about the house, a dread fear rising within me. Down the hallway I went, tripping into one room and then another. I was a reckless visitor, an intruder really, a shivering man in search of his son. And after all these years, down one dead end and then another, moving through back streets, through alleyways and lanes, through tears, prevarications, bitter arguments, hospital appointments and Christmas dinners, here we were; here I was, walking through a stranger's house at night.

It did not seem the kind of house Garrick would live in; it had none of his style. Besides: what was he doing in Ireland in the first place?

The last room I came to, at the end of the corridor, was Dillon's. I just knew it. It was a small, rectangular room. There was no furniture but for a small single bed and a chair in the corner. Some books lay beside the bed. On the floor a box of toys was turned over, and clothes were scattered on the chair. I walked into the room and felt a strange quiver run through my body. I was overcome with exhaustion.

I climbed into the bed and covered myself with the Spider-Man duvet.

The bedroom was flooded with an otherworldly moonlight. I took the gun from my pocket and placed its cold steel beneath my shirt, on my chest. How cold, how

comforting. More comforting than I would have imagined. I felt it sink into my skin. I felt it imprint itself,
tattooing itself into my being. It was heavy, and with the
rising and falling of my chest it seemed to almost become
a part of me.

I felt myself drifting. Instead, I took a long drink of
whiskey, let it course through my veins. It didn't give me
the energy I wanted. It sent me in the other direction. It
sent me to sleep, the deep stone of the gun weighing on
my heart. Before I dropped off to sleep, I made one last
call to Cozimo. Was he my last friend? The last friend I
had in the world? How I missed him then. The phone
seemed to ring more slowly than it might have in real time.
This didn't seem to be real time. This was something else.

A woman answered. 'Yes?'

'Cozimo?'

'Who is this?'

'It's Harry for Coz.'

'He's not here.'

'When will he be back?'

'He . . .'

'Who is this? Is this Maya?'

'Yes.'

'I want to speak to my friend.'

But I knew it before she even said it. I knew it from the
pause on the line – that tiny silence, the blood in my ears
rushing in to fill the space.

'Harry, I'm sorry. Cozimo is gone.'

I couldn't speak, pushed to the very edge of something
dark and consuming.

'He passed earlier tonight.'

I'm not sure what else she said or what I said. The darkness thickened. My mind was fading or breaking apart, like a meteor entering the earth's atmosphere. Or something, I don't know. It was all coming apart, reaching an ending. With Cozimo gone, I felt the last vestiges of my happiness in Tangier trickle away. I had never been more estranged from what I thought was my life. Cozimo, dear friend, how could you take your leave of me now?

Outside, the stars shone bright, brighter in the countryside than the city. The silence of the night had a texture to it. I could touch it. I could sink into it. My arms and legs felt like dead weight, and they brought me down gently, gradually, like heavy anchors to the bottom of a dream-sleep sea.

It was strange, though. I knew my son was here. Or did I? I had not seen him. I had no idea what to do. I may have pretended not to have expected this moment, this time, this day, but there was something in me, from day one, from before I had even met Robin, my beloved Robin, something from before that suggested yes, he is here, alive, waiting, ready for me, always.

I sank my head into his pillow and inhaled. I dreamed of Garrick painting my portrait. *Keep still*, he is telling me. *Keep still. Now hold it.* I am caught by his gaze, caught in it, held there, suspended, paralysed like some wild animal in a cage – and then I am a panther pacing. Keep still, he warns. At one moment, he is raising the paintbrush; at another, he is pointing a gun. Will he fire? And then suddenly, it is Spencer who is aiming the gun at me, painting me, and then as quickly it is Dillon, ablaze. He has a deep and serious voice. Not his voice; it's the voice of a thwarted older man. It is Jim's voice. And there is Cozimo holding his two hands to me, intoning the words 'It's so good to see you.' The dream spins and whirrs and takes me deeper into the dark and questioning caverns of my mind or some other place I cannot even name.

I emerge, still in sleep, at some other place, some other time. Tangier, of course. Our old bedroom. The curtains are blowing in the breeze. The sky is a burnished blue. The buildings are chipped and flaking, falling apart. The sun loves me here, but the afternoon is not for walking. The afternoon in Tangier can be bedtime. With Robin. Robin, my love. In my arms again. Then. When we made love, I closed my eyes. Open them, she said to me. Brave, brazen Robin. Look into my eyes. Open them. And I did and I would lose myself there. Into the deep oval greyness of her mysterious eyes. And we would move this way and that, shadowing each other, knowing where and how, as if we were following directions, but it was intuitive, it was natural, and then I would move deeper inside her and she would hold me in her gaze, and bite me and twist and turn, and we moved like that, as if we knew every move there was, and still she held me in her gaze, but I could not hold hers, and before our lovemaking ended I would close my eyes and travel, it seemed into another galaxy, travelling at speed through space and time, and Robin would grip me tighter and release me and let out the sigh that said both pleasure but disappointment too, because I had not managed to keep my eyes open. And she would drape her arms over me and chastise me. *You didn't keep them open*, she would say, gulping for air, laughing, inhaling the entire world. That's how it felt back then, but for that one time, the night we made Dillon.

Outside there was rain. I remember the coolness it brought with it, a temporary coolness. That night, I knew we had done something, made something, someone. In those years, we seemed to have all the time in the world to make love. And after Dillon, in Ireland, it had gone, all that sensuousness, all that passion. My dream avoided the dullness of Dublin and tunnelled through to its own Tangier heart, the hot and heavy days when our mouths sought each other out and our tongues were insatiable. It was the kind of intimacy that felt like nourishment. And in the afternoon, lazily out of bed, we drank mint tea, and later in the evening, we left the city for where the roads were lined with trees and sunflowers.

When I woke, I didn't know where I was. My mouth was parched. I reached for water, but what I noticed was that the gun had shifted from my chest. I did not know where it was. And I must have been sweating. My clothes had stiffened, and I was shivering. And most surprising of all was that when I rubbed the sleep from my eyes and looked up, above me stood Garrick.

# 16. Robin

I drove with my foot to the floor, heedless, reckless, a tightness running the length of my body, all the muscles and sinews taut with fear. Already, I knew that I was too late; that somewhere in the snowy stillness of the Wicklow Hills, Harry had got there before me, venturing into an unfamiliar place, opening up the Pandora's box of my past. I had a flash, then, of his face, pale and shadowy, his voice a hoarse shell of bewilderment. Oh God, I thought, please let it be all right. Please let it not be too late. But in a way I knew that I was beyond all that. For I knew that I would have to tell him.

I thought about how to tell him, how to ease him into understanding. I wanted to say that I remembered it as a series of happenings, a sequence of events. The time we had together was so short. And yet, things grow in memory, don't they? Small things become magnified, take on a new significance. There was so much intensity.

I wanted to tell him how I found it difficult, all these years later, to put my finger on when it started. There must have been a point at which I made a decision. I realized that. I didn't fall into it – people don't, however much they like to protest their innocence in these things. You make a choice. At some point, you get to decide. All of this, I wanted to tell him.

As I drove out of Dublin and saw the jagged rock of the Sugarloaf gleaming white on that cold, snowy morning, I began to imagine how I might explain it to Harry, and all at once I was transported back to another time, another place, when I was a different person, when all of this began.

You won't want to hear this, Harry. But I know you. You will ask for details, bravely claiming that you want to know, that you need to know. Only I wonder if, deep down, that is true. Can you cope with the sharp pain of such intimacies? Can anyone? You once told me that truth is in the details. We were talking about art – a very safe conversation. This is so much deeper than that. In real life, details can cut you to the quick, wound you beyond all repair.

A crackle on the line. Interference, like thunder in the air.

'This evening,' he said. 'Will you come?'

I twisted the phone's cord around my finger. I looked around, but the bar was almost empty. There was no one to overhear.

'Where?'

'The Mendoubia Gardens. Under the arch. After the call to prayer.'

I drew in my breath. A trickle of sweat ran over my chest. I felt it tracing a path down my breastbone.

'So, you'll be there?'

'I'll be there.'

*

All day it had been still and dry. Now a cool breeze was coming in off the ocean. A line of pink clouds hovered above the horizon. I hurried through the tumbling streets of the medina, listening to the noises coming from the windows above me that opened out on to the alleyways: raised voices, the clatter of pots and pans. Cooking smells reached me, fishy and spicy. Close by, the imam had ascended the minaret, and I heard the call to prayer echoing above the roofs.

I reached the Grand Socco and made my way to the gardens. I was there before him and took my place beneath the archway, trying to look casual and inconspicuous. A group of teenage boys were hanging around nearby, whispering and giggling and casting glances in my direction. I pulled my scarf up over my head and tried to look aloof. The blood was thundering in my head.

I moved away from the arch and took a seat on a bench, among the fig trees and dragon trees, and watched for him with a growing sense of anxiety. He arrived just as I was about to give up on him. I saw him entering the gardens, scanning the shaded space, looking for me. He had his hands in his pockets. He sauntered, with a kind of rolling gait. His expression didn't change when his eyes settled on me, and he sat down next to me.

We didn't speak. Instead, we sat side by side, watching the comings and goings underneath the archway. I felt one of us should say something, but I was afraid to speak, afraid my voice would emerge as a nervous squeak. Wordlessly, he offered me a cigarette, and I leaned in to his lighter, cupping my hand around his. The touch was brief and electrifying. We drew away from each other. The shadows thrown on the ground grew long as the sun sank behind the buildings. My heart was beating loudly; I was tense with trying to appear casual. I was utterly aware of his breathing next to me. When he reached out and took my hand, it was so startling, I almost recoiled. His hand was large and cool. It held mine loosely, carelessly. A squeeze then, and he leaned towards me, his face so close to mine I could feel his breath along my cheek, along my collarbone.

'Let's get out of here,' he said.

He took me through unfamiliar streets. We passed strangers who barely registered us. My cheeks were burning. I was terrified we would meet someone who knew me, who knew you. He held my hand the whole time. His step was longer than mine, and I had to hurry to keep up. Just once, he turned and looked at me, and I managed the briefest of smiles.

At that point, I still had a choice. I had not strayed so far that I couldn't go back. The most I was guilty of was an error of judgement, a momentary weakness. My infidelity did not go beyond the holding of hands. My mind was flying on ahead, tumbling recklessly into the future, into the next few hours. I allowed myself to be led in that way, without question; I was surrendering to my desires, and to his. I was no innocent. I was not naive. I knew well what would come next. When he led me up the stairs and into the dim shadowy space of his rooms, I was breathless with expectation. When he pushed the door shut behind him and took hold of me roughly, slamming me against the wall, and I felt the length of his body pressing urgently against mine, I knew that every word spoken, every look exchanged between us from the moment we'd first met, had been leading, inevitably, inexorably, to this.

There was a light on when I got home. I saw it as I reached the return and climbed the last few steps. I stopped at the door, taking one breath and then another, trying to calm myself. My hand went to my hair, and I smoothed it down, arranging it about my shoulders. I touched my neck, the place where it pulsed, where he had fixed his mouth. I touched it as though my fingers could trace the raised outline of a kiss, sweet and savage.

I pushed open the door. The light was too bright; it hurt my eyes, and I turned it off. The room was empty. I put down my bag and crossed the floor to the bedroom. You were passed out, Harry, splayed across the bed, lying over the covers. I made no attempt to move you. When I climbed into bed, you didn't stir. There was whiskey on your breath. I looked at you through the darkness. Your animated face was at peace.

Yes, there was guilt. It lingered, but it was not enough. I pulled my gaze away from you and turned over on to my side. I think I slept.

The next time, I went straight to his apartment, where he was waiting for me. As soon as we were upstairs, the door closed behind us, he grabbed my arm and spun me around, his face on mine, hungry, greedy. He peeled my T-shirt off, then slid my skirt up my thighs, pushing me back on to the bed. We did not speak. His desire was urgent and tinged with aggression; it veered towards violence. He wrapped his hand in a swatch of my hair and yanked my head back, so that my neck was arched and offered up to him, and he sank his teeth into it. It left a mark that I would have to hide later.

The sun had moved across, leaving the room dim and shadowy. In the distance there were sounds of traffic, the angry whine of a scooter. But in that small, hot room, with its blank walls and twisted sheets, there was silence. My breath and his, entwined, laboured, gasping. He reached up to cover my mouth.

In company, I did not look at him. I refused to catch his eye. I laughed at other people's jokes, smiled at whoever was talking. I engaged in conversation furiously, manically. I heard my own laughter, and it sounded false. The ghost of his mouth was on my breast, sweat on my back. My conscience like an iron band tightening about my head.

I lost interest in my art. Blank canvases stared back at me, accusingly. The brushes felt wrong in my hand. The hours passed like slow beasts. I was bored and restless. I couldn't see anything clearly; everything was cloudy, blurred. My faith in myself was draining away.

I dropped a jar of olives. The glass shattered into pieces on the tiled floor, the fruits careering off into every corner, like marbles bouncing and rolling.

'What is with you?' you asked.

'Nothing.'

'You're not yourself.'

'I don't know what you mean.'

'You're distracted. And clumsy.'

Your eyes swept over the mess on the floor.

'Are you okay?'

Your hand on my back was solicitous and concerned.

'I'm fine, Harry,' I said, and moved away.

I bent down to hide my face from you, kneeling to clean up the mess.

A darkening room, a hush drawing over it. I lay beneath the slow whirr of the fan, my head resting on his chest, his hand in my hair, idly stroking. A brief moment of peace before I would have to rise up from those sheets and step into my clothes and go out into the dry night, leaving him behind me.

'I want you to stay,' he said.

'I know.'

'But you won't.'

'I can't.'

His silence was bullish, irritated. His body remained still, and yet I felt the stirrings of discontent within it.

This was a new thing. This growing need. This desire to linger afterwards. I felt the pull of him. My leave-taking was draining, weakening. I felt myself breaking up into pieces, disassembling. He had brought me to this.

'You could leave him,' he said.

The words hung over us, pulsing in the dry heat of the bedroom.

How long did it go on? A couple of months? Ten weeks? Not long. Not in the grand scheme of things, in the course of a whole adult life. Why is it that we measure our love affairs in temporal terms? A marriage that lasts forty years is viewed a success. But some things that are short can be more meaningful, in some ways more lasting than those that stretch out for a lifetime.

An evening at home. Cozimo came to our apartment for dinner. You and he sat and discussed a forthcoming trip to Seville while I prepared the meal. Lamb stew, dumplings, my fingers covered in flour. Lately, I had been concentrating my domestic efforts in the kitchen. Some need to nourish you, build you up, fortify you for what might break between us. Again, the guilt – it presented itself in strange ways.

I could hear your voices; I half-listened to the conversation, my attention drifting between the rooms, until my interest was snagged by a name.

'Garrick gave it to me,' Cozimo said.

I heard you let out a whistle of appreciation.

'Jameson 1780,' you said. 'Not bad. Not bad at all.'

'If you say so. I never developed much of a taste for whiskey. But I have never been one to look a gift horse in the mouth, either, so . . .'

His low voice, a dry chuckle.

'So what was the occasion for the gift?'

'He was clearing out his things. Giving away anything he didn't want to take with him.'

I stopped what I was doing. I stood dead still, my whole being straining toward this conversation.

'He's left?'

'Yes. I understand he took the boat last night.'

'Do you know where he's gone?'

'He didn't say. Home, perhaps.'

'Wherever that is.'

'Indeed.'

'Do you think he will come back?'

I ached to hear the reply, but there was none. Not a verbal one, anyway. A shake of the head, perhaps, or a shrug of the shoulders.

'Well, that's just like him, isn't it?' you said, a sneer in your voice. 'The mystery man. Disappearing without a trace.'

'Yes.'

'So what was his deal, Cozimo, hmm?'

'I really could not say. But I think . . . I don't know.'

'What?'

'I think there is a woman involved.'

'Really?' You perked up, interested now.

In the kitchen, my legs began to tremble.

'Who? Someone here?'

'No. Well, I'm sure he's had his little trysts here. Who hasn't? No, I mean back home, wherever home is for him. I always had the impression that he had someone waiting for him.'

A noise escaped from me. A cry of anguish, of betrayal.

It was involuntary, and I put my hand to my mouth to stifle it.

'Let me get some glasses,' Cozimo said.

I turned away as he stepped behind me. I busied myself chopping onions so that he wouldn't see my distress, my shaking hands.

He fumbled in a cupboard, searching for glasses. I couldn't look at him. There was an ache in my stomach. I wanted to bend over and cry out. I heard the clink of glasses on the countertop, the unscrewing of a bottle. His hand was on my shoulder.

'An aperitif, my dear?'

I looked at it, the gleam of light through the honey-coloured whiskey, the sweet, musky smell of it in my nostrils, and a wave of nausea surged up from deep inside me. I barely made it to the sink before I threw up.

The pain was physical, acute. A wound that had split open. The days stretched out endlessly. I was at turns furious, then weepy, then panicked. The sight of food turned my stomach. I was exhausted all the time. I called in sick to work and spent hours wrapped in the blankets, lying face down on our bed. I was too tired, too wrung out, to cry any more.

You worried. You sat on the edge of the bed, testing my brow for a fever.

'We should get a doctor.'

'What for?' I asked. 'It's just a flu or something.'

'You should eat something.'

'Later, maybe.'

'Some tea and toast, at least.'

'Please, Harry, I just need to rest.'

What I wanted was to be left alone in a darkened room to wallow. I was depressed, broken-hearted. A doctor couldn't do anything about that.

You looked down at me, worry lines furrowing your brow.

'You're not pregnant, are you?'

As soon as you said it, I knew it was true.

'Are you?' you repeated, eyebrows raised.

I drew myself up on to my elbows, stared at the pillow, furiously calculating dates.

Your hand was on my back. I turned to look at you, a slow smile starting on your face.

'Robin?' you asked softly. 'Could you be?'

'I . . . I don't know.'

'Fuck!' you exclaimed, running your hands through your hair. You couldn't chase the grin from your face.

'Harry . . .'

'How late are you?'

'I'm not sure.'

'But you are late?'

'Yes, I think so.' Although, in truth, I had never been this late before.

You were up off the bed, reaching for your wallet on the floor.

'What're you doing?'

'Getting a test.'

'No, wait . . .'

I watched you checking for cash, then stuffing the

wallet in your back pocket. It was all happening way too fast. My mind was a tangle of questions; it teemed with worries, and possible explanations.

'Best to just find out, eh?'

You leaned down and kissed me – a long, lingering kiss. I felt your lips full and hard against my mouth, your hand holding the back of my head, fingers in my hair. When you drew away, you looked deep into my eyes, and I got a glimpse of all the love and hope that lay within you. I wanted you to leave quickly, before the bitter pang of guilt came over me. I waited to hear the door slam, then sank my head into the pillow.

It was love. Pure, untainted and frighteningly powerful. I looked upon his small, triangular, catlike face, his curled fingers, the soft silky hair of his head, and I couldn't believe my luck. He was so utterly perfect. Throughout my pregnancy, guilt had hovered close to me, a hangover of my Catholic upbringing. I couldn't forget what I had done. As the baby grew within me, so did my conviction that there would be something wrong with him or her. An underlying illness or some deformity. Punishment for my terrible deceit.

The moment when I might have told you came and went. You fell in love with my pregnancy so fast, fixated upon the child growing in my womb. That the child might not be yours never entered your head. I found it unbearable, at times, the naked love you felt for this unborn baby, your raw excitement at the prospect of becoming a father. For a man who had lived his whole life endeavouring to be free of the shackles of ordinary commitments, you showed no signs of panic at the impending responsibilities, but, rather, embraced them wholeheartedly. The prospect enlivened and inspired you.

I never heard from Garrick. I couldn't understand how he could go and not say goodbye. He had disappeared like a wisp of smoke in the wind. The pain lingered, then lessened, and when I looked at my newborn son, I saw him there. It was unmistakable. His appearance only confirmed what I had already guessed. I had been careless for months before anything started with Garrick. Careless, and yet nothing had happened. All the occasions of our lovemaking – yours and mine, Harry – had never produced a child. And then the month of my affair, a month where you and I hardly seemed to touch each other, let alone make love, those precious weeks when I gave myself wholeheartedly to my lover, that was the time I conceived. It could not be a coincidence. When I looked at Dillon's face, I knew as much. That chin dimple, those wide, staring eyes. His features were soft, but they held the promise of sharpness in the future, when all the baby fat had fallen away. I saw it so clearly, but, to my surprise and relief, no one else identified the likeness. Least of all you.

'He's like his mother,' you said proudly whenever someone peered inquisitively into the bassinet.

He had Garrick's colouring, which was also mine. In time, people remarked that he was like me, with a trace of you about his mouth, a theory I was all too willing to go along with. Even you proclaimed to see it. Funny, how the mind plays these little tricks.

Dillon. He was my consolation. And I felt I could not have wished for anything better, or more perfect. I could not have loved anyone more. I thanked the gods and my lucky stars for the escape I had had, for letting me get away with it, and being rewarded with my beautiful child. What I didn't know was that my punishment lay in wait for me, that it would come for me when I least expected it.

On a warm breezy afternoon in the spring of 2003, I walked on to the terrace of a beachside café and saw him there. He was sitting with Cozimo, Elena and Blanca, half-reclining, his shades pushed back off his forehead – as if he had never left. I stopped behind a chair. My heart gave out a single deadened thump, and then I recovered.

'Hey,' he said, rising out of his chair.

'Hello again,' I said. 'Please don't get up.'

Cozimo had leaned forwards, arms outstretched, beckoning to Dillon, who dropped my hand and tottered towards his favoured uncle, smiling as he was swept up into the old guy's arms and plonked firmly in his lap. The others were making a fuss over him as they always did, and I was grateful for the distraction. It allowed me time to get over my shock, to pull myself together.

His eyes were on me, and I looked up to meet them in a challenging way. I was deeply unsettled, my anger at his leaving flaring up suddenly, bringing a dull pain from the past. His eyes flickered briefly towards the boy, then to me.

'So, you're back, then?' I said brightly, casually.

'For a little while.'

I nodded sagely. I couldn't think of what to say. For

business or pleasure? Are you travelling alone or in company? Any question I might ask, no matter how innocent, could betray a neediness on my part, an old desire. So I said nothing to him. Instead, I took a seat next to Elena. She was only too happy to share with me the latest crisis in her love life. We became absorbed in this half-whispered conversation. I couldn't look at him, and yet I was aware of him all the time, aware of that lean, angular frame slouching in his chair, aware of those deep-set, light-coloured eyes fixed on the ocean. Occasionally, he made a remark or offered an opinion, always in that slow drawl of his. Calmness emanated from him, or was it boredom? I envied his coolness, his nonchalance, his customary reserve, while inside I churned with emotion.

More than two years had passed since last I had seen him, since we had sat in such close proximity to each other, and when I thought of the intimacy that had once existed between us, replaced now by this cold and awkward distance, I felt overwhelmed.

Dillon was restless. He had abandoned Cozimo and was looking for some way to escape. He whined when corralled back to the group, and I took this opportunity to leave.

'He needs some exercise,' I explained.

'Do you want me to take him?' Elena asked.

'No, no. That's okay. I'll bring him down to the beach.'

We went, the two of us, hand in hand. He jabbered away in his own language. I could barely answer him, could barely listen, so consumed was I by what had just happened.

It was cooler by the sea. We kicked off our shoes and

felt the sand warm between our toes. The wind whipped our hair about our faces, and I pulled a strand of it from my mouth. His hair was long, too long for a boy, but I couldn't bear to cut it yet, the springy golden locks that curled about his neck. He played at gathering shells, putting them in his shoes and mine, then spilling them out and starting afresh. I sat in the sand and watched him. He chattered as he played, a curious babble with intonations he mimicked from my own speech, peppered with the occasional word I recognized: Mama, Dada, Didi – the name he'd given himself.

A shadow fell across us. I knew who it was before I looked up. I had known all along that he would follow us down here, that he would seek me out.

'Is it okay if I sit here?' he asked.

'Sure.'

He sat next to me but not too close, as if sensing my wariness.

'He's cute,' he said, nodding towards Dillon.

I didn't answer. I stayed within the walls of injured silence.

Dillon regarded him strangely, giving him that guarded look he treated all strangers to. And then he decided to trust this man, for he came forwards and offered him Ted, his best buddy, the toy he had had since birth.

'Wow, thanks, little guy. And who's this?'

Dillon's eyes stared back at him from beneath a frown.

'That's Ted,' I said.

'Well, hello, Ted,' he said, turning the toy to face him. 'Aren't you a fine fellow?'

He handed the toy back, and Dillon, satisfied or bored with this exchange, turned his back on us and resumed his shell hunting.

We watched him in silence. I wanted to say something but didn't want it to be casual or trite. And yet I was afraid of blurting out anything revealing, anything that might let him see how broken up I'd been at his departure, how painful it had been for me. As it happened, he was the first to speak.

'I feel I owe you an explanation,' he said.

'Yes, you do,' I said drily. 'At the very least, an apology.'

'Sure. You're right.'

I sensed him nodding slowly. Still, I couldn't bring myself to look at him.

'It was crazy, what we were doing,' he told me. 'I'd never done anything like that. I'd never felt anything like it.' He said this softly, and I felt the words coming at me like arrows. 'Things got serious between us, quicker than I ever intended. You were married, and I . . .'

I turned and saw him staring at the sand between his shoes.

'You were married, too,' I said, finishing the sentence for him.

I saw it clearly, what I had been blind to before.

He nodded, his eyes averted, almost shamefaced.

A puff of laughter escaped from me, laughter at my own foolishness. It made him turn and look at me.

'What?'

'It's just so . . . I dunno. So prosaic.'

He took that in, nodding slowly.

'That's one way of looking at it, I guess.'

'You could have told me then that you were married.'

'Would it have made a difference?'

'At least it would have given me a reason, instead of that awful blankness, not knowing what to think. Feeling abandoned and not understanding why.'

I bit my lip, silently berating myself for revealing too much.

'You're right,' he said quietly. 'I should have told you. It was just . . .'

He paused, and I waited. Then he said, 'It was just so fucking hard to leave you.'

Those words pierced deep inside me. They swept away all the hatred and resentment I had built up towards him. In one fell swoop, those words sent it all crashing down.

'I loved you. I never told you that.'

'Stop,' I told him. 'Please don't.'

'Okay,' he said, watching me carefully, backing off.

He thought about it for a moment, then added, 'I don't know why I thought it would help for you to know that now.'

My face was turned from him. I wiped the corners of my eyes with the back of my hand.

'It doesn't matter,' I said, trying to sound like I meant it. 'It's all in the past.'

Still, he stared at me.

'What about your wife?' I asked, trying to summon some dignity after the tears. 'Where is she?'

'She's in the States. Although she's Irish by birth. I guess I have a type, huh?'

I let that go.

Then, after a moment, I asked, 'Does she know?'

He nodded.

'Yeah. We were separated, you see. And then she wanted a reconciliation. I thought it was the right thing to do. Things were so crazy here. I just wanted to make something in my life right. And in the spirit of starting over . . .'

'You told her.'

'I told her. You never told Harry?'

I shook my head.

Then I asked him, 'You and your wife, are you still together?'

He nodded. 'We have a son. Felix. He's not much younger than Dillon.'

He sat and stared ahead of him. His eyes fixed on Dillon, who had moved a little bit away from us, closer to the water's edge. I called to him to step back a bit, and he did what I asked. There was tiredness in the slump of his little shoulders. I saw him rubbing at one eye. Soon, we would have to leave.

'He's mine. Isn't he?'

The words were shocking. I couldn't answer. I pulled my legs in close to my chest and hugged them to myself. I felt him looking at me, reading the reply in my silent refusal to utter the words.

'Harry doesn't know about that either, does he?'

I shook my head. In a voice that came out low and whispery and broken with emotion, I said, 'He must never know.'

He drew in his breath.

273

The sun was low in the sky, and there was a chill on the breeze. I knew you would be home by now and wondering where we were. I gathered up our shoes and got to my feet. He caught hold of my wrist.

'Can I see you again? Before I leave?'

'No,' I said, shaking my head with a firm resolve.

It hurt to refuse him. His hand around my wrist. The first touch since we'd parted.

He held me there for a moment, then let go.

We walked in silence up the beach. I carried Dillon, drawing strength from the warmth and weight of his little body in my arms.

Before we parted again, he reached into his pocket and drew out a business card.

'It's got my e-mail and cell phone on it,' he said.

I looked at the card he offered me, needing to get away from him, now, before my emotions surfaced again.

'I'd like to stay in touch,' he said, the card still in his outstretched hand. He was gazing intently at me, his face in shadow now that the sun was going down.

'I don't know. It's not a good idea.'

'I understand. But if there was any way you could. Just the odd e-mail. So I could know how you and Dillon are doing. So I could know that you are both okay. I won't get in touch with you – not if you don't want me to.'

When I took the card, my movements were rushed, fuelled by nerves and indecision, so that I snatched it from him, turning away as I did, feeling him looking after us as I walked away from him, the only sound in the street the hush of the ocean and the soles of my shoes slapping against the dusty pavement.

I pulled the car into the narrow driveway and felt the gravel beneath the tyres. The garden lay in a deep silence under a quilt of snow. Drawing up outside the house, I saw that the front door was open, and braked hard. There was no sign of life, no evidence of activity, and in the stillness of the car after the engine had died, I listened to the eerie silence. Something about it made me grow cold. A kind of dread came over me then at what awaited me once I passed through that open door. But it lasted for only an instant. And then I was out of the car and racing up those steps, impatient now to know, to see what turn our story was about to take.

# 17. Harry

I stared at the gun in his hand. He was holding it steady, his grip firm, his gaze cool, the snout of the barrel pointing straight at my head. The air about us was still and heavy. I might have felt fear at that point – fear that he was going to kill me – but more than anything, I felt a terrible impatience. I needed answers. Where was my son? What had he done with him? Anger raced through my veins. I was so close to finding Dillon, but Garrick, with his implacable stare and humourless, down-turned mouth, was trying to stop me. I bit down on the bile rising up from my stomach and pushed myself up slowly, my head still clogged with alcohol and sleep, until I was sitting up in that narrow bed.

'So,' I said slowly. 'Are you going to shoot me, or what?'

'I don't know,' came his cool reply. 'I could. No one would blame me. You're an intruder in my home. It's self-defence.'

'No shit,' I said. Somehow I knew that he wouldn't pull the trigger. The moment for that had passed. I didn't feel any fear at that point. More than anything, he irritated me. I swung my legs off the bed and got to my feet. He took a step back, still pointing the gun, and for an instant the room seemed to whirl around me.

'Not one more step,' he said, the instruction delivered in a cool, steady tone.

I stopped.

He thought for a moment, weighing the situation, and then, slowly, he brought his hand down, the gun at his side. His jaw tensed, and his eyes narrowed, and the electricity in the room remained.

'You gonna tell me what you're doing here? Or do I have to guess?'

'I've come for Dillon.'

His eyes flickered over my face. 'I don't know what you mean.'

'I think you do.'

'There's no one here. Just me.'

No sooner were the words spoken than a car pulled up outside. From where I stood, I could not see it.

'Wait here,' Garrick said, cool as you like. His face betrayed no fear or anxiety as he closed the door behind him.

I listened to him walking down the hall, his footfall firm and unrushed. I put my head to the door and listened. Muffled voices – Garrick's and a woman's. It was impossible to make out a single thing they were saying. My irritation grew, and my impatience. If it was the woman I had seen with Dillon, then I wanted to confront her – demand to know what she had done with him, where she had hidden him away. The memory of her blue scarf rising like smoke on the wind came back to me, the way she had hurried away, pulling the boy after her, and I was taken then by a new fury.

They were standing in front of the open door, and with the porch light behind them, their forms were cast in silhouette. It was only as I got close to them, only as she turned to look at me, that I saw it was not the woman I had glimpsed the day of the march.

It was Robin.

'What are you doing here?' I asked, my mouth dry as paper.

'Harry. Thank God you're all right,' she exclaimed, coming towards me, reaching out for me.

Her forehead was knotted with anxiety; her voice was shaky with emotion. Her arms went about me, and I pulled her into my embrace. The sudden warmth of her body caused an ache within me, a creeping fatigue, and I recognized it for what it was: relief. All this time I had been labouring alone in the dark, frightened of my own thoughts and convictions, yet compelled to plough on regardless of who might get hurt in the process. Robin, my love, my only one – how I had yearned for her to believe me, how I had strived to make her see that I was not crazy, that our son really was alive. And now she was here, by my side, with me at the end. All the bitterness of the past, the words spoken in anger, the wounds and recriminations – all would be forgotten, blown away in the wind. What mattered now was that we were together, and soon we would have our son.

'Come home,' she whispered, her face against my neck.

'Soon this will all be over,' I told her. Then quietly, speaking the words into her hair so that Garrick could not hear, I said, 'Be careful. He has a gun.'

'What?'

She drew back, a look of horror coming over her face, and, turning to Garrick, she saw the gun and, just as swiftly, broke free of my embrace, crossed the floor, and reached for the weapon, claiming it easily. At first, I didn't understand what was happening. He surrendered it to her without a question, without any kind of struggle. She said something to him, something I couldn't catch, and I watched her put the gun into the pocket of her overcoat.

'Harry. Sweetheart,' she said, returning to me. 'Come away from here.'

But I just stood there, rooted to the spot, troubled by something I couldn't identify.

'Our son, Robin. We're not leaving without him.'

'Please, love. Come away. There's nothing for us here. Only more pain.'

The strain in her voice nagged at me, and I heard the echo of another voice rising up from the hollows within me: Cozimo saying, *There were things I knew which perhaps I should have told you.*

Tangier. The shadows. The dark. The murky depths of the waters lapping the harbour. I felt the wound in my leg clawing at me, pulling me down, my head swimming in confusion. It was a struggle now to stay focused, to hold it together until I got what I'd come here for.

A question flitted through my brain, and I looked at her. How had she known to come here?

'Did Spencer tell you?' I asked.

'Spencer?' The confusion misting her gaze told me that it had not been him. That she had discovered this house some other way. It didn't matter. All that mattered now was Dillon.

I turned to Garrick. 'Tell me where he is. Tell me what you have done with my son.'

'You don't know what you're talking about.'

'Don't give me that crap. I know what I saw. I have proof.'

'Proof? What proof?'

'A photograph. CCTV footage. A licence plate.'

Robin's hand was in mine, and I heard her say my name, but still I went on.

'You were there, weren't you, that night in Tangier? I know you took him. I know it was you. But I don't know why. That's what I can't figure out. I'm not sure I even care any more. I just want him back. We both do.'

I squeezed Robin's hand in mine, drawing strength from it, the strength to keep going, to hold on until this would all be over.

'Harry,' she said again, her voice more insistent this time, and when I looked down at her, her grey oval eyes were full of fear. 'You're not well, sweetheart. You need to come with me now.'

'What? No. Just wait, Robin. You'll see.'

'But –'

'Trust me. I saw him, Robin. I saw Dillon.'

'No,' she said then.

The conviction in her voice gave me pause. I looked at her, the shadow of confusion starting to clear, but still I did not see it. Did not want to see it.

'You saw Felix,' she said softly.

'Who?'

'Felix,' Garrick repeated. 'My son.'

'No,' I said, shaking my head, refusing to believe them, remembering again the boy's face, the instant recognition I had experienced that day, coming at me suddenly with a plunging sensation. 'It was Dillon. I know it was him. I saw him.'

'You only think it was him,' Garrick said, 'because of the resemblance.'

'The resemblance?' I repeated, something cold pooling in the pit of my stomach.

'Dave,' Robin said to him, a warning in her voice, and when I heard her use his name like that — his Christian name — I felt myself reeling away from her.

Maybe he heard the warning in her voice and decided to ignore it, because he said it anyway: 'Dillon and Felix are brothers.'

His words dissolved in the air, escaped into the ether. Nobody spoke. They both stood watching me, wary of me, afraid of what I would do next.

'Brothers?' I said slowly, looking at Robin.

Her eyes filled with tears and she shook her head, but it was not a refusal, more a helpless gesture of surrender.

'Dillon was my son,' Garrick said. Then Robin swung around and said to him with real ferocity, 'Shut up, for God's sake!'

Just like that it came together for me, and I finally understood. Images of them tangled in each other's arms, naked limbs, sweat, a ferocious hunger for each other, all of it cramming into the corners of my consciousness, sending me spinning away into a kind of delirium.

She was coming at me now, fear in her eyes as she reached out and took my face in her hands, saying my name, trying to drag me back to the present, trying to hold me within the safety of her gaze.

'Listen to me, sweetheart. I'm so sorry. Words can't say how sorry I am.'

'It's not true,' I said, still not believing, still resisting the tug of knowledge. 'Tell me it's not true.'

'I love you, Harry. That's all that matters. Our future. The baby inside me. Please, sweetheart, I can't lose you now.'

Still, I couldn't grasp it. This woman I had known since I was a young man, sixteen or more years ago, looked suddenly like a stranger to me. A stranger, pale and forlorn, not someone I trusted, not the person I cared for and loved, but a weary woman, regretful and grieving, confronted by her past when she had hoped it was behind her.

I could have told her there was no escaping it.

Her hands were hot on my face – I felt the tremble within them.

'I'm not Dillon's father?'

'Sweetheart,' she said, her voice breaking, sudden tears filling her eyes. 'You were. In every way that mattered.'

'What?'

She was crying hard now, her voice shaking with fear.

'I made a terrible mistake, Harry. So help me God, I

wish I hadn't. Except it gave me Dillon. But believe this, I beg you: in my heart, I always thought of you as his father.'

She wrapped her arms around me then, and I stood there, immobile, feeling her body shake with the force of her weeping. Over her shoulder, I saw Garrick, hands in his pockets, staring thoughtfully at the floor, and a well of anger deep within me was tapped. I wanted to push her away from me, shove her aside so I could get at him, but instead I opened my arms to accept her embrace. Drawing her to me, I felt the shudder of her sobs, the brush of her hair against my face. I wrapped my arms around her, whispered to her to hush, and then I reached into her coat pocket.

I heard the sharp intake of her breath as she felt it, but she was not quick enough. Moving swiftly, I pushed her aside, drew back my hand, then struck Garrick across the face with the butt of the gun.

'No!' she screamed as Garrick fell to the ground.

I stood above him, watching as he writhed and moaned, blood seeping out from a gash across his cheek.

'What are you doing?' she cried out. 'Oh my God.'

She went to kneel by his side, but I pulled her away.

'For Christ's sake, Harry. He's bleeding!'

'He's lucky I didn't put a bullet in his head,' I said, stung by fury. Then I turned and kicked him hard in the gut. It was shocking how soft his belly felt as my foot connected with it.

He wheezed, his body curling around the pain. I could hear Robin crying, her hysteria growing.

'Where's Dillon?' I demanded.

He grabbed hold of my leg, pulling himself around my ankle, and I leaned down and put the gun to his temple. He was saying something, but his words were inaudible through his laboured breathing and the gurgle of blood in his mouth. I leaned in to hear him.

'You should have taken better care of him,' Garrick wheezed.

I could see Robin wringing her hands, running them through her hair, her worried eyes ranging around the room as she began to pace back and forth. I told her to keep still.

The gun was still pressed to Garrick's temple and I increased the pressure, feeling the trigger hot against my finger.

'You should have taken better care of Dillon,' he repeated. 'You shouldn't have left him before the earthquake, asleep, alone. You shouldn't have drugged a small boy like that, Harry, and you know it.'

I felt myself recoil at the truth within his statements. A great roll of sadness came over me, and I took the gun away, noting the round indent it had left on his skin. Garrick coughed and spluttered, and I turned aside.

'I just want him back,' I said then, but all the threat, all the anger, had drained from me.

Robin came to me, but I raised a hand to stop her, to warn her away. If she touched me, I might fall apart, disintegrate, and it would all have been for nothing.

'Where is he, Garrick? For the love of God, would you just tell me?'

He lay on the floor, still gasping for breath. Every inch

of me ached from holding myself upright. I couldn't remember the last time I had slept a dreamless sleep, the last time I had laid my head down and felt the comfort of oblivion. My eyes were closing, lids weighted with the dragging desire for sleep, and it took everything I had to fight it. Soon this will be over, I told myself. Just hang on.

I brought the gun up again and aimed it at his head. He rolled on to his back on the floor, staring up at me, no fear on his face, his mouth set in a grim line of determination. The fucker was willing me to shoot him, and I, God help me, felt myself being pushed to the edge. I could see it happening. I could feel it: the pressure of the trigger, the sudden snapping and then the glorious release of the bullet, the wild bang, the smell of burning and the tearing of flesh and the shattering of bone. An instant and it would all be over. My whole arm shook with the tremble of possibility. There was nothing else for it.

And then, just as I was about to do it, just as I felt the last vestige of self-control escape me, there was a clatter on the steps outside, a flickering light behind me. I turned and saw him – a young boy, running up the steps and crossing the threshold into this madhouse. He held a lantern in his hands. 'Daddy, Daddy,' he was calling. The lantern was lit. The light wavered, and I blinked in disbelief. At the end of this long, lonely journey, here he was, my boy, my Dillon, and still somehow I didn't quite believe it.

I heard something then, a shout, and Garrick struggled to his knees, saying, 'Out! Dillon, get out!'

And then another, stranger sound – a cry, like that of a

wounded animal, so gut-wrenching and forceful it seemed like a sort of violence. Turning, I saw my wife fall to her knees, her face a white page of furious disbelief, her eyes round and dark with shock. She looked at him, at the boy she had thought dead, giving up this sound like the last offering of grief within her, and for a moment we all fell silent – me, Garrick, the boy – watching her as the room around us wavered and rocked in its burning brightness.

# 18. Garrick

They say there are two sides to every story. Sometimes, there are three.

He held the boy's hand in his. That is what he remembers. Afterwards, when it was done, when everyone else had left the room, he sat there with the boy's hand clasped in his own. He stared hard at it and marvelled at how small it seemed. There was a freckle between the knuckles of the index and middle fingers. A small detail. Still – how had he not noticed it before?

Through the open doorway, he could hear his wife, her voice low and weary, cracked with the effort of imparting the news – an impossible task, but one that she had readily assumed. It wasn't even discussed between them. She had just leaned down and taken her phone from her bag and then left the room. She was better than he was at handling the situation. Always more in control of her emotions, even now, when they were being tested beyond anything they had imagined. Below her voice, the regular sounds of the hospital filtered through: the screeching of trolleys, the monotone of the voice coming over the speakers, the footfalls and laughter, the whoosh of the swinging doors, the sudden slap of running feet – noises so familiar to him now, after all the time they had spent here. It occurred to him then that he would not hear them again. Once they left here today, they would not return. He thought of this and began to see his future differently. He thought of all the days and weeks and months to come, and it was like peering down a long, dark tunnel.

Through the window that gave out on to the corridor, between the slatted blinds, he could see his wife bring her hand to her face. She was pressing the back of her hand against her mouth, and her body seemed to shudder. He hadn't quite got there yet. He hadn't reached that point. But he would catch up with her soon enough. For now, he sat there with the boy. He didn't want him to be there alone. The silence that filled in the space around them was like stone – solid and immovable. He felt the heft of finality weighing down on him. His fingers tightened around the boy's hand, but there was no answering squeeze, no flutter of life. He looked down at the hand and realized that this was the last he would see of it. Already, it was going cold.

Felix, meaning happiness, joy. Once he was gone, all the joy and happiness in their lives seemed to slip away. The world around them was leached of colour. Felix died as the seasons were changing. All summer, Garrick had spent his time shuttling back and forth between the hospital and home. Such was his state of mind that he hardly noticed the blossoming trees, the lushness of the grass, the burgeoning fruit trees that lined the avenue that led to his house. It was only after the boy had gone that his eyes cast around, looking for something to fix upon other than the gloomy images in his head that fought for his attention. New England in the fall is a sight to behold, but he was impervious to its charms that year. The deep red and fiery orange and brilliant gold of the leaves seemed lurid and showy and overdone. Nature at its most boastful. Rubbing his nose in it. What was it anyway but a gaudy façade to cover up death and decay? He looked at it and felt a new anger stirring inside him. For how could such beauty continue to exist, year after year, now that his son was no longer in the world?

He didn't say this to his wife. They said little to each other in the weeks and months that followed. Communication between them existed at the level of necessity. They avoided conversation with each other, each circling the other cautiously, like those who are wary of touching an open wound, although, privately, he talked with other people, opening up to friends, to barely friends, to strangers in a bar about his grief and pain. He did this, and he knew that she did too, and yet still it felt like a betrayal.

It was nobody's fault. Felix got sick and he died. There was no clue, no warning. There were no previous instances of the illness within either of their families; it had not been a time bomb lurking in their DNA. He had not died as a result of an accident; there was no negligence involved on either of their parts. And yet Garrick felt responsible. He felt guilty.

They were naturally quiet people, both of them. With Felix gone, the silence in the house grew eerie. Eva held herself apart from him. Rarely did he see her grief come to the surface. On only a couple of occasions did it erupt, and when it did, it astonished him. It gushed, it spurted and leaped out with a terrible ferocity. Always, after these episodes, she returned to her calm, quiet self, yet the shadow of her furious grief remained, prowling the quiet corners of their home. Their sadness should have brought them together, but he felt, instead, that it divided them. He watched his wife pull away from him, aloof and imperious and alone in her sadness.

There was a beauty to her solitude. However much it frustrated him, he felt a grudging admiration for her. But in her solitude, he read something else. Blame. She never said it. After all, what was he to blame for? He had loved his son. He had done everything a father could do to save him. What had happened was beyond his control. And yet he read in her silence an unspoken accusation. And he knew it had nothing to do with this. It was because he had another son, and she could not forgive him for it.

He told her about Dillon when he returned home from his visit to Tangier. There was no reason to do so, only an urge on his part to purge himself of the knowledge. Somehow, he couldn't bear to think of her existing in the world, living her life as his wife, as the mother of his child, and not knowing. To keep it from her would seem like an insult to her dignity and intelligence. She was a strong woman, quiet and determined and sure of herself. There was something in the quality of her stillness that drew out of him his darkest secrets, his most hidden and shameful fears. With Eva, he always felt the urge to confess and, by

290

confessing, to have her absolve him from whatever misdemeanour he had committed. And so he had told her. He knew it was a risk. At the time, he had worried that it might drive a wedge between them too great to bridge. After her initial fury, there was a long period of frosty silence. He waited for it to thaw, constantly anxious about whether he had made the right decision in telling her. In time, things softened between them, and, perversely, it seemed to renew their interest in each other. He tried hard to be a good husband and father. He looked at his wife and their beautiful son and gave thanks for what he had. They never mentioned the other boy.

The time that passed was bleak and slow. Winter came, and with the advance of Christmas, they decided to go away. There were invitations from Eva's family in Ireland, and from his in Oregon – their relatives seeking to draw them in and offer comfort and solace. But both of them resisted. They were both still crawling out from under the chaos of emotions that surrounded Felix's illness and death. His wife's face had grown thin and white. She would sit for hours staring out at the garden with deadened eyes, her folded hands held still on her lap. There was a fragility about her that frightened him. She, who'd once been so strong, now seemed threatened by the slightest thing. He couldn't bear the prospect of an ill-judged remark, or an unwanted display of sympathy that might break her apart and shatter her into little pieces.

Instead, they drove to New York and checked into a hotel on Madison Avenue. They took long walks in Central Park. They visited the Guggenheim and the Met. He brought her to Tiffany's and picked out a platinum band studded with diamonds, which she wore alongside her wedding rings. Over glasses of wine in dimly lit restaurants, they held hands and tried to remember what it was like to be just the two of them again, without a child to occupy their attention. They went to Mass on Christmas morning in St Patrick's Cathedral because that was what she wanted. They exchanged gifts and afterwards lay on the big bed in their hotel room and stared at the Yule log burning on the TV screen. Always, the boy was with them. A shadow at the periphery of their vision. A ghostly form walking quietly behind them.

The night before they left New York, he was scrolling through his e-mails while Eva was in the shower when he came across one from Robin. In the period since Felix's death, he had become lax about communications with the outside world, only checking his inbox once a week, at best. This e-mail was five days old. He opened it and read the message there. A brief, almost terse account of how life was for her and Harry and the boy, wishing a merry Christmas to him and Eva and Felix. He read that, and his heart gave a lurch. She did not know. How could she, as he had not told her? He closed his laptop and called through the bathroom door to Eva, telling her that he was popping out for some cigarettes.

Downstairs, in the lobby, he found a chair in a quiet corner and took out his phone. He never did this. It was one of the unspoken rules between them. No phone calls; no contact unless she initiated it. He keyed in the number and listened to the foreign dial tone, and then she was there on the line, her voice distant and curt.

'Hello?'

'It's me,' he said.

'Yes, I recognized the number.'

'Can you talk?'

'Hang on.'

The sound of footsteps and a door slamming. When she came back on the line, she seemed closer, calmer.

'There,' she said, breathing out a small sigh. 'Is everything all right?'

'Yeah. I just got your e-mail and I . . . I dunno. It's Christmas, so I thought I'd ring and say hi. See how you're doing. That's all.'

He knew then that he wasn't going to tell her about Felix. Not yet.

'Dave, this isn't a good idea. What if someone else had picked up the phone? How would I have explained it?'

He shrugged, although she couldn't see it. 'Well, that didn't happen, so I guess you don't have to worry about it.'

A brief pause.

'I guess not.'

'So, how are you? How's Dillon?'

'He's good. He's getting big. Tall and gangly.'

'Like me.'

'Yes,' she said cautiously. 'Like you.'

'So, what's he like? Is he a good kid?'

What was he asking this for? Why was he doing this? He felt her tense up on the line.

'Dave, what's this about?'

293

'Nothing. Just, like I said, I wanted to get in touch . . .'

'You sound strange. Are you sure everything's all right?'

The concern in her voice made him stop suddenly. Tears sprang into his eyes without warning. Emotion crowded his throat. He felt a line of sweat running the length of his spine. His hands were shaking. He sat there, taking deep breaths, sucking in the air, trying to regain his composure.

She must have read something in his silence, for when she began talking again, her voice had changed. It had grown softer, kinder. He felt a seam of compassion opening up within her. She didn't question him further. Instead, she spoke about Dillon, about how talkative he had become, about the blueness of his eyes and the length of his eyelashes. She described how curious he was about everything, and fearless, too, with a reckless tendency to climb furniture and jump from heights. He was forever getting lost amid the narrow streets, the warrens of houses. She told him it scared her witless. He was animated and sociable, she said, although she worried that he spent too much time among adults. Lately, she had been making an effort to seek out other children his age for him to befriend.

He listened to her voice and felt himself grow calm. Part of him reasoned that it should upset him to hear her speak of this boy – this second son – that he didn't know, that he would never know, while Felix lay beneath the frozen New England soil. But there was comfort in the fact that this child was alive and thriving on the other side of the world. The soft timbre of Robin's voice filtered down the line and soothed him.

When he asked her about herself, about her own life, he noticed that her voice changed again. A note of tiredness crept into it. She was still working in the bar, she said, and still painting when she had the time, which was not as often as she would like. He had the impression that she was unhappy. Disappointed, perhaps, with the way things had turned out for her. He could sense that the life she was living was not the one she had envisioned for herself, and yet, somehow, to admit that to him would be a betrayal.

'And Harry?' he asked. 'How are things with him?'

'He's fine. He's working. His painting is going well, although . . .'

Her hesitation was momentary, but he felt all the doubt pooling within it.

'Although what?'

'Things are difficult right now.'

'How so?'

'Harry and I aren't together any more.'

The news rocked him. For some reason, he had never considered this a possibility.

'You broke up?'

She laughed – a brief, flat burst of mirthless laughter. 'Broke up. When you say it like that, it sounds almost civilized. No, I wouldn't say we broke up.'

'He left you?'

'More like I threw him out.'

'But why? What happened?'

And there it was again – the hesitation.

Curiosity drew him towards it; he sensed a chink in the brave façade, a weak spot.

'Something happened. I found out . . . he was . . .'

He pictured her sitting on a darkened doorstep, biting her lip, jiggling her crossed legs, trying to decide whether to trust him or not. Whether to say the words out loud.

'It's okay, Robin,' he said softly. 'You can tell me. I'm not going to judge you.'

'The thing is, Dillon doesn't sleep. Not much, at any rate. And we're so tired, all the time.'

'Really? But he's, what? Three years old?'

'I know. Ridiculous, isn't it? I suppose Felix has slept through the night since he was three months old, right?'

He felt the tightening in his chest again and focused on the pattern of the carpet beneath his feet.

'Right.'

'I can't imagine what that's like. I've forgotten what it means to get more than four hours of sleep at a stretch. That's if I'm lucky.'

'How come he doesn't sleep?'

She sighed then, and began a litany of explanations: colic, sensitivity to noise, some gastric problem that had since been resolved. Now she felt he was waking out of habit. She blamed herself for not being stricter with him, for not leaving him to cry it out while he was still young and pliable enough to get into a routine.

'But?' he said, softly nudging her toward revealing to him what was really on her mind.

'It was getting too much for Harry — the sleeplessness. I think . . . I think he was pushed to do something about it.'

'Like what?'

Something sharp gathered in the pit of his stomach. It had a taste to it, acidic, like bile. The taste of an old anxiety stirring up again. He waited for her to continue. When she did, it was in a quiet voice, almost a whisper.

'A couple of times, when I was working late and Harry had people over, well, those nights Dillon slept through. A deep, heavy sleep lasting well into the morning. I can't tell you how unusual that is for him. At first, I thought that he had turned a corner, that he had finally grown out of his sleeplessness. But then . . .'

'Then?'

She gave a defeated sigh and told him.

'I found these pills down the side of the couch. Sleeping pills. He said they were Cozimo's and they must have slipped out of his pocket.'

'You think he had been giving Dillon sleeping pills?' he asked, trying to keep his voice level, but a hoarseness crept into it, something akin to an enraged disbelief.

'Maybe. Yes. When I confronted him about it, he denied it, of course, but I didn't believe him. I was so furious.'

'And the sleeping? How did he explain that?' He was working hard now to keep the anger from his voice. What had once been mere dislike for Harry was now bubbling over into something darker and more dangerous.

'He said Dillon was up late, playing games with the adults. That he had just exhausted himself, and we should be thankful. But it was just bullshit. You know what they're like – Harry and Cozimo – when they get together. They probably thought it was harmless. No doubt they persuaded themselves that it would actually do Dillon good, or some such bullshit.'

'So you threw him out?'

'Yes.'

'When did all this happen?'

She sighed again. 'A couple of weeks ago.'

'And what are you going to do now?'

'I don't know. I really don't. Harry's staying at Cozimo's for now. He wants to come back. Swears he will do anything to make amends if I will just take him back.'

'Are you going to?'

She gave out a sigh, long and weary, and he felt the indecision within her and also that she was tired of turning it over in her mind, fed up with the swinging doubts.

'I don't know. I really don't. Anyhow,' she continued, as if giving herself a shake, and he felt the closing down of that strand of conversation, 'it isn't your concern.'

She had started something, though. That one short conversation planted a seed of anger within him. He carried it around inside him that last night in New York, and when he awoke the next morning in his hotel bed, he found that the seed had swollen in size and had gathered heat in it. On the drive home, he thought about it, and the more he thought about it, the angrier he became. This guy, this jerk, doping his kid without any thought to the possible consequences, just so he could get a few hours to kick back with his friends and drink or smoke weed. It was reckless; no, it was downright criminal. When he thought of how he had kept vigil by Felix's bed all those days and nights, listening to the *bleep bleep* of the machines that were keeping his son alive, all the tubes and bags hanging off his son's small body, when he thought about that and then thought of Harry, his hands tightened around the steering wheel, his knuckles whitening with the strain of containing his indignant rage.

He and Eva didn't speak throughout the long journey home. But when he pulled into the driveway and switched off the engine and felt the tension in his arms begin to ease, Eva said to him, 'I can't go inside.'

She was looking straight ahead at the darkened windows and the leafless creeper clinging to the walls of the house that had been their home for the last four years.

'I can't,' she repeated, giving her head the slightest shake.

She was holding herself carefully. It was a bad day, and she was laid low by her sorrow. But now she broke her gaze away from the house and looked at him, and the voice she addressed him with was clear and sure. She told him that the house held too many reminders: Felix's room, the toy box in the corner of the kitchen, the paintings on the fridge, his toothbrush in the bathroom. She couldn't sweep a floor without unearthing some small piece of a toy or jigsaw to remind her of him. The remnants of his short life trailed into every corner of the house. Even if they were to clean out the place entirely, it would make no difference. His memory inhabited every room. She felt at times, when entering the house, that she could smell him. It was unbearable. They could not stay there.

'Take me away from here,' she told him. 'I need you to take me someplace where I am not constantly reminded of him. Where I don't turn a corner and still half-hope I will see him.'

Garrick listened. He looked into his wife's clear grey eyes, and what he felt was relief. At last she had opened up to him, expressing a weakness that, until now, she had kept remote from him. A step had been taken, albeit a small one, towards mending what was broken between them. And what she wanted – what she needed from him – was within his gift. In that moment, he knew that it was the right thing – the only thing – to do.

He put his hand to her face and saw the shadow of the woman she had once been. He held her there in his gaze for a moment. Then he slotted the key back into the ignition and slowly backed out of the driveway.

They went to London first. He had suggested Ireland, the country of her birth, where her mother still lived, but Eva had not wanted that. She wanted to lose herself in places where no one knew them, where no one knew of the tragedy they had suffered. Landing early one morning at Heathrow, he opened the travel pouch Eva habitually carried and felt a jolt of shock when he saw three passports there, not two. It unnerved him, caused a quiver of grief to pass through him, sudden and unexpected. Later, sitting in their hotel drinking bitter coffee, he felt drawn to ask the question: why was his wife still carrying the passport of their dead son? She looked at him then, her eyes rimmed with tiredness in the early-morning light, and when she spoke, her voice seemed laden with a kind of weary dread.

'I couldn't do it,' she said quietly. 'I couldn't bring myself to throw it away or to leave it behind. Just the thought of taking his passport and separating it from ours, it seemed so . . . so final. So desperately final. I couldn't.'

He looked down at the passports grouped together, the three of them fitting snugly together in the pouch.

'I'm not ready for that yet,' she said. 'Please, Dave. Please, don't ask me to.'

He said no more about it and put the pouch away.

After London, they went to Paris, then slowly began a meandering route south, down through the hills and valleys of central France to Provence and the Mediterranean. In the cities, they visited cathedrals and art galleries and palaces, staring at paintings, at stained glass windows, at statues lit from below by the flickering candles of faith. Miles and miles they walked, their eyes and minds filling up with images of beauty and reverence and majesty. They drove through towns and villages and countrysides, past fields and forests and red tiled roofs and cobbled squares. They ate endless meals and drank countless cups of coffee and bottles of wine. They became expert at filling the silence with talk. The weather warmed, and they made their way across the Pyrenees, into Spain.

In Seville, they sat under the wide awning of a café on the Plaza del Triunfo, sipping beer and staring at the shoppers and tourists passing by. All morning Eva had been distracted, holding herself at a distance. She hadn't spoken while they had taken their seats, while they'd waited for the girl to bring their drinks. She had sat, large sunglasses obscuring her face, as she kept her gaze fixed on the square and the activity it held. Now, as her slender fingers traced the shape of her glass, he saw that she was working herself up to something.

'What?' he asked, curious and wary, too, as he often was on the days when her grief was pulling her down.

'I want to go there,' she said. 'To Tangier.'

She took off her sunglasses and regarded him directly, and he understood the purpose that lay there.

'Why?' he asked, although he knew already.

'I want to go. I want to see what it is like, so that I can have some knowledge, some understanding of what held you there.'

He listened to those words, knowing that they were false. Behind her gaze lurked the shadow of an old accusation. Fearful as he was of going back there again, he did not attempt to cajole her from the idea. He needed to protect her, to do what he could to dispel her melancholy. That was what he had committed to. He drained his glass and returned it to the table, nodding his agreement, his acquiescence. She put out her hand and touched his wrist.

Later that day, they booked their tickets, and before the week ended, they left Spain on a ferry bound for Tangier.

They arrived late in the afternoon, the sun beginning its languorous descent, and took a room in a hotel on the seafront. Eva had a blinding headache, so after they had checked in, he settled her in their room and made sure she had painkillers and enough water; then, leaving her to sleep, he slipped out into the early-evening sun.

For a while, he walked along the front, the slightest breeze whispering in the air, the exercise going some way toward relaxing the ache that had attached itself to his upper back and shoulders. When he reached the American Steps, he veered off to the left, past the mosque, and found himself in the warren of half-familiar little streets that crowded around the back of the Petit Socco. Every corner he turned, every shop front and street reminded him of Robin. He felt dogged by nostalgia. Somewhere nearby was the building where his apartment had been. At each turn, he thought he would stumble across it, but each time he was disappointed. He couldn't help but think about her, and this led him on to thoughts of the boy. Dangerous thoughts, for somehow they had become linked with his memories of Felix, and he shied away from them, afraid that they would lead him to unravel.

He had the half-formed notion of seeking out Cozimo, that wizened old man with the sharp eyes and wry sense of humour. He looked for Cozimo in a handful of places and eventually walked into a café near the Spanish Cathedral, where, sure enough, his old friend was holding court to a bunch of expats Garrick didn't recognize. As he approached, he saw the expression on Cozimo's face change, surprise briefly flitting over his features before being chased away by a broad smile.

'Garrick, my old friend,' he said graciously, rising to beckon him with outstretched arms. 'It has been too long.'

He stayed for an hour, not wanting to leave Eva alone for too long, and in that time they sat and talked about old times, and the creep of nostalgia made him melancholy. Cozimo was the same, and yet Garrick felt different. He recognized the change in himself and felt aged and weary. Where once he had enjoyed these smoke-filled surroundings and the lull of Cozimo's endless anecdotes, louche and outrageous and fictitious as they were, on that night he saw the emptiness at the heart of it all. He looked at his old friend and beheld a sad old man, still spinning his yarns – a spider weaving his network of lies – and the hollowness of it all hit him. One thing he did learn: Harry and Robin were back together. He was not told, nor did he ask, about how they had patched things up. All he knew was that they were still living together in the apartment above Cozimo's bookshop. Somehow the news disappointed him, and he walked back to his hotel feeling a little sad and depressed.

The next evening, after he and Eva had spent hours wandering around the medina, visiting the Church of St Andrew and the American Legation museum, Eva again declared her exhaustion, and for a second night, he left her in the hotel and went out alone to wander the narrow streets and alleyways, letting the sounds and smells of Tangier penetrate his senses. He found himself drawn to the street where Robin and Harry lived, and from a place in the shadows, he looked up at the lit windows of their apartment, watchful for movement, for the sight of a familiar silhouette, hoping to catch a glimpse . . . of what? Of whom? Something had started inside him, and it was not just curiosity. It surprised him how much he was bothered by the news that she had taken Harry back. It infuriated him. How could she? After what he had done? The seed of anger inside Garrick glowed brightly all the time he stood there in the shadows, and on the long walk back to his hotel.

On the third night, he again left Eva alone, and this time he walked purposefully towards his destination. He knew now that he was going to confront them. The anger inside him had not gone away. Without having said a word to his wife, he made his way towards a confrontation – a revelation – his need of which he could barely understand himself, let alone try to explain to Eva. Darkness was falling, and the city seemed quieter than he remembered. The air had a strange quality to it, the stillness unnerving. His anger drew him on, although the night was advancing and his doubts lingered and the need to get back to the hotel and Eva was strong.

When he reached the bookshop, he found the door unlocked. He hesitated, then pushed through and entered. The smell of the place was familiar. The mustiness of those old books gathered in that dim space struck a match in his memory, and he thought of all the afternoons he had sat in here with Cozimo, drinking tea and smoking Turkish cigarettes and discussing art or philosophy or politics. He reached out and brought his fingertips to the spines of the books and thought back to that younger version of himself with a kind of fond regret. So much had changed in only a few years. Upstairs, Robin and Harry might be preparing dinner, or playing with their son, or painting, or resting. For a moment, he had a vision of what he was about to do. He was going to go upstairs and burst into their home, burst back into their lives and tear apart any peace they had found. For a fleeting moment, he caught a glimpse of what might happen, of how far he might go, how much he might reveal, and a quiver of fear stopped him in his tracks, made him hold himself back, unsure. It was while he lingered there, in the back of the shop, riven with indecision, that he heard the sudden clamour of footsteps descending the stairs and he looked up to see Harry rush past to the doorway. Unnoticed, he stood in the shadows and watched Harry lock the door and hasten away, and then Garrick was alone.

Harry had moved too fast for him to react. Too fast for him to step out of the shadows and announce himself, while he was still wrestling with his indecision. Now he stood alone among the books, berating himself for his hesitation. Robin and the boy were upstairs. The thought struck him, and this time he did not pause; curiosity drew him to the stairwell, and he began to climb. Silence greeted each step, and it felt as though he was the only occupant of the place, although still he hoped to find Robin there. Disappointment touched him as he pushed open the door and surveyed the empty living room. She was not there. Nor was the boy.

Garrick looked around at the low couch, the paintings stacked in the corner. Cooking smells greeted him, and he saw evidence of Harry's efforts in the kitchen: the chopping board, the couscous, the half-full bottle of gin. And it was as he was contemplating the bottle that the earthquake hit. It slammed against the foundation of the building, sending shock waves up through his feet, into his body. Thrown against a wall, he staggered to the nearest doorway, a bolt of alarm charging through him as the walls wavered and swayed around him. Every pot and plate in the kitchen was flung to the floor. The oven door flew open and a joint of meat tumbled out of it. The crashing and splintering of crockery and glass continued in the living room, where plates hanging on the wall slid down to the floor and the glass-topped coffee table shattered. Great cracks appeared in the walls and the ceiling, fissures that moved at an alarming speed. Skidding and swerving, he made his way back the way he had come, fuelled now by the knowledge that the place was going to collapse. He was sure of it. And just before he reached the stairs, he glanced down the corridor and saw the door open into the bedroom and the sleeping form that lay there.

The earthquake stopped. The building seemed to rock on its hinges, and Garrick moved quickly to the bedroom. He looked down at the boy, his sleeping son, but the stillness was momentary. Around him, the walls continued to creak and moan, and there was another sound coming up beneath it – the breaking apart of the very masonry that held the place together.

Did he know what he was doing? Even now, he cannot be sure. Perhaps. Some half-baked notion of saving one son's life where he had been powerless to save the other. It was not heroic. It was instinctive. Garrick had no other thought in his head than to snatch the child from that damn building and get him outside, to safety. Swiftly, he bundled the boy in the sheet and hurried down the steps. He needed to get him away from here, and as he passed through the bookshop and reached the door, he heard the rending of wood above his head and felt the walls around him crumble. He slammed his body against the door with all the force he could muster, and they found themselves outside in the night air, where he heard the first screams and cries from the street beyond.

He didn't look back at the fallen building. Instead, he began to run, no thought in his head but to get away from there. All of Tangier, it seemed, was running. A river of people flowing down the hill, tributaries streaming down lanes and alleyways.

Sweat had matted his hair to his forehead; his lungs were on fire. But still he ran, pressed by an urgent need to get the boy to safety. On and on he went, pressing through the dust and the smoke that filled the air, not stopping for anything, no thought in his mind about right or wrong. He was powered, now, by a new emotion. Rage. Convinced already of Harry's negligence, his culpability, he ran through the streets of the old quarter, past the shops and the cafés – so much of it a shattered mess of detritus left by the quake – not stopping until he reached the seafront.

He should bring the boy to a hospital, he thought. He should try to find Robin. But instead he found himself back at his hotel, which remained standing, a testament to its solidity. The guests were huddled in frightened groups in the lobby, and as he scanned their faces for Eva, his heart hammering loudly in his chest, he saw her coming towards him, her face pale, her eyes fixed on the boy. Neither of them said a word, and they slipped away from the others, unnoticed.

Their room was in darkness, the electricity having failed. Leaning back, he closed the door behind himself, then advanced into the room. He laid the boy gently on the bed, and as he did so, Eva struck a match. From somewhere, she had found a candle, and in the wavering light, the white coverlet seemed to glow. She came and stood beside him, and it was only then, as he looked at her stricken face and then at the boy asleep in front of them, that he drew his hands over his face and sucked breath into his gasping lungs and thought to himself, Jesus Christ, what the hell have I done?

They talked deep into the night. In whispered conversation, he explained to her what had happened, about going back to Cozimo's shop, about the earthquake hitting and about finding the boy. He told her how he had run and kept on running until he got back here. She did not say to him: why? Why on earth did you risk your life? Nor did she ask what he'd been doing going back to that place, or why he had brought the boy here, instead of returning him to his parents. She just watched as he spoke, her face calm and inscrutable, nodding slowly to draw him on.

'We should contact his mother,' she said.

'Yes.'

But he just sat in his chair, and she didn't mention it again.

The boy lay still on the bed. Garrick watched as his wife went over to check on him for the sixth or seventh time in the hour since he had laid him down. She pulled the sheet up to his chin, adjusting the coverlet. Her hand went instinctively to his sleeping head, her fingers in the soft curls, and he remembered how she had done this with Felix, and the gesture seemed completely natural and, at the same time, so unbearably sad that he had to look away.

'Should we call a doctor?' she asked anxiously.

'He seems okay. We should let him sleep.'

She kept her eyes fixed on the boy, her arms folded across her chest as she lingered by the bed.

'He's sound asleep.'

'Yeah.'

'And he didn't wake when you picked him up?'

'Nope.'

'He stayed asleep the whole way back here?'

He stared at the floor, feeling the ache in his muscles and bones. He knew that she was staring at him, waiting for an answer. The incredulity was there in her voice.

'I think he's been given a sleeping pill.'

'*What?*'

The word shot out of her like an accusation. He raised his head to meet her gaze, furious and indignant and disbelieving, as he had been.

'How do you know this?' she demanded.

He twisted his watch around his wrist.

'Dave?' she said, and he knew that he would have to tell her.

So he went to the minibar and fixed two whiskey and sodas, and she came and sat by him and listened with her drink cradled in her hand while he explained about Robin, about the phone call in New York, about what she had told him.

In the hush of the room, her shock was palpable.

'To do that to a child,' she intoned, shaking her head. 'And the earthquake. He might have been killed.'

'I know.'

'Such negligence,' she went on, her gaze again drawn back to the boy.

'Yes,' he said.

'And she *knew* about it and still took him back?' Eva asked, her head whipping around to face him, as if it had only just occurred to her.

He nodded, and she gave out a sharp exhalation, a little huff of fury, and he felt the ripples of her anger, as well as the unspoken thing: *What kind of mother would leave her child open to such a risk?*

He was aware of the awkwardness between them that occurred whenever they spoke of Robin – his own shame and her low, simmering anger at the mention of this other woman. But that evening, there were no recriminations, no cool silences between them. Outside, the city was on fire. Sirens screamed all night. But inside their hotel room, he felt the tightening of a bond, each of them drawing towards the other, towards the unexpected thing that had presented itself to them.

She asked him about Harry, and he gave her a broad outline of his character, as he had perceived it during that time when he and Harry had been on friendly, if somewhat distant, terms.

'He's not a bad guy, I guess. Just a bit caught up in himself.'

'Hmm. Sounds like a real gem.'

Encouraged by her sarcasm, by her implicit refusal to see Harry as anything but the bad guy, he began to tell her of his distrust, his niggling doubts about the man who was raising his son. Not that there was anything he could have done about it. Just little things.

'Like what?' she asked.

In the dimness of the room, her eyes were sharp and glinting. They were observing him closely, hungry for all he was telling her, the idea being nourished by every character flaw, every little mistake and misdemeanour he could summon about Harry.

Neither of them had given voice to the idea yet, but it was there between them. Already it was taking shape.

After a while, he told her she should get some sleep. The truth was, he was so overwhelmed that the room seemed to tip and veer about him. The enormity of what they were contemplating disoriented him; he was afraid that if he stood up, he might fall over. He told her to sleep in the bed with the boy, while he stretched out on the couch. It was not long before sleep took them, but just before it did, he observed his wife nestling up against the small, curled shape in the bed, her arm briefly suspended over the boy, a hesitation there lest the weight of her arm about him wake him up. Instead, her hand rested briefly on his little shoulder, tracing down to the crook of his arm and then silently withdrawing.

He didn't know how long he slept. But when he woke, she was standing over him.

'What?' he asked, for he sensed the tension in her, a slow uncertainty about her face. 'Is something wrong?'

She was wearing one of his T-shirts over her underwear, and his eyes passed down her long, slim body, and then he saw that there was something in her hand.

'Here,' she said, giving it to him.

He sat up, rubbing the sleep from his eyes. There were serious aches in three places along his spine, as if his body had been folded up like a piece of cardboard and was now trying to unfold itself. He looked down at the passport in his hand.

She was biting her lip, a kind of wild anxiety in her eyes as she watched him open the passport. Felix's photograph stared out at him from the pages. Eva turned away and slunk back to the bed.

He had taken the photograph himself. Remembering it now, he flinched at his irritation, his growing frustration with the child, who had refused to sit still for him, who wouldn't face the camera or, when he did, could not keep his face expressionless; that impish grin kept returning and spoiling the shot.

'Goddamn it, Felix!' he had shouted at the boy.

He thought of that and flushed with shame and

remorse. He would give anything to have that moment back.

Eva was sitting, now, on the bed by the boy, whose little chest was rising and falling with his steady breathing.

'Amazing, isn't it?' she said to him. 'How alike they look.'

The passport was in his hand. He checked. It was still valid.

In the bed, the boy was stirring. Garrick held his breath as he watched the boy's eyes opening, his little body drawing up, his fists rubbing the sleep from his face. And when he looked about himself at the unfamiliar room, and then at Eva and Garrick, the sleep fell away, and his expression became fearful.

'Where's my mummy?' he asked, and something plunged within Garrick at the little voice emerging hoarse with sleep and panic.

If Eva felt any such misgivings, she hid them well beneath a blanket of composure.

'Your mummy and daddy can't be here right now,' she said, her voice soft yet firm with reassurance. 'They've asked us to mind you for a little while.'

The lie was delivered so gently, so easily, it left Garrick breathless.

She told him their names, and Garrick watched as the boy drew his legs up under the sheet, hugging his knees to his chest – a defensive gesture. He looked out at them beneath a fringe of brown hair, his eyes large and watchful. His chin trembled, and tears sprang suddenly within his eyes, and Garrick felt something sharp in his chest.

Eva moved closer to the boy, her voice bright with cheerful reassurance.

'Are you hungry, Dillon? What would you like for breakfast? Do you like croissants? Toast?'

He stared at her with suspicion, but the trembling in his chin seemed to have stopped – for now, at least.

'How about a glass of milk and a nice sticky bun?'

He gave a little nod and hugged his knees in closer to his chest. She went to reach for him and he drew back instantly, and Garrick watched as his wife's hands fell back into her lap, but her face held that same brightness, that sunny optimism.

'Do you like boats, Dillon?' she asked. The boy didn't answer, just squirmed a little under the sheet and stared hard at the little hump that was his bent legs. Eva continued: 'Later today, we might take a little trip on a boat – just the three of us. Would you enjoy that? And if you like, we can sit up on deck and watch all the other boats and the gulls and the waves. Wouldn't that be fun?'

Then she looked up at Garrick, and the fullness of her unspoken proposal struck him forcibly. He didn't think of the consequences. Not then. Neither of them did. They told themselves that it was in the boy's best interests. He would be better off with them, away from his parents and their negligence, their recklessness. They could give him a better life than the one he'd had, living in a hovel, a death trap, surrounded by hippies and potheads. They would love and cherish him and never take him for granted. With them, his life would be full of opportunities; he could achieve his potential, and nothing would be beyond his grasp. That was what they told themselves. But beneath all that was the knowledge of their own pain, of how they had been at rock bottom, and now there was this opportunity, this most unexpected way that they could be rescued.

How do you explain it to someone – the way to go about rebuilding your life around such a grand deception? Were he to read it himself in a paper – a shocking headline: COUPLE STEALS CHILD TO REPLACE DEAD SON – he would imagine it as a sordid affair, both plotted and calculating. But it wasn't like that. It was more the slow and steady accumulation of several small deceptions, one leading to another, until you became accustomed to it. A trickle of lies, each one told not out of any malice but out of an overwhelming need to protect the boy, to shield him from further pain. A period of grieving, of readjustment, until they could start on the serious yet joyful work of building their lives together – that little unit of three.

At first, there were tears. They came regularly. Garrick learned to read the signs. That watchful look that came over the boy, the stony silence that would suddenly grow up around him, and then a frown line would appear and his lower lip would turn out, his face rapidly becoming liquid as the crying took over. Questions about his mother, about his father, about his home. The insistent tone, the tantrums. Flailing limbs lashing out, bursts of shocking violence. Every time it erupted, they would wait it out. Eva was better at it than he was. She would stay there, murmuring words of comfort, soft noises to calm him, purring terms of endearment, pet names that she had, until then, reserved for Felix. Often, Garrick found that he couldn't stay and listen to it. He had to walk away. But not Eva. Never once did she crack. Her resolve was stronger. The tenacity she showed in the face of such overwhelming grief, anger, and confusion was fascinating. He watched her with a kind of frightened awe, ashamed of his bouts of cold feet, his trembling admissions of doubt. But all she had to do was remind him of that night in Tangier to pull him back to her.

'He left the boy alone,' she would say coldly, and all at once he was back there in that room, the walls quaking and crumbling about him, looking down at the small shape of the boy, drugged and abandoned, alone as the earth fell. He remembered it and sucked in his breath. It was as if some other force were at work, as if there were a reason why he'd been in Tangier that night, a design that had brought him back to Cozimo's, that had drawn him up the stairs like a thief in the night and sent him running through the crazed streets clutching the sleeping child in his arms.

They answered Dillon's questions patiently. His mum and dad were not well, and they had asked Eva and Garrick to mind him. No, they did not know when he would see them again. No, they couldn't call on the telephone – it was not possible. And then they waited for the crying to abate, and they would shower him with affection and spoil him with gifts, a tremendous effort to fight the tide of his grief and confusion. They were in too deep now to go back.

'Remember the holiday we had in Oregon?' Eva said to Garrick one night.

It had been a bad day. The boy's tears had erupted several times, and Garrick had felt all day on the verge of giving in and surrendering Dillon to the authorities, confessing to his crime, ending it all there and then.

'The last one,' she said, clarifying.

He nodded. Of course he remembered. The last holiday before Felix got sick.

'Remember how we were in the car, on the road three or four hours already, when Felix started to wail in the backseat? He had forgotten Bo.'

He smiled at the memory. A sad, nostalgic smile. Bo, that grubby, greasy, mangy-looking stuffed cat that Felix had inexplicably formed a passionate attachment to.

'The panic that came over us – don't you remember?'

'I remember. I nearly crashed the damn car.'

'Right! We were both so freaked! What were we going to do without Bo? How the hell were we going to handle Felix for a whole month without his beloved Bo?'

'That's right.'

'And it was hell at first, wasn't it?'

'Yeah.'

'All that sobbing and wailing. The sulks and tantrums.'

'He got over it, though.'

'He did. And quickly too,' she said, with a brightness in her eyes. 'After the second week of the holiday, he didn't even mention him. And by the time we got home, it was as if he had never had Bo. He was clean forgotten.'

'Eva,' Garrick said, serious now, keeping his voice quiet,

318

and yet the warning was still there. 'This isn't some stuffed toy we're dealing with. They're his parents.'

'*You're* his parent,' she replied, quick as a flash.

Just as quickly, she looked away.

He reached for her hand, held it in his, and let the silence drift in around them.

It was understood between them, anyway. As time passed, memory would fade, and those thoughts the boy had for his parents would diminish. He was only three years old. He would forget.

Weeks passed. They moved on. Every time they crossed a border, he felt his hands grow sweaty, a narrow band of tension tightened about his skull. They were careful not to use Dillon's name when addressing him. They never slipped up.

Their house in the States was put on the market, the decision made: they were not going back. A distance had crept in between them and their families, their friends. They had held themselves apart in their grief after Felix. Now they had to explain the boy. Letters were written, carefully worded e-mails, quiet phone calls late at night, when Dillon was asleep. They'd agreed upon a story: Dillon's mother had died in the Tangier earthquake. It had fallen to Garrick, the boy's father, to take care of him. There would be raised eyebrows at that, gossip, speculation, the calculation of dates. It wouldn't take a genius to figure out Garrick's infidelity. But Eva was prepared to live with the humiliation. And he could live with the shame. They had suffered through far worse. And at least, in this instance, there was a point to their pain, something they could both accept, if it meant they could keep Dillon.

A wet afternoon some months after they had taken him. Newly arrived in Canada, where they had chosen to settle in a quiet suburb of Toronto, a place where no one knew them, where they could begin again. In the rental house, Garrick and Dillon sat on the couch, watching a movie they had both seen before, *Finding Nemo*. It was the boy's favourite. Sitting side by side, unspeaking, an amicable silence gathering around them, they watched. And then Dillon turned to him, a solemn look coming over his face, and asked in a quiet voice:

'Is my mum dead?'

His heart had seized with sudden fright, and he'd tried to keep his features still and calm as he looked into the boy's pale and watchful face.

The boy hardly blinked.

Garrick nodded slowly.

'And my dad?'

'Yes.' His mouth dry as dust.

The boy held him there for a moment with that solemn gaze, and Garrick found that he was holding his breath, waiting for the tears to come. But instead, the boy turned back to the movie, and they watched it together on the couch, in silence.

The worst lie he had told. How easily he had done it. It frightened him, in a way — the enormity of it, the untold consequences. And yet, once it was done, he felt lighter somehow, as if the way ahead had suddenly been cleared of a giant obstacle.

The questions dried up after that. Dillon still grieved for them, but it was different now, as if his moods were tempered by an understanding. Slowly, almost without them noticing, a calm seemed to come over their home. Weeks became months. Months grew into years. The steady accumulation of time bringing them closer together, tightening their bond, fixing it so that it was just the three of them against the world. They had no need of any others.

How long might it have continued like that? Who can say? The writing was on the wall from the moment they learned that Eva's mother was seriously ill. He remembers the night clearly. Eva pacing the floor, her face wet with tears, her arms crossed tightly over her chest, torn between grief and indecision.

'You've got to go back,' he told her. 'She's your mom. You'll regret it if you don't.'

'Will you come with me?' she asked.

'It's a risk.'

'After all this time? You still think that?'

'What if someone sees him? What if someone recognizes him?'

'What are the chances? And besides, he's changed. It's been five years. He looks different. He's like you now. Not her.'

He let that pass, but he felt the cold, hard silence that slipped between them whenever Robin was mentioned. He gave in to her after that. He had to. His guilt, her grief and the promise they had made each other when first they had taken him: to stay together. The three of them were a family. They would not be separated.

Going through passport control at Dublin Airport, he felt the sweat breaking out all over his body, a prickle of nerves running over his skin. Not until they were sitting in a taxi bound for Wicklow did he begin to relax a little.

Eva's mother was in the hospital in Dublin, and they spent those weeks shuttling back and forth between the Wicklow Hills and the city. Eva liked to take the boy with her when she visited, but Garrick rarely joined them. His aversion to hospitals, honed during the long season of Felix's illness, held fast. At first, their excursions into the city made him nervous, but in time he relaxed, let his guard down. They seemed to exist in a sort of limbo – waiting for the woman to die. They knew it would not be long.

A morning in November. He remembered it clearly. Snow piled up on the verges of the roads as they made their way north, towards the city. Slow traffic on a Saturday morning held up by the road closures and diversions. A protest march. It had taken time to find parking. Then there was the long walk to the hospital. On that day, the old woman was barely lucid, slipping in and out of consciousness. She didn't seem to recognize any of them, and Garrick's presence alarmed her.

In the corridor, Eva squeezed his arm.

'Don't take it personally,' she told him. 'She's confused, that's all.'

'I'll go get the car,' Garrick said.

He had planned to pick them up at the entrance, but

when he reached the car, he realized that it would take at least an hour for him to drive back to the hospital. The march had moved south, towards the quays, blocking the roads that led to his destination. It would be quicker for Eva and Dillon to walk towards him, and he could pick them up halfway.

And so he called his wife's cell phone and made the arrangements. One phone call. One snap decision.

In the time it took them to reach him, the damage was done. The slip-up made. After five careful years, all it took was a phone call, and the whole plan came undone.

'If you believe nothing else, believe this: we didn't go to Tangier with the intention of taking Dillon,' he said. 'That was not what we had intended, however bad it looks.'

A chance came, and they took it.

That was what he told them, when he reached that part of the story.

# 19. Harry

His voice as he told us his story seemed distant, the tone almost private, as he brought us down the meandering route that led to his terrible act. I tried to listen, Dillon. I tried hard to concentrate, to fix my attention on the story, for it was important to me to know what had happened to you. But the words just fluttered past me, barely brushing against me. In no way did they penetrate the surface of my thoughts. The truth was, I couldn't take my gaze off you. My eyes feasted on your very being. To see you again, Dillon, to know that you were alive – I felt overcome. You stood next to him – Garrick – with a stillness I found admirable in such a young boy. A grave look had taken hold of your face, and the wariness in your stare pained me, Dillon. I could hardly wait for a time when all of this would be behind you, the healing done. For now, his arm was around you, and I saw your pyjama bottoms peeking out from under your jeans.

Robin's eyes were on me and, turning to meet them, I could see that the fear was gone from them. Her gaze was steady, sincere, and even though it remained unspoken, I knew that I had been vindicated. She leaned forwards, straining towards you, Dillon; she ached to hold you, as I did, but was frightened of overwhelming you, of scaring you away. I looked at her, experiencing that whole range of emotions, and all the love I had ever felt for her suddenly burst back into my heart.

And then the words dried up. Garrick's story had reached its end. A silence came over the room. I realized that you were all looking at me, wondering what I would do, and I remembered with a kind of hot jolt that I was holding the gun. No sooner had I been scalded with that realization than a shadow moved across the doorway, and we all turned to stare at the woman who stood there.

We had all forgotten about Eva. But there she was, her face a pale oval in the gloom. She took a moment to assess the situation, then cried out in fright. Rushing to Garrick's side, she knelt by you and grabbed you into her embrace. There was something feral about her action, the way she swooped you up into her arms – protective and defensive all at once, like an animal snatching her young from a predator. She turned on me then, her eyes bright and cold as snow, her voice a snarl: 'You can't have him.'

We all scrambled to our feet, the air charged with this new electricity, and I felt the gun heavy in my hand, felt all the possibility contained within it, how I could use it to take control. And yet, she had you in her arms, Dillon. I could not wave a weapon at my own son.

Garrick was the first to speak, his tone low and careful.

'Eva, stay calm, honey. We will get this all straightened out, but you gotta stay calm, okay?'

Only she was well beyond that. Shaking and scared, her eyes brimming with tears, she clutched at you tighter, Dillon.

'We shouldn't have come back here,' she said, convulsing with emotion. 'We shouldn't have taken the risk.'

'Eva . . .'

'It's all my fault. I shouldn't have brought you both with me.'

Garrick seemed reluctant to say anything, but he obviously did not want to see Eva in distress. 'We agreed, Eva. Your mother . . .'

She dropped her head and dipped her face so that it rested on your crown, her arms about you, Dillon, and she seemed to drink in your whole being. In a disquieting way, I suppose, she was already taking her leave of you, already preparing herself for that unbearable loss, trying to gather up as much of you as she could so that she could save her memories of you in these final minutes, to make them rich and solid enough to last a lifetime. I knew all that and felt the slow corrosion of pity working away at my resolve. Dillon, it almost worked.

In that moment, Garrick moved around her, and I had to focus suddenly as he was coming towards me, slowly, carefully, his palms held up as if to show that he meant me no harm. But we were well past that. I tightened my grip on the gun.

'Not another step,' I told him.

'Let them go, Harry,' he said quietly. 'The rest of them. Let them go. Let's you and me sit down together, alone, and work this thing through.'

'No.'

'Come on. Be reasonable. Let Eva and Robin take

Dillon outside, where it's safe.' And then, in a lower voice, he said, 'I don't want him here in this room with that gun.'

As he spoke those words, my eyes flickered to your face, Dillon, and I saw how it was pale with fear, and I felt a moment of crushing shame, to think that my actions had inspired that fear. And all at once the years were falling away, and I was back there on that street in Tangier, dust in my eyes, blinking in disbelief at the emptiness, the terrible vacuum that stood in place of my home, my sleeping son.

I bent my head and closed my eyes, passing a hand over my forehead. I was a mess. What a way for you to see me, Dillon. Bedraggled, beaten, sore. I don't think I would have recognized myself. A hand pressed gently against the small of my back, and my eyes flared open, my hand shaking, and I saw Robin there, leaning into me, her arm about me.

'Please, Harry,' she said gently. 'Let him go. I promise I won't take my eyes off him. I won't let her take him. Not again.'

I gazed into the warmth of her eyes and I swear, in that moment, I could have fallen into her arms. She looked at me again, and I could feel the love, the old love. Wherever it had gone, it was back. It was like something physical in my gut, a presence in my blood.

'All right,' I said, my voice breaking. It was the thought of being parted from you again, Dillon, even for just a few moments. The thought of you leaving my sight once more filled me with a deep foreboding.

You looked at me, then to Eva and Garrick.

Garrick managed to whisper to you: 'It's okay, Dillon. This will all be over soon. Go with Mom. You'll be fine. I'll be fine. I will see you soon.' His eyes widened.

Eva was shaking. I couldn't look at Robin, lest I lose my resolve.

Eva went to embrace Garrick, and then you looked at him one last time. Maybe you did get on with him, maybe he was good to you, but you did not walk over to him. Instead, you turned and gazed into your mother's eyes. You seemed to know what was happening.

'I'll be okay,' you said, your voice clear and calm. How brave you were, Dillon. I imagined holding you then for the first time in years. I leaned towards you and took in your every sinew, inhaled the smell from your hair. You did not resist. Even when I kissed your cheek.

'Dillon,' I said, but I could not finish what I wanted to say. I was overcome. And then you let yourself be taken by your mother, away and into the night. My heart lurched. I ached, every pore of me ached, at seeing you leave again.

We watched you silently – Garrick and I. He was slumped in the corner by the stairs, one hand pressed against his ruined face. I was by the door. Together we watched the backs of the three figures as they descended the steps, down into the darkened slope of the garden. I had my back to Garrick, which wasn't wise, but the fight seemed to have gone out of him the moment I'd agreed to let you leave. He seemed spent. And so I followed the shapes of the ones I loved for as long as I could. Distantly, I heard a car, and saw the sweep of headlights across the driveway. But the distraction was fleeting. I kept watching until the darkness swallowed you up – until there was nothing left of you.

You probably want to know what happened then. You may already know. Or you may have worked it out for yourself.

Either way – this is how it went for me.

The car zoomed into the driveway, spitting up gravel on all sides. It drew to a sudden halt, and Spencer got out. His face had a toughness about it, a knowing fierceness, but there was apprehension there, too. 'Harry what's going on?'

I knew from the tenor of his voice that he was frightened, and that scared me even more. I experienced a fleeting moment of clarity, as if I had stepped outside my own body and could see precisely the mess I had got myself into. The gun pressed hotly in my palm.

'Stay back,' I shouted from the doorway.

He came forwards. 'Harry, for fuck's sake, put that thing down.'

I didn't. Instead, I aimed it at him. There was a scream, a cry of fright. Whose voice was it? Robin's? Eva's? For all I know, it could have been my own. Retreating quickly, I slammed the door shut, my hands shaking. Then, leaning in to steady myself, I pressed my forehead against the hardwood door.

It was almost as if I had forgotten about Garrick.

I had found you again, Dillon. That one thought played through my head. And then the strike came, a sharp blow to the back of my head. I felt it acutely and fiercely, and I dropped to the ground. Blood was pouring into my ear. A soupy, disorientating flow. I lay there, paralysed.

He stepped over me, pulled open the door, and I stirred from my fearful paralysis, tackling Garrick and rolling him on to the ground. I had thought he was spent, but I felt the strength in his body, sinewy and tough. He gripped my arms and pulled me under him, and I reached up and clawed at the wound on his face, causing him to cry out in rage and pain. And I, too, was enraged. Incensed. My ear was full and my hair was matted with more and more blood, and as it dripped into my mouth, I spat at the man who had taken you.

The door was half-open, our bodies jammed against it, and then, out of the corner of my eye, I saw half a dozen Chinese lanterns float into the air.

'What the fuck?' Spencer came running towards me and Garrick, but he was stopped in his tracks by the gunshot.

At first I thought it was fireworks or one of the Chinese lanterns exploding into the night. But there was no fantastic spillage of light and magic. Garrick must have prised the gun from my hand or picked it up after it had fallen; I don't know. But I do know that this time the first sensation was not visual. The bullet went through me so quickly that the first thing I felt was lightness.

It felt like I was floating.

How could the knuckle of lead have done any damage travelling through me so fast, this little package propelled by gunpowder – but it did, Dillon.

And it was amazing, the tumbling mélange of images that came to me then.

Garrick's face retreated, and Spencer cradled my head in his arms.

Sound and sense revolved into each other and what came to me was the Egyptian boy prince, the boy on a horse, the red flag, the sun and the dry cobbles of Tangier. Your singing, gurgling childish sounds, your whimper and your playful digs. Your night-time embrace, your 'Dada' in the dark, your tickles and giggles and rousing temper, your tears and your laughter. Your paint-stained hands in Tangier, Dillon. All of it a boon and precious cargo carried to me then – its happy host.

So now you know, Dillon. That is what happened.

A cold, white day of protest in Dublin is how it started, and as I drifted into another state of being, into the cold embrace of another winter, I was not saddened, Dillon; I had found you after all. Instead, the one burning, shining desire within me as my life left me was to paint one more canvas. Can you believe it, Dillon?

And what is the image, what was the image to be? From whence does it come? My dying imagination or a faint memory of our first times together?

Dearest Dillon, does it matter?

# 20. Robin

On a late afternoon in September, I find myself sitting alone outside a café in the heart of the medina. It is the kind of place that appeals to the tide of tourists who browse through the stalls of the Petit Socco, looking for a refuge from the fierce trade of that market, the haggling and the hassling, the guides and the touts, seeking out a chair in which to sip mint tea while watching the world go about its business here in Tangier. The waiter, a young Moroccan with a quick smile and distracted eyes, listens while I tell him my order, then gives a dismissive nod and wanders off in an unhurried manner. All around me are Americans, Italians, French nationals and Australians, some still bearing enthusiastic looks, others with the slump of the weary traveller, all on plastic seats pulled up to rickety tables that front the square, bathed now in the gentle heat of the declining sun, the shadows lengthening as evening draws in.

Of all the people in this busy place, I am the only one who sits alone.

The coffee I ordered comes, plonked down without ceremony.

'*De rien*,' my waiter intones without feeling when I thank him, then drifts away to another table, his tray held aloft, skimming the heads of the customers seated around me.

I take a sip, then fiddle with my mobile. One of the

women at the next table leans in to impart some confidential information to her partner, who then swivels in his chair and gives me a brief, appraising look before turning away. I am distinctly aware, in this moment, that I am a woman alone in this place. It is at once strange and yet familiar, too. The sights and smells reach some inner part of me, caressing the touchstone of memory, stirring it up again. The grand silhouettes of the tall palm trees that line the perimeter of the Petit Socco, black against the evening sky and its puckering of grey clouds scudding the horizon, the gentle lull in commerce that takes place at this hour of the day before the evening traders arrive to set up their stalls, the smell of exhaust fumes from waspish mopeds mingling with the sharp cleansing scent of the mint tea being brewed up and down this strip of cafés — all of it blends and rises up around me in a miasma of familiarity. And yet there is something profoundly wrong about being alone here in this place, in this city, where so often I had been with Harry.

But then, of course, I am not alone. My children are with me. Right now, they are at the Mendoubia Gardens with their uncle Mark and his girlfriend, Suki. An hour has passed since I watched them go, that happy group, the boy carried aloft on his uncle's shoulders, the baby kicking her legs in her pram. I had kept my eyes on them until they disappeared from view, an involuntary clutch about my heart as I lost sight of them. An hour, and only now, with the coffee warming my throat, do I start to relax. Yet still I keep my mobile within easy reach, one eye watchful for an incoming call or text.

'Take some time to yourself,' Mark had said to me. 'Make the most of us while we're still here.'

'I don't know,' I had said, chewing my lip, reluctance pulling me back.

'We'll be gone tomorrow, and then you'll be wishing you had let us take the children off your hands while you still had a chance.'

And so I had put my fear aside and let them go.

I am unused to being alone, not quite sure of what to do with myself. There is no book in my hands to amuse or distract me. I fiddle with a sachet of sugar, sip from my cup and all at once, without warning, I am back there, on that cold winter day, in that lonely abandoned place, pulled by the drag of memory, and I recall with piercing rawness the events of that terrible day.

We hurried down the steps, down, down into the shadowy garden, grey in the dim light. The snow lay thickly about the house, and I laboured to plough my way through it, my heart beating high and light in my chest, the metallic taste of blood in my mouth from where I had chewed the inside of my cheek in those nervous moments before fleeing the house. My coat was too hot, the sheer weight of it hampering my movements. Sweat formed under my clothing. My whole body felt liquid and heavy. And underneath my ribs, my heart hammered away with fear and uncertainty. Every step I took put distance between us and the danger that was contained within that house. But I had left Harry behind.

I looked about myself, at the scrubby bushes and wiry

trees black against the snow, and had no idea where to go, or what to do then. Eva had stopped, and I felt a corresponding hesitation within her, as she paused and stared back at the house, her arm still held protectively about the boy. When I saw the fear and suspicion in his eyes, it caused a tightening about my heart. I couldn't stop looking at him, couldn't resist the urge to glance down at his face, to check again that it was really him, that it was really my son, the boy who was dead. Eva held his hand, avoiding my gaze, and yet I felt no anger towards her. That would come later, when it was all over and I realized the great wrong that had been done to us, the theft of those precious years, the breaking of a bond that might forever be beyond repair. But in that moment, I was still occupying a place of disbelief and a surging emotion that I couldn't quite identify: relief? Joy? The blasting away of all my sorrow? The boy who was dead, the boy who had been claimed by the earth, now returned to me, older, changed, but living, breathing. At that moment, it was all that mattered.

I stayed close. I didn't want to take my eyes off them, and yet something made me look back – a sense of foreboding, perhaps – and as I did so I saw Harry standing there at the top of the steps, his tall body framed by the shadow of the doorway, and every particle of my being strained to go to him. It was all I could do to hold myself back. Just a glimpse was all I got. Then a car drew up, and there were raised voices, slamming doors. Everything happened too quickly. I saw the glint of gunmetal in my husband's hand, watched in horror as he raised and pointed that weapon at a man bounding up the steps towards him. The man paused, his hands held up in a gesture of surrender. Then Harry took a step back and the door closed and the house swallowed him up and a plunge of terror went through me – a shiver of dread – as I realized with an empty gravity that I might not see him alive again.

The man turned and bounded down the steps toward us, and I saw Spencer's sagging features contorted into a grimace of anxiety.

'Get down!' he shouted as he came, and I felt the urgency in his voice and the weight of his body pressing on me, pinning me down. Eva, Dillon – all three of us were held there by his grip as he kept shouting at us to stay down, his voice enraged, it seemed to me, or maybe it was fear I heard. The cold dampness of the snow clawed its way through my clothing. I felt nauseous and weak and dreadfully scared. At the same time, I was in the grip of a surreal sensation – that this was happening not to me but to someone else. That I was merely watching another woman flung on to the snow, in the grip of near hysteria. That it was not me who kept glancing fearfully across at the son she had presumed dead, but someone else, someone ghostly and drawn, someone whose foundations had just been rocked.

And then the clouds above us seemed to part, the hard brightness of the winter moon breaking through and falling on the snow. It made me feel dizzy, disoriented, as if my head had been held underwater for a time and now emerged, gasping for breath, panicked and unsure of everything. The door was half-open suddenly, and Spencer was moving quickly back towards it, and it was as I watched him bounding up those steps that I heard it. A sharp crack in the middle distance that disturbed the air. I looked up at the house. Holding my breath, I could hear nothing, only the boy's breathing beside me. A cold, hard fear came down over me then, and my body began to tremble and shake.

'Oh Jesus,' I heard Eva say. 'Oh Jesus Christ.'

I caught the urgency and high note of fear in her voice, and, seized by a new panic, I stared hard at the house, at the door that was ajar, at the shadows that moved there, shapes coming out of the darkness, announcing themselves as figures. Spencer was inside now, kneeling by the door. All that was visible of him was his hunched form, the soles of his shoes. He turned then, and I saw his face as a streak of fear.

'Call an ambulance!' he cried out, before twisting away from us.

'Oh God!' Eva cried. 'Oh my God!'

She fumbled for her phone and began punching in digits and I heard the shrill panic in her voice, and I knew all about that panic, that innate fear realized, yet still I didn't give voice to it.

In my head, I was willing him to stand up, willing the door to swing back and reveal my husband to me, standing, unharmed, safe. Someone was lying on the floor – I couldn't see who – and a voice inside me repeated over and over with the pleading insistence of a prayer, *Let it not be Harry. Let it not be him.*

How long did I wait there? How long did I kneel in the snow, straining with hope and fear? My whole life stilled and condensed and sharpened down to that one moment in time, that one fervent desire.

And then the door opened a little more and a face announced itself from within the gloom, and I saw Garrick standing there, his face drawn, his hand to his mouth, bewildered, uncertain. I saw him, and the knowledge hit me with full force.

My heart clenched, and I opened my mouth wide and felt the screams coming out of me and filling the air, echoing off every tree and wall and icy surface in that cold, wintry space and coming back at me redoubled.

'*C'est fini?*'

I look up at the waiter pointing to my empty cup, his voice shattering my reverie and claiming my attention, drawing me mercifully back to the present.

'*Oui,*' I say, then order another.

He casts his eyes briefly over me. I feel that he is looking at me properly for the first time and try to rearrange my features accordingly, smoothing them out to a flat expression, bringing them back from the shadowy depths of the past.

The people at the next table are lively, their voices raised, a farewell of some kind or other. A sudden crash and the shattering of glass as a waiter in the next café drops his tray, and all along the strip, the other waiters pause to cheer and applaud the mishap, drawing indulgent smiles from the tourists. My eyes follow them, flickering with interest, picking out the many faces among them in an involuntary sweep of the crowd.

The world is a different place for me now. I see it with fresh eyes. Danger lurks in familiar places. Harry is gone, killed instantly by a bullet that penetrated his heart. An accident, or so Garrick's lawyers are pleading. The gun went off as the two men tussled for control of it. I try to imagine that moment: the charged atmosphere in that house, the two of them grappling, the sudden violence of the gun going off and the shock it must have caused. When I picture it, I see Harry's eyes flying open, a look of naked surprise there before the pain clouds his face and his body folds in around the sharp, burning point of it. Luck was not on Harry's side that day. There is a painful irony to his fate. It might have been either of them.

The child I had lost has been returned to me, changed, damaged, the bond between us broken. Every day is a battle to win his trust. The suspicion in his eyes that greets me causes my heart to clench with pain. And there is a new child – a girl – a living reminder of her father, with his dark hair and his wide, round eyes, solemn and appraising. She clings to me and I to her. She is my greatest comfort in all of this.

The baby was born in July, and it was a few weeks later, on a warm September afternoon, that I made my decision. We were sitting together, my mother and I, in the kitchen of my parents' house, looking out at the garden dappled in golden sunlight. My father was hunkered down beside the flower beds, pulling weeds and deadheading sweet peas. Dillon attended him, watching with a grave expression, dutifully handing over tools when they were called for. I studied the tension in his narrow shoulders, his quiet obedience, and felt vaguely unsettled. He had none of the mischief or vigour that a young boy should have. His stillness and compliance – the good boy that he was – worried me greatly. My head was swimming with exhaustion; every limb felt sodden and swamped, as if I were submerged in water, fully clothed, my soaked garments weighing me down. All I wanted was to let go of these thoughts and fears and constant anxieties and just sleep for more than three hours together. But I was also afraid of what might happen were I to let my guard down. My grief had not hit me yet, and I feared that a lowering of my defences would merely provide it with an opportunity to creep in and engulf me.

'What about Hazel?' my mother said, snagging my attention.

The baby was asleep in her arms, swaddled in a blanket, my mother's eyes locked on her little face.

'Hazel?'

'Yes. I've always thought it a lovely name.'

'I don't think she's a Hazel.'

'Alannah then?'

'No.'

'Well, you have to call her something,' my mother said after a moment, a note of impatience creeping into her voice. 'We can't go on calling her "baby". She's almost two months old.'

I felt her voice like a tiny hammer pinging against

the roof of my skull and turned back to gaze out the window.

She was right, of course. I would have to give the child a name. But since I had lost Harry, I had become unmoored. My pregnancy had been a blur of confusion, the birth an episode of pain and distress and sudden joy arising from my grief. Since then, I had been drifting through the days and weeks. Things happened around me, but I found it difficult to focus my attention, to lock down hard on any one thing. A form of running away, I suppose, by refusing to confront what was there. But it was the only way I could cope with everything that had happened. Sometimes, a hazy oblivion seemed like a form of solace. I felt the weight of responsibilities tugging at me, but making a decision, one as important as the name my daughter would bear for the rest of her life, seemed beyond me.

Outside, my father was holding his cupped hand out to Dillon, and the boy peered down into it, his neck straining with curiosity. It must have been a worm, or an insect of some kind, for suddenly my father brought his hand close to Dillon's face, which sent the boy reeling backwards, and then they both started laughing, and it was so surprising to see my son happy, so rare and unexpected, that my eyes filled with tears, and I had to look away.

There was a hand on mine then, and I looked down at my mother's fingers, diamonds sparkling above her wedding ring.

'He'll be all right,' she said softly, and I felt the emotion break within me, and the tears fell freely, and my voice, when I spoke, came out liquid and choked.

'He's so broken,' I said.

'He's safe now. That's all that matters.'

'He won't talk to me. He can hardly even bring himself to look at me.'

'It will take time, Robin, but he will come back to you. He's your son.'

I shook my head and drew my hand away, pressing my fingertips against my eyelids.

'I feel like he blames me – for everything. For letting him be taken from me in the first place. And then, once he had forgotten me, once he had formed new bonds, I came along and broke those bonds, and he blames me for that, too.'

My mother drew in her breath, and I opened my eyes and saw the worry lines creasing her forehead, her lower lip sucked in in that anxious way of hers.

'Remember what the counsellor said: it will take time – who knows how much time. Months, even years. But children are resilient. And he is tougher than he looks. Just like his mother.'

'I'm not tough. I'm barely hanging on, Mum.'

'Oh, Robin. My poor pet.'

She squeezed my hand again, and there was love and fear in that reassuring gesture, and I felt like a child again, a thirty-five-year-old child returned home and needing to be cared for and nourished, protected and guided all over again, and with this thought came a rising impatience with myself. I needed to do something. I needed to regain my life.

After Harry died, I'd been unable to go back to the

house. I couldn't face returning to the home we had shared and all the memories it contained, both good and bad. I'd had Dillon with me by then, and I couldn't cope with him alone, his rejection of me, his unassailable anger and resentment towards me. I'd needed help. It was my father who'd suggested that we move back in with them.

'Just until the baby arrives,' he had said, 'and you get back on your feet again.'

At the time, it had felt like a defeat of sorts, but then I'd felt defeated at so many levels that one more hardly made a difference. I'd told myself it would be best for Dillon, and that truth had been borne out as I'd watched him drawing close to my mother and father, accepting hugs from them, slowly opening up to them, a little voice emerging unsteadily from his mouth as they eased him into a routine. But with me he'd remained silent. Cold and distant. Resentment emanated from him in waves, and it amazed me, the patience with which he kept it going. Months had passed, and still there was no sign of any softening towards me. I'd thought that once the baby arrived, things might change, but while he showed an interest in his little sister, it never extended beyond her to me.

The feeling had been growing within me for some time that we needed to get away. There were too many memories here. I was dogged by nostalgia – and by gossip. The press had got hold of the story and had a field day with it. And while things had died down, I knew it would all start up again once the trial began. I felt too old to be living in my parents' house. Were I to have any chance of rebuilding my relationship with my son, it would have to be done

343

somewhere far away, without any help from my parents or anyone else. This was something I needed to do alone. I had the sense that were we to be thrown together in isolation, he would have no choice but to learn to trust me again.

Sitting there with my mother, staring out at the garden in the last flush of summer, I had a thought. It was unbidden and surprising, and yet, in that moment, it felt completely right. It felt like a gift. Tangier. The place of Dillon's birth. But more than that, it was the one place where Harry had felt truly alive. The one place he had called home. I'd realized, in the weeks after I'd lost him, that he had never really settled in Dublin. The house had not been home to him, a place of refuge, a harbour. Instead, it had been a shell, lacking a centre. A hollow space within which we had rattled around, circling each other, a cold cavern within which our suspicions of each other had been nurtured and allowed to grow.

Tangier was where he had left his heart. It was as if he had exacted an unspoken promise from me in the longing of his gaze that last time I'd looked upon him. To go back there. To bring the boy home.

Resolve formed within me, and I felt it strengthen and harden, and for the first time in all those long months, a feeling of excitement caught tightly in my chest. It glowed inside, and I looked up to tell my mother, but then decided against it. She was not ready for that. She would not understand my need to go, and I hadn't the strength yet to persuade her of it. Instead I looked at her gently cradling her granddaughter in her arms.

'Martha,' I said softly. 'That's her name.'

My mother's eyes clouded, and she offered me a watery smile before looking down at the sleeping child.

'Martha,' she said gently, trying it out.

Then she brought her face down to the baby and pressed her lips against Martha's head.

She had not understood, but she had let us go. And since I've arrived back in this old familiar town, with my two small children and my broken heart, I have spoken to my mother often. I know she thinks that this is just a passing phase, that I will return home once the seasons change. I haven't the heart to tell her otherwise. Tomorrow, my brother and his girlfriend will leave, and there is an attendant fear about striking out on my own. I acknowledge the fear and then try to put it aside, sipping my coffee and watching the leaves of the giant palms flutter and sway in the warm evening breeze.

A trial date has been set. Eight months from now, I will sit in a courtroom and listen as the drama of my life and Harry's death is played out for the gallery. Garrick, I am told, has hired a specialist legal team. He has dipped into his family's wealth, which, as it turns out, is considerable – the Garricks are brewing multimillionaires, and their sphere of influence is broad – and he is employing the very best lawyers to explore and exploit all legal loopholes to ensure that he and his wife escape justice. So far, he has been successful. In Ireland, he was awarded bail. I neither know nor care where he is living. Here in Morocco, there seems to be no appetite to dredge up the horrors of that night, to open the old wounds of many who lived through that earthquake, not to mention the legal and political hoops that would have to be gone through in order to extradite Garrick and Eva. I am not sure I have the energy for that fight. Everything I have is taken up with survival, with reconnecting with the boy I lost and getting to know this new little girl I have been blessed with.

Certain things will have to happen now. For one thing, I will have to put my house in Dublin on the market. My father will baulk at it not achieving its true value. Still, I need the money. And I have come to believe that it is the best thing for me and Dillon and Martha. I hope my parents will understand that.

The other thing I will have to tell them is that there is to be a posthumous exhibition of Harry's work in Dublin in a couple of months. It was Diane's idea, and I must admit that I was surprised when she contacted me about it. I was sceptical at first; it seemed too soon for such a gesture, and I worried whether it might also be too maudlin for Harry's tastes. Would his spirit rile and protest at being remembered by a roomful of stiffs in suits and stuffy art bores clutching glasses of cheap wine, and others present merely out of a prurient curiosity, drawn by the whiff of scandal that attached itself to his name after death? I don't know. Still, the decision has been made.

My phone rings. It is Mark, telling me that the children are tired so he and Suki are taking them home. I tell him that I will join them, but he urges me to relax. There is no rush.

I finish my coffee and pay my bill and walk away from the square. The peasant women in their striped robes and wide-brimmed hats have gone, taking their wares with them, replaced now by merchants setting up their stalls for the night market. I wander past, ignoring any calls to peruse and purchase, keeping my eyes fixed on a point in the distance, feeling the night air sweeping in off the Strait of Gibraltar. I wear my solitude lightly here, sensing, with a degree of pleasure, the anonymity it brings.

Close by, in the warren of streets that huddle and spread over this part of the medina, is the place where Garrick had lived – the place we used to go to together. I have a fleeting recollection of lying next to him, staring up at the lazy revolutions of a ceiling fan. Immediately, I put that thought away.

Instead, I think of Harry, of his conviction in those last days of his life and how he discovered the truth purely by chance and through his own dogged determination and unshakeable belief that Dillon was still alive. I try to imagine how it was for him that day on a street in Dublin when he set eyes on a boy and felt the frightening jolt of recognition. It had seemed to me a fantasy, that he was merely imagining the boy to life by virtue of the fact that his mind could not bridge the gaping chasm of loss. And I remember how I had doubted him, how my doubt had been the very worst kind of betrayal, and when I remember it, I feel the shame rise through me and I need to concentrate very hard on the ground in front of me to prevent my emotions from claiming me.

I am aware, too, that my grieving has not started

347

yet – not properly. It lies in wait around a corner, lurking in the shadows, ready to jump out and catch me unawares. I cannot yet conceive of a world without Harry in it. For now, when I think of him, what I feel most is gratitude. All-encompassing and overwhelming gratitude. For his stubborn belief, his refusal to be swayed from the crazy notion that our boy had been stolen when everything pointed so clearly to his death. Had he not held on to that belief, had he not trusted his instincts and pursued them against all the odds, then . . . No. It does not bear thinking about.

Sometimes, in the nights I have spent here, I've dreamed that Harry is with me, and that we are lying alongside each other in a companionable silence. When I wake, it is a renewed shock to see the empty space on the pillow next to me, and in those moments, the longing I feel is achingly physical, and I want to draw the covers up over my head and surrender to it all. But then I hear Martha crying in her cot and I force myself to swing my legs out of bed and press my feet into my sandals.

On the Rue es Siaghin I get caught behind a group of tourists milling about outside the Spanish Cathedral. For a moment they stand looking around themselves, consulting maps and trying to find their bearings, and the cries from the street sellers rise in pitch. The place, all at once, is too crowded, too loud and oppressive. Time to go home.

The sky above the medina is streaked with bands of gold. Gulls wheel and swoop, their echoing cries carried aloft.

I turn to go, and it is in the motion of turning that I feel it – the sense that someone is watching me, a sensation like a feather passing over the skin at the nape of my neck, goose-bumps crawling over the space between my shoulders. I stop, my eyes scouring the crowd. And then I see him. Tall, rangy, his intense gaze fixed on me. That face so familiar and yet impossible. Disbelief plunges to the very depths of my stomach. Impossible. It cannot be.

He turns away quickly, pushing hurriedly through the crowd.

I need to go after him, but I am paralysed.

I need to shout out his name, but it catches in my throat.

Emotion bubbles and roils within me, filling my inner spaces, drowning out sense and reason.

'Harry!' I call out, my voice a hoarse shout of fear.

He turns a corner without looking back.

Quickly now, I begin to move, my legs weak, my breath shallow.

A frantic impatience grows within me.

And then I turn the corner on to a street I don't know. My eyes scan it quickly: the dusty pavement, the intricate wrought-iron railings that enclose balconies overhead, awnings stretching and casting the street in shadow. At every corner there is an exit – a warren of alleys shooting off into the *ville nouvelle*. A woman's laughter drifts down from above. At a drain, a dog sniffs at something, the only living being here.

I stand there, looking down the empty street, feeling the pulse in my head, that rhythmic thumping, my eyes casting about, uncertain, wavering. It couldn't be. It couldn't. Grief begins to clamour at the edges of my thoughts, threatening to break through, and with it comes the doubt that clouds my judgement, telling me it cannot be – it cannot. But I am not yet ready to let the grief in. It lasts only an instant before being overshadowed by a new, insistent urgency. I suck in my breath. Then I start to run.

# Acknowledgements

We would like to thank the teams at Curtis Brown, ICM Partners, Penguin UK/Michael Joseph and Henry Holt. In particular, we wish to thank: Jonathan Lloyd, an inspiring agent; his assistant Lucia Rae; Melissa Pimentel and her superb work as translation agent; Kari Stuart for her wise guidance; Stefanie Bierwerth for championing this book from the start and for her unflagging enthusiasm; Mari Evans for her careful steering; Steve Rubin and Aaron Schlechter for their vision for the book and consummate professionalism.

Finally, we would like to thank Aoife Perry and Conor Sweeney for their love, patience and support.

# Reading Group Questions

1. Do you agree with Harry that he was a bad father? Does one mistake deserve such devastating consequences, or was he just unlucky?

2. The story is set in two very different locations and atmospheres – Tangier and Dublin. Did you think that the characters changed as their locations did? Cozimo, for example, seemed to fade back in the confines of a London apartment.

3. What did you think about Harry's infidelity? Was his and Robin's marriage already damaged beyond repair?

4. Did you, like many of the characters, think that Harry was simply delusional with guilt? Was there a turning point at which you began to question your initial thoughts?

5. Did you blame or sympathize with Robin? How did your thoughts about her change towards the end of the novel?

6. How did you feel when the boy's identity was revealed? Was it a celebratory or tragic moment?

7. Do you think it was the right thing for Dillon to be returned to his real parents by the end of the novel?

8. Did you sympathize with Garrick and Eva? Can their actions be forgiven?
9. If circumstances had been different do you think that Harry and Robin could have regained their trust in each other and gone on to be a happy family?
10. Who, if any, do you think are the victims and the villains in *The Boy That Never Was*?

The new novel from Karen Perry

# Only We Know

is coming in June 2015. Read an extract now . . .

# Prologue

## *Kenya, 1982*

A woman lies in a field, sunning herself. The grass grows long around her, and from it she hears the sibilant hum of unseen insects. Nearby, the children sit in the grass, restless and bored, but content to leave her be. Above her, the air shimmers with heat. It is almost noon.

She has flattened out a patch of grass with the tarpaulin they have used beneath their tent. It gives off a stale tang of sweat or mould, but right now that doesn't bother her as she stretches out, legs crossed at the ankles, a paperback novel unread and flattened against her belly, sunglasses covering her eyes from the white glare of the sun. For now, all she wants is to lie still and soak up the heat.

She breathes in the heavy air, feels the baking earth beneath her, and takes in the hush of the great plains that stretch out around her. The others left half an hour ago, down the worn track towards the Maasai village and she, Sally, has stayed behind to watch over the children. But the children are of an age that resists parental supervision. All summer long they have held her at a distance, absorbing themselves in their new-found alliance, forming their own secret games, their own clandestine code. She feels driven

357

out by their new demands for privacy. Even now, she can hear them stirring, getting to their feet, a resolve formed between them. She sits up and watches the three of them moving purposefully towards the downward slope of the field.

'Boys!' she calls to them, and when she calls a second time, they stop, Luke turning to look up at her, Nicky mumbling something to Katie.

'What?'

She has to shade her eyes to see her eldest son's face, and even though it is in shadow, she can still see the sullen set of his features, that suspicious look he has been giving her for some time now. Lately, whenever she is with him, she gets the sense that the boy is faintly disgusted by her.

'Where are you off to?'

'The river.'

'No, Luke, it's dangerous.'

'Dad lets us.'

'Even so, I'm not happy with –'

'Oh, for Christ's sake.'

'Luke!' she shouts, suddenly enraged.

He opens his mouth to say something, thinks better of it and stands there chewing his lip, waiting. Sally feels prickly and uncomfortable, the vast heat rising around her. When she thinks of the trees that flank the river, the relief of shade there, she finds she hasn't the heart to stand up to him.

'Oh, very well,' she says, trying to sound firm and purposeful. She wishes she wasn't seated. Her authority seems diminished, stretched out on her sheet of tarpaulin, her son gazing imperiously down on her. Ten years old with the haughtiness of an aristocrat. 'But you're to be careful, do you understand? All of you.'

She casts her voice out so that the other two will take note. Katie glances back but Nicky keeps his gaze fixed firmly on the dusty ground.

'Luke,' she says sharply, as he turns to go. 'I'm counting on you to watch out for the others. All right?'

He gives her a look – closed and unreadable, and there it is again, this feeling she has lately that during every exchange, he is holding himself back from blurting something out and confronting her.

'All right?' she says again.

He shrugs, then turns away. She watches him catching up with the others, then overtake them; his shoulders set with a grim determination, moving towards the shady banks with a purposeful air while the others lope along in his wake. How different they are – her two sons. Where one is bold and enlivened with a kind of animal energy, the other hangs back, dreamy and shy. And she, Sally – their mother – finds it hard sometimes to negotiate the role of parent to two such different children. If she is honest with herself, she knows she leans towards her younger son, finding she understands him innately, that she can identify with his dreaminess, with the rich inner life that occupies him. Whereas her older son remains a mystery – an enigma – even though he lives his life so openly, almost aggressively, with an energy that sometimes baffles her, not knowing how she might contain and control it. A wave of feeling overtakes her as she watches them until they reach the trees and disappear into the shadows – her two sons, her beautiful boys.

The sun is too bright, and the stifling heat makes it impossible to linger here. She can feel her body becoming desiccated like the baked earth around her. Besides, there are things to be done before the others return. She gets to her feet and moves back towards the camp, leaving her book and the tarpaulin behind her – she will get them later, when Ken and Helen return with another driver.

The tents have already been collapsed, but the job of folding and packing them away was abandoned once Albert came back and they discovered he was drunk. God, what a scene. Sally doesn't even want to think about it – not in this heat. She stops by the white van to check on him before she tackles the tents. Peeping in through the cab window she sees him stretched out on the seat, one arm thrown over his head, the other dangling down into the footwell, the steady rise and fall of his chest as he sleeps it off. She cannot see his face as it is turned away into the backrest.

'I don't like him,' she had said to Jim that first day.

They were in the office in Kianda, the two of them. Albert had just left.

'Why not?' Jim had asked, looking up at her, surprised.

'I don't trust him,' she replied, and Jim had laughed and shook his head before returning his gaze to his paperwork, one hand tapping out a rhythm with his pen.

'You don't trust anyone,' he had said, but there was fondness in his tone, a light-hearted mockery which took the sting out of it.

But it was true – she didn't trust Albert – although she had nothing to base it on; only her own gut instinct. Within minutes of him stepping inside the office she had felt it – the nudge of wariness. He was a small man, thin shoulders braced with tension. Square-faced and flat-nosed, nostrils that seemed permanently flared, she had watched him lighting up, puffing away on his cigarette the whole time they were making the arrangements, his small eyes flicking around the room but hardly ever alighting on her. He directed his comments to Father Jim, as if Sally wasn't even there. The whites of his eyes were tinged yellow like nicotine stains, and he never once looked her in the eye.

'He seems shifty,' she had said.

'Look,' said Jim, trying to sound reasonable, 'he knows the road well, and he knows the safari routes out there like the back of his hand. By all means, look for someone else, but you won't find anyone who can sniff out the big game like Albert, believe me.'

She had gone along with it, despite her instincts telling her otherwise. So when they woke on the last day of their three-day safari to find their driver missing, it was, in a way, her fault.

It was mid-morning by the time the white van came skidding up the track, coughing up dust around it as it drew to an unsteady halt. She knew, as soon as Albert stepped out of his van, that he was drunk. The angle of his cap, the unsteady weave of his gait as he came towards them, the way he heaved in his breath as if trying to push down on the rising bile inside him.

'Oh, Christ,' Ken had said. 'He's pissed.'

361

And he was. Astonishingly and outstandingly drunk. He staggered towards them and tried to string a few words together but they emerged an incoherent mash-up of an excuse. Helen, a witness to Albert's inebriation, blew up. Ken lost all his patience and decorum, and Sally felt a rage ripping through her like she wanted to kill someone. The row that ensued was awful. It was like Albert's drunkenness had put a match to a highly flammable atmosphere, one that had been smouldering for days, setting it ablaze.

In the searing heat of the midday sun, as Sally bends to her knees and begins folding away the tents, she feels suffused with a sense of shame. She should never have let it get so far. The words she had spoken, the things she had said – in front of her own children, in front of Helen's daughter – unforgivable.

She would have to patch things up with Helen, although time was not on her side. They would drive back to Nairobi tonight – if they could find a driver – and the next day Helen and Katie would be boarding their flight for home. And then what would happen?

She packs away the tents, stacks the neat bundles alongside their bags, and looks around for any stray belongings. There is still no sign of the others.

Shouts erupt from the trees down by the river – yelps of joy and delight, alongside sounds of taunting. Helen's words come back at her – *you'll keep an eye on Katie, won't you?* She feels a small stab of guilt. The shouts draw her on, as does the need to get out of the glare of the sun.

Even here, under the shade of the acacias, it's still hot as Hell. Sweat beads on her brow and she wipes it away with the back of her forearm, looks down into the gloom, her eyes adjusting to the sudden plunging loss of sunlight. A great whoop of delight catches her off guard – shrieked out through the shadows, it causes her to step back involuntarily – followed by the sound of a deep splash. She looks down into the water, sees it ripple and rock in the half-light, before Luke's blond head emerges, then his naked torso. Stripped off to the waist, his skin glistens and when she calls to him, for just an instant she sees the look on his face – that of unabashed glee – as he turns, before the mask comes down, extinguishing the glittering light of his joy.

'What?' he asks sullenly.

'I told you not to go into the river,' she says.

'No you didn't.'

'Luke, I did. It's not safe.'

'You said to be careful, and we are. But you never said not to go in.'

She hesitates – a fatal mistake. Her authority leaks away and he lowers himself back into the water, keeping his eyes locked on her, challenging her.

'Where's Nicky?' she asks.

'There.' She follows the direction of his outstretched arm, sees the dark hair of her younger son a little way down. He is crouched among the shallows and there are two girls with him, but neither one is Katie.

'Hello,' she says tentatively, feeling her way carefully down to the bank. 'I see you've made new friends, Nicky.'

The boy doesn't look up, just stays there hugging his knees to his chest and staring into the water, a strange little smile on his face.

'Hello, lady!' the girl next to him shouts up.

Sally laughs at the salutation, and looks down at this girl – white blonde hair in pigtails, two big square front teeth shining in their newness, gaps on either side where the adult teeth are yet but stubs. A rabbitty face. A face busy with freckles, rounded cheeks, her smile is open and warm but there is something about her that Sally is unsure of. Gormless. That is the word she alights on. A look in the girl's eye that is dull and slow. 'Not the full shilling,' as her father might have said.

'What's your name?' she asks brightly.

'Cora.'

'Hello, Cora.'

'And she's Amy.'

A jerked thumb indicates the presence of a smaller girl hovering behind her. A tatty-looking dress tucked in knickers, the same white blonde hair as her sister, but her eyes are sharper, the gaze more discerning. Sally guesses this child is about four or five.

'Are you allowed play here by the river?' she asks, wondering about the younger child, wary somehow of leaving her in the care of this slow-witted lumbering older girl.

'Oh, yeah. Pops says it's fine.'

Sally glances behind the girl, up past the bank of trees on the other side of the river. There is a clearing there, the vague outline of some kind of house. Over the past few nights they have seen the glow of a campfire through the perimeter of trees, smoke rising into the night. When they asked him about it, Albert had snorted dismissively, saying: 'Gypsies.'

Sally looks down at these girls with their washed-out dresses, dirty faces and feet, and feels a jab of uncertainty.

'Where's Katie?' she asks.

'Here I am.'

The voice, directly behind her, causes Sally to jump. She swings around, sees the girl sitting still in the shadows, sandaled feet together, hands clasped around her knees, and those big round eyes, solemn and staring up at her through the gloom.

'What are you doing?' Sally asks, unreasonably sharp, but she is still recovering from the fright.

'Nothing,' Katie says, keeping her eyes fixed on Sally.

'Well, it's time to go back to camp now,' she says firmly.

'Is Dad back yet?' Luke asks.

'No. But he will be soon.'

'Ten more minutes.'

'Now.'

'Aw, please, Mum,' he says, a plaintive whine in his voice and it strikes Sally forcefully that, for the first time in days, he has addressed her as Mum. Something inside her falters.

'All right then.'

What is the point in arguing anyway? Best to leave them here, playing, where they are happily entertaining themselves, than have them under her feet, whining and moaning and questioning her constantly about when the others will return.

She scrambles up the bank, stops to take one look back at them – Luke gliding through the water, Nicky

365

turned to the girl with the buck teeth, whispering something to her, Katie sitting and gazing down at them, still and impassive. Sally watches them for no more than a minute before turning away. And as she steps back out into the blinding heat, feeling the dryness of the grass brushing her ankles, she has no idea that this is the last time she will see them as innocent children, the last time she will feel such uncompromising love. She doesn't know it yet, but in less than an hour, her whole life will have changed.

Everything is packed and ready now, but still the others have not returned. Sally lies down on the tarpaulin, resting on her front, and tries to read her book. But the words blur on the page, sweat running down into her eyes; soon enough she gives up, rolls over on to her back and closes her eyes.

The others will come back soon and then they will all pile into the van for the long difficult journey back to Nairobi. Tomorrow, Helen and Katie will leave Kenya, and what then? Sally feels her body swamped in heat, imagines herself as a tiny insect trapped beneath the searing gaze of the African sun. Three years they have been here, and now that Ken is coming to the end of his contract, a decision must be made. Do they return to Ireland or will he push to extend his contract over another year? The boys are growing up and there is their education to consider. There is also Sally's own work in Kianda, and the growing pull it has on her life. She thinks of the house back in Ireland, remote in the Wicklow hills, each room crowded with inherited antiques, and tries to imagine going back there, picking up where she had left off, but somehow she can't. Africa has changed her. She is not the same person as the woman who kept house in those rooms. A door has been opened inside her and she fears returning to Ireland will mean slamming that door shut.

Tiredness pulls at her limbs, dragging her towards sleep. She should go and fetch the children. Five more minutes, and she'll get up and go to the river.

A decision needs to be made – Ken will begin to push her on it soon. The truth is, she had hoped to know by now, had thought that somehow it would grow clear to her what she should do. But her thoughts are so muddy and opaque. She cannot seem to think clearly. And there is another decision that pulls at her conscience – an ultimatum delivered before they left for the Maasai Mara, an ultimatum from someone else entirely.

'I have to know,' the man had said. 'I can't hang on here for ever.'

The three days away on safari was supposed to be time spent thinking it over. But somehow, whenever she has a quiet moment to herself, the last thing she wants to do is think about it.

Sleep comes to her then, swooping down and taking her; under the burning sun, she lets it all go – the argument this morning, her decaying friendship, the ultimatum delivered, the indecision and dread that she has been dogged by lately – all of it obliterated by the blanketing darkness of sleep.

A scream.

The shrill note of terror.

It comes to her through her dream. Instantly, she opens

her eyes, squints under the glare of the sun, feels the tightness of sunburn across her forehead and cheeks.

Another scream. She pulls herself up, head heavy and swimming with sleep, she looks about her, confused, the searing knot of a headache announcing itself at the back of her eyes.

Silence surrounds her. Only the gentle hissing of a breeze through the grass, the click and hum of insects. Birds in the trees. And yet the absence of any other sound strikes a chord of urgency within her. She cannot hear the children now, but remembering the scream, her heart gives out a sudden beat of fright. She knows it wasn't imagined.

She stumbles to her feet, looks around her at the empty field, and turns towards the river. She moves swiftly, the ground hard and unforgiving beneath the soles of her feet, propelled by a fear that has come alive inside her.

The silence seems to deepen, to gather density as the dark clutch of trees looms in front of her.

A voice whispers in her head.

*The boys*, it says.

And then it starts – the stream of frightening possibilities: a fall, a broken limb, a gashed head, a snakebite – all of them run through her as she beats a ragged path through the bush; the silence seems to roar around her now and a warning voice sounds in her head, a voice that tells her to hold steady, to steel herself for whatever is to come.

Another scream – this time from the opposite bank – stops her in her tracks.

And it comes to Sally then, with a striking clarity, an insight so clear that she knows it to be true.

The river.

A child underwater.

Momentarily the fear drains away as she reels from the impact, coldness flushing through her body. It lasts but a second. Then, she starts to run.

# dead good

*For all of you who find*
*a crime story irresistible.*

Discover the very best crime and thriller books on our dedicated website — hand-picked by our editorial team so you have tailored recommendations to help you choose what to read next.

We'll introduce you to our favourite authors and the brightest new talent. Read exclusive interviews and specially commissioned features on everything from the best classic crime to our top ten TV detectives, join live webchats and speak to authors directly.

Plus our monthly book competition offers you the chance to win the latest crime fiction, and there are DVD box sets and digital devices to be won too.

## Sign up for our newsletter at
## www.deadgoodbooks.co.uk/signup

Join the conversation on:

# NICCI FRENCH

**BLUE MONDAY**

Monday: five-year-old Matthew Faraday is abducted. His face is splashed across newspaper front pages. His parents and the police are desperate. Can anyone help find their little boy before it is too late?

Psychotherapist Frieda Klein just might know something.

One of her patients describes dreams of seizing a boy who is the spitting image of Matthew. Convinced at first the police will dismiss her fears out of hand, Frieda reluctantly finds herself drawn into the heart of the case. A previous abduction, from twenty years ago, suggests a new lead - one that only Frieda, an expert on the minds of disturbed individuals, can uncover.

Struggling to make sense of this terrifying investigation, Frieda will face her darkest fears in the hunt for a clever and brutal killer . . .

'A brilliantly crafted new crime series' *Daily Mirror*

'Both a frightening and gripping read' *Easy Living*'

# NICCI FRENCH

## TUESDAY'S GONE

When a decomposing body is found in the flat of Michelle Doyce, a woman who is plainly deranged, the police call in psychotherapist Frieda Klein. They need Frieda to help Michelle identify the corpse. But the name Frieda eventually uncovers is that of a master conman whose victims turn out to be as numerous as the possible motives for his murder. The police need Frieda to figure out who might be telling the truth – or lying – as they draw closer to identifying the killer. But someone is determined to silence her . . . and will stop at nothing to do so.

'Will keep you on the edge of your seat. Even more gripping than *Blue Monday*' *Daily Express*

'Rattles along briskly and has real depth' *Metro*

'Reassuringly terrifying' *Red*

# TIM WEAVER

**VANISHED**

**No life is perfect. Everyone has secrets.**

For millions of Londoners, the morning of 17 December is just like any other. But not for Sam Wren. An hour after leaving home, he gets onto a tube train - and never gets off again. No eyewitnesses. No trace of him on security cameras. Six months later, he's still missing.

Out of options and desperate for answers, Sam's wife Julia hires David Raker to track him down. Raker has made a career out of finding the lost. He knows how they think. And, in missing person cases, the only certainty is that everyone has something to hide.

But in this case the secrets go deeper than anyone imagined.

For, as Raker starts to suspect that even the police are lying to him, someone is watching. Someone who knows what happened on the tube that day. And, with Raker in his sights, he'll do anything to keep Sam's secrets to himself . . .

'Fans of Mo Hayder will be in seventh hell' *Guardian*

'Weaver has delivered another cracking crime thriller' *Daily Mail*

# JAMES OSWALD

## NATURAL CAUSES

Sixty years ago a young girl was brutally murdered – her internal organs were removed and her body mutilated. Until now she lay undiscovered, sealed in an underground chamber.

For the Edinburgh police force the six-decade-old case is not a priority, but Detective Inspector McLean is haunted by the dead girl's ritualistic murder and the six trinkets placed carefully around the body.

As a wave of high-profile and bloody murders hits the city of Edinburgh – each one bearing an uncanny resemblance to the last – the same name begins to recur. As McLean digs deeper he must question just how many coincidences there can be, realising that the most irrational answer might be the only one possible . . .

*Natural Causes* is the first Inspector McLean Novel.

# DAVID BELL

---

## THE HIDING PLACE

Sometimes it's easier to believe a lie . . .

Twenty-five years ago, four-year-old Justin Manning disappeared. Two months later his body was found in a shallow grave in the woods, shocking the small town of Dove Point, Ohio.

Janet Manning has been haunted by her brother's death since the day she lost sight of him in the park. Now, a detective and a reporter are asking questions, raising new suspicions and opening old wounds. But if the man jailed for murder is innocent, who did kill Justin?

At the same time a stranger appears at Janet's door claiming to know the truth, and a high-school friend returns with his own confused memories of what happened. Janet thought she'd put the past and guilt behind her. But now the truth about her brother is heartbreakingly close – has she the courage to find it?

'Utterly compelling, absolutely riveting, not to be missed' **Lisa Unger**, *New York Times* bestselling author of *Heartbroken*

'A fast, mean head-trip of a thriller. A winner on every level' **Will Lavender**, *New York Times* bestselling author of *Dominance*

---

# ALEX GRECIAN

**THE YARD**

1889. One year on from Jack the Ripper, a new killer stalks London's streets . . .

But he has not reckoned on Scotland Yard's newly formed Murder Squad and the team of new-recruit Walter Day and the world's first forensic pathologist, Dr Kingsley . . .

'Will keep you riveted from page one' **Jefferey Deaver**

'CSI: Victorian London' *Daily Express*

'Throw in deranged prostitutes, poisonings and throat slitting galore, amidst lashings of London fog. Gory, lurid and tons of guilty fun' *Guardian*

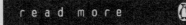

# MARY BURTON

**DYING SCREAM**

NO ONE WILL FIND YOU

An aspiring artist. A high-school senior. A stripper. Three women who seemed to
have nothing in common except their sudden disappearance. But one man knew
them all. Wealthy, privileged Craig Thornton even claimed to love them. And for
that, they paid the ultimate price.

NO ONE WILL SAVE YOU

When Adrianna Barrington receives an anniversary card from her husband Craig,
she assumes it's a sick joke. After all Craig is dead. But then come the whispered
phone calls and beautiful flowers, all reminding her how much Craig misses
her. While Adrianna begins to doubt her sanity, grisly remains are found on the
Thornton estate. Detective Gage Hudson is convinced the bodies are linked to
Craig. But the biggest shocks are yet to come.

NO ONE WILL HEAR YOU

A psychopath has taken up his chilling work again, each death a prelude to the
moment when Adrianna is under his control at last. And the only way for Gage
and Adrianna to stop him is to uncover the truth about a family's dark past and a
twisted love that someone will kill for again and again . . .